Luise Mühlbach, Nathaniel Greene

The Daughter of an Empress

An Historical Novel

Luise Mühlbach, Nathaniel Greene

The Daughter of an Empress
An Historical Novel

ISBN/EAN: 9783337048211

Printed in Europe, USA, Canada, Australia, Japan

Cover: Foto ©Andreas Hilbeck / pixelio.de

More available books at **www.hansebooks.com**

THE

DAUGHTER OF AN EMPRESS.

AN HISTORICAL NOVEL.

BY

L. MÜHLBACH,

AUTHOR OF "MARIE ANTOINETTE," "JOSEPH II. AND HIS COURT," "FREDERICK THE GREAT
AND HIS FAMILY," "BERLIN AND SANS-SOUCI," ETC., ETC.

TRANSLATED FROM THE GERMAN, BY
NATHANIEL GREENE.

COMPLETE IN ONE VOLUME.

With Illustrations.

NEW YORK:
D. APPLETON AND COMPANY,
549 & 551 BROADWAY.
1875.
EL.

CONTENTS.

THE DAUGHTER OF AN EMPRESS.

CHAPTER I.

COUNTESS NATALIE DOLGORUCKI.

"No, Natalie, weep no more! Quick, dry your tears. Let not my executioner see that we can feel pain or weep for sorrow!"

Drying her tears, she attempted a smile, but it was an unnatural, painful smile.

"Ivan," said she, "we will forget, forget all, excepting that we love each other, and thus only can I become cheerful. And tell me, Ivan, have I not always been in good spirits? Have not these long eight years in Siberia passed away like a pleasant summer day? Have not our hearts remained warm, and has not our love continued undisturbed by the inclement Siberian cold? You may, therefore, well see that I have the courage to bear all that can be borne. But you, my beloved, you my husband, to see you die, without being able to save you, without being permitted to die with you, is a cruel and unnatural sacrifice! Ivan, let me weep; let your murderer see that I yet have tears. Oh, my God, I have no longer any pride, I am nothing but a poor heart-broken woman! Your widow, I weep over the yet living corpse of my husband!" With convulsive sobs the trembling young wife fell upon her knees and with frantic grief clung to her husband's feet.

Count Ivan Dolgorucki no longer felt the ability to stand aloof from her sorrow. He bent down to his wife, raised her in his arms, and with her he wept his youth, his lost life, the vanishing happiness of his love, and the shame of his fatherland.

"I should joyfully go to my death, were it for the benefit of my country," said he. "But to fall a sacrifice to a cabal, to the jealousy of an insidious, knavish favorite, is what makes the death-hour fearful. Ah, I die for naught, I die that Münnich, Ostermann, and Biron, may remain securely in power. It is horrible thus to die!"

Natalie's eyes flashed with a fanatic glow. "You die," said she, "and I shall live, will live, to see how God will avenge you upon these evil-doers. I will live, that I may constantly think of you, and in every hour of the day address to God my prayers for vengeance and retribution!"

"Live and pray for our fatherland!" said Ivan.

"No," she angrily cried, "rather let God's curse rest upon this Russia, which delivers over its noblest men to the executioner, and raises its ignoblest women to the throne. No blessing for Russia, which is cursed in all generations and for all time—no blessing for Russia, whose bloodthirsty czarina permits the slaughter of the noble Ivan and his brothers!"

"Ah," said Ivan, "how beautiful you now are—how flash your eyes, and how radiantly glow your cheeks! Would that my executioner were now come, that he might see in you the heroine, Natalie, and not the sorrow-stricken woman!"

"Ah, your prayer is granted; hear you not the rattling of the bolts, the roll of the drum? They are coming, Ivan, they are coming!"

"Farewell, Natalie;—farewell, forever!"

And, mutually embracing, they took one last, long kiss, but wept not.

"Hear me, Natalie! when they bind me upon the wheel, weep not. Be resolute, my wife, and pray that their torments may not render me weak, and that no cry may escape my lips!"

"I will pray, Ivan."

In half an hour all was over. The noble and virtuous Count Ivan Dolgorucki had been broken upon the wheel, and three of his brothers beheaded, and for what?—Because Count Münnich, fearing that the noble and respected brothers Dolgorucki might dispossess him of his usurped power, had persuaded the Czarina Anna that they were plotting her overthrow for the purpose of raising Katharina Ivanovna to the imperial throne. No proof or conviction was required; Münnich had said it, and that sufficed; the Dolgoruckis were annihilated!

But Natalie Dolgorucki still lived, and from the bloody scene of her husband's execution she repaired to Kiew. There would she live in the cloister of the Penitents, preserving the memory of the being she loved, and imploring the vengeance of Heaven upon his murderers!

It was in the twilight of a clear summer night when Natalie reached the cloister in which she was on the next day to take the vows and exchange her ordinary dress for the robe of hair-cloth and the nun's veil.

Foaming rushed the Dnieper within its steep banks, hissing broke the waves upon the gigantic boulders, and in the air was heard the sound as of howling thunder and a roaring storm.

"I will take my leave of nature and of the world," murmured Natalie, motioning her attendants to remain at a distance, and with firm feet climbing the steep rocky bank of the rushing Dnieper. Upon their knees her servants prayed below, glancing up to the rock upon which they saw the tall form of their mistress in the moonlight, which surrounded it with a halo; the stars laid a radiant crown upon her pure brow, and her locks, floating in the wind, resembled wings; to her servants she seemed an angel borne upon air and light and love upward to her heavenly home! Natalie stood there tranquil and tearless. The thoughtful glances of her large eyes swept over the whole surrounding region. She took leave of the world, of the trees and flowers, of the heavens and the earth. Below, at her feet, lay the cloister, and Natalie, stretching forth her arms toward it, exclaimed: "That is my grave! Happy, blessed Ivan, thou diedst ere being coffined; but I shall be coffined while yet alive! I stand here by thy tomb, mine Ivan. They have bedded thy noble form in the cold waves of the Dnieper, whose rushing and roaring was thy funeral knell, mine Ivan! I shall dwell by thy grave, and in the deathlike stillness of my cell shall hear the tones of the solemn hymn with which the impetuous stream will rock thee to thine eternal rest! Receive, then, ye sacred waves of the Dnieper, receive thou, mine Ivan, in thy cold grave, thy wife's vow of fidelity to thee. Again will I espouse thee—in life as in death, am I thine!"

And, drawing from her finger the wedding-ring which her beloved husband had once placed upon it, she threw it into the foaming waves.*

Bending down, she saw the ring sinking in the waters and murmured: "I greet thee, Ivan, I greet thee! Take my ring—forever am I thine!"

Then, rising proudly up, and stretching forth her arms toward heaven, she exclaimed aloud: "I now go to pray that God may send thee vengeance. Woe to Russia, woe!" and the stream with its boisterous waves howled and thundered after her the words: "Woe to Russia, woe!"

---

* "Notice sur les Principales Familles de la Russie. Par le Prince Pierre Dolgorouky," p. 30.

CHAPTER II.

COUNT MÜNNICH.

The Empress Anna was dead, and—an unheard-of case in Russian imperial history—she had even died a natural death. Again was the Russian imperial throne vacated! Who is there to mount it? whom has the empress named as her successor? No one dared to speak of it; the question was read in all eyes, but no lips ventured to open for the utterance of an answer, as every conjecture, every expression, if unfounded and unfulfilled, would be construed into the crime of high-treason as soon as another than the one thus indicated should be called to the throne!

Who will obtain that throne? So asked each man in his heart. The courtiers and great men of the realm asked it with shuddering and despair. For, to whom should they now go to pay their homage and thus recommend themselves to favor in advance? Should they go to Biron, the Duke of Courland? Was it not possible that the dying empress had chosen him, her warmly-beloved favorite, her darling minion, as her successor to the throne of all the Russias? But how, if she had not done so? If, instead, she had chosen her niece, the wife of Prince Anton Ulrich, of Brunswick, as her successor? Or was it not also possible that she had declared the Princess Elizabeth, the daughter of Czar Peter the Great, as empress? The latter, indeed, had the greatest, the most incontestable right to the imperial throne of Russia; was she not the sole lawful heir of her father? How, if one therefore went to her and congratulated her as empress? But if one should make a mistake, how then?

The courtiers, as before said, shuddered and hesitated, and, in order to avoid making a mistake, did nothing at all. They remained in their palaces, ostensibly giving themselves up to deep mourning for the decease of the beloved czarina, whom every one of them secretly hated so long as she was yet alive.

There were but a few who were not in uncertainty respecting the immediate future, and conspicuous among that few was Field-Marshal Count Münnich.

While all hesitated and wavered in anxious doubt, Münnich alone was calm. He knew what was coming, because he had had a hand in shaping the event.

"Oh," said he, while walking his room with folded arms, "we have at length attained the object of our wishes, and this bright emblem for which I have so long striven will now finally become mine. I shall be the ruler of this land, and in the unrestricted exercise of royal power I shall behold these millions of venal slaves grovelling at my feet, and whimpering for a glance or a smile. Ah, how sweet is this governing power!"

"But," he then continued, with a darkened brow, "what is the good of being the ruler if I cannot bear the name of ruler?—what is it to govern, if another is to be publicly recognized as regent and receive homage as such? The kernel of this glory will be mine, but the shell,—I also languish for the shell. But no, this is not the time for such thoughts, now, when the circumstances demand a cheerful mien and every outward indication of satisfaction! My time will also come, and, when it comes, the shell as well as the kernel shall be mine! But this is the hour for waiting upon the Duke of Courland! I shall be the first to wish him joy, and shall at the same time remind him that he has given me his ducal word that he will grant the first request I shall make to him as regent. Well, well, I will ask now, that I may hereafter command."

The field-marshal ordered his carriage and proceeded to the palace of the Duke of Courland.

A deathlike stillness prevailed in the streets through which he rode. On every hand were to be seen only curtained windows and closed palaces; it seemed as if this usually so brilliant and noisy quarter of St. Petersburg had suddenly become deserted and desolate. The usual equipages, with their gold and silver-laced attendants, were nowhere to be seen.

The count's carriage thundered through the deserted streets, but wherever he passed curious faces were seen peeping from the curtained windows of the palaces; all doors were hastily opened behind him, and he was followed by the runners of the counts and princes, charged with the duty of espying his movements.

Count Münnich saw all that, and smiled.

"I have now given them the signal," said he, "and this servile Russian nobility will rush hither, like fawning hounds, to bow before a new idol and pay it their venal homage."

The carriage now stopped before the palace of the Duke of Courland, and with an humble and reverential mien Münnich ascended the stairs to the brilliant apartments of Biron.

He found the duke alone; absorbed in thought, he was standing at the window looking down into streets which were henceforth to be subjected to his sway.

"Your highness is surveying your realm," said Münnich, with a smile. "Wait but a little, and you will soon see all the great nobility flocking here to pay you homage. My carriage stops before your door, and these sharp-scenting hounds now know which way to turn with their abject adoration."

"Ah," sadly responded Biron, "I dread the coming hour. I have a misfortune-prophesying heart, and this night, in a dream, I saw myself in a miserable hut, covered with beggarly rags, shivering with cold and fainting with hunger!"

"That dream indicates prosperity and happiness, your highness," laughingly responded Münnich, "for dreams are always interpreted by contraries. You saw yourself as a beggar because you were to become our ruler—because a purple mantle will this day be placed upon your shoulders."

"Blood also is purple," gloomily remarked the duke, "and a sharp poniard may also convert a beggar's blouse into a purple mantle! Oh, my friend, would that I had never become what I am! One sleeps ill when one must constantly watch his happiness lest it escape him. And think of it, my fortunes are dependent upon the eyes of a child, a nurseling, that with its mother's milk imbibes hatred to me, and whose first use of speech will be, perhaps, to curse me!"

"Then it must be your task to teach the young emperor Ivan to speak," exclaimed Münnich—"in that case he will learn to bless you."

"I shall not be able to snatch him from his parents," said Biron. "But those parents certainly hate me, and indeed very naturally, as they, it seems, were, next to me, designated as the guardians of their son Ivan. The Duchess Anna Leopoldowna of Brunswick is ambitious."

"Bah! for the present she is in love," exclaimed Münnich, with a laugh, "and women, when in love, think of nothing but their love. But only look, your highness, did I not prophesy correctly? Only see the numerous equipages now stopping before your door! The street will soon be too narrow to contain them."

And in the street below was really to be seen the rapid arrival of a great number of the most splendid equipages, from which alighted beautiful and richly-dressed women, whose male companions were covered with orders, and who were all hastening into the palace. There was a pressing and pushing which produced the greatest possible confusion. Every one wished to be the first to congratulate the new ruler, and to assure him of their unbounded devotion.

The duke's halls were soon filled with Russian magnates, and when at length the duke himself made his appearance among them, he everywhere saw only happy, beaming faces, and encountered only glances of love and admiration. The warmest wishes of all these hundreds seemed to have been fulfilled, and Biron was precisely the man whom all had desired for their emperor.

And, standing in the centre of these halls, they read to Biron the testament of the deceased Empress Anna: that testament designated Ivan, the son of the Duchess Anna Leopoldowna and Prince Ulrich of Brunswick, as emperor, and him, Duke Biron of Courland, as absolute regent of the empire during the minority of the emperor, who had now just reached the age of seven months. The joy of the magnates was indescribable; they sank into each other's arms with tears of joy. At this moment old enemies were reconciled; women who had long nourished a mutual hatred, now tenderly pressed each other's hands; tears of joy were trembling in eyes which had never before been known to weep; friendly smiles were seen on lips which had usually been curled with anger; and every one extolled with ecstasy the happiness of Russia, and humbly bowed before the new sun now rising over that blessed realm.

With the utmost enthusiasm they all took the oath of fidelity to the new ruler, and then hastened to the palace of the Prince of Brunswick, there with the humblest subjection to kiss the delicate little hand of the child-emperor Ivan.

Münnich was again alone with the duke, who, forgetting all his ill-boding dreams, now gave himself up to the proud feeling of his greatness and power.

"Let them all go," said he, "these magnates, to kiss the hand of this emperor of seven months, and wallow in the dust before the cradle of a whimpering nurseling! I shall nevertheless be the real emperor, and both sceptre and crown will remain in my hands!"

"But in your greatness and splendor you will not forget your faithful and devoted friends," said Münnich; "your highness will remember that it was I who chiefly induced the empress to name you as regent during the minority of Ivan, and that you gave me your word of honor that you would grant me the first request I should make to you."

"I know, I know," said Biron, with a sly smile, thoughtfully pacing the room with his hands behind his back. But, suddenly stopping, he remained standing before Münnich, and, looking him sharply in the eye, said: "Shall I for once interpret your thoughts, Field-Marshal Count Münnich? Shall I for once tell you why you used all your influence to decide the Empress Anna to name me for the regency? Ah, you had a sharp eye, a sure glance, and conse- quently discovered that Anna had long since resolved in her heart to name me for the regency, before you undertook to confirm her in this resolve by your sage counsels. But you said to yourself: 'This good empress loves the Duke of Courland; hence she will undoubtedly desire to render him great and happy in spite of all opposition, and if I aid in this by my advice I shall bind both parties to myself; the empress, by appearing to be devoted to her favorite, and the favorite, by aiding him in the accomplishment of his ambitious plans. I shall therefore secure my own position, both for the present and future!' Confess to me, field-marshal, that these were your thoughts and calculations."

"The regent, Sir Duke of Courland, has a great knowledge of human nature, and hence I dare not contradict him," said Münnich, with a constrained laugh. "Your highness therefore recognizes the service that I, from whatever motive, have rendered you, and hence you will not refuse to grant my request?"

"Let me hear it," said the duke, stretching himself out on a divan, and negligently playing with a portrait of the Empress Anna, splendidly ornamented with brilliants, and suspended from his neck by a heavy gold chain.

"Name me generalissimo of all the troops," said Münnich, with solemnity.

"Of all the troops?" asked Biron. "Including those on the water, or only those on land?"

"The troops on the water as well as those on land." *

* Levecque, "Histoire de la Russie," vol. v p. 209.

"Ah, that means, I am to give you unlimited power, and thus place you at the head of all affairs!" Then, suddenly rising from his reclining position, and striding directly to Münnich, the duke threateningly said: "In my first observation I forgot to interpret a few of your thoughts and plans. I will now tell you why you wished for my appointment as regent. You desired it for the advancement of your own ambitious plans. You knew Biron as an effeminate, yielding, pleasure-seeking favorite of the empress—you saw him devoted only to amusement and enjoyment, and you said to yourself: 'That is the man I need. As I cannot myself be named regent, let it be him! I will govern through him; and while this voluptuous devotee of pleasure gives himself up to the intoxication of enjoyments, I will rule in his stead.' Well, Mr. Field-Marshal, were not those your thoughts?"

Münnich had turned very pale while the duke was thus speaking, and a sombre inquietude was depicted on his features.

"I know not," he stammered, with embarrassment.

"But *I* know!" thundered the duke, "and in your terror-struck face I read the confirmation of what I have said. Look in the glass, sir count, and you will make no further attempt at denial."

"But the question here is not about what I might have once thought, but of what you promised me. Your highness, I have made my first request! It is for you to grant it. I implore you on the strength of your ducal word to name me as the generalissimo of your troops!"

"No, never!" exclaimed the duke.

"You gave me your word!"

"I gave it as Duke of Courland! The regent is not bound by the promise of the duke."

"I made you regent!"

"And I do *not* make you generalissimo!"

"You forfeit your word of honor?"

"No, ask something else, and I will grant it. But this is not feasible. I must myself be the generalissimo of my own troops, or I should no longer be the ruler! Ask, therefore, for something else."

Münnich was silent. His features indicated a frightful commotion, and his bosom heaved violently.

"I have nothing further to ask," said he, after a pause.

"But I will confer upon you a favor without your asking it!" proudly responded the duke. "Count Münnich, I confirm you in your offices and dignities, and, to prove to you my unlimited confidence, you shall continue to be what you were under the Empress Anna, field-marshal in the Russian army!"

"I thank you, sir duke," calmly replied Münnich. "It is very noble in you that you do not send me into banishment for my presumptuous demand."

Clasping the offered hand of the duke, he respectfully pressed it to his lips.

"And now go, to kiss the hand of the young emperor, that you may not be accused of disrespect," smilingly added

Biron; "one must always preserve appearances."

Münnich silently bowed, while walking backward toward the door.

"We part as friends?" asked the duke, nodding an adieu.

"As friends for life and death!" said Münnich, with a smile.

But no sooner had the door closed behind him than the smile vanished from his features, and was replaced by an expression of furious rage. He threateningly shook his fist toward the door which separated him from the duke, and with convulsively compressed lips and grating teeth he said: "Yes, we now part as friends, but we shall yet meet as enemies! I shall remember this hour, sir duke, and shall do my best to prevent your forgetting it. Ah, you have not sent me to Siberia, but I will send you there! And now to the Emperor Ivan. I shall there meet his parents, the shamefully-slighted Ulrich of Brunswick, and his wife Anna Leopoldowna. I think they will welcome me."

With a firm step, rage and vengeance in his heart, but outwardly smiling and submissive, Field-Marshal Count Münnich betook himself to the palace of the Duke of Brunswick, to kiss the hand of the cradled Emperor Ivan.

CHAPTER III.

COUNT OSTERMANN.

FOUR weeks had passed since Biron, Duke of Courland, had commenced his rule over Russia, as regent, in the name of the infant Emperor Ivan. . The Russian people had with indifference submitted to this new ruler, and manifested the same subjection to him as to his predecessor. It was all the same to them whoever sat in godlike splendor upon the magnificent imperial throne—what care that mass of degraded slaves, who are crawling in the dust, for the name by which their tyrants are called? They remain what they are, slaves; and the one upon the throne remains what he is, their absolute lord and tyrant, who has the right to-day to scourge them with whips, to-morrow to make them barons and counts, and perhaps the next day to send them to Siberia, or subject them to the infliction of the fatal knout. Whoever proclaims himself emperor or dictator, is greeted by the Russian people, that horde of creeping slaves, as their lord and master, the supreme disposer of life and death, while they crawl in the dust at his feet.

They had sworn allegiance to the Regent Biron, as they had to the Empress Anna; they threw themselves upon the earth when they met him, they humbly bared their heads when passing his palace; and when the magnates of the realm, the princes and counts of Russia, in their proud equipages, discovered the regent's carriage in the distance, they ordered a halt, descended from their vehicles, and bowed themselves to the ground before their passing lord. In Russia, all distinctions of rank cease in the presence of the ruler; there is but one lord, and one trembling slave, be he prince or beggar, and that lord must be obeyed, whether he commands a murder or any other crime. The word and the will of the emperor purify and sanctify every act, blessing it and making it honorable.

Biron was emperor, although he bore only the name of regent; he had the power and the dominion; the infant nurseling Ivan, the minor emperor, was but a shadow, a phantom, having the appearance but not the reality of lordship; he was a thing unworthy of notice; he could make no one tremble with fear, and therefore it was unnecessary to crawl in the dust before him.

Homage was paid to the Regent Biron, Duke of Courland; the palace of Prince Ulrich of Brunswick, and his son, the Emperor Ivan, stood empty and desolate. No one regarded it, and yet perhaps it was worthy of regard.

Yet many repaired to this quiet, silent palace, to know whom Biron would perhaps have given princedoms and millions! But no one was there to betray them to the regent; they were very silent and very cautious in the palace of the Prince of Brunswick and his wife the Princess Anna Leopoldowna.

It was, as we have said, about four weeks after the commencement of the regency of the Duke of Courland, when a sedan-chair was set down before a small back door of the Duchess Anna Leopoldowna's palace; it had been borne and accompanied by four serfs, over whose gold-embroidered liveries, as if to protect them from the weather, had been laid a tolerably thick coat of dust and sweat. Equally splendid, elegant, and unclean was the chair which the servants now opened for the purpose of aiding their age-enfeebled master to emerge from it. That person, who now made his appearance, was a shrunken, trembling, coughing old gentleman; his small, bent, distorted form was wrapped in a fur cloak which, somewhat tattered, permitted a soiled and faded under-dress to make itself perceptible, giving to the old man the appearance of indigence and slovenliness. Nothing, not even the face, or the thin and meagre hands he extended to his servants, was neat and cleanly; nothing about him shone but his eyes, those gray, piercing eyes with their fiery side-glances and their now kind and now sly and subtle expression. This ragged and untidy old man might have been taken for a beggar, had not his dirty fingers and his faded neck-tie, whose original color was hardly discoverable, flashed with brilliants of an unusual size, and had not the arms emblazoned upon the door of his chair, in spite of the dust and dirt, betrayed a noble rank. The arms were those of the Ostermann family, and this dirty old man in the ragged cloak was Count Ostermann, the famous Russian statesman, the son of a German preacher, who had managed by wisdom, cunning, and intrigue to continue in place under five successive Russian emperors or regents, most of whom had usually been thrust from power by some bloody means. Czar Peter, who first appointed him as a minister of state, and confided to him the department of foreign affairs, on his death-bed said to his successor, the first Catharine, that Ostermann was the only one who had never made a false step, and recommended him to his wife as a prop to the empire. Catharine appointed him imperial chancellor and tutor of Peter II.; he knew how to secure and preserve the favor of both, and the successor of Peter II., the Empress Anna, was glad to retain the services of the celebrated statesman and diplomatist who had so faithfully served her predecessors. From Anna he came to her favorite, Biron of Courland, who did not venture to remove one whose talents had gained for him so distinguished a reputation, and who in any case might prove a very dangerous enemy.

But with Count Ostermann it had gone as with Count Münnich. Neither of them had been able to obtain from the regent any thing more than a confirmation of their offices and dignities, to which Biron, jealous of power, had been unwilling to make any addition. Deceived in their expectations, vexed at this frustration of their plans, they had both come to the determination to overthrow the man who was unwilling to advance them; they had become Biron's enemies because he did not show himself their friend, and, openly devoted to him and bowing in the dust before him, they had secretly repaired to his bitterest enemy, the Duchess Anna Leopoldowna, to offer her their services against the haughty regent who swayed the iron sceptre of his despotic power over Russia.*

A decisive conversation was this day to be held with the duchess and her husband, Prince Ulrich of Brunswick, and therefore, an unheard-of case, had even Count Ostermann resolved to leave his dusty room for some hours and repair to the palace of the Duchess Anna Leopoldowna.

"Slowly, slowly, ye knaves," groaned Ostermann, as he ascended the narrow winding stairs with the aid of his servants. "See you not, you hounds, that every one of your movements causes me insufferable pain? Ah, a fearful illness is evidently coming; it is already attacking my limbs, and pierces and agonizes every part of my system! Let my bed be prepared at home, you scamps, and have a strengthening soup made ready for me. And now away, fellows, and woe to you if, during my absence, either one of you should dare to break into the store-room or wine-cellar! You know that I have good eyes, and am cognizant of every article on hand, even to its exact weight and measure. Take care, therefore, take care! for if but an ounce of meat or a glass of wine is missing, I will have you whipped, you hounds, until the blood flows. That you may depend upon!"

And, dismissing his assistants with a kick, Count Ostermann ascended the last steps of the winding stairs alone and unaided. But, before opening the door

---

* Levecqua, "Histoire de Russie," vol. v., p. 241.

at the head of the stairs, he took time for reflection.

"Hem! perhaps it would have been better for me to have been already taken ill, for if this plan should miscarry, and the regent discover that I was in this palace to-day, how then? Ah, I already seem to feel a draught of Siberian air! But no, it will succeed, and how would that ambitious Münnich triumph should it succeed without me! No, for this time I must be present, to the vexation of Münnich, that he may not put all Russia in his pocket! The good man has such large pockets and such grasping hands!"

Nodding and smiling to himself, Ostermann opened the door of the ante-room. A rapid, searching glance satisfied him that he was alone there, but his brow darkened when he observed Count Münnich's mantle lying upon a chair.

"Ah, he has preceded me," peevishly murmured Ostermann. "Well, well, we can afford once more to yield the precedence to him. To-day he—to-morrow I! My turn will come to-morrow!"

Quite forgetting his illness and his pretended pains, he rapidly crossed the spacious room, and, throwing his ragged fur cloak upon Münnich's mantle, said:

"A poor old cloak like this is yet in condition to render that resplendent uniform invisible. Not a spangle of that magnificent gold embroidery can be seen, it is all overshadowed by the ragged old cloak which Münnich so much despises! Oh, the good field-marshal will rejoice to find his mantle in such good company, and I hope my old cloak may leave some visible memento upon its embroidered companion. Well, the field-marshal is a brave man, and I have given him an opportunity to make a campaign against his own mantle! The fool, why does he dislike these good little animals, and would yet be a Russian!"

As, however, he opened the door of the next room, his form again took its former shrunken, frail appearance, and his features again bore the expression of suffering and exhaustion.

"Ah, it is you," said Prince Ulrich, advancing to meet the count, while Münnich stood near a writing-table, in earnest conversation with Anna Leopoldowna, to whom he seemed to be explaining something upon a sheet of paper.

"We have waited long for you, my dear count," continued the prince, offering his hand to the new-comer, with a smile.

"The old and the sick always have the misfortune to arrive too late," said Count Ostermann, "pain and suffering are such hinderances, your grace. And, moreover, I have come only in obedience to the wishes of your highness, well knowing that I am superfluous here. What has the feeble old man to do in the councils of the strong?"

"To represent wisdom in council," said the prince, "and for that, you are precisely the man, count."

"Ah, Count Ostermann," at this moment interposed Münnich, "it is well you have come. You will be best able to tell their excellencies whether I am right or not."

"Field-Marshal Münnich is always right," said Ostermann, with a pleasant smile. "I unconditionally say 'yes' to whatever you may have proposed, provided that it is not a proposition of which my judgment cannot approve."

"That is a very conditional yes!" exclaimed the duchess, laughing.

"A 'yes,' all perforated with little back doors through which a 'no' may conveniently enter," laughed the prince.

"The back doors are in all cases of the greatest importance," said Count Ostermann, earnestly. "Through back doors one often attains to the rooms of state, and had your palace here accidentally had no back door for the admission of us, your devoted servants, who knows, your highness Anna, whether you would on this very night become regent!"

"On this night!" suddenly exclaimed Münnich. "You see, your highness, that Count Ostermann is wholly of my opinion. It must be done this night!"

"That would be overhaste," cried the duchess; "we are not yet prepared!"

"Nor is the regent, Biron of Courland," thoughtfully interposed Ostermann; "and, therefore, our overhaste would take Biron by surprise."

"Decidedly my own opinion," said Münnich. "All is lost if we give the regent time and leisure to make his arrangements. If we do not annihilate him to-day, he may, perhaps, send us to Siberia to-morrow."

The duchess turned pale; a trembling ran through her tall, noble form.

"I so much dread the shedding of blood!" said she.

"Oh, I am not at all vain," said Ostermann. "I find it much less unpleasant to see the blood of others flowing than my own. It may be egotism, but I prefer keeping my blood in my veins to exposing it to the gaping curiosity of an astonished crowd!"

"You think, then, that he already suspects, and would murder us?"

"You, us, and also your son, the Emperor Ivan."

"Also my son!" exclaimed Leopoldowna, her eyes flashing like those of an enraged lioness. "Ah, I should know how to defend my son. Let Biron fall this night!"

"So be it!" unanimously exclaimed the three men.

"He has driven us to this extremity," said the princess. "Not enough that he has banished our friends and faithful servants, surrounding us with his miserable creatures and spies—not enough that he wounds and humiliates us in every way—he would rend the young emperor from us, his parents, his natural protectors. We are attacked in our holiest rights, and must, therefore, defend ourselves."

"But what shall we do with this small Biron, when he is no longer the great regent?" asked Ostermann.

"We will make him by a head smaller," said Münnich, laughing.

"No," vehemently exclaimed Leopoldowna—"no, no blood shall flow! Not with blood shall our own and our son's rights be secured! Swear this, gentlemen, or I will never give my consent to the undertaking."

"I well knew that your highness would so decide," said Münnich, with a smile, drawing a folded paper from his bosom. "In proof of which I hand this paper to your highness."

"Ah, what is this?" said the duchess, unfolding the paper; "it is the ground plan of a house!"

"Of the house we will have built for Biron in Siberia," said Münnich; "I have drawn the plan myself."*

"In fact, you are a skilful architect, Count Munnich," said Ostermann, laughing, while casting an interrogating glance at the paper which Anna was still thoughtfully examining. "How well you have arranged it all! How delightful these snug little chambers will be! There will be just space enough in them to turn around in. But these small chambers seem to be a little too low. They are evidently not more than five feet high. As Biron, however, has about your height, he will not be able to stand upright in them."

"Bah! for that very reason!" said Münnich, with a cruel laugh. "He has carried his head high long enough; now he may learn to bow."

"But that will be a continual torment!" exclaimed the Duke of Brunswick.

"Oh, has he not tormented us?" angrily responded Münnich. "We need reprisals."

"How strange and horrible!" said Anna Leopoldowna, shuddering; "this man is now standing here clothed with unlimited power, and we are already holding in our hands the plan of his prison!"

"Yes, yes, and with this plan in his pocket will Count Münnich now go to dine with Biron and enjoy his hospitality!" laughingly exclaimed Oster-

mann. "Ah, that must make the dinner particularly piquant! How agreeable it must be to press the regent's hand, and at the same time feel the rustling in your pocket of the paper upon which you have drawn the plan of his Siberian prison! But you are in the right. The regent has deeply offended you. How could he dare refuse to make you his generalissimo?"

"Ah, it is not for that," said Münnich with embarrassment; and, seeking to give the conversation a different turn, he continued—"ah, see, Count Ostermann, what a terrible animal is crawling there upon your dress!"

"Policy, nothing but policy," tranquilly responded Ostermann, while the princess turned away with an expression of repugnance.

"Well," cried the prince, laughing, "explain to us, Count Ostermann, what those disgusting insects have to do with policy or politics?"

"We are all four Germans," said Ostermann, "and consequently are all familiar with the common saying, 'Tell me the company you keep, and I will tell you what you are!' I have always kept that in mind since I have been in Russia; and to make this good people forget that I am a foreigner, I have taken particular pains to furnish myself with a supply of their dirt and of these delicate insects. If any one asks me who I am, I show him these creatures with whom I associate, and he immediately concludes that I am a Russian."

Ostermann joined in the laugh that followed this explanation, but suddenly he uttered a piercing cry, and sank down upon a chair.

* Leveeque, vol. v., p. 214.

"Ah, these pains will be the death of me!" he moaned—"ah, I already feel the ravages of death in my blood; yes, I have long known that a dangerous malady was hovering over me, and my death-bed is already prepared at home! I am a poor failing old man, and who knows whether I shall outlive the evening of this day?"

While Ostermann was thus lamenting, and the prince with kindly sympathy was occupied about him, Münnich had returned the drawing to his pocket, and was speaking in a low tone to the duchess of some yet necessary preparations for the night. Count Ostermann, notwithstanding his lamentations and his pretended pains, had yet a sharp ear for every word they spoke. He very distinctly heard the duchess say: "Well, I am satisfied! I shall expect you at about two o'clock in the morning, and if the affair is successful, you, Count Münnich, may be sure of my most fervent gratitude; you will then have liberated Russia, the young emperor, and myself, from a cruel and despotic tyrant, and I shall be eternally beholden to you."

Count Münnich's brow beamed with inward satisfaction. "I shall, then, attain my ends," thought he. Aloud he said: "Your highness, I have but one wish and one request; if you are willing to fulfil this, then will there be nothing left on earth for me to desire."

"Then name your request at once, that I may grant it in advance!" said the princess, with a smile.

"The man is getting on rapidly, and will even now get the appointment of generalissimo," thought Ostermann.

"That must never be; I must prevent it!"

And just as Münnich was opening his mouth to prefer his request, Ostermann suddenly uttered so loud and piteous a cry of anguish that the compassionate and alarmed princess hastened to offer him her sympathy and aid.

At this moment the clock upon the wall struck four. That was the hour for which Münnich was invited to dine with the regent. It would not do to fail of his engagement to-day—he must be punctual, to avoid exciting suspicion. He, therefore, had no longer the time to lay his request before the princess; consequently Count Ostermann had accomplished his object, and secretly triumphing, he loudly groaned and complained of his sufferings.

Count Münnich took his leave.

"I go now," he smilingly said, "to take my last dinner with the Duke of Courland. I shall return this night at the appointed hour. We shall then convert the duke into a Siberian convict, which, at all events, will be a very interesting operation."

Thus he departed, with a horrible laugh upon his lips, to keep his appointment with the regent.

Count Ostermann had again attained his end—he remained alone with the princely pair. Had Münnich been the first who came, Ostermann was the last to go.

"Ah," said he, rising with apparent difficulty, "I will now bear my old, diseased body to my dwelling, to repose and perhaps to die upon my bed of pain."

"Not to die, I hope," said Anna.

"You must live, that you may see us in our greatness," said the prince.

Ostermann feebly shook his head. "I see, I see it all," said he. "You will liberate yourself from one tyrant, your highness, to become the prey of another. The eyes of the dying see clear, and I tell you, duchess, you were already on the point of giving away the power you have attained. Know you what Münnich's demand will be?"

"Well?"

"He will demand what Biron refused him, and for which refusal Münnich became his enemy. He will ask you to appoint him generalissimo of all your forces by land and sea."

"Then will he demand what naturally belongs to me," said the prince, excitedly, "and we shall of course refuse it."

"Yes, we must refuse it," repeated the princess.

"And in that you will do well," said Count Ostermann. "I may venture to say so, as I have no longer the least ambition—death will soon relieve me from all participation in affairs of state. I am a feeble old man, and desire nothing more than to be allowed occasionally to impart good counsels to my benefactors. And this is now my advice: Guard yourselves against the ambition of Count Münnich."

"We shall bear your counsel in mind," said the prince.

"We will not appoint him generalissimo!" exclaimed the princess. "He must never forget that he is our servant, and we his masters."

"And now permit me to go, your highness," said Ostermann. "Will you have the kindness, prince, to command your lackeys to bear me to my sedan-chair? It is impossible for me to walk a step. Yes, yes, while you are this night contending for a throne, I shall, perhaps, be struggling with death!"

And, with a groan, sinking back into the arms of the lackeys whom the prince had called, Ostermann suffered himself to be carried down to his chair, which awaited him at the door.

He groaned and cried out as they placed him in it, but as soon as its door was closed and his serfs were trotting with him toward his own palace, the suffering expression vanished from Ostermann's face, and a sly smile of satisfaction played upon his lips.

"I think I have well employed my time," he muttered to himself. "The good Münnich will never become generalissimo, and poor old failing Ostermann may now, unsuspected, go quietly to bed and comfortably await the coming events. Such an illness, at the right time, is an insurance against all accidents and miscarriages. I learned that after the death of Peter II. Who knows what would then have become of me had I not been careful to remain sick in bed until Anne had mounted the throne? I will, therefore, again be sick, and in the morning we shall see! Should this conjuration succeed, very well; then, perhaps, old Ostermann will gradually recover sufficient health to take yet a few of the burdens of state upon his own shoulders, and thus relieve the good Münnich of a part of his cares!"

CHAPTER IV.

THE NIGHT OF THE CONSPIRACY.

It was a splendid dinner, that which the regent had this day prepared for his guests. Count Münnich was very much devoted to the pleasures of the table, and, sitting near the regent, he gave himself wholly up to the cheerful humor which the excellent viands and delicate wines were calculated to stimulate. At times he entirely forgot his deep-laid plans for the coming night, and then again he would suddenly recollect them in the midst of his gayest conversation with his host, and while volunteering a toast in praise of the noble regent, and closing it by crying—"A long life and reign to the great regent, Biron von Courland!" he secretly and with a malicious pleasure thought: "This is thy last dinner, sir duke! A few hours, and those lips, now smiling with happiness, will be forever silenced by our blows!"

These thoughts made the field-marshal unusually gay and talkative, and the regent protested that Münnich had never been a more agreeable *convive* than precisely to-day. Therefore, when the other guests retired, he begged of Münnich to remain with him awhile; and the field-marshal, thinking it might possibly enable him to prevent any warning reaching the regent, consented to stay.

They spoke of past times, of the happy days when the Empress Anne yet reigned, and when all breathed of pleasure and enjoyment at that happy court; and perhaps it was these recollections that rendered Biron sad and thoughtful. He was absent and low-spirited, and his large, flashing eyes often rested with piercing glances upon the calm and smiling face of Münnich.

"You all envy me on account of my power and dominion," said he to Münnich; "of that I am not ignorant. But you know not with what secret pain and anguish these few hours of splendor are purchased!—the sleepless nights in which one fears seeing the doors open to give admission to murderers, and then the dreams in which blood is seen flowing, and nothing is heard but death-shrieks and lamentations! Ah, I hate the nights, which are inimical to all happiness. In the night will misfortune at some time overtake me—in the night the evil spirit reigns!"

With a drooping head the regent had spoken half to himself; but suddenly raising his head and looking Münnich sharply in the .eye, he said: "Have you, Mr. Field-Marshal, during your campaigns, never in the night foreseen any important event?"

Münnich shuddered slightly, and

the color forsook his cheeks. "He knows all, and I am lost," thought he, and his hand involuntarily sought his sword. "I will defend myself to the last drop of my blood," was his first idea.

But Biron, although surprised, saw nothing of the field-marshal's strange commotion—he was wholly occupied with his own thoughts, and only awaited an answer to his question.

"Well, Mr. Field-Marshal," he repeated, "tell me whether in the night you have ever had the presentiment of any important event?"

"I was just considering," he calmly said. "At this moment I do not recollect ever having foreseen any extraordinary event by night. But it has always been a principle of mine to take advantage of every favorable opportunity, whether by day or night." *

Münnich remained with the regent until eleven o'clock in the evening, and then they separated with the greatest kindness and the heartiest assurances of mutual friendship and devotion.

"Ah, that was a hard trial!" said Münnich, breathing easier and deeper, as he left the palace of the duke behind him. "I was already convinced that all was lost, but this Biron is unsuspecting as a child! Sleep now, Biron, sleep!—in a few hours I shall come to awaken you, and realize your bloody dream!"

With winged steps he hastened to his own palace. Arrived there, he summoned his adjutant, Captain von Maunstein, and, after having briefly given

him the necessary orders, took him with him into his carriage for the purpose of repairing to the palace of the Prince of Brunswick.

It was a cold November night of the year 1740. The deserted streets were hushed in silence, and no one of the occupants of the dark houses, no one on earth, dreamed that this carriage, whose rumbling was only half heard in sleep, was in a manner the thundering herald of new times and new lords.

Münnich had chosen his time well. For if it was forbidden to admit any one whatever, during the night, to the palace occupied by the young czar, and if also the regent had given the guards strict orders to shoot any one who might attempt, in spite of these commands, to penetrate into the forbidden precincts, this day made an exception for Münnich, as a portion of one of his own regiments was to-day on duty at the imperial palace.

Unimpeded, stayed by no one, Münnich penetrated to the apartments of Anna Leopoldowna. She was awaiting him, and at his side she descended to receive the homage of the officers and soldiers, who had been commanded by Münnich to submit themselves to her.

With glowing words she described to the listening soldiers all the insults and injuries to which the regent had subjected herself, her husband, and their son the emperor.

"Who can say that this miserable, low-born Biron is called to fill so exalted a place, and to lord it over you, my beloved friends and brothers? To me, as the niece of the blessed Empress

* Mannstein's, Memoirs p. 211; Levecque, vol. v., p. 240.

Anne, to me, as the mother of Ivan, chosen as emperor by Anne, to me alone belongs the regency, and by Heaven I will reconquer that of which I have been nefariously robbed! I will punish this insolent upstart whose shameful tyranny we have endured long enough, and I hope you, my friends, will stand by me and obey the commands of your generals!"*

A loud *viva* followed this speech of Anna Leopoldowna, who tenderly embraced the enraptured officers, commanding them to follow her.

Accompanied by Marshal Münnich and eighty soldiers, Anna then went out into the streets. In silence they advanced to within a hundred steps of Biron's palace. Here, making a halt, Mannstein alone approached the palace to command the officers of the guard in the name of the new regent, Anna Leopoldowna, to submit and pay homage to her. No opposition was made; accustomed always to obey, they had not the courage to dispute the commands of the new ruler, and declared themselves ready to assist her in the arrest of the regent.

Mannstein returned to Anna and Münnich with this joyful intelligence, and received orders to penetrate into the palace with twenty men, to capture the duke, and even kill him if he made resistance.

Without opposition Mannstein again returned to the palace with his small band, carefully avoiding making the least noise in his approach. All the soldiers in the palace knew him; and as the watch below had permitted him to pass, they supposed he must have an important message for the duke, and no one stopped him.

He had already wandered through several rooms, when an unforeseen difficulty presented itself. Where is the sleeping-room of the duke? Which way must he turn, in order to find him? He stood there undecided, not daring to ask any of the attendants in the anterooms, lest perhaps they might suspect him and awaken the duke! He finally resolved to go forward and trust to accident. He passed two or three chambers—all were empty, all was still!

Now he stands before a closed door! What if that should prove the chamber of the duke? He thinks he hears a breathing.

He cautiously tries the door. Slightly closed, it yields to his pressure, and he enters. There stands a large bed with hanging curtains, which are boldly drawn aside by Mannstein.

Before him lies the regent, Duke Biron of Courland, with his wife by his side.

"Duke Biron, awake!" called Mannstein, with a loud voice. The ducal pair started up from their slumber with a shriek of terror.

Biron leaps from the bed, but Mannstein overpowers him and holds him fast until his soldiers come. The duke defends himself with his hands, but is beaten down with musket-stocks. They bind his hands with an officer's scarf, they wrap him in a soldier's mantle, and so convey him down to Field-Marshal Münnich's carriage which is waiting, below, to transport him to the winter palace.

---

* Levecque, vol. v., p. 241.

While Mannstein and the soldiers were occupied with the duke, his duchess had found an opportunity to make her escape. With only her light nightdress, shrieking and lamenting, she had rushed into the street.

She was seized by a soldier, who, conducting her to Mannstein, asked what he should do with her.

"Take her back into the palace!" said Mannstein, hastening past.

But the soldier, only anxious to rid himself of an encumbrance, threw the now insensible duchess into the snow, and hurried away.

In this situation she was found by a captain of the guard, who lifted her up and conveyed her into the palace to give her over to the care of her women, that she might be restored to consciousness and dressed. But she no longer had either women or servants! Her reign is over; they have all fled in terror, as from the house of death, that they may not be involved in the disaster of those whose good fortunes they have shared. The slaves had all decamped in search of new masters, and the regent's palace, so often humbly and reverently sought, is now avoided as a pest-house.

With trembling hands the duchess enveloped herself in her clothes, and then followed her husband to the winter palace.

And while all this was taking place the court and nation yet trembled at the names of these two persons who had just been so deeply humbled. The Princess Anna Leopoldowna, accompanied by the shouting soldiery, made a triumphant progress through the streets of the city, stopping at all the caserns to receive the oaths and homage of the regiments.

This palace-revolution was consummated without the shedding of blood, and the awaking people of St. Petersburg found themselves with astonishment under a new regency and new masters! *

But a population of slaves venture no opposition. Whoever may have the power to declare and maintain himself their ruler, he is their master, and the slavish horde bow humbly before him.

As, hardly four weeks previously, the great magnates of the realm had hurried to the Duke of Courland to pay their homage and prostrate themselves in the dust before him, so did they now hasten to the palace of the new regent, humbly to pay their court to her. The same lips that even yesterday swore eternal fidelity to the Regent Biron, and sounded his praise to the skies, now condemned him, and as loudly commended their august new mistress, Anna Leopoldowna! The same knees which had yesterday bent to Biron, now bent before Anna; and, with tears of joy, men now again sank into the arms of each other, loudly congratulating their noble Russia upon which the sun of happiness had now risen, giving her Anna Leopoldowna as regent!

And while all was jubilation in the palace of the new regent, that of the great man of yesterday stood silent and deserted—no one dared to raise a voice in his favor! Those who yesterday revelled at his table and sang his praises,

* Levecque, vol. v., p. 241, and following.

were to-day his bitterest enemies, cursing him the louder the more they had landed him yesterday.

Magnificent festivals were celebrated in St. Petersburg in honor of the new regent, while they were at the same time trying the old one and condemning him to death. But Anna Lepoldowna mitigated his punishment—what a mitigation!—by changing the sentence of death into that of perpetual banishment to Siberia!

CHAPTER V.

HOPES DECEIVED.

TRANQUILLITY was again established in Russia. Once again all faces were lighted up with joy at this new state of affairs, and again the people congratulated themselves on the good fortune of the Russian empire! All this was done four weeks previously, when Biron took upon himself the regency, and the same will be done again when another comes to overthrow the regent Anna!

It was on the day after this new revolution, when Münnich, entering the palace with a proud step and elevated head, requested an interview with the regent.

"Your highness," he said, not bending the knee before his sovereign as custom demanded, but only slightly pressing her hand to his lips—"your highness, I have redeemed my word and fulfilled my promise. I promised to liberate you from Biron and make you regent, and I have kept my word. Now, madame, it is for you to fulfil your pledge! You solemnly promised that when I should succeed in making you regent, you would immediately and unconditionally grant me whatever I might demand. Well, now, you are regent, and I come to proffer my request!"

"It will make me happy, field-marshal, to discharge a small part of my obligations toward you, by yielding to your demand. Ask quickly, that I may the sooner give!" said Anna Leopoldowna, with an engaging smile.

"Make me the generalissimo of your forces!" responded Münnich in an almost commanding tone.

A cloud gathered over the smiling features of the regent.

"Why must you ask precisely this—this one only favor which it is no longer in my power to bestow?" she sadly said. "There are so many offices, so many influential positions—ah, I could prove my gratitude to you in so many ways! Ask for money, treasures, landed estates—all these it is in my power to give. Why must you demand precisely that which is no longer mine!"

Münnich stared at her with widely-

opened eyes, trembling lips, and pallid
cheeks. His head swam, and he thought
he could not have rightly heard.

"I hope this is only a misunderstanding!" he stammered. "I must have
heard wrong; it cannot be your intention to refuse me."

"Would to God it were yet in my
power to gratify you!" sighed the regent. "But I cannot give what is no
longer mine! Why came you not a few
hours earlier, field-marshal? then would
it have been yet possible to comply
with your request. But now it is too
late!"

"You have, then, appointed another generalissimo?" shrieked Münnich,
quivering with rage.

"Yes," said Anna, smiling; "and
see, there comes my generalissimo!"

It was the regent's husband, Prince
Ulrich von Brunswick, who that moment entered the room and calmly
greeted Münnich.

"You have here a rival, my husband," said the princess, without embarrassment; "and had I not already
signed your diploma, it is very ques-
tionable whether I should now do it,
now that I know Count Münnich desires the appointment."

"I hope," proudly responded the
prince, "Count Münnich will comprehend that this position, which places
the whole power of the empire in the
hands of him who holds it, is suitable
only for the father of the emperor!"

Count Münnich made no answer.
Already so near the attainment of his
end, he saw it again elude his grasp.
Again had he labored, struggled, in
vain. This was the second revolution
which he had brought about, with this
his favorite plan in view: two regents
were indebted to him for their greatness, and both had refused him the one
thing for which he had made them regents; neither had been willing to create him generalissimo!

In this moment Münnich felt unable
to conceal his rage under an assumed
tranquillity; pretending a sudden attack
of illness, he begged permission to retire.

Tottering, scarcely in possession of
his senses, he hastened through the hall
thronged with petitioners. All bowed
before him, all reverently saluted him;
but to him it seemed that he could read
nothing but mockery and malicious joy
upon all those smiling faces. Ah, he
could have crushed them all, and trodden them under his feet, in his inex-
tinguishable rage!

When he finally reached his carriage,
and his proud steeds were bearing him
swiftly away—when none could any
longer see him—then he gave vent to
furious execrations, and tears of rage
flowed from his eyes; he tore out his
hair and smote his breast; he felt himself wandering, frantic with rage and
despair. One thought, one wish had
occupied him for many long years; he
had labored and striven for it. He
wished to be the first, the most powerful man in the Russian empire; he
would control the military force, and
in his hands should rest the means of
giving the country peace or war! That
was what he wanted; that was what
he had labored for—and now. . . . .

"Oh, Biron, Biron," he faintly
groaned, "why must I overthrow you?

You loved me, and perhaps would one day have accorded me what you at first refused! Biron, I have betrayed you with a kiss. It is your guardian angel who is now avenging you!"

Thus he reached his palace, and the servants who opened the door of his carriage started back with alarm at the fearful expression of their master's face. It had become of an ashen gray, his blue lips quivered, and his gloomily-gleaming eyes seemed to threaten those who dared approach him.

Alighting in silence, he strode on through the rows of his trembling servants. Suddenly two of his lackeys fell upon their knees before him, weeping and sobbing; they stretched forth their hands to him, begging for mercy.

"What have they done?" asked he of his major-domo.

"Feodor has had the misfortune to break your excellency's drinking-cup, and Ivanovitch bears the blame of suffering your greyhound Artemisia to escape."

A strange joy suddenly lighted up the brow of the count.

"Ah," said he, breathing more freely, and stretching himself up—"ah, I thank God that I now have some one on whom I can wreak my vengeance!"

And kicking the unfortunate weeping and writhing servants, who were crawling in the dust before him, Münnich cried:

"No mercy, you hounds—no, no mercy! You shall be scourged until you have breathed out your miserable lives! The knout here! Strike! I will look on from my windows, and see that my commands are executed! Ah,

I will teach you to break my cups and let my hounds escape! Scourge them unto death! I will see their blood—their red, smoking blood!"

The field-marshal stationed himself at his open window. The servants had formed a close circle around the unhappy beings who were receiving their punishment in the court below. The air was filled with the shrieks of the tortured men, blood flowed in streams over their flayed backs, and at every new stroke of the knout they howled and shrieked for mercy; while at every new shriek Münnich cried out to his executioners:

"No, no mercy, no pity! Scourge the culprits! I would, I must see blood! Scourge them to death!"

Trembling, the band of servants looked on with folded hands; with a savage smile upon his face, stood Count Münnich at his window above.

Weaker and weaker grew the cries of the unhappy sufferers—they no longer prayed for mercy. The knout continued to flay their bodies, but their blood no longer flowed—they were dead!

The surrounding servants folded their hands in prayer for the souls of the deceased, and then loudly commended the mild justice of their master!

Retiring from the window, Count Münnich ordered his breakfast to be served! *

---

* Such horribly cruel punishments of the serfs were at that time no uncommon occurrence in Russia. Unhappy serfs were daily scourged to death at the command of their masters. Moreover, princes and generals, and even respectable ladies, were scourged with the knout at the command of the emperor. Yet these punishments in Russia had nothing dishonoring in them. The Empress Catharine II. had three of her court ladies stripped and scourged in the presence of the

From that time forward, however, Münnich's life was a continuous chain of vexations and mortifications. As his inordinate ambition was known, he was constantly suspected, and was reprehended with inexorable severity for every fault.

It is true the regent raised him to the post of first minister; but Ostermann, who recovered his health after the successful termination of the revolutionary enterprise, by various intrigues attained to the position of minister of foreign affairs; while to Golopkin was given the department of the interior, so that only the war department remained to the first minister, Münnich. He had originated and accomplished two revolutions that he might become generalissimo, and had obtained nothing but mortifications and humiliations that embittered every moment of his life!

whole court, for having drawn some offensive caricatures of the great empress. One of these scourged ladies, afterward married to a Russian magnate, was sent by Catharine as a sort of ambassadress to Sweden, for the purpose of inducing the King of Sweden to favor some of her political plans.—"Mémoires Secrets sur la Russie, par Masson," vol. iii., p. 392.

CHAPTER VI.

THE REGENT ANNA LEOPOLDOWNA.

ANNA had succeeded, she was regent; she had shaken off the burden of the Bironic tutelage, and her word was all-powerful throughout the immeasurable provinces of the Russian empire. Was she now happy, this proud and powerful Anna Leopoldowna? No one had ever yet been happy and free from care upon this Russian throne, and how, then, could Anna Leopoldowna be so? She had read the books of Russian political history, and that history was written with blood! Anna was a woman, and she trembled when thinking of the poison, the dagger, the throttling hands, and flaying sword, which had constantly beset the throne of Russia, and in a manner been the means in the hands of Providence of clearing it from one tyrant, only, indeed, to make room for another. Anna, as we have said, trembled before this means of Providence; and when her eyes fell upon Münnich—upon his dark, angry brow and his secretly threatening glance—she then with inward terror asked herself: "May not Providence have chosen him for my murderer? Will he not overthrow me, as he overthrew his former master and friend Duke Biron?"

Anna now feared him whom she had chiefly to thank for her greatness. At the time when he had made her regent he had satisfactorily shown that his arm was sufficiently powerful to displace one regent and hurl him to the dust! What he had once done, might he not now be able to accomplish again?

She surrounded this feared field-marshal with spies and listeners; she caused all his actions to be watched, every one of his words to be repeated to her, in order to ascertain whether it had not some concealed sense, some threatening secret; she doubled the guards of her palace, and, always trembling with fear, she no longer dared to occupy any one of her apartments continuously. Nomadically wandered they about in their own palace, this Regent Anna Leopoldowna and her husband Prince Ulrich of Brunswick; remembering the sleeping-chamber of Biron, she dared not select any one distinct apartment for constant occupation; every evening found her in a new room, every night she reposed in a different bed, and even her most trusted servant often knew not in which wing of the castle the princely pair were to pass the night.*

She, before whom these millions of Russian subjects humbled themselves in the dust, trembled every night in her bed at the slightest rustling, at the whisperings of the wind, at every breath of air that beat against her closed and bolted doors.

She might, it is true, have released herself from these torments with the utterance of only one word of command; it required only a wave of her hand to send this haughty and dangerous Münnich to Siberia! Nor was an excuse for such a proceeding wanting. Count Münnich's pride and presump-

tion daily gave occasion for anger; he daily gave offence by his reckless disregard of and disrespect for his chief, the generalissimo, Prince Ulrich; daily was it necessary to correct him and to confine him within his own proper official boundaries.

And such refractory conduct toward a Russian master, had it not in all times been a terrible and execrable crime—a crime for which banishment to Siberia had always been considered a mild punishment?

Poor Anna! called to rule over Russia, she lacked only the first and most necessary qualification for her position —a Russian heart! There was, in this German woman's disposition, too much gentleness and mildness, too much confiding goodness. To a less barbarous people she might have been a blessing, a merciful ruler and gracious benefactor!

But her arm was too weak to wield the knout instead of the sceptre over this people of slaves, her heart too soft to judge with inexorable severity according to the barbarous Russian laws which, never pardoning, always condemn and flay.

It was this which gradually estranged from her the hearts of the Russians. They felt that it was no Russian who reigned over them; and because they had no occasion to tremble and creep in the dust before her, they almost despised her, and derided the idyllic sentiments of this good German princess who wished to realize her fantastic dreams by treating a horde of barbarians as a civilized people!

The slaves longed for their former

* Levecque, vol. v., p. 218.

yoke; they looked around them with a feeling of strangeness, and to them it seemed unnatural not everywhere to see the brandished knout, the avenging scaffold, and the transport-carriages departing for Siberia!

Much as Ostermann importuned her, often as her own husband warned her, Anna nevertheless refused; she would not banish Field-Marshal Münnich to Siberia, but remained firm in her determination to leave him in possession of his liberty and his dignities.

But when Münnich himself, excited and fatigued with these never-ending annoyances, and moreover believing that Anna could not do without him, and therefore would not grant his request, finally demanded his dismission, Anna granted it with joy; and Münnich, deceived in all his ambitious plans and expectations, angrily left the court to betake himself to his palace beyond the Neva.

Anna now breathed easier; she now felt herself powerful and free, for Münnich was at least removed farther from her; his residence was no longer separated from hers only by a wall, she had no longer to fear his breaking through in the night—ah, Münnich dwelt beyond the Neva, and a whole regiment guarded its banks and bridges by night! Münnich could no longer fall upon her by surprise, as she could have him always watched.

Anna no longer trembled with fear; she could yield to her natural indolence, and if she sometimes, from fear of Münnich, troubled herself about state affairs and labored with her ministers, she now felt it to be an oppressive burden, to which she could no longer consent to subject herself.

Satiated and exhausted, she in some measure left the wielding of the sceptre to her first and confidential minister, Count Golopkin. He ruled in her name, as Count Ostermann was generalissimo in the name of her husband the Prince of Brunswick. Why trouble themselves with the pains and cares of governing, when it was permitted them to only enjoy the pleasures of their all-powerful position?

The minister might flourish the knout and proclaim the Siberian banishment over the trembling people; the scourged might howl, and the banished might lament, the great and powerful might dispose of the souls and bodies of their serfs; rare honesty might be oppressed by consuming usury; offices, honors, and titles might be gambled for; justice and punishment might be bought and sold; vice and immorality might universally prevail—Anna would not know it. She would neither see nor hear any thing of the outside world! The palace is her world, in which she is happy, in which she revels!

Ah, that charming, silent little boudoir, with its soft Turkish carpet, with its elastic divans and heavily curtained windows and doors—that little boudoir is now her paradise, the temple of her happiness! In it she lingers, and in it is she blessed. There she reposes, dreaming of past delightful hours, or smiling with the intoxication of the still more delightful present in the arms of the one she loves.

CHAPTER VII.

THE FAVORITE.

SEE how her eyes flash, how her heart beats—how beautiful she is in the warm glow of excitement, this beautiful Anna Leopoldowna!

The door opens, and a smiling young maiden looks in with many a nod of her little head.

"Ah, is it you, my Julia?" calls the princess, opening her arms to press the young girl to her heart. "Come, I will kiss you, and imagine it is he who receives the kiss! Ah, what would this poor Anna Leopoldowna be if deprived of her dear friend, Julia von Mengden?" And, drawing her favorite down into her lap, she continued: "Now relate to me, Julia. Set your tongue in motion, that I may hear one of your very pleasantest stories. That will divert me, and cause the long hours before his coming to pass more quickly."

Julia von Mengden roguishly shook her beautifully curling locks with a comic earnestness, and, very aptly and unmistakably imitating the somewhat hoarse and nasal voice of Prince Ulrich, said :

" Your grace forgets that you are regent, and have to hold the reins of government in the name of the illustrious imperial squaller, your son, since his imperial grace still remains in his swaddling-clothes, and has much less to do with state affairs than with many other little occupations !"

Anna Leopoldowna, breaking out in joyous laughter, exultingly clapped her little hands, which were sparkling with brilliants.

"This is superb," said she. "You play the part of my very worthy husband to perfection. It is as if one saw and heard him. Ah, I would that he resembled you a little, as he would then be less insupportable, and it would be somewhat easier to endure him."

Julia von Mengden, making no answer to this remark, continued with her nasal voice and comic pathos :

"Your grace, this is not the time to analyze our diverting little domestic dissensions, and occupy ourselves with the quiet joys of our happy union! Your grace is, above all things, regent, and must give your attention to state affairs. Without are standing three most worthy, corpulent, tobacco-scented ambassadors, who desire an audience. Your grace is, above all things, regent, and must receive them."

"Must!" exclaimed Anna, suddenly contracting her brows. "We will first hear what they desire of us."

"The first is the envoy of the great Persian conqueror, Thamas-Kouli-Khan,

3

who comes to lay at your feet the magnificent presents of his master."

"Bah! they are presents for the young Emperor Ivan. He may, therefore, be conducted to the cradle of my son, and there display his presents. It does not interest me."

"The second is a messenger from our camp. He brings news of a great victory obtained by one of your brave generals over the Swedes!"

"But what does that concern me?" angrily cried the regent. "Let them conquer or be defeated, it is all the same to me. That concerns my husband the generalissimo! Let me be spared the sight of the warlike and blood-dripping messenger!"

"The third is the ambassador of the wavering and shaking young Austrian Empress Maria Theresa. He comes, he says, upon a secret mission, and pretends to have discovered a sort of conspiracy that is hatching against you."

"Let him go with his discovery to Golopkin, our minister of the interior. That is his business!"

"Your grace is, above all things, regent, and should remember—"

"Nothing—I will remember nothing!" exclaimed Anna Leopoldowna, interrupting her favorite. "I will not be annoyed, that is all."

"Well, thank God!" now cried Julia von Mengden, in her natural tone—"thank God, that such is your determination, princess! you are then, in earnest, and I am to send these three amiable persons to the devil, or, what is just the same, to your husband?"

"That is my meaning."

"And this is beautiful in you," continued Julia, cowering down before her mistress. "These eternal, tiresome and intolerable state affairs would make your face prematurely old and wrinkled, my dear princess. Ah, there is nothing more tedious than governing. I am heartily sick of it! At first I was amused when we two sat together and settled who should be sent to prison and who should be pardoned; whom we should make counts and princes, or degrade to the ranks as common soldiers. But all that pleased only for a short time; now it is annoying, and why should we take upon ourselves this trouble? Have we not the power to act and live according to our own good pleasure? Bah! that is the least compensation you should receive for allowing these horrid Russians the privilege of calling you their regent and mistress!"

"But, my little chatterer, you forget the three envoys who are waiting without," said Anna, with a smile.

"Ah, that is true! I must first send those wig-blocks away!" cried Julia, springing up and fluttering out of the room as lightly as a bird.

. "How lovely she is, and how agreeable it is to have her with me!" said Anna, tenderly looking after her departing favorite. "She is, indeed, my good genius, who drives away the cares from my poor brain."

"So, it is done!" cried Julia, quickly returning to the room. "I have sent the gentlemen away. To the Persian envoy I said: 'Go to our emperor, Ivan. He feeds upon brilliants, and, as he has had no breakfast this morning, his appetite will be good. Go, therefore, and give him your diamonds for breakfast. Anna Leopoldowna wants them not; she is already satiated with them!'—To the second I said: 'Go and announce your glorious victory to our sublime generalissimo. He is at his toilet, and as he every morning touches his noble cheeks with rouge, your new paint, prepared from the purple blood of the enemy, will doubtless be very welcome to him!'—'And as to what concerns your secret mission and your discovered conspiracy,' said I to the Austrian ambassador, 'I am sorry that you cannot here give birth to the dear children of your inventive head; go with them to our midwife, Minister Golopkin, and hasten a little, for I see in your face that you are already in the pangs of parturition!'"

"Well," asked Anna Leopoldowna, loudly laughing, "what said their worships to that?"

"What did they say? They said nothing! They were dumb and looked astonished. They made exactly such eyes as I have seen made at home, upon my father's estate in Liefland, by the calves when the butcher knocked them upon the head. But now," continued Julia, nestling again at the feet of her mistress, "now give me a token of your favor, and forget for a while that you are regent. Let us chat a little like a couple of real genuine women—that is, of our husbands and lovers. Oh, I have very important news for you!"

"Well, speak quickly," said Anna, with eagerness. "What have you to tell me?"

Julia assumed a very serious and important countenance. "The first and most important piece of news is, that your husband, Prince Ulrich of Brunswick, is very jealous of me, and yet of one other!"

"Bah!" said Anna, contemptuously, "let him be jealous. I do not trouble myself about it, and shall always do as I please."

"No, no, that will not do," seriously responded Julia. "It is so tiresome to always hear the wrangling and growling of a jealous husband! I tell your grace that I must have quiet in his presence; I can no longer bear his grim looks and his constant anger and abuse. You must soothe him, Princess Anna, or I will run away from this horrible court, where a poor maiden is not allowed to love her friend and mistress, the charming Princess Anna Leopoldowna, with all her heart and soul!"

The regent's eyes filled with tears. "My Julia," she tremulously said, "can you seriously think of leaving me? See you not that I should be thereby rendered very solitary and miserable?"

And, raising up her favorite into her arms, she kissed her.

Julia's bright eyes also filled with tears. "Think you, then, princess, that I could ever leave, ever be separated from you?" she tenderly asked. "No, my Princess Anna has such entire possession of my heart, that it has no room for any other feeling than the most unbounded love and devotion to my dear, my adored princess. But for the very reason that I love you, I cannot bear to have your husband fill the palace with his jealous complaints, and thus publishing to St. Petersburg and all the world your unfaithfulness and criminal intrigues. Oh, I tell you I see through this generalissimo, I know all his plans and secret designs. He would gladly be able to convict you of infidelity to him—then, with the help of the army he commands, declare his criminal wife unfit for the regency, and then make himself regent! He has a cunningly devised plan, but which my superior cunning shall bring to naught! I will play him a trick!—But no, I will tell you no more now! At the right time you shall know all. Now, Princess Anna, now answer me one question. Do you, then, so very much love this Count Lynar?"

The princess looked up with a dreamy smile. "Do I love him!" she then murmured low. "Oh, my God, Thou knowest how truly, how glowingly my heart clings to him. Thou knowest that of all the world I have never loved any other man than him alone! And you, Julia, you who know every emotion and palpitation of my heart, you yet ask me if I love him? Do you remember, child, when, four years ago, I first saw him—when he stood before me in all his proud manly beauty, with his conquering glance, his heart-winning smile? Ah, my whole heart already then flew to meet him. I revelled in the sight of him, I thought only of him, I spoke to him in my thoughts, and my prayers, I lived only when I saw him; and that happy, that never-to-be-forgotten day when he confessed his love, when he lay at my feet and swore eternal truth to me—ah, why could I not have died on that day? I was then so happy!"

"Poor Princess Anna," said Julia, sympathetically, "they soon grudged you that happiness!"

"Yes," continued Anna with a bitter smile, "yes, the virtuous Empress Anna blushed in the arms of her lover, Biron, at this aberration of her sold and coupled niece. She found it very revolting that the poor sixteen-year-old Anna Leopoldowna dared to have a heart of her own and to feel a real love. They must therefore rob her of the only happiness Heaven had vouchsafed her. Consequently, they wrote to Warsaw, asking, nay, commanding the recall of the ambassador, and Lynar was compelled to leave me."

"Ah, I well know how unhappy you were at that time," said Julia, pressing the hand of the princess to her bosom; "how you wept, how you wrung your hands—"

"And how I nowhere found mercy or commiseration," interposed Anna, with bitterness, "neither on earth nor in heaven. I was and remained deserted and solitary, and was compelled to marry this Prince Ulrich of Brunswick, for whom I felt nothing but a chilling, mortal indifference. But you must know, Julia, that when I stood with this man at the altar, and was compelled to become his wife, I thought only of him I loved; I vowed eternal truth only to Lynar, and when the prince folded me in his arms as his wife, then was my God gracious to me, and in a happy deception it seemed to me that it was my lover who held me in his arms—I thought only of him and breathed only his name, and loved him, kissed him, and became his wife, although he was far, alas, so immeasurably far from me! And when

I felt a second self under my heart, I then loved with redoubled warmth the distant one whom I had not seen for years; and when Ivan was born, it seemed to me that the eyes of my lover looked at me through his, and blessed my son whose spiritual father he was! And, my child, what think you gave me the courage to overthrow Biron and assume the regency? Ah, it was only that I might have the power to recall Lynar to my side! I would and must be regent, that I might demand the return of Lynar as ambassador from Warsaw. That gave me courage and decision; that enabled me to overcome all timidity and anxiety. I thought only of him, and when the end was attained, when I was declared regent, the first exercise of my power was to recall Lynar to court. Julia, what a happy day was that when I saw him again!"

And the princess, wholly absorbed in her delightful reminiscences, smilingly and silently reclined upon the cushions of the divan.

"Ah, it must be love that so thinks and feels," thoughtfully observed Julia. "I no longer ask you, Princess Anna, if you love the count, I now know you do. But answer me yet one question. Have you confidence in me—full, unlimited confidence? Will you never mistake, never doubt me?"

"Never!" said Anna Leopoldowna, confidently. "And if all the world should tell me that Julia von Mengden is a traitress, I would nevertheless firmly rely upon you, and reply to the whole world: 'That is false! Julia von Mengden is true and pure as gold. I shall always love her.'"

Julia gratefully glanced up to the heavens, and her eyes filled with tears.

"I thank you, princess," she then said, with a happy smile. "I now have courage for all. You shall now be enabled to love your Lynar without fear or trembling, and your husband's clouded brow and reproaching tongue shall molest us no more. Confide in me and ask no questions. It is all decided and arranged in my mind. But hark! do you hear nothing?"

Anna's face was transfused with a purple glow, and her eyes flashed.

"It is my beloved," said she. "Yes, it is he. I know his step!"

Julia smilingly opened the concealed door, and Count Lynar, with a cry of joy, rushed to the feet of his beloved.

"At length!" he exclaimed, clasping her feet, and pressing them to his bosom.

"Yes, at length!" murmured Anna, looking down upon him with a celestial smile.

Julia stood at a distance, contemplating them with thoughtful glances.

"They should be happy," she murmured low, and then asked aloud: "Count Lynar, did you receive my letter?"

"I did receive it," said the count, "and may God reward you for the sacrifice you are so generously disposed to make for us! Anna, your friend Julia is our good angel. To her we shall owe it if our happiness is henceforth indestructible and indissoluble. Do you know the immense sacrifice this young maiden proposes to make for us?"

"No, Princess Anna knows nothing, and shall know nothing of it," said Julia, with a grand air. "Princess Anna shall only know that I love her, and am ready to give my life for her. And now," she continued, with her natural gayety, "forget me, ye happy lovers! Lull yourselves in the sweet enjoyment of nameless ecstasies! I go to watch the spies, and especially your husband, lest he break in upon you without notice!"

And Julia suddenly left the room, shutting the door upon Anna Leopoldowna and her lover, the Polish Count Lynar.

CHAPTER VIII.

NO LOVE.

Prince Ulrich of Brunswick, the husband of the regent, had assembled the officers of his general staff for a secret conference. Their dark, threatening glances were prophetic of mischief, and angrily flashed the eyes of the prince, who, standing in their midst, had spoken to them in glowing words of his domestic unhappiness, and of the idle, dreamy, and amatory indolence into which the regent had fallen.

"She writes amorous complainings," he now said, with a voice of rage, in closing his long speech—"she writes sonnets to her lover, instead of governing and reading the petitions, reports, and other documents that come to her from the different ministries and bureaus, which she constantly returns unread. You are men, and are you willing to bear the humiliation of being governed by a woman who dishonors you by disregarding her first and holiest duties, and setting before your wives and daughters the shameful example of a criminal love, thus disgracing her own son, your emperor and master?"

"No, no, we will not bear it!" cried the wildly excited men, grasping the hilts of their swords. "Give us proof of her unfaithfulness, and we shall know how to act as becomes men over whom an adulterous woman would reign!"

"It is an unnatural and unendurable law that commands man to obey a woman. It is contrary to nature that the mother should rule in the name of her son, when the father is living—the father, whom nature and universal custom acknowledge as the lord and head of his wife and children!" cried the prince.

"Give us proof of her guilt," cried the soldiers, "and we will this very hour proclaim you regent in her stead!"

A confidential servant of the prince, who entered at this moment, now whispered a few words in his ear.

The prince's face flamed up. "Well, then, gentlemen," said he, straightening himself up, "you demand proof. In this very hour will I furnish it to you. But I do it upon one condition. No personal violence! In the person of your present regent you must respect the mother of your emperor, the wife of your future regent! Anna will yield to our just representations, and voluntarily sign the act of abdication in my favor. That is all we ought to demand of her. She will retain her sacred and inviolable rights as the wife of your regent, as the mother of your emperor. Forget not that!"

"First of all, give us the proof of her guilt!" impatiently cried the men.

"I shall, alas, be able to give it you!" said the prince, with dignity. "Far be it from me to desire the conviction of an innocent person! Believe me, nothing but her guilt could induce me to take action against her; were she innocent, I would be the first to kneel and renew to her my oath of fidelity and obedience. But you cannot desire that I, your generalissimo, should be the subject of a wife who shamefully treads under foot her first and holiest duty! The honor of you all is wounded in mine. Come, follow me now. I will show you Count Lynar in the arms of his mistress, the Regent Anna Leopoldowna!"

The prince strode forth, cautiously followed by his generals. They thus passed noiselessly through the long corridor leading from the wing of the palace inhabited by the prince to that occupied by the regent.

In the boudoir of the Regent Anna a somewhat singular scene was now presented.

The tender caresses of the lovers were suddenly interrupted by Julia von Mengden, who slipped in through the secret door in a white satin robe, and with a myrtle crown upon her head.

"Princess Anna, it is time for you to know all!" she hurriedly said. "Your husband is now coming here through the corridor with his generals; they hope to surprise you in your lover's arms, that they may have an excuse for deposing you from the regency and substituting your husband. Struggle against struggle! We will outwit them, and cure your husband of his jealousy! From this hour he shall be compelled to acknowledge that he was mistaken, and that it is for him to implore your pardon. Anna Leopoldowna, I love no one in the world but you, and therefore I am ready to do all that love can do for you. I will marry Count Lynar for the purpose of preserving you from suspicion and slander. I will bear the name of his wife, as a screen for the concealment of your loves." *

Anna's eyes overflowed with tears of emotion and transport.

"Weep not, my love," whispered the count, "be strong and great in this eventful hour! Now will you be forever mine, for this magnanimous friend veils and protects our union."

Julia opened the door and waved her hand.

A Russian pope in sacred vestments, followed by two other servants of the Church, entered the room. With them

* Levecque, "Histoire de la Russie," vol. v., p. 222.

came the most trusted maid-servants of Julia.

Clasping the count's hand and advancing to Anna, Julia said: "Grant, illustrious princess, that we may celebrate our solemn espousal in thy high presence, which is the best blessing of our union!"

Anna opened wide her arms to her favorite, and, pressing her to her bosom, whispered: "I will never forget thee, my Julia. My blessing upon thee, my angel!"

"I will be a true sister to him," whispered Julia in return; "always believe in me and trust me. And now, my Anna, calmness and self-possession! I already hear your husband's approach. Be strong and great. Let no feature of your dear face betray your inward commotion!"

And, stepping back to the count, Julia made a sign to the priest to commence the marriage ceremony.

Hand in hand the bridal pair knelt before the priest, the servants folded their hands in prayer, and, proudly erect, with a heavenly transfiguration of her noble face, stood Anna Leopoldowna—the priest commenced the ceremony.

A slight noise was heard at the closed, concealed door. The priest calmly continued to speak, the bridal pair remained in their kneeling position, and, calmly smiling, stood the regent by their side.

The door opened, and, followed by his generals, the enraged prince appeared upon the threshold.

No one suffered himself to be disturbed; the priest continued the service, the parties remained upon their knees, and Anna Leopoldowna stood looking on with a proud and tranquil smile.

Motionless, benumbed, as if struck by lightning, remained the prince upon the threshold; behind him were seen the astonished faces of his generals, who, on tiptoe, stretched their necks to gaze, over each other's shoulders, upon this singular and unexpected spectacle!

At length a murmur arose, they pressed farther forward toward the door, and, overcoming his momentary stupefaction, the prince ventured into the room.

An angry glance of the priest commanded silence; with a louder voice he continued his prayer. Anna Leopoldowna smilingly beckoned her husband to her side, and slightly nodded to the generals.

They bowed to the ground before their august mistress, the regent.

Now came the closing prayer and the dispensation of the blessing. The priest pronounced it kneeling,—the regent also bent the knee, and drew the prince down beside her. Following the example of the generalissimo, the other generals also sank upon their knees,—it was a general prayer, which no one dared disturb.

The ceremony was ended. The priest kissed and blessed the bridal pair, and then departed with his assistants; he was followed by the servants of the favorite.

Anna now turned with a proud smile to the prince.

"Accident, my husband, has made

you a witness of this marriage," said she. "May I ask your highness what procures me this unexpected and somewhat intrusive visit, and why my generals, unannounced, accompany you to their regent and mistress?"

The embarrassed prince stammered some unintelligible words, to which Anna paid no attention.

Stepping forward, she motioned the generals to enter, and with her most fascinating smile said: "Ah, I think I now know the reason of your coming, gentlemen! Your loyal and faithful hearts yearn for a sight of your young emperor. It is true, his faithful subjects have not seen him for a long time! Even a sovereign is not guaranteed against the evil influences of the weather, which has lately been very rough, and for that reason the young czar has been unable to show himself to his people. Ah, it pleases me that you have come, and I am obliged to my husband for bringing you to me so unexpectedly. You may now satisfy yourselves that the emperor lives and is growing fast. Julia, bring us the young emperor!"

Julia von Mengden silently departed, while Count Lynar, respectfully approaching the regent, said a few words to her in a low tone.

"You are quite right, sir count," said the regent aloud, and, turning to her husband and the generals, continued: "Count Lynar is in some trouble about the unexpected publicity given to his marriage. There are, however, important reasons for keeping it still a secret. The family of my maid of honor are opposed to this alliance with a for-

eigner, and insist that Julia shall marry another whom they have destined for her. On the other hand, certain family considerations render secrecy the duty of the count. Julia, oppressed by her inexorable relations, disclosed the state of affairs to me, and as I love Julia, and as I saw that she was wasting away with grief without the possession of her lover, I favored her connection with Count Lynar. They daily saw each other in my apartments, and, finally yielding to their united prayers, I consented that they should this day be legally united by the priest, and thus defeat the opposition of their respective families.

"This, gentlemen," continued Anna, raising her voice, "is the simple explanation of this mystery. I owed this explanation to myself, well knowing that secret slander and malicious insinuations might seek to implicate me in this affair, and that a certain inimical and evil-disposed party, displeased that you should have a woman for regent, would be glad to prove to you that all women are weak, faulty, and sinful creatures! Be careful how you credit such miserable tales!"

Silent, with downcast eyes, stood the generals under the flashing glance of the regent, who now turned to her husband with a mocking smile. "You, my prince and husband," said she, "you I have to thank!—your tenderness of heart induced you generously to furnish me with this opportunity to justify my conduct to my most distinguished and best-beloved subjects and servants, and thus to break the point of the weapon with which calumny threatened my breast! I therefore thank you, my husband. But see! there comes the emperor."

In fact, the folding-doors were at this moment thrown open, and a long train of palace officials and servants approached. At the head of the train was Julia von Mengden, bearing a velvet cushion bespangled with brilliants, upon which reposed the child in a dress of gold brocade. On both sides were seen the richly adorned nurses and attendants, and near them the major-domo, bearing upon a golden cushion the imperial crown and other insignia of empire.

Anna Leopoldowna took young Ivan in her arms; the child smiled in her face, and stretched forth his hand toward the sparkling crown.

With her son upon her arm, Anna majestically advanced to the centre of the hall, and, lifting up the child, said: "Behold your emperor! Respect and reverence for your illustrious master! Upon your knees in the presence of your emperor!"

It was as if all, servants, attendants, and generals, had been struck with a magic wand. They all fell upon their knees, and bowed their heads to the earth—venal slaves, one word from the ruler sufficed to set them all grovelling in the dust!

With a proud smile Anna enjoyed this triumph. Near her stood the prince, the father of the emperor, with rage and shame in his heart.

"Long live the emperor!" resounded from all lips, and the child Ivan, Emperor of all the Russias, screeched for joy at the noise and at the splendor of the assemblage.

"Long live our noble regent, Anna Leopoldowna!" now loudly cried Julia von Mengden.

Like a thundering cry of jubilation it was instantly echoed through the hall.

The generals were the first to join in this enthusiastic *viva!*

A quarter of an hour later the generals were permitted to retire, and the emperor was reconveyed to his apartments.

Anna Leopoldowna remained alone with her husband and the newly-married pair, who had retreated to the recess of a window and were whispering together.

Anna now turned to her husband, and, with cutting coldness in her tone, said:

"You must understand, my husband, that I am very generous. It was in my power to arrest you as a traitor, but I preferred only to shame you, because you, unhappily, are the father of my child."

"You think, then," asked the prince, with a scornful smile, "that I shall take the buffoonery you have just had played before us for truth?"

"That, my prince, must wholly depend upon your own good pleasure. But for the present I must request you to retire to your own apartments! I feel myself much moved and exhausted, and have also to prepare some secret dispatches for Count Lynar to take with him in his journey."

"Count Lynar is, then, to leave us?" quickly asked the prince, in an evidently more friendly tone.

"Yes," said Anna, "he leaves us for

some weeks to visit the estate in Liefland which I have given to Julia as a
bridal present, and to make there the
necessary preparations for the proper
reception of his wife."

Julia clasped the hands of her mistress, and bathed them with tears of
joy and gratitude.

"Anna," whispered Prince Ulrich,
" I did you wrong. Pardon me."

Anna coldly responded: "I will pardon you if you will be generous enough
to allow me a little repose."

The prince silently and respectfully
withdrew.

Anna finally, left alone with her lover
and her favorite, sank exhausted upon a
divan.

"Close the doors, Julia, that no one
may surprise us," she faintly murmured.
"I will take leave. Oh, I would be left
for at least a quarter of an hour undisturbed in my unhappiness."

"Then it is true that you intend
to drive me away?" asked Count Lynar, kneeling and clasping her hands.
"You are determined to send me into
banishment?"

Anna gave him a glance of tenderness.

"No," said she, "I will send myself
into banishment, for I shall not see you,
dearest. But I felt that this sacrifice
was necessary. Julia has sacrificed herself for us. With another love in her
heart, she has magnanimously thrown
away her freedom and given up her
maiden love for the promotion of our
happiness. We owe it to her to preserve her honor untarnished, that the
calumnious crowd may not pry into the
motives of her generous act. For Ju-

lia's sake, the world must and shall believe that she is in fact your wife, and
that it was love that united you. We
must, therefore, preserve appearances,
and you must conduct your wife to
your estate in triumph. Decency requires it, and we cannot disregard
its requirements."

"Princess Anna is in the right," said
Julia; "you must absent yourself for
a few weeks—not for my sake, who little desire any such triumph, but that
the world may believe the tale, and no
longer suspect my princess."

It was a sweetly painful hour—a farewell so tearful, and yet so full of deeply-
felt happiness. On that very night was
the count to commence his journey to
Liefland and Warsaw. As they wished
to make no secret of the marriage, the
count needed the consent of his court
and his family.

Anna provided him with letters and
passports. The best and fairest of the
estates of the crown in Liefland was assigned to Julia as a bridal present, and
the count was furnished with the proper
documents to enable him to take possession of it.[*]

And finally came the parting moment! For the last time they lay in each
other's arms; they mutually swore eternal love, unconquerable fidelity—all that
a loving couple could swear !

Tearing himself from her embrace, he
rushed to the door.

Anna stretches out her arms toward
him, her brow is pallid, her eyes fixed.
The door opens, he turns for one last
look, and nods a farewell. Ah, with

* Levecque, vol. v., p. 222.

her last glance she would forever enchain that noble and beautiful face—with her extended arms she would forever retain that majestic form.

"Farewell, Anna, farewell!"

The door closes behind him—he is gone!

A cold shudder convulsed Anna's form, a bodeful fear took possession of her mind. It lay upon her heart like a dark mourning-veil.

"I shall never, never see him again!" she shrieked, sinking unconscious into Julia's arms.

CHAPTER IX.

PRINCESS ELIZABETH.

WHILE a Mecklenburg princess had attained to the regency of Russia, and while her son was hailed as emperor, the Princess Elizabeth lived alone and unnoticed in her small and modestly-furnished palace. German princes sat upon the Russian throne, and yet in St. Petersburg was living the only rightful heir to the empire, the daughter of Czar Peter the Great! And as she was young, beautiful, and amiable, how came she to be set aside to make room for a stranger upon the throne of her father, which belonged to her alone?

Princess Elizabeth had voluntarily kept aloof from all political intrigues and all revolutions. In the interior of her palace she passed happy days; her world, her life, and her pleasures were there. Princess Elizabeth desired not to reign; her only wish was to love and be loved. The intoxicating splendor of worldly greatness was not so inviting to her as the more intoxicating pleasure of blessed and happy love. She would,

above all things, be a woman, and enjoy the full possession of her youth and happiness.

What cared she that her own rightful throne was occupied by a stranger—what cared she for the blinding shimmer of a crown? Ah, it troubled her not that she was poor, and possessed not even the means of bestowing presents upon her favorites and friends. But she felt happy in her poverty, for she was free to love whom she would, to raise to herself whomsoever she might please.

It was a festival day that they were celebrating in the humble palace of the emperor's daughter Elizabeth—certainly a festival day, for it was the name-day of the princess.

The rooms were adorned with festoons and garlands, and all her dependants and friends were gathered around her. Elizabeth saw not the limited number of this band; she enjoyed herself with those who were there, and lamented not the much greater number of those who had forgotten her.

She was among her friends, in her little reception-room. Evening' had come, the household and the less trusted and favored of her adherents had withdrawn, and only the most intimate, most favored friends now remained with the princess.

They had conversed so long that they now recurred to the enjoyment of that always-ready, always-pleasing art, music. A young man sang to the accompaniment of a guitar.

Elizabeth listened, listlessly reclining upon her divan. Behind her stood two gentlemen, who, like her, were delightedly listening to the singing of the youth.

Elizabeth was a blooming, beautiful woman. She was to-day charming to the eye in the crimson-velvet robe, embroidered with silver, that enveloped her full, voluptuous form, leaving her neck and *gorge* free, and displaying the delicate whiteness of her skin in beautiful contrast with the purple of her robe. Perhaps a severe judge might not have pronounced her face handsome according to the rules of the antique, but it was one of those faces that please and bewitch the other sex; one of those beauties whose charm consists not so much in the regularity of the lines as in the ever-varying expression. There was so much that was winning, enticing, supercilious, much-promising, and warm-glowing, in the face of this woman! The full, swelling, deep-red lips, how charming were they when she smiled; those dark, sparkling eyes, how seducing were they when shaded by a soft veil

of emotional enthusiasm; those faintly-blushing cheeks, that heaving bosom, that voluptuous form, yet resplendent with youthful gayety—for Elizabeth had not yet reached her thirtieth year—whom would she not have animated, excited, transported?

Elizabeth knew she was beautiful and attractive, and this was her pride and her joy. She could easily pardon the German princess, Anna Leopoldowna, for occupying the throne that was rightfully her own, but she would never have forgiven the regent had she been handsomer than herself. Anna Leopoldowna was the most powerful woman in Russia, but she, Elizabeth, was the handsomest woman in Russia, which was all she coveted, and she had nothing more to desire.

But at this moment she thought neither of Anna Leopoldowna nor of her own beauty, but only of the singer who was warbling to her those Russian popular songs so full of love and sadness that they bring tears into the eyes and fill the heart with yearning.

Elizabeth had forgotten all around her—she heard only him, saw only him; her whole soul lay in the glances with which she observed him, and around her mouth played one of those bewitching smiles peculiar to her in moments of joy and satisfaction, and which her courtiers knew and observed.

He was very handsome, this young singer, and as Elizabeth saw him in this moment, she congratulated herself that her connoisseur-glance had quickly remarked him, when, some weeks previously, she had first seen him as the precentor of the imperial chapel.

Surprised and excited by the beauty of his form and the sweetness of his voice, Elizabeth had begged him of the lord-marshal for her private service, and since then Alexis Razumovsky had entered her house as her private secretary and the manager of her small estate.*

While Alexis was singing with his sweetly-melting tones, Elizabeth turned her swimming eyes to the two men who were standing in respectful silence behind her.

"You must acknowledge," said she in a low tone, and as if oppressed by internal commotion, "that you never saw nor heard any thing finer than my Alexis."

"Oh, yes," said one of these men, with a low bow, "we have seen *you!*"

"And did we not yesterday hear you sing this same charming slumber-song, princess?" asked the other.

Elizabeth smiled. "It is already well known that Woronzow and Grünstein must always flatter!" said she.

"No, we do not flatter," responded Woronzow, the chamberlain of the princess, "we only love truth! You ask if we have ever seen any thing more beautiful than your private secretary, and we answer that we have seen *you!*"

"Well, now, you have all so often assured me that I am the handsomest woman in Russia, that at length I am compelled to believe you. But Alexis is fortunately a man, and therefore not my rival; you may, then, fearlessly confess that Alexis is the handsomest of all men? But how is this?" exclaimed

the princess, interrupting herself, as the handsome young singer suddenly sprang up and threw his guitar aside with an indignant movement; "do you sing no more, Alexis?"

"No," frowardly responded the young man, "I sing no more, when my princess no longer listens!"

"There, see the ungrateful man," said the princess, with a charming smile—"he was occupying all my thoughts, and yet he dares complain! You are a malefactor deserving punishment. Come here to me, Alexis; kneel, kiss my hand, and beg for pardon, you calumniator!"

"That is a punishment for which angels might be grateful!" responded Alexis Razumovsky, kneeling to the princess and pressing her hand to his burning lips. "Ah, that I might oftener incur such punishment!"

"Do you then prefer punishment to reward?" asked Elizabeth, tenderly bending down to him and looking deep into his eyes.

"She loves him!" whispered Grünstein to the chamberlain Woronzow. "She certainly loves him!"

Elizabeth's fine ear caught these words, and, slowly turning her head, she slightly nodded. "Yes," said she, "Grünstein is right—she loves him! Congratulate me, therefore, my friends, that the desert void in my heart is at length filled—congratulate me for loving him. Ah, nothing is sweeter, holier, or more precious than love; and I can tell you that we women are happy only when we are under the influence of that divine passion. Congratulate me, then, my friends, for, thank God, I am in

* Masson, "Mémoires Secretes," vol. I.

love! Now, Alexis, what have you to say?"

"There are no words to express such a happiness," cried Alexis, pressing the feet of the princess to his bosom.

"Happiness, then, strikes you dumb," laughed the princess, "and will not allow you to say that you love me? Such are all you men. You envelope yourselves with a convenient silence, and would make us poor women believe the superabundance of feeling deprives you of utterance."

At this moment the door was softly opened, and a lackey, who made his appearance at the threshold, beckoned to Woronzow.

"What is it, Woronzow?" asked the princess, while, wholly unembarrassed by the presence of the lackey, she played with the profuse dark locks of the kneeling Razumovsky.

"An invitation from the Regent Anna to a court-ball, which is to take place fourteen days hence," said Woronzow.

"Ah, our good cousin is, then, so gracious as to remember us," cried the princess, with a somewhat clouded brow. "It will certainly be a very magnificent festival, as we are invited so many days in advance. How sad that I cannot have the pleasure of being present!"

"And why not, if one may be allowed to ask, princess?" asked Woronzow.

"Why?" sighed Elizabeth. "Ask my waiting-woman; she will tell you that the Princess Elizabeth, daughter of the great Czar Peter, has not one single robe splendid enough to render her presentable, without mortification, at a court-ball of the regent."

"Whatever robe you may wear," passionately interposed Alexis, "you will still be resplendent, for your beauty will impart a divine halo to any dress!"

That was precisely the kind of flattery pleasing to Elizabeth.

"Think you so, flatterer?" asked Elizabeth. "Well, for once I will believe your words, and assume that the Princess Elizabeth may be fair without the aid of splendor in dress. We therefore accept the invitation, Woronzow. Announce that to the regent's messenger. But still it is sad and humiliating," continued Elizabeth after a pause, a cloud passing over her usually so cheerful countenance, "yes, it is still a melancholy circumstance for the daughter of the great Peter to be so poor that she is not able to dress herself suitably to her rank. Ah, how humiliating is the elevation of my high position, when I cannot even properly reward you, my friends, for your fidelity and attachment!"

"You will one day be able to reward us," significantly remarked Grünstein. "One day, when an imperial crown surmounts your fair brows, then will your generous heart be able to act according to its noble instincts."

"Still the same old dreams!" said Elizabeth, shaking her head and letting Razumovsky's long locks glide through her fingers. "Pay no attention to him, Alexis, he is an enthusiast who dreams of imperial crowns, while I desire nothing but a ball-dress, that in it I may please you, my friend!"

"Oh, you always please me," whispered Alexis, and most pleasing are you when—"

The conclusion of his flattering speech he whispered so low that it was heard by no one but the princess.

Patting his cheek with her little round hand, she blushed, but not for shame, as she did not cast down her eyes, but answered with a glowing glance the tender looks of her lover. She blushed only from an internal passionate excitement, while her bosom stormily rose and fell.

"You are very saucy, Alexis," said she, but at the same time lightly kissing him upon the forehead, and smiling; but then her brow was suddenly clouded, for the door was again opened and once more the lackey appeared upon the threshold.

"The French ambassador," said he, "the Marquis de la Chetardie, begs the favor of an audience."

"Ah, the good marquis!" cried the princess, rising from her reclining position. "Conduct him in, he is very welcome."

The lackey opened both wings of the folding-door, and the marquis entered, followed by several servants with boxes and packets.

"Ah, you come very much like a milliner," laughingly exclaimed Elizabeth, graciously advancing to receive the ambassador.

Dropping upon one knee, the marquis kissed her offered hand.

"I come, illustrious Princess Elizabeth, to beg a favor of you!" he said.

"You wish to mortify me," responded Elizabeth. "How can the ambassador of a great and powerful nation have a favor to ask of the poor, repudiated, and forgotten Princess Elizabeth?"

"In the name of the king my master come I to demand this favor!" solemnly answered the marquis.

"Well, if you really speak in earnest," said the princess, "then I have only to respond that it will make me very happy to comply with any request which your august king or yourself may have to make of me."

"Then I may be allowed, on this occasion of the celebration of your name-day, to lay at your feet these trifling presents of my royal master," said the ambassador of France, rising to take the boxes and packages from the lackeys and place them before Elizabeth.

"They are only trifles," continued he, while assiduously occupied in opening the boxes, "trifles of little value—only interesting, perhaps, because they are novelties that have as yet been worn in Paris by no lady except the queen and madame!"

"This mantelet of Valenciennes lace," continued the busy marquis, unfolding before the princess a magically fine lace texture, "this mantelet is sent by the Queen of France to the illustrious Princess Elizabeth. Only two such mantelets have been made, and her majesty has strictly commanded that no more of a similar pattern shall be commenced."

Princess Elizabeth's eyes sparkled with delight. Like a curious child she fluttered from one box to the other, and in fact they were very costly, tasteful and charming things which their majesties of France had sent to the Princess Elizabeth, who prized nothing higher than splendor in dress and ornaments.

There were the most beautiful gold-embroidered velvet robes, light crape and lace dresses, and hats and topknots of charming elegance.

Elizabeth examined and admired all; she clapped her hands with delight when any one of these precious presents especially pleased her, calling Alexis, Grünstein, and Woronzow to share her joy and admiration.

"Now will it be a triumph for me to appear at this ball!" said Elizabeth, exultingly; "ah, how beautiful it is of your king that he has sent me these magnificent presents to-day, and not eight days later! I shall excite the envy of the regent and all the court ladies with these charming things, which no one besides myself will possess."

And the princess was constantly renewing her examination of the presents, and breaking out into ecstasies over their beauty.

The Marquis de la Chetardie smilingly listened to her, told her much about Paris and its splendors, declaring that even in Paris there was no lady who could be compared to the fair Princess Elizabeth.

"Ah," remarked Elizabeth, smilingly threatening him with her finger, "you would speak differently if the queen or some other lady of your court were standing by my side!"

"No," seriously replied the marquis, "I would fall at the feet of my queen and say: 'You are my queen, judge me, condemn me, my life is in your hand. You are the Queen of France, and as such I bend before you; but Princess Elizabeth is the queen of beauty, and as such I adore her!'"

Princess Elizabeth smiled, and with

harmless unconstraint chatted yet a long time with the shrewd and versatile ambassador of the French king.

"I have yet one more request to make," said the marquis, when about to take leave. "But it is a request that no one but yourself must hear, princess!"

Elizabeth signed to her friends to withdraw into the open anteroom.

"Well, marquis," she then said with some curiosity, "let me now hear what else you have to ask."

"My king and master has learned with regret that the noble Princess Elizabeth is not surrounded with that wealth and splendor which is her due as the daughter of the great emperor and the rightful heir to the Russian throne. My king begs the favor of being allowed to make good the delinquency toward you of the present Russian regency, and that he may have the pleasure of providing you with the means necessary to enable you to establish a court suitable to your birth and position. I am provided with sufficient funds for these purposes. You have only to send me by your physician in ordinary, Lestocq, a quittance signed by you, and any sum you may require will be immediately paid!"*

"Oh," said the princess, with emotion, "I shall never be able sufficiently to testify my gratitude to the generous King of France. I am a poor, insignificant woman, who can thankfully accept but never requite his kindness."

"Who knows!" said the marquis significantly. "you may one day become the most powerful woman in En-

* Levecque, vol. v., p. 224.

4

rope, for your birth and your destiny call you to the throne."

"Oh, I know you are Lestocq's friend, and share his dreams," said the princess. "But let us not now speak of impossibilities, nor idly jest, while I am deeply touched by the generous friendship of your sovereign. That I accept his offer, may prove to him and you how much I love and respect him: for we willingly incur obligations only to those who are so highly estimated that we gratefully subordinate ourselves to them. Write this to your king."

"And may I also write to him," asked the marquis, "that this conversation will remain a secret, of which, above all things, the regent, Anna Leopoldowna, is to know nothing?"

"My imperial word of honor," said the princess, "that no one except ourselves and Lestocq, whom you yourself propose as a medium, shall know any thing of this great generosity of your sovereign. God grant that a time may one day come when I may loudly and publicly acknowledge my great obligations to him!"

"That time will have come when you are Empress of Russia!" said the ambassador, taking his leave.

"Already one more who has taken it into his head to make an empress of me," said the princess, as her three favorites again entered. "Foolish people that you are! It does not satisfy you to be the friend of a Princess Elizabeth, but I must become an empress for your sakes."

"How well the diadem would become that proud pure brow!" exclaimed Alexis, with animation.

"How happy would this poor Russia be under your mild sceptre!" said the chamberlain, Woronzow.

."Yes, you owe it to all of us, to yourself and your people, to mount the throne of your fathers," said Grünstein.

"But if I say to you that I will not?" cried the princess, reclining again upon her divan. "The duties of an empress are very difficult and wearing. I love quiet and enjoyment; and, moreover, this throne of my father, of which you speak so pathetically, is already occupied, and awaits me not. See you not your sublime Emperor Ivan, whom the regent-mother is rocking in his cradle? That is your emperor, before whom you can bow, and leave me unmolested with your imperial crown.—Come, Alexis, sit down by me upon this tabouret. We will take another look at these magnificent presents. Ah! truly they are dearer to me than the possession of empire."

"The Princess Elizabeth can thus speak only in jest!" said an earnest voice behind them.

"Ah, Lestocq!" cried the princess, with a friendly nod. "You come very late, my friend."

"And yet too soon to bring you bad news!" said Lestocq, with a profound and respectful bow to the princess.

"Bad news?" repeated Elizabeth, turning pale. "*Mon Dieu*, am I, then, one too many for them here? Would they kill me, or send me in exile to Siberia?"

"Yet worse!" laconically responded Lestocq. "But, first of all, let us be cautious, and take care that we have no listeners. And, crossing the room, Lestocq closed all the doors, and carefully looked behind the window curtains to make sure that no one was concealed there. "Now, princess," he commenced, in a tone of solemnity, "now listen to what I have to say to you."

CHAPTER X.

A CONSPIRACY.

A MOMENTARY pause followed. Princess Elizabeth silently motioned her friends to be seated, and drew her favorite Alexis nearer to her.

Lestocq, her physician and confidant, with a solemn countenance, took a place opposite her.

"We are ready to hear your bad news," said the princess.

"The regent, Anna Leopoldowna, will have herself crowned as empress," laconically responded Lestocq.

Elizabeth looked at him interrogatively and with curiosity for the continuation of his bad news. But as Lestocq remained silent, she asked with astonishment: "Is that all you have to tell us?"

"Preliminarily, that is all," answered Lestocq.

Princess Elizabeth broke out with a joyous laugh.

"Well, this is, in fact, very comic. With a real Job's mien you announce to us the worst news, and then inform us that Anna Leopoldowna is to be crowned empress! Let her be crowned! No one will interfere to prevent it, and she will be none the happier for it. No woman who has taken possession of the Russian throne as an independent princess has ever yet been happy. Or do you think that Catharine, my lofty stepmother, was so? Believe me, upon the throne she trembled with fear of assassins; for it is well known that this Russian throne is surrounded by murderers, awaiting only the favorable moment. Ah, whenever I have stood in front of this imperial throne, it has always seemed to me that I saw the points of a thousand daggers peeping forth from its soft cushions! And you would have me seat myself upon such a dagger-beset throne? No, no, leave me my peace and my repose. Let Anna Leopoldowna declare herself empress—what should I care? I should have to bend before her with my congratulations. That is all!"

And the princess, letting her head glide upon Razumovsky's shoulder, as if exhausted by this long speech, closed her fatigued eyelids.

"Ah, if Czar Peter, your great father, could hear you," sadly exclaimed Lestocq, "he would spurn you for such pusillanimity, princess."

"It is, therefore, fortunate for me that he is dead," said the princess, with a smile. "And now, my dear Lestocq, if you know nothing further, let this suffice you: I tell you, once for all, that I have no desire for this imperial throne. I would crown my head with roses and myrtles, but not with that golden circle which would crush me to the earth. Therefore, trouble me no more on this subject. Be content with what I am, and if you cannot, well—then must I be reconciled to being abandoned by you!"

"I will never desert you, even if I must follow you to suffering and death!" exclaimed Alexis Razumovsky, casting himself at the feet of the princess.

"We will remain true and faithful to you unto death!" cried Woronzow and Grünstein.

"Well, and you alone remain silent, Lestocq?" asked the princess, with tears in her eyes.

"I have not yet come to the end of my bad news," said Lestocq, with a clouded brow.

"Ah!" jestingly interposed the princess, "you would, perhaps, as further bad news, inform us that the Emperor Ivan has cut his first tooth!"

"No," said Lestocq, "I would only say to you, that the 18th of December, the day on which the regent is to be crowned as empress, the 18th of December is the day assigned for the marriage of the Princess Elizabeth with Prince Louis of Brunswick, the new Duke of Courland!"

The princess sprang up from her seat as if stung by an adder. Alexis Razumovsky, who still knelt at her feet, uttered loud lamentations, in which Wo-

ronzow and Grünstein soon joined. With calm triumph Lestocq observed the effect produced by his words.

"What are you saying there?" at length Elizabeth breathlessly asked.

"I say that on the 18th of December the Princess Elizabeth is to be married to Prince Louis of Brunswick, who has already come to St. Petersburg for that purpose," calmly answered Lestocq.

"And I say," cried the princess, "that no such marriage will ever take place!"

Lestocq shrugged his shoulders. "Princess Elizabeth is a gentle, peace-loving, always suffering lamb," he said.

"But Princess Elizabeth can become a tigress when it concerns the defence of her holiest rights!" exclaimed the princess, pacing the room in violent excitement.

"Ah," she continued, "they are not then satisfied with delivering me over to poverty and abandonment; it does not suffice them to see me so deeply humiliated as to receive alms from this regent who occupies the throne that belongs to me. They would rob me of my last and only remaining blessing, my personal freedom! They would make my poor heart a prisoner, and bind it with the chains and fetters of a marriage which I abhor! No, no, I tell you that shall they never do."

And the princess, quite beside herself with rage, stamped her feet and doubled up her little hands into fists. Now was she her father's real and not unworthy daughter; Czar Peter's bold and savage spirit flashed from her eyes, his scorn and courageous determination spoke from her wildly excited features. She saw not, she heard not what was passing around her; she was wholly occupied with her own angry thoughts, and with those dreadful images which the mere idea of marriage had conjured up.

Her four favorites stood together at some distance, observing her with silent sympathy.

"It is now for you, Alexis Razumovsky, to complete the work we have begun," whispered Lestocq to him. "Elizabeth loves you; you must nourish in her this abhorrence of a marriage with the prince. You must make yourself so loved, that she will dare all rather than lose you! We have long enough remained in a state of abjectness; it is time to labor for our advancement. To the work, to the work, Alexis Razumovsky! We must make an empress of this Elizabeth, that she may raise us to wealth and dignities!"

"Rely upon me," whispered Alexis, "she must and shall join in our plans."

He approached the princess, who was walking the room in a state of the most violent agitation, giving vent to her internal excitement and anger in loud exclamations and bitter curses.

"I must therefore die!" sighed Alexis, pressing Elizabeth's trembling hand to his lips. "Kill me, princess, thrust a dagger in my heart, that I at least may not live to see you married to another!"

"No, you shall not die," cried Elizabeth, with fierce vehemence, throwing her arms around Razumovsky's neck. "I will know how to defend you and myself, Alexis! Ah, they would shackle me,—they would force me to marry, because they know I hate marriage. Yes, I hate those unnatural fetters which would command my heart, force it into obedience to an unnatural law, and degrade divine free love, which would flutter from flower to flower, into a necessity and a duty. It is an unnatural law which would compel us forever to love a man because he pleased us yesterday or may please us to-day, and who perhaps may not please us to-morrow, while on the next day he may excite only repugnance! Would they forge these matrimonial chains for me? Ah, Regent Anna, you are this time mistaken; you may be all-powerful in this empire, but you cannot and shall not extend that power over me!"

"And how," asked Lestocq, shrugging his shoulders, "how will Princess Elizabeth oppose the regent or empress? What weapon has she with which to contend?"

"If it must be so, I will oppose power to power!" passionately exclaimed the princess. "Yes, when it comes to the defence of my freedom and my personal rights I will then have the courage to dare all, defy all; then will I shake off the lethargy of contented mediocrity, and upon the throne will find that freedom which Anna would tread under foot!"

"Long live our future empress! Long live Elizabeth!" cried the men with wild excitement.

"I have long withstood you, my friends," said Elizabeth, "I have not coveted this imperial Russian crown, but much less have I desired that crown of thorns a compulsory marriage. I am now ready for the struggle, and, if it must be so, let a revolution, let streams of blood decide whether the Regent Anna Leopoldowna or the daughter of Peter the Great has the best right to govern this land and prescribe its laws!"

"Ah, now are you really your great father's great daughter!" cried Lestocq, and bending a knee before the princess, he continued: "Let me be the first to pay you homage, the first to swear eternal fidelity to you, our Empress Elizabeth."

"Receive also my oath, Empress Elizabeth," said Alexis, falling upon his knees before her, "receive the oaths of your slaves who desire nothing but to devote their bodies and souls to your service!"

"Let me, also, do homage to you, Empress Elizabeth?" exclaimed Woronzow, falling to the earth.

"And I, too, will lie at your feet and declare myself your slave, Empress Elizabeth!" said Grünstein, kneeling with the others.

But Elizabeth's anger was already past; only a momentary storm-wind had lashed her gently flowing blood into the high foaming waves of rage; now all was again calm within her, and consequently this solemn homage scene of her four kneeling friends made only a comic impression upon her.

She burst into a loud laugh; astonished and half angry, the kneeling men looked up to her, and that only increased her hilarity.

"Ah, this is infinitely amusing," said the princess, continuing to laugh; "there lie my vassals, and what vassals! Herr Lestocq, a physician; Herr Grünstein, a bankrupt shopkeeper and now under-

officer; Herr Woronzow, chamberlain; and Alexis Razumovsky, my private secretary. And here am I, the empress of such vassals, and what sort of an empress? An empress of four subjects, an empress without a throne and without a crown, without land and without a people—an empress who never was and never will be an empress! And in this solemn buffoonery you cut such serious faces as might make one die with laughter."

The princess threw herself upon the divan and laughed until the tears ran down her cheeks.

"Princess," said Lestocq, rising, "these four men, at whom you now laugh, will make you empress, and then it will be in your power to convert this chirurgeon into a privy councillor and court physician, this bankrupt merchant into a rich banker, this chamberlain into an imperial lord-marshal, and your private secretary into a count or prince of the empire."

The eyes of the princess shone yet brighter, and with a tender glance at Alexis Razumovsky she said: "Yes, I will make him a prince and overload him with presents and honors. Ah, that is an object worth the pains of struggling for an imperial crown."

"No, no," interposed Alexis, kissing her hand, "I need neither wealth nor titles; I need nothing, desire nothing but to be near you, to be able to breathe the air that has fanned your cheek. I desire nothing for myself, but every thing for my friends here, with whose faithful aid we shall soon be enabled to greet you a real empress."

Elizabeth's brow beamed with the

purest blessedness. "You are as un-selfish as the angels in heaven, my Alexis," said she. "It suffices you that I am Elizabeth, you languish not for this imperial title which these others would force upon me."

Alexis smilingly shook his fine head. "You err, princess," said he; "I would freely and joyfully give my heart's blood, could I this day but salute you as empress! I should then, at least, have no more to fear from this strange prince whom they would compel you to marry!"

A cloud passed over the brow of the princess. "Yes, you are right," said she, "we must avoid that at all events, and if there are no other means, very well, I shall know what to decide upon —I shall venture an attempt to dethrone the regent and make myself empress! But, my friends, let that now suffice. I need rest. Call my women to undress me, Woronzow. Good-night, good-night, my high and lofty vassals, your great and powerful empress allows you to kiss her hand!"

With a pleasing graciousness she ex-tended her fair hands to her friends, who respectfully pressed them to their lips and then departed.

"Alexis!" called the princess, as Razumovsky was about to withdraw with the others—"Alexis, you will re-main awhile. While my women are undressing me, you shall sing me to sleep with that charming slumber-song you sing so splendidly!"

Alexis smiled and remained.

A quarter of an hour later deep si-lence prevailed in the dark palace of Elizabeth, and through the stillness of the night was heard only the sweetly-melodious voice of the handsome Alexis, who was singing his slumber-song to the princess.

From this day forward her four trusted friends left the princess no peace. They so stormed her with pray-ers and supplications, Alexis so well knew how to represent his despair at her approaching and unavoidable mar-riage, that the amiable princess, to sat-isfy her friends and be left herself at peace, declared herself ready to sanction the plans of her confidants and enter into a conspiracy against the regent.

Soon a small party was formed for the cause of the princess. Grünstein—who, as the princess had said, from a bankrupt merchant had attained the position of subordinate officer—Grün-stein had succeeded in winning for the cause of the princess some fifty grena-diers of the Preobrajensky regiment, to which he belonged; and these people, drunkards and dissolute fellows, were the principal props upon which Eliza-beth's throne was to be established! They were neither particular about the means resorted to for the accomplish-ment of the proposed revolution, nor careful to envelop their movements in secrecy.

Elizabeth soon began to find pleasure and distraction in exciting the enthu-siasm of the soldiers. She often re-paired to the caserns of the guards, and her mildness and affability won for her the hearts of the rough soldiers accus-tomed to slavish subjection. When she rode through the streets, it was not an unusual occurrence to see common soldiers approach her sledge and converse familiarly with her. Wherever she showed herself, there the soldiers received her with shouts, and the palace of the princess was always open to them. In this way Elizabeth made herself popular, and the Regent Anna, who was informed of it, smiled at it with indifference.

Just as incautiously did Elizabeth's fanatical political manager, Lestocq, set about his work. He made no secret of his intercourse with the French ambassador, and in the public coffee-houses he was often heard in a loud voice to prophesy an approaching politics' change.

But with regard to all these imprudences it seemed as if the court and the regent were blinded by the most careless confidence, as if they could not see what was directly before their eyes. It was as if destiny covered those eyes with a veil, that they might not see, and against destiny even the great and the powerful of the earth struggle in vain.

CHAPTER XI.

THE WARNING.

THE 4th of December, the day of the court-ball, to which Elizabeth had looked forward with a longing heart because of her anxiety to display at court her new Parisian dresses, at length had come. A most active movement prevailed in the palace of the regent. The lord-marshal and the chamberlains on service passed up and down through the rooms, overlooking with sharp eyes the various ornaments, festoons, garlands, and draperies, to make sure that all was splendid, and tasteful, and magnificent.

Anna Leopoldowna troubled herself very little about these busy movements in her palace. She was in her boudoir, delightedly reading a letter from her distant lover, which had just been received under Julia's address. She had already read this letter several times, but ever recommenced it, and ever found some new word, some new phrase that proved to her the glowing love of her absent friend.

"Ah, he still loves me," murmured she, pressing the letter to her lips; "he really loves me, and this short separation will not estrange his heart, but cause it to glow with warmer passion! Oh, what a happiness will it be when he again returns! And he will return! Yes, he will be with me again on the 18th of December, and, animated by his glances, I shall for the first time appear in all the splendor of an imperial crown. Ah, they have no presentiment, my councillors and ministers, that I have selected the 18th of December for the ceremony precisely because it is the birthday of my beloved! He will know it, he will understand why his Anna has chosen this particular day, and he will thank me with one of those proud and glowing glances which always make my heart tremulous with overpowering happiness. Oh, my Lynar, what a blessed moment will be that when I see you again!"

A slight knock at the door interrupted the imaginings of the princess. It was Julia von Mengden, who came to announce the old Count Ostermann.

"And is it for him that you disturb my delightful solitude?" asked the princess, somewhat reproachfully. "Is this Count Ostermann, is this whole miserable realm of so much importance to me as the sweet contemplation of a letter from my friend? When I am reading his letter it seems to me that my beloved himself is at my side, and therefore you must clearly see that I cannot receive Count Ostermann, as Lynar is with me!"

"Put your letter and your lover in your bosom," said Julia, with a laugh; "he will be very happy there, and then you can receive the old count without betraying your lover's presence! The count has so pressingly begged for an audience that I finally promised to intercede with you for him."

"Ah, this eternal business!" angrily exclaimed the princess. "They will never let me have any peace; they harass me the whole day. Even now, when it is time to be making my toilet for the ball—even now I must be tormented with affairs of state."

"Shall I, then, send away Count Ostermann?" sulkily asked Julia.

"That I may, consequently, for the whole evening see you with a dissatisfied face? No, let him come; but forget not that I submit to this annoyance only to please you."

With a grateful smile, Julia kissed the regent's hand, and then hastened to bear to Count Ostermann the favorable answer.

In a few minutes, Count Ostermann, painfully supporting himself upon two crutches, entered the regent's cabinet.

Anna Leopoldowna received him, sitting in an arm-chair, and listlessly rummaging in a band-box filled with various articles of dress and embroidery, which had just been brought to her.

"Well," said she, raising her eyes for a moment to glance at Ostermann, "you come at a very inconvenient hour, Herr Minister Count Ostermann. You see that I am already occupied with my toilet, and am endeavoring to find a suitable head-dress. Will you aid me in the choice, sir count?"

Ostermann had until now, painfully and with many suppressed groans, sustained himself upon his feet; at a silent nod from the princess he glided down into a chair, and staring at Anna with his piercing and wonderfully-flashing eyes, he said:

"Your highness would select a head-dress? Well, as you ask my advice in the matter, I will give it; choose a head-dress so firm and solid as to prove a fortification for the defence of your head. Choose a head-dress that will protect you against conspiracies and revolutions, against false friends and smiling enemies! Choose a head-dress that will keep your head upon your shoulders!"

"Count Ostermann speaks in riddles," said Anna, smiling, and at the same time arranging a wreath of artificial roses. "Or no, it was not Count Ostermann, but a toad singing his hoarse song. Drive away that toad, Ostermann, it is broad day—why, then, have we the croaking of such night-birds?"

"Listen to the croaking of this toad," anxiously responded the old man. "Believe me, princess, when the toads croak in broad daylight, it betokens an approaching misfortune. Let it warn you, Madame Regent Anna! You have called me a toad—very well, toads always have correctly prophesied misfortune, and if they can never avert it, it is because overwise people will not listen to such oracular voices of all-wise Nature! Let me be your toad, your highness, and listen to me! I foresee misfortune for you. Believe my prophecy, and that misfortune may yet be averted. Mark the signs by which fate would warn you! Did you not yesterday see Elizabeth driving through the streets, chatting and jesting with the soldiers, who crowded around her sledge? Have you not heard how the grenadiers of the Preobrajensky regiment shouted after her? Has it not been told you that Lestocq holds secret intercourse with the French ambassador, and know you not that Lestocq is the confidential servant of the princess? Guard yourself against Princess Elizabeth, your highness!"

"Are you in earnest?" smilingly asked Anna, drawing her silver toilet-glass nearer to her person, and placing a bouquet of flowers in her hair to examine its effect in the glass.

"Oh, Heavens!" cried Count Ostermann, "you adorn yourself with flowers, while I am telling you that you are threatened with a conspiracy!"

"A conspiracy!" laughed the regent, "and Princess Elizabeth to be at the head of it! Believe me, you overwise men, with all your wisdom, never learn rightly to understand women. I, however, am a woman, and I understand Elizabeth. You think that when she kindly chats with the soldiers, and admits the handsome stately grenadiers into her house, it is done for the purpose of conspiring with them. Go to, Count Ostermann, you are very innocent. Princess Elizabeth has but one passion, but it is not the desire of ruling; and when she chats with handsome men, she speaks not of conspiracy, believe me." And, laughing, the regent essayed a new head-dress.

"And how do you explain the secret meetings of Lestocq and the Marquis de la Chetardie?" asked Ostermann, with painfully-suppressed agitation.

"Explain? Why should I seek an explanation for things that do not at all interest me? What is it to me what the surgeon Lestocq has to do with the constantly-ailing French ambassador? Or do you think I should trouble myself about the *lavements* administered to an ambassador by a surgeon?"

"Well, then, your highness will allow me to explain their meetings from a less medical point of view? France is your enemy, France meditates your destruction, and the Marquis de la Chetardie is exciting the princess and Lestocq to an insurrection!"

"And to what end, if I may be allowed to ask?" scornfully inquired Anna.

"France, struggling with internal and foreign enemies, at war with Austria, involved in disputes with Holland and Spain, France would wish at any price to see the Russian government so occupied with her own domestic difficulties as to have no time to devote to international affairs. She would provide you with plenty of occupation at home, that you may not actively interfere with the affairs of the rest of the world. That is the shrewd policy of France, and it would fill me with admiration were it not fraught with the most terrible danger to us. The Marquis de la Chetardie has it in charge to bring about a revolution here at any price, and as an expert diplomatist, he very well comprehends that Princess Elizabeth is the best means he can employ for that purpose; for she, as the daughter of Czar Peter, has the sympathies of the old Russians in her favor, and they will flock to her with shouts of joy whenever she may announce to the people that she is ready to drive the foreign rulers from Russia!"

"Ah, our good Russians," laughingly exclaimed the regent, "they shout only for those who make them drunk, and for that the poor princess lacks the means!"

"The Marquis de la Chetardie has, in the name of his king, offered her an unlimited credit, and she is already provided with almost a million of silver rubles."

"You have a reason for every thing," laughed the regent. "The princess is poor; let the French ambassador quickly provide her with his millions. The good princess, I wish she had these millions, and then she could indulge her love of ornaments and magnificent dresses."

"The marquis has brought her rich dresses and stuffs from Paris," said Ostermann, laconically.

The regent burst into a clear, ringing laugh.

"The marquis is a real *deus ex machina*," exclaimed she. "Wherever you need him, he appears and helps you out of your trouble. But seriously, my dear count, let it now suffice with these gloomy suspicions. They are already commencing the dance-music, and you will put me out of tune with your croaking. A ball, my dear count, requires that one should be in and not out of tune, and you are pursuing the best course to frighten the smiles from my lips."

"Oh, could I but do that!" cried Ostermann, wringing his hands—"could I but cry in your ear with a voice of thunder: 'Princess, awake from this slumber of indifference, force yourself to act, save your son, your husband, your friends; for we are all, all lost with you!'"

"Oh, speaking of my son," smilingly interposed the regent, "you must see a splendid present which the Emperor Ivan has this day received."

With this she took from a cartoon a small child's dress, embroidered with gold and sparkling with brilliants, which she handed to the count.*

"Only look at this splendor," said she. "The ladies of Moscow have embroidered this for the young emperor, and it has to-day been presented by a deputation. Will not the little emperor make a magnificent appearance in this brilliant dress?"

Count Ostermann did not answer immediately. His face had assumed a very painful expression, and deep sighs escaped his agitated breast. Slowly rising from his seat, with a sad glance at the princess, he said:

"I see that your destruction is inevitable, and I cannot save you; you will be ruined, and we all with you. Well, I am an old man, and I pardon your highness, for you act not thus from an evil disposition, but because you have a noble and confiding heart. Believe me, generosity and confidence are the worst failings with which a man can be tainted.in this world—failings which always insure destruction, and have only mockery and derision for an epitaph. You

---

* Levecque, vol. v., p. 225.

are no longer to be helped, duchess. You are on the borders of an abyss, into which you will smilingly plunge, dragging us all after you. Well, peace be with you! My sufferings have lately been so great, that I can only thank you for furnishing me with the means of quickly ending them! Madame, we shall meet again on the scaffold, or in Siberia! Until then, farewell!"

And, without waiting for an answer from the regent, the old man, groaning, tottered out of the room.

"Thank Heaven that he is gone!" said Anna, drawing a long breath when the door closed behind him. "This old ghost-seer has tormented me for months with his strange vagaries, which weigh upon his soul like the nightmare! Happily, thy letter, my beloved, has filled my whole heart with the ecstasy of joy, else would his dark and foolish prophecies be sufficient to sadden me."

Thus speaking, the princess again drew Count Lynar's letter from her bosom and pressed it to her lips. Then she called her women to dress her for the ball.

CHAPTER XII.

THE COURT BALL.

SOME hours later the *élite* of the higher Russian nobility were assembled in the magnificent halls of the regent. Princes and counts, generals and diplomatists, beautiful women and blooming maidens, all moved in a confused intermixture, jesting and laughing with each other. They were all very gay on this evening, as the regent had herself set the example. With the most unconstrained cheerfulness, radiant with joy, did she wander through the rooms, dispensing smiles and agreeable words among all whom she approached. She bore in her bosom the glowing and cherished letter of her lover, and at its lightest rustling she seemed to feel the immediate presence of the writer. That was the secret of her gayety and her joyous smiles. People, perhaps, knew not this secret, but they saw its effects, and, as the all-powerful regent deigned this day to be cheerful and smiling, it was natural for this host of slavish nobility, who breathe nothing but the air of the court, to adopt for this evening's motto, "Gayety and smiles."

As we have said, only smiling lips and faces beaming with joy were to be seen; all breathed pleasure and enjoyment, all jested and laughed; it seemed as if all care and sorrow had fled from this happy, select circle, to give place to the delights of life. They had, with submissive humility, repressed all discontent and disaffection, all envyings and enmities; they chatted and laughed, while every one knew or suspected that they were standing on a volcano, whose overwhelming eruptions might be expected at any moment, and yet every one feigned the most perfect innocence and unconstraint. The ladies scrutinized each other's magnificent and costly toilets, jesting and exchanging amorous glances with the gentlemen displaying orders and diamond crosses.

A movement suddenly arose in the rooms, the crowd divided and respectfully withdrew to the sides, and through the rows of smiling, humbly bowing courtiers passed the Princess Elizabeth, followed by her chamberlain Woronzow, her private secretary Alexis Razumovsky, and her physician Lestocq, in the splendor of her beauty and grace, all kindness, all smiles. She was to-day wonderfully charming in her gold-spangled lace dress, which flowed like a breath over her under-dress of heavy white satin. Her widely-bared, full and luxuriant shoulders were partially covered by a costly lace mantelet, the present of the French queen, and her long, floating ringlets were surmounted by a wreath of white roses such as only Parisian artistic skill could offer in such perfect imitation of nature. Thus eveloped as it were in a veil of white mist and floating vapors, Elizabeth's beauty appeared only the more full and voluptuous. She looked like a purple rose standing out from a cloud of fluttering snow-flakes, wonderfully charming, wonderfully seductive. Princess Elizabeth was fully conscious of the impression she made, and this internal satisfaction manifested itself in a sweet smile which increased the charm of her appearance. With pride and pleasure she enjoyed the triumph of being the fairest of all the beauties present, and this triumph contented her heart.

The princess now approached her cousin, the Regent Anna, who came from the adjoining room to meet and welcome her, and for one short moment the courtiers forgot her smiles and her inoffensiveness. All eyes were with the most intense anxiety directed toward these two women; all conversation, jesting, and laughing were at once suspended. There was a deep pause, all breathing was smothered, all feared that the loud beating of their hearts might betray them and cause them to be suspected.

The two princesses now approached each other—Princess Elizabeth would have bent a knee to the regent—Anna, with charming kindness, raising and kissing her, tenderly reproached her for coming so late.

"I feared coming too early," said Elizabeth, pressing the regent's hand to her lips, "for I doubted whether my fair cousin would find time to be-

stow a friendly word upon her poor re lation, Princess Elizabeth!"

"How could Elizabeth fear that when she knows I love her like a sis ter?" tenderly asked the regent, and, taking the arm of the princess, she made with her a round through the rooms.

Now again came life and movement in this lately so silent and anxiously expectant assemblage; they now knew how they were to deport themselves: Princess Elizabeth was in the good graces of the regent, and therefore they could receive her polite greetings with the most reverential thankfulness; they could approach her and admire her beauty without incurring suspicion. The stereotyped smile had reappeared upon all faces, cheerful and lively conversation was again resumed, and wherever the two arm-in-arm wandering princesses appeared, they were greeted with endless shouts of ecstasy.

As we have said, it was a gay and very splendid festival. Only occasionally did something like a dark shadow pass through the rooms; only here and there did the chattering guests forget their wonted smiles; only occasionally did the mask of cheerfulness fall from many a face, discovering serious, anxious features, and suspicious, lurking glances. Every one felt that a catastrophe was impending, but, as no one could know its result in advance, all wished to keep as clear of it as possible, and seem perfectly unconscious and unaffected by these things. As they could not foresee which party would triumph, they found it advisable to join neither while awaiting coming events, after which they would hail as lords and masters those who might succeed in attaining to power.

For the present, Anna Leopoldowna was the ruler, and, as they were her subjects, they must in humble submissiveness pay homage to her; but Elizabeth might become empress, and therefore they must likewise pay homage to her, with a prudent avoidance of the too much, which might cause them to be suspected in case the regent should still continue in power.

These were the dangerous rocks between which this proud and elegant assemblage had to find their winding way, and they did it with smiles and outward ease, with open admiration of both princesses, before whom they bowed to the ground with slavish submission.

But suddenly something like a panic-terror, like an unnatural awe, flew through all these splendid halls; the smiles were arrested on all faces, the harmless jests on all lips; the pallor of beautiful women became visible through their paint, and generals staggered to and fro as if a thunderbolt had fallen. As if touched by a magic wand, every one stood motionless like statues modelled in clay, no one daring to speak to his neighbor or make a sign to a friend. They would not see, they would not hear, they only wished to seem to be indifferent and unobserving.

As we said, a panic-terror pervaded the halls, and like an evil-announcing night-spectre passed over the heads of the stiffened, lifeless crowd the dismal rumor—"The regent and the princess are at variance; the regent is speaking to her with vehemence, and the princess weeps!"

This certainly was a terrible announcement. But if the regent was angry, it must be because she knew of the intrigues and machinations of the princess, and knowing them she could counteract and nullify them; consequently the plans of the princess were upset, Anna Leopoldowna would remain ruler, and her son Ivan the Czar of all the Russias.

Now the touch, the vicinity of Elizabeth's friends became an evil-breathing pest, a death-bringing terror; they anxiously avoided the vicinity of Lestocq, they crowded back from Woronzow and Razumovsky, whom they had before sought with every demonstration of friendliness; they even avoided looking at the French ambassador; for, if the regent knew all, she must know of the intimate relations of Lestocq with the Marquis de la Chetardie, and he was therefore doomed like the other three.

And moreover, this pernicious rumor had not lied; the two princesses were at this moment no longer so tender and friendly disposed as shortly before.

They had long wandered through the halls, confidingly chatting and smiling, and Anna, leaning upon Elizabeth's arm —Anna who this day saw every thing *couleur de rose*—felt a sort of disquiet that people should suspect her who was walking by her side with such innocent candor and unconstraint, seeming not to have the least presentiment of the dark cloud gathering over her head.

"She is inconsiderate," thought the regent; "she allows herself to be carried away by her temperament, and behind her inclination and her weakness for handsome grenadiers and soldiers, her enemies seek to discover an insidious and well-considered conspiracy; this is cruel and unjust! This good Elizabeth must be warned, that she may become more cautious, and give her numerous enemies no occasion for suspecting her. Poor innocent child, so gay and ingenuous, she plays with roses under which serpents lie concealed! It is my duty to warn her, and I will."

Wholly penetrated with this noble and generous resolution, the regent drew her cousin Elizabeth into the little boudoir which lay at the end of the hall, offering a convenient resting-place for a confidential conversation.

But at this moment Anna's eyes fell upon the lace mantelet of the princess, and quite involuntarily came to her mind the warning words of Ostermann, who had said to her: "The French ambassador, by command of his government, provides the princess not only with money, but also with the newest modes and most costly stuffs." This lace mantelet could surely only come from Paris; nothing similar to it had been seen in St. Petersburg; it certainly required especial sources and especial means for the procurement of such a rare and magnificent exemplar.

A cloud drew over the regent's brow, and in a rather sharp and cutting tone she said : "One question, princess! How came you by this admirable lace veil, the like of which I have not seen here in St. Petersburg?"

While putting this question, the regent's eyes were fixed with a piercing, interrogating expression upon the face of the princess: she wished to observe the slightest shrinking, the least movement of her features.

But Elizabeth was prepared for the question; she had already considered her answer with the marquis and Lestocq. Her features therefore betrayed not the least disturbance or disquiet; raising her bright and child-like eyes, she said, with an unconstrained smile: "You wonder, do you not, how I came by this costly ornament? Ah, I have for the last eight days rejoiced in the expectation of surprising you to-day with the sight of it ! "

"But you have not yet told me whence you have these costly laces?" asked the regent in a sharper tone.

"It is a wager I have won of the good Marquis de la Chetardie," said Elizabeth, without embarrassment, "and your highness must confess that this French ambassador has paid his wager with much taste."

The regent had constantly become more serious and gloomy. A dark, fatal suspicion for a moment overclouded her soul, and in her usually unsuspicious mind arose the questions: "What if Ostermann was right, if Elizabeth is really conspiring, and the French ambassador is her confederate?"

"And what, if one may ask, was the subject of the wager?" she asked, with the tone of an inquisitor.

"Ah, this good marquis," said the princess, laughing, "had never yet experienced the rigor of a Russian winter, and he would not believe that our Neva with its rushing streams and rapid current would in winter be changed into a very commodious highway. I wagered that I would convince him of the fact, and be the first to cross it on the ice; he would not believe me, and declared that I should lack the courage. Well, of course I did it, and won my wager!"

The regent had not turned her eyes from the princess while she was thus speaking. This serene calmness, this unembarrassed childishness, completely disarmed her. The dark suspicion vanished from her mind; Anna breathed freer, and laid her hand upon her heart as if she would restrain its violent beating. The letter of Lynar slightly rustled under her hand.

A ray of sunshine became visible in Anna's face; she thought of her beloved; she felt his presence, and immediately all the vapors of mistrust were scattered—Anna feared no more, she suspected no more, she again became cheerful and happy—for she thought of her distant lover, his affectionate words rested upon her bosom—how, therefore, could she feel anger?

She only now recollected that she had intended to warn Elizabeth. She therefore threw her arms around the neck of the princess, and, sitting with her upon the divan, said: "Do you know, Elizabeth, that you have many enemies at my court, and that they would excite my suspicions against you?"

"Ah, I may well believe they would be glad to do so, but they cannot," said Elizabeth, laughing; "I am a foolish, trifling woman, who, unfortunately for them, do nothing to my enemies that can render me suspected, as, in reality, I do nothing at all. I am indolent, Anna, very indolent; you ought to have raised me better, my dear lady regent!"

And with an amiable roguishness Elizabeth kissed the tips of Anna's fingers.

"No, no, be serious for once," said Anna; "laugh not, Elizabeth, but listen to me!"

And she related to the listening princess how people came from all sides to warn her; that she was told of secret meetings which Lestocq, in Elizabeth's name, held with the French ambassador, and that the object of these meetings was the removal of the regent and her son, and the elevation of Elizabeth to the imperial throne.

Elizabeth remained perfectly cheerful, perfectly unembarrassed, and even laughingly exclaimed—"What a silly story!"

"I believe nothing of it," said Anna, "but at last my ministers will compel me to imprison Lestocq and bring him to trial, in order to get the truth out of him."

"Ah, they will torture him, and yet he is innocent!" cried Elizabeth, bursting into tears. And, clasping the regent's neck, she anxiously exclaimed: "Ah, Anna, dear Anna, save me from my enemies! Let them not steal away my friends and ruin me! They would also torture me and send me to Siberia; Anna, my friend, my sovereign, save me! You alone can do it, for you know me, and know that I am innocent! The idea that I should conspire against you, against you whom I love, and to whom, upon the sacred books of our religion, I have sworn eternal fidelity and devotion! Anna, Anna, I swear to you by the soul of my father, I am innocent, as also is my friend. Lestocq has never passed the threshold of the French ambassador's hotel! Oh, dear, dear Anna, have mercy on me, and do not permit them to torture me and wrench my poor members!"

With a loud cry of anguish, with streaming tears, pale and trembling, Elizabeth sank down at the regent's feet.

It was this cry of anguish that rang through the hall, and spread everywhere astonishment and consternation. And this shrieking, and weeping, and trembling, was no mask, but truth. Elizabeth was frightened, she wept and trembled from fear, but she had sufficient presence of mind not to betray herself in words. It was fear even that gave her that presence of mind and enabled her to play her part in a manner so masterly that the regent was completely deceived. Taking the princess in her arms, she pressed her to her bosom, at the same time endeavoring to reassure and console her with tender and affectionate words, with reiterated promises of her protection and her love.

But it was a long time before the trembling and weeping princess could be tranquillized—before she could be made to believe Anna's asseverations that she had always loved and never mistrusted her.

"What most deeply saddens me," said Elizabeth, with feeling, "is the idea that you, my Anna, could believe these calumnies, and suppose me capable of such black treason. Ah, I should be as bad as Judas Iscariot could I betray my noble and generous mistress."

Tears of emotion stood in Anna's eyes. She impressed a tender kiss upon Elizabeth's lips, and with her own hand wiped the tears from the cheeks of the princess.

"Weep no more, Elizabeth," she tenderly said—"nay, I beg of you, weep no more. It is indeed all right and good between us, and no cloud shall disturb our love or our mutual confidence. Come, let us smile and be cheerful again, that this listening and curious court may know nothing of your tears. They would make a prodigious affair of it, and we will not give them occasion to say we have been at variance."

"No, they shall all see that I love, that I adore you," said Elizabeth, covering Anna's hand with kisses.

"They shall see that we love each other," said Anna, taking the arm of the princess. "Be of good cheer, my friend, and take my imperial word for it that I, whatever people may say of you, will believe no one but yourself; that I will truly inform you of all calumnies, and give you an opportunity to disarm your enemies and defend yourself. Now come, and let us make another tour through the halls."

Arm in arm the two princesses returned to the nearest hall. This was empty, no one daring to remain there lest they might incur the blame of having overheard and understood some word of the princesses, and thus acquired a knowledge of their private conversation. People had therefore withdrawn to the more distant rooms, where they still preserved a breathless silence.

Suddenly the two princesses, arm in arm, again appeared in the halls, pleasantly conversing, and instantly the scene was again changed, as if by the stroke of a magic wand. The chilling silence melted into an agreeable smile, and all recovered their breaths and former joviality.

All was again sunshine and pleasure, for the princesses were again there, and the princesses smiled—must they not laugh and be beside themselves with joy?

Elizabeth's tender glances sought her friend, the handsome Alexis Razumovsky. Suddenly her brow was darkened and her cheeks paled, for she saw him, and saw that his eyes did not seek hers!

He stood leaning against a pillar, his eyes fixed upon a lady who had just then entered the hall, and whose wonderful beauty had everywhere called forth a murmur of astonishment and admiration. This lady was the Countess Lapuschkin, the wife of the commissary-general of marine, from whose family came the first wife of Czar Peter the Great, the beautiful Eudoxia Lapuschkin.

Eleonore Lapuschkin was more beautiful than Eudoxia. An infinite magic of youth and loveliness, of purity and energy, was shed over her regular features. She had the traits of a Hebe, and the form of a Juno. When she smiled and displayed her dazzlingly white teeth, she was irresistibly charming. When, in a serious mood, she raised her large dark eyes, full of nobleness and spirit, then might people fall at her feet with adoration. Countess Lapuschkin had often been compared and equalled to the Princess Elizabeth, and yet nothing could be more dissimi-

lar or incomparable than these two beauties. Elizabeth's was wholly earthly, voluptuous, glowing with youth and love, but Eleonore's was chaste and sublime, pure and maidenly. Elizabeth allured to love, Eleonore to adoration.

The princess had long hated the young Countess Eleonore Lapuschkin, and considered her as a rival; but that this rival should now gain an interest in the heart of her favorite, that filled Elizabeth's soul with anger and agitation, that caused her eyes to flash and her blood to boil.

Staringly as Alexis Razumovsky's eyes were fixed upon the countess, she, unconscious of this double observation, stood cheerful and unembarrassed in the circle of her admiring friends and adorers.

Anna Leopoldowna followed the glance of the princess, and, observing the beautiful Lapuschkin, said, without thinking of Elizabeth's very susceptible vanity:

"Leonore Lapuschkin is an admirably beautiful woman, is she not? I never saw a handsomer one. To look at her is like a morning dream; her appearance diffuses light and splendor. Do you not find it so, Elizabeth?"

"Oh, yes, I find it so," said Elizabeth, with a constrained smile. "She is the handsomest woman in your realm."

"Yourself excepted, Elizabeth," kindly subjoined the regent.

"Oh, no, she is handsomer than I!" murmured Elizabeth.

Poor Leonore! In this moment hath the princess pronounced your sentence of condemnation, and in her heart subscribed the stern order for your execution.

A longer view of this triumph of the countess became insufferable; alleging a sudden attack of illness, she immediately took leave of the regent, and ordered her carriage.

Tears of anger and love stood in her eyes as Razumovsky approached to aid her in entering it. Hurling away his hand, she entered the carriage without assistance.

"And may I not accompany you in the carriage as usual?" asked Alexis, with tenderness in his tone.

"No," she curtly said, "go back into the hall, and again admire the handsomest woman in the empire!"

Then, jealousy getting the better of anger, she beckoned to Alexis, who was about departing in sadness, and commanded him to enter the carriage without delay.

As soon as the carriage door was closed, with an angry movement she seized both of Razumovsky's hands.

"Look at me," said she—"look me directly in the eye, and then tell me, is Eleonore Lapuschkin handsomer than I?"

CHAPTER XIII.

THE PENCIL-SKETCH.

It was the day after the court ball. Princess Elizabeth was in her dressing-room, and occupied in enveloping herself in a very charming and seductive *négligé*. She was to-day in very good humor, very happy and free from care, for Alexis Razumovsky had, with the most solemn asseverations, assured her of his truth and devotion, and Elizabeth had been soothed and reconciled by his glowing language. It was for him that she wished to appear especially attractive to-day, that Alexis, by the sight of her, might be made utterly to forget the Countess Eleonore Lapuschkin. In these coquettish efforts of her vanity she had utterly forgotten all the plans and projects of her friends and adherents; she thought no more of becoming empress, but she would be the queen of beauty, and in that realm she would reign alone with an absolute sway.

A servant announced Lestocq.

A cloud of displeasure lowered on the brow of the princess. Startled from her sweet dreams by this name, she now for the first time recollected the fatal conversation she had had on the previous evening with the regent. In her love and jealousy she had totally forgotten the occurrence, but now that she was reminded of it, she felt her head throb with anxiety and terror.

Dismissing her attendants with an

imperious nod, she hastened to meet the entering physician.

"Lestocq," said she, "it is well you have come at this moment, else, perhaps, I might have forgotten to say to you that it is all over with the conjuration spun and woven by you and the French marquis. We must give it up, for the affair is more dangerous than you think it, and I may say that you have reason to be thankful to me for having, by my foresight and intrepidity, saved you from the torture, and a possible transportation to Siberia. Ah, it is very cold in Siberia, my dear Lestocq, and you will do well silently and discreetly to build a warm nest here, instead of inventing ambitious projects dangerous to all of us."

"And whence do you foresee danger, princess?" asked Lestocq.

"The regent knows all! She knows our plans and combinations. In a word, she knows that we conspire, and that you are the principal agent in this conspiracy."

"Then I am lost!" sighed Lestocq, gliding down upon a chair.

"No, not quite," said Elizabeth, with a smile, "for I have saved you. Ah, I should never have believed that the playing of comedy was so easy, but I tell you I have played one in a masterly manner. Fear was my teacher; it taught me to appear so innocent, to implore so affectingly, that Anna herself was touched. Ah, and I wept whole streams of tears, I tell you. That quite disarmed the regent. But you must bear the blame if my eyes to-day are yet red with weeping, and not so brilliant as usual."

And Princess Elizabeth ran to the toilet-table to examine critically her face in the glass.

"Yes, indeed," she cried, with a sort of terror, "it is as I feared. My eyes are quite dull. Lestocq, you must give me a means, a quick and sure means, to restore their brightness."

Thus speaking, Elizabeth looked constantly in the glass, full of care and anxiety about her eyes.

"I shall appear less beautiful to him to-day," she murmured; "he will, in thought, compare me with Eleonore Lapuschkin, and find her handsomer than I. Lestocq, Lestocq!" she then called aloud, impatiently stamping with her little foot, "I tell you that you must immediately prescribe a remedy that will restore the brilliancy of my eyes."

"Princess," said Lestocq, with solemnity, "I beseech you for a moment to forget your incomparable beauty and the unequalled brilliancy of your eyes. Be not only a woman, but be, as you can, the great czar's great daughter. Princess, the question here is not only of the diminished brilliancy of your eyes, but of a real danger with which you are threatened. Be merciful, be gracious, and relate to me the exact words of your yesterday's conversation with the regent."

The princess looked up from her mirror, and turned her head toward Lestocq.

"Ah, I forgot," she carelessly said, "you are not merely my physician, but also a revolutionist, and that is of much greater importance to you."

"The question is of your head, princess, and as a true physician I would help you to preserve it. Therefore, dearest princess, I beseech you, repeat to me that conversation with the regent."

"Will you then immediately give me a recipe for my eyes?"

"Yes, I will."

"Well, listen, then."

And the princess repeated, word for word, to the breathless Lestocq, her conversation with Anna Leopoldowna. Lestocq listened to her with most intense interest, taking a piece of paper from the table and mechanically writing some unmeaning lines upon it with an appearance of heedlessness. Perhaps it was this mechanical occupation that enabled him to remain so calm and circumspect. During the narration of the princess his features again assumed their expression of firmness and determination; his eyes again flashed, and around his mouth played a saucy, scornful smile, such as was usually seen there when, conscious of his superiority, he had formed a bold resolution.

"This good regent has executed a stroke of policy for which Ostermann will never forgive her," said he, after the princess had finished her narration. "She should have kept silence and appeared unconstrained—then *we* should have been lost; but now it is *she*."

"No," exclaimed the princess, with generous emotion, "the regent has chosen precisely the best means for disarming us! She has manifested a noble confidence in me, she has discredited the whisperings of her minister and counsellors, and instead of destroying me, as she could have done, she has warned me with the kindness and affection of a sister. I shall never forget that, Lestocq; I shall ever be grateful for that! Henceforth the Regent or Empress Anna Leopoldowna shall have no truer or more obedient subject than I, the Princess Elizabeth!"

"By this you would not say, princess—"

"By this I mean to say," interposed Elizabeth, "that this conspiracy is brought to a bloodless conclusion, and that, from this hour, there is but one woman in this great Russian realm who has any claim to the title of empress, and that woman is the Regent Anna Leopoldowna!"

"You will therefore renounce your sacred and well-grounded claims to the imperial throne?" asked Lestocq, continuing his scribbling.

"Yes, that will I," responded Elizabeth. "I will no longer be plagued with your plans and machinations—I will have repose. In the interior of my palace I will be empress; there will I establish a realm, a realm of peace and enjoyable happiness; there will I erect the temple of love, and consecrate myself as its priestess! No, speak no more of revolutions and conspiracies. I am not made to sit upon a throne as the feared and thundering goddess of cowardly slaves, causing millions to tremble at every word and glance! I will not be empress, not the bugbear of a quaking, kneeling people; I will be a woman, who has nothing to do with the business and drudgery of men; I will not be plagued with labor and care, but will enjoy and rejoice in my existence!"

"For that you will be allowed no time!" said Lestocq, with solemnity. "When you give up your plans and renounce your rights, then, princess, it will be all over with the days of enjoyment and happiness. It will then no longer be permitted you to convert your palace into a temple of pleasure, and thenceforth you will be known only as the priestess of misfortune and misery!"

"You have again your fever-dreams," said Elizabeth, smiling. "Come, I will awaken you! I have told you my story; it is now for you to give me a recipe for my inflamed eyes."

"Here it is," earnestly answered Lestocq, handing to the princess the paper upon which he had been scribbling.

Elizabeth took it and at first regarded it with smiling curiosity; but her features gradually assumed a more serious and even terrified expression, and the roses faded from her cheeks.

"You call this a recipe for eyes reddened with weeping," said she, with a shudder, "and yet it presents two pictures which make my hair bristle with terror, and might cause one to weep himself blind!"

"They represent our future!" said Lestocq, with decision. "You see that man bound upon the wheel—that is myself! Now look at the second. This young woman who is wringing her hands, and whose head one of these nuns is shearing, while the other is endeavoring, in spite of her struggling resistance, to envelop her in the black veil;—that is you, princess. For you the cloister, for me the wheel! That will be our future, Princess Elizabeth, if you now hesitate in your forward march in the path upon which you have once entered."

"And to persevere in this conspiracy is to give ourselves up to certain destruction, for doubt not they will be able to convict us. Among Grünstein's enlisted friends there are drunkards enough who would betray you for a flask of brandy! Princess Elizabeth, would you be a nun or an empress? Choose between these two destinations. There is no middle course."

"Then I would be an empress!" said Elizabeth, with flashing eyes, trembling with anxiety and excitement, and still examining the two drawings. "Ah, you are an accomplished artist, Lestocq, you have designed this picture with a horrible truth of resemblance. How I stand there! how I wring my hands, the pale lips opened for a cry of terror, and yet silenced by a view of those dreadful shears before whose deadly operations my hair falls to the earth, and that veil entombs me while yet living!"

And casting away the drawings, the princess trod them under foot, declaring in a loud and imperious tone: "These drawings are false, Lestocq, and that will I prove to you—I, the Empress Elizabeth!"

"All hail, my empress!" cried Lestocq, throwing himself at her feet and kissing the hem of her robe; "blessings upon you, for you have now rescued me from the hands of the executioner! You have saved my life, in return for which I will this day place an imperial crown upon your heavenly brows."

* Levecque, vol. v., p. 227.—"Voyage en Sibérie, par l'Abbé Chappe d'Auteroche," vol. i., p. 184.

"This day?" asked Elizabeth, with a shudder.

"Yes, it must be done this very night! We must improve the moment, for only the moment is ours. Every hour of delay but brings us nearer to our destruction. Yet one night of hesitation, and they will already have rendered our success impossible. Ah, the Regent Auna has sworn to believe only you, and never to doubt you, and yet she has ordered three battalions of the guards to march early in the morning to join the army in Viborg. Our friends and confidants are in these three battalions. Judge, then, how very much Anna Leopoldowna confides in you!"

"Ah, if it be really so," said Elizabeth, "then can I no longer have any regard for her. Anna will remove my friends from here, and that is a betrayal of the friendship she has sworn for me. I have therefore no further obligations toward her! I am free to act as I think best. Lestocq, I will be no nun, but an empress! You now have my word, and are at liberty to make all necessary arrangements. If it must be done, let it be done quickly and unhesitatingly. I have yet to-day the courage to dare any enormity, therefore let us utilize this day!"

"Expect me to-night at twelve o'clock!" said Lestocq, rising; "I will then be here to bring you the imperial crown."

This firm confidence made Elizabeth tremble again. Until now all had seemed like a dream, a play of the imagination; but when she read in Lestocq's bold and resolved features that it was a reality, she shook with terror, and an anxious fear overpowered her soul.

"And if it miscarry?" said she, thoughtfully.

"It will not and cannot miscarry!" responded Lestocq. "The right is on your side, and God will watch over the daughter of the great czar."

"And then, when I am really empress," said Elizabeth, thoughtfully, to herself, "what then? There is no happiness in it! They will give me another title, they will place a crown upon my head, and bind me to a throne. I shall be no longer free to act according to my will, to live as I would. Thousands of spies will lurk around me. Thousands of eyes will follow my steps, thousands of ears will listen for my every word, in order to interpret and attach a secret meaning to it! They will call me an empress, but I shall be a slave bound with golden fetters, upon whose head sits a golden crown of thorns. And this toil and weariness! These tiresome sittings of the ministers, this law-making and the signing of orders and commands! How horrible!—Lestocq," suddenly cried the princess, aloud, "if I must always labor, and make laws, and subscribe my name, and command and govern, then will I be no empress, no, never!"

"You shall be empress only to enjoy life in its highest splendor. We, your servants and slaves, we will work and govern for you!" said Lestocq.

"Swear that to me! Swear to me that I shall not be constrained to labor, swear that you will govern for me, that I may devote my time to the enjoyment of life!"

"I swear it to you by all that is most sacred to me."

"Well, then, I will be your empress!" said Elizabeth, satisfied.

At this moment a secret door opened and gave admission to Alexis Razumovsky.

By his entrance Elizabeth was reminded of her inflamed eyes, and of the fair Countess Eleanore Lapuschkin.

She gave Alexis a searching, scrutinizing glance, and it seemed to her that he appeared less tender and ardent than usual.

"Oh," she proudly said, motioning her favorite to approach her and lightly kissing him upon the forehead, "oh, I will yet compel you to adore me. When an imperial crown encircles my brow, then will you be obliged to confess that I am the fairest of women! Alexis, on this night shall I become an empress!"

With a cry of joy Alexis sank to her feet.

"Hail to my adored empress!" he exclaimed, with enthusiasm. "Hail Elizabeth, the fairest of all women!"

"With the exception of the beautiful Countess Lapuschkin!" said Elizabeth, with a bitter smile—"ah, when I am empress, I shall at least have the power to render that woman harmless, and to annihilate her!—You turn pale, Alexis," she continued with more vehemence—"your hand trembles in mine! You must therefore love her very much, this exalted queen of godlike beauty? Ah, I shall know how to punish her for it!"

"Princess!" reproachfully exclaimed Alexis—"Elizabeth, you, my august and gentle empress, you will not sacrifice an innocent woman to a momentary jealous vagary!"

"Ah, he ventures to intercede for her!" cried Elizabeth, with a hoarse laugh, and, turning to Lestocq, she continued, with anger-flashing eyes: "Lestocq, I have yet a condition to make before consenting to become an empress."

"Name your condition, princess, and if it be within the compass of human power it shall be fulfilled."

Casting an angry glance at Razumovsky, Elizabeth said, with a sinister smile:

"Swear to me, by all you hold most sacred, to find some fault in this Countess Lapuschkin which shall give me the right to condemn her to death!"

"I swear it by all I hold most sacred," solemnly responded Lestocq.

"And you will do well in that!" exclaimed Alexis. "For when a crime rests upon her, and she, only with a word or look, offends against my fair and noble empress, she will deserve such condemnation."

"You will, then, defend her no longer?" asked the somewhat appeased princess, bending down to her kneeling lover.

"What is Countess Lapuschkin to me?" tenderly responded Alexis. "For me there is but one woman, one empress, and one beauty, and that is Elizabeth!"

The princess smiled with satisfaction. "Lestocq," said she, "this time I keep my word. I am ready to dare all, in order to place the imperial crown upon my head. I must and will be empress, that I may have the power to reward you all, and to raise you, my Alexis, to me!"

And, drawing the handsome Alexis up to herself, she gave him her hand to kiss.

"I now go to make all necessary preparations," said Lestocq. "At midnight I will come for you. Be ready at that time, Elizabeth!"

"I will then be ready!" said Princess Elizabeth, nodding a farewell to Lestocq.

"At midnight!" she then thoughtfully continued. "Well, we have twelve hours until then, which will suffice for the invention of a suitable toilet. Alexis, tell me what sort of dress I shall wear. What color best becomes me and in what shall I best please the soldiers? The toilet, my Alexis, is often decisive in such cases; an unsuitable costume might cause me to displease the conspirators, and lead them to give up the enterprise. You must aid me, Alexis, in choosing a costume. Come, let us repair to the wardrobe, and call my women. I will try on all my dresses, one after the other; then you shall decide which is most becoming, and that will we choose."

The princess and her lover betook themselves to the wardrobe, and called her women to assist in selecting a suitable revolution-toilet.

CHAPTER XIV.

THE REVOLUTION.

NIGHT had come. The lights in palaces and houses were gradually extinguished. St. Petersburg began to sleep, or at least to give itself the appearance of sleeping. The regent, Anna Leopoldowna, also, had already dismissed her household, and withdrawn into her private apartments.

It was a fine starlight night. Anna leaned upon the window-frame, thoughtfully and dreamily glancing up at the heavens. Her eyes gradually filled with tears, which slowly rolled down over her cheeks and fell upon her hands. She was startled by the falling of these warm, glowing drops. She had been unconscious of her weeping, as her thoughts had diverted her attention from her tears. She was thinking of Lynar, of the distant, warmly-desired one, to whom she would gladly have devoted her whole existence, but to whom she could belong only through falsehood. She thought it would be nobler and greater to renounce him, that her love might be consecrated by her abnegation, while actually devoting her life to the duties enjoined by the laws and the Church. But these thoughts filled her bosom with a nameless sorrow, and it was involuntarily that she wept.

"No," she murmured low, "I cannot make this sacrifice; I cannot make an offering of my love to my virtue; for this bughear of a compulsory marriage I cannot give up a love which God Himself has inspired in my heart. Then let it be so! Let the world judge and the priests condemn me. I will not sacrifice my love to a prejudice. I know that this is sinful, but God will have compassion on the sinner who has no other happiness on earth than this only one—a love that controls her whole being. And if this sin must be punished, oh, my Maker, I pray you to pardon him, and let the punishment fall on me alone!"

Thus speaking, she raised her arms and directed her eyes toward the heavens in fervent prayer. Suddenly a brilliant light flashed through the air—a star had shot from its sphere, and, after a short course, had become extinguished.

"That bodes misfortune," said Anna, with a shudder, her head sinking upon her breast.

At this moment there was a loud knocking at her door, and Prince Ulrich, Anna's husband, earnestly demanded admission.

Anna hastened to open, asking with surprise the cause of his unusual visit.

"Anna," said the prince, hastily entering, "I come to warn you once more. Again has a warning letter been mysteriously conveyed to me. I have just found it upon my night-table. See for yourself. It implores us to be on our guard. It informs us that we are threatened with a frightful danger, that Elizabeth conspires, and that we are lost if we do not instantly take preventive measures."

Anna read the warning letter, and then smilingly gave it back to her husband.

"Always the same old song, the same croaking of the toad," said she. "Count Ostermann has taken it into his head that Elizabeth is conspiring, and doubtless all these warning letters come from him. Read them no more in future; my husband, and now let us retire to rest."

"And what if it were, nevertheless, true," said the prince, pressingly—"if we are really threatened with a great danger? A word from you can turn it away. Let us, therefore, be careful! Remember your son, Anna—his life is also threatened! Protect him, mother of an emperor! Allow me, the generalissimo of your forces, to take measures of precaution! Let me establish patrols, and cause a regiment, for whose fidelity I can be answerable, to guard the entrances of the palace!"

Anna smilingly shook her head. "No," said she, "nothing of all that shall be done! Such precautions manifest suspicion, and would wound the feelings of this good Elizabeth. She is innocent, believe me. I yesterday sharply observed her, and she came out from the trial pure. It would be ignoble to distrust her now. Moreover, she has my princely word that I will always listen only to herself, and believe no one but her. In the morning I will go to her and show her this letter, that she may have an opportunity to justify herself."

" You therefore consider her wholly innocent?" asked the prince, with a sigh.

" Yes, perfectly innocent. Her firm demeanor, her asseverations, her tears, have convinced me that it was unjust in us to believe the hateful rumors they had spread concerning her.* Let us therefore retire in peace and quiet. No danger threatens us from Elizabeth!"

There was something convincing and tranquillizing in Anna's immovable conviction; the prince felt his inability to oppose her, and was ashamed of his feminine fears in the face of her masculine intrepidity.

With a sigh he took his leave and returned to his own room.

At the door he turned once again.

"Anna," said he, with solemnity, "you have decided upon our destiny, and God grant that it may all eventuate happily! But should it be otherwise, should the monstrous and terrible break in upon you, then, at least, remember this hour, in which I warned you, and confess that I am free from all blame!"

Without awaiting an answer, with a drooping head and deep sigh, the prince left the room.

Anna looked after him with a compassionate smile.

"Poor prince!" she murmured low, "he is always so timid and trembling; that indicates unhappiness! He loves me, and I cannot force my heart to return the feeling. Poor prince, it must be very sad to love and be unloved!"

With a sigh she closed the door through which her husband had passed.

* Levecque, vol. v., p. 227.

"I will now sleep," said she. "Yes, sleep! Possibly Heaven may send me a pleasant dream, and I may see my Lynar! But no, I must first go to Ivan, to ascertain whether his slumber is tranquil."

With hasty steps she repaired to the adjacent chamber, which was that of the young emperor.

There all was still. Before the door opening upon the corridor she heard the regular step of the soldier on guard. The waiters upon the emperor were slumbering upon mattresses around him. It was a picture of profound tranquillity.

With light steps Anna approached the cradle of her son, and, bending down over him, regarded him with tender maternal glances, while his still and peaceful slumber seemed to touch her heart with a sweet emotion.

"Sleep, my dear child, my charming little emperor," she murmured—"sleep, and in your dreams may you play with angels as beautiful as yourself!"

Bending again over the cradle, she breathed a light kiss upon the rosy lips of her child, and then noiselessly returned to her own chamber.

"And now," said she, drawing a long breath, "now will I, also, sleep and dream! Good-night, my beloved; good-night, Lynar!"

With a happy smile she reclined upon her couch, and soon slumbered.

At this moment the clock in the next chamber struck the twelfth hour. Slowly and solemnly resounded the tones of the striking clocks that announced the midnight.

At this same hour a lively movement

commenced in the palace of the Princess Elizabeth. Lights were seen glancing from window to window, hurrying shadows were seen coming and going in the rooms, every thing there announced an activity unusual for the hour, and certainly it was a signal good fortune for Elizabeth that Anna had forbidden her husband's sending a patrol through the streets. One single patrol passing the palace might have frustrated the whole conspiracy!

But the streets were perfectly quiet; nowhere was a sentinel or watchman to be seen.

The slight creaking and whizzing of a sledge upon the crackling snow was now heard; it came nearer and nearer, and then there was a knocking at the palace gate. The porter opened, and two sledges drove into the court.

The first, with a rich covering and magnificent ornaments, was empty. But Lestocq was seen to spring out of the second, and hurriedly enter the palace.

Elizabeth, splendidly dressed, sparkling with brilliants, was waiting in her small reception-room. No one but Alexis Razumovsky was with her. Neither of them spoke, and their visages plainly discovered that they were in a state of painfully uncomfortable suspense.

Elizabeth was pale and had a convulsive twitching about her mouth, her form trembled feverishly, and she was obliged to cling to Razumovsky, to prevent falling.

"Did you hear the opening of the court-yard gate?" she breathed low. "Lestocq is not yet here, and it is past midnight. "Certainly he is arrested, all is discovered, and we are lost! I am fearfully anxious, Alexis; I already seem to feel the sword at my throat. Ah, hear you not steps in the corridor? They come this way. They are my pursuers. They come to conduct me to the scaffold! Save me, Alexis, save me!"

And with a shrill cry of anguish the princess clung to the neck of her favorite.

The door was now hastily opened, and upon the threshold appeared Lestocq and Woronzow.

"Princess Elizabeth!" exclaimed Lestocq, with solemnity, "I have come for you. The throne awaits its empress!"

"Up, Princess Elizabeth," said Alexis, "take courage, my fair empress, give us an example of spirit and resolution!"

The princess slowly raised her pale face from Razumovsky's shoulder, and looking around with timid glances, faintly said: "I suffer fearfully! This anguish will kill me! My destiny is so cruel, I am so tormented. Why must I be an empress?"

"That you may be no nun," laconically responded Lestocq.

"And to become the greatest and loftiest woman in the world!" said Woronzow.

"To raise to your own elevation the man you love," whispered Alexis.

With a glance of tenderness, Elizabeth nodded to him.

"Yes," said she, "for your sake, my Alexis, I will become an empress! Come, let us go. But where is Grünstein?"

"With his faithful followers he awaits

us before the casern of his regiment. We go there first."

"Then let us go!" said Elizabeth, striding forward. But she stopped on seeing that Alexis followed with the other two.

"No," said she, "you must not go with us. Alexis. If I am to have courage to act and speak, I must know that you are not mingled in the strife—I must not have to tremble for your life! No, no, only when I know that you are concealed and in safety, can I have courage to struggle for an imperial crown. Promise me, therefore, Alexis, that you will quietly remain here until I send a messenger for you!"

Razumovsky begged and implored in vain—in vain he knelt before her, and covered her hands with tears and kisses.

Elizabeth remained inflexible, and, as Alexis yet persisted in his prayers, she earnestly and proudly said: "Alexis Razumovsky, I command you to remain here. You will obey the first command of your empress!"

"I will remain," sighed Alexis, "and the world will point the finger of scorn at me, calling me a coward!"

"And I will compel the world to honor you as a king!" said Elizabeth, with tenderness, beckoning to Lestocq and Woronzow to follow her from the room.

Silently they hastened down the stairs—silently was Elizabeth handed into her sledge, while Lestocq and Woronzow took their places in the second.

"Forward!" thundered Lestocq's powerful voice, and the train rushed through the dark and deserted streets.

St. Petersburg slept. No one appeared at the darkened windows of the silent palaces, no one boded that a new empress was passing through the streets,—an empress, who at this time had but two subjects in her train!

They had now reached the casern of the Peobrajensky regiment. There they halted. In the open door stands Grünstein with his thirty recruits.

They silently approached the sledge of the princess and prostrated themselves before her.

"Hail to our empress!" whispered Grünstein low, and as low was it repeated by the soldiers.

"Let us enter the casern, call the soldiers and awaken the officers; I myself will address them!" said Elizabeth, alighting from her sledge. She was now full of courage and resolution. In the face of danger now no longer to be avoided, she had suddenly steeled her heart; her father's spirit was awakened in her.

With a firm step she entered the casern; the conspirators had already raised an alarm there, and the suddenly aroused soldiers rushed from all the corridors, with wonder and admiration staring at this noble and beautiful woman who, radiant in the splendor of her beauty, and sparkling with jewels, stood in their midst.

"Soldiers," cried Elizabeth, with a firm voice, "I come to implore your support in my attempt to obtain justice in the realm of my father! I am the daughter of the great Emperor Peter, the rightful heir to the throne of Russia, and I claim what is mine! I will no longer suffer a German princess to give laws to you, my beloved brethren and countrymen! Follow me therefore, and let us drive away these foreign intruders who have usurped the throne of your lawful sovereign!"

"All hail, Elizabeth, our empress!" cried the conspirators, prostrating themselves.

Surprised, benumbed, and overpowered, the others made no opposition. Miserable slaves, they were accustomed to obey whoever dared assume the command over them,—and they therefore submitted. Falling upon their knees, they took the oath of allegiance to the new empress!

Elizabeth was now the empress of three hundred soldiers.

"Up, now, my friends, to the palace of the czar, where these usurpers dwell and inflict upon you the shame of calling a cradled infant your emperor. Come, and let us punish them for this insult, by thrusting them from their usurped power!"

"We will follow our empress in life and death!" cried the soldiers.

They therefore started again, and once more hastened through the silent streets until, at length, they reached the imperial palace, where dwelt the Emperor Ivan with his parents.

Elizabeth, with her confidential partisans in four sledges, had hastened on in advance of the others. With renewed courage they approached the principal entrance of the palace.

The guard took to their arms, and the drummer was preparing to beat an alarm, when a single blow of Lestocq's fist broke through the skin of the drum. The terrified drummer fell, and over his body passed the band of conspirators, Elizabeth at their head.

No one ventured to oppose them; the slaves fell upon their knees in homage to her who announced herself as their mistress and empress!

Thus meeting with universal submission and obedience, they approached the wing of the palace occupied by the Emperor Ivan and his mother the regent. Here is stationed an officer of the guard. He alone ventures defiance to the intruders. He meets them with his sword drawn, and swears to strike down the first person who attempts to enter the corridor.

"Unhappy man, what is it you dare!" said Lestocq, boldly advancing. "You are guilty of high-treason. Fall upon your knees and implore pardon of your empress, Elizabeth!"

The officer shrank back in terror. It was an empress who stood before him, and he had dared to defy her!

Begging for forgiveness and mercy, he dropped his sword and fell upon his knees.* The Russian slave was awakened in him, and he bent before the one who had the power to command.

Unobstructed, retained by no one, Elizabeth and her followers now strode through the corridor leading to the private apartments of the regent. Sentinels were placed at every door, with strict commands to strike down any one who should dare to oppose them.

In this manner they reached the anteroom of the regent's chamber.

Elizabeth had not the courage to go any farther. She hesitatingly stopped.

* "Voyage en Sibérie, par l'Abbe Chappe d'Auteroche," vol. i., p. 185.

A deep shame and repentance came over her when she thought of the noble confidence Anna had shown, and which she was now on the point of repaying with the blackest treason.

Lestocq, whose sharp, observing glance constantly rested upon her, divined her thoughts and the cause of her irresolution. He privately whispered some words to Grünstein, who, with thirty grenadiers, immediately approached the door of Anna's sleeping-room.

With a single push the door was forced, and with a wild cry the soldiers rushed to the couch upon which Anna Leopoldowna was reposing.

With a cry of anguish Anna springs up from her slumber, and shudderingly stares at the soldiers by whom she is encompassed, who, with rough voices, command her to rise and follow them. They scarcely give her time to put on a robe, and encase her little feet in shoes.

But Anna has become perfectly calm and self-possessed. She knows she is lost, and, too proud to weep or complain, she finds in herself courage to be tranquil.

"I beg only to be allowed to speak to Elizabeth," said she, aloud. "I will do all you command me. I will follow you wherever you wish, only let me first see your empress, Elizabeth."

Elizabeth, leaning against the door-post, had heard these words; yielding to an involuntary impulse of her heart, she pushed open the door and appeared upon the threshold of Anna Leopoldowna's chamber.

On perceiving her, a faint smile passed over Anna's features.

"Ah, come you thus to me, Elizabeth?" she said, reproachfully, with a proud glance at the princess.

Elizabeth could not support that glance. She cast down her eyes, and again Anna Leopoldowna smiled. She was conquered, but before her, blushing with shame, stood her momentarily subdued conqueror. But Anna now remembered her son, and, folding her hands, she said, in an imploring tone:

"Elizabeth, kill not my son! Have compassion upon him!"

Elizabeth turned away with a shudder, she felt her heart rent, she had not strength for an answer.

Lestocq beckoned the soldiers, and commanded them to remove the traitress, Anna Leopoldowna.

Thirty warriors took possession of the regent, who calmly and proudly submitted herself to them and suffered herself to be led away.

In the corridor they encountered another troop of soldiers, who were escorting the regent's husband, Prince Ulrich of Brunswick, and Anna's favorite, Julia von Mengden.

"Anna!" sorrowfully exclaimed the prince, "oh, had you but listened to my warning! Why did I not, in spite of your commands, what I ought to have done? I alone am to blame for this sad misfortune."

"It is no one's fault but mine," calmly responded Anna. "Pardon me, my husband; pardon me, Julia."

And so they descended to the sledges in waiting below. They placed the prince in one, and the regent, with Julia, in the other.

"Ah," said Julia, throwing her arms

around Anna's neck, "we shall at least suffer together."

Anna reclined her head upon her friend's shoulder.

"God is just and good," said she. "He punishes me for my criminal love, and mercifully spares the object of my affections. I thank God for my sufferings. Julia, should you one day be liberated and allowed to see him again, then bear to him my warmest greetings; then tell him that I shall love him eternally, and that my last sigh shall be a prayer for his happiness. I shall never see him again. Bear to him my blessing, Julia!"

Julia dissolved in tears, and, clinging to her friend, she sobbed: "No, no, they will not dare to kill you."

"Then they will condemn me to a life-long imprisonment," calmly responded Anna.

"No, no, your head is sacred, and so is your freedom. They dare not attack either."

"Nothing is sacred in Russia," laconically responded Anna.

The sledges stopped at the palace of the Princess Elizabeth. Hardly two hours had passed since Elizabeth, in those same sledges, had left her palace as a poor, trembling princess; and now, as reigning empress, she sent them back with the dethroned regent.

The latter entered the palace of the princess as a prisoner, while Elizabeth, as empress, took possession of the palace of the czars;

CHAPTER XV.

THE SLEEP OF INNOCENCE.

ANNA LEOPOLDOWNA had hardly left the room in which she had been surprised and captured, when Lestocq turned to Grünstein with a new order.

"Now," said he, in an undertone to him—"now hasten to seize the emperor. This little Ivan must be annihilated."

Elizabeth had overheard these words, and remembering Anna's last prayer, she exclaimed with vehemence:

"No, no, I say, he shall not be annihilated! Woe to him who injures a hair of his head! I will not be the murderer of an innocent child! Take him prisoner, get him in your power, but in him respect the child and the emperor! Tear him not forcibly from his slumber, but protect his sleep! Poor child, destined to suffer so early!"

"No weakness now, princess," whispered Lestocq; "show yourself great and firm, else all is lost! Come away from here, that the sight of this child may not yet more enfeeble your heart.

6

Come, much more still remains to be done."

And, reverently taking Elizabeth's hand, he led her to the door.

"Now do your duty," said he to Grünstein. "Seize young Ivan."

"But remember my command, and spare him," said Elizabeth, slowly and hesitatingly leaving the chamber.

"Now to Ivan!" Grünstein commanded his soldiers, and with them he hastened to the sleeping-room of the young emperor.

There deep stillness and undisturbed peace yet prevailed. Only the waiting-women were awakened, and had hastily fled in search of concealment and safety. They had left the young emperor entirely alone, and he had not been awakened by the disturbance all around him.

He lay quietly in his splendid cradle, which was placed upon a sort of estrade in the centre of the room, dimly lighted by a lamp suspended from the ceiling by golden chains. This slumbering, smiling, childish face, peeping forth from the green silk coverings of the pillows, resembled a fresh, bursting rose-bud. It was a sight that inspired respect even in those rough soldiers.

Devoutly staring, they at first remained at the door of the room; then slowly, and stepping on the points of their toes, they approached nearer and surrounded the cradle. But, remembering the words of their new empress, "Spare his sleep," no one dared to touch the child, or awaken him from his slumber.

In close order the bearded warriors pressed around the cradle of the imperial child, leaning upon their halberds, watching for his awaking.[*]

It was a rare and admirable picture. In the centre, upon its estrade, was the splendid cradle of the slumbering child, and all around, upon the steps of this child-throne, these soldiers with their wild and threatening faces, all eyes expectantly resting upon the smiling infantile brow.

The door now opened, and, her face pallid with terror, Ivan's nurse rushed into the room and to the cradle of her imperial nursling. The soldiers, with imperious glances, beckoned her to await in silence, like themselves, the awaking of the emperor. The poor woman spoke not, but her fast-flowing tears indicated the depth of her grief.

Time passes. As if under enchantment, earnest, immovable, silent, stand the soldiers. Behind the cradle, her eyes and arms raised imploringly toward heaven, stands the nurse, while the child continues to slumber, smiling in its sleep.

At the expiration of an hour thus passed, the imperial infant moves, throws up its little rosy arms, opens its eyes—it is awake!

A cry of triumph escapes the lips of the soldiers—all arms are stretched forth to seize him who, an hour before, had been their lord and emperor.

The child, frightened by the aspect of these rough soldiers, bursts out into a cry of alarm, and stretches out its little arms toward its nurse.

She takes him in her arms and weeps over him. The frightened child buries its little face in the bosom of his nurse,

* Levecque, vol. v., p. 227.

THE SLEEP OF INNOCENCE.

p. 82.

and the soldiers now convey them both to the waiting sledges. The dethroned emperor is quickly transported to the dethroned regent at Elizabeth's palace, who, with hot tears, clasps her son to her heart.

CHAPTER XVI.

THE RECOMPENSING.

MEANWHILE, Elizabeth had made herself absolute mistress of the imperial palace. Hastening to the throne-room, she had taken possession of the throne of her father, and administered the oath of allegiance to the guards surrounding her.

They lay upon their knees before her, these cowardly instruments of despotism; they bowed their heads in the dust, and these four or five thousand slaves, to which number the followers of the empress already amounted, swore fealty to Elizabeth, ready to strangle the regent and the young emperor at her command, or to serve her the same if, peradventure, the regent should regain a momentary power.[*]

While the guards were doing homage in the palace, Grünstein and Woronzow, by Lestocq's command, led their men to Münnich's and Ostermann's, and both were imprisoned; with them, a great number of leading and suspected persons, who, perhaps, might have been disposed to draw the sword for Anna Leopoldowna. Lestocq had thought of every thing, had considered every thing; at the same time that he entered the regent's palace with Elizabeth, he sent to the printer the manifesto which proclaimed Elizabeth as empress. With the appearance of the sun in the horizon, Elizabeth was recognized as empress in the capital, and soon after throughout the whole empire. Who were they who recognized her? It was not the people, for in Russia there are no people—there are only masters and slaves. Elizabeth had become empress because fortune and Anna Leopoldowna's generous confidence had favored her; not the exigencies of the people, nor the tyranny of her predecessor had called her to the throne, but she had attained to it by the cunning and intrigues of some few confederates. She had become empress because Lestocq was tired of being only physician to a poor princess; because Grünstein thought the position of under-officer was far too humble for him, and because Alexis Razumovsky, the former precentor in the imperial chapel, found it desirable to add to his name the title of count or prince!

When St. Petersburg awoke it heard

---

[*] "L'Abbé Chappe d'Auteroche," vol. i., p. 138.

with astonishment the news of a new revolution. From mouth to mouth flew this astounding announcement: "We have changed our rulers! We are no longer the servants of the Emperor Ivan, but of the Empress Elizabeth! A new dynasty has arisen, and we have a new oath of allegiance to take!"

At first only a few ventured to spread this extraordinary intelligence, and these few were tremblingly and anxiously avoided; it was dangerous to listen to them; people fled from them without answering. But as the rumors became constantly louder and more significant, as at length their truth could be no longer doubted, as it became certain that the regent and her son were dethroned and Elizabeth was established in power, all the doubting and anxious faces were, as by an electric spark, lighted up with joy; then nothing was heard but the cry of triumph and jubilation; then was Anna Leopoldowna loudly cursed by those who had blessed her on the preceding day; then was the new Empress Elizabeth loudly lauded by those who yesterday had smiled with contempt at her powerlessness.

All again hastened to the imperial palace; the great and the noble again brought out their state coaches for the purpose of throwing themselves at the feet of the new possessor of power and swearing a new allegiance; again nothing was heard but the sound of universal rejoicing, nothing seen but faces lighted up by ecstasy and eyes glistening with tears of joy. And this was, in fourteen months, the third time that they had done homage to a new ruler who had as regularly dethroned his predecessor, and they had each time gone through the ceremony with the same evidences of joy, the same ecstasies, the same slavish humility, not commiserating the defeated party, but professing love and devotion to the victor!

And as the day dawned on St. Petersburg, as it gloriously beamed upon the young empress, as she saw these thousands of worshipping slaves at her feet, Elizabeth's heart swelled with a proud joy, and looking down upon the masses of humble and devoted subjects, whose mistress she was, she felt herself momentarily overcome by a deep and holy emotion.

"I will be a mother to this people," thought she; "I will love and spare them; I will govern them with mildness; they shall not curse, but adore me!"

Yielding to this first generous impulse of her heart, Elizabeth rose from the throne, and with uplifted hands loudly and solemnly swore that she would be a mother to her subjects—a mother who, when compelled to punish, would never forget love and forbearance!

"No one, however great his crime," said she, with flashing eyes—"no one shall be punished with death so long as I sit upon this throne! From this day the punishment of death is abolished in my realm! I will punish crime, but I will spare the life of the criminal!"

When Elizabeth had thus spoken, the large hall again resounded with the rejoicing shouts of the great and noble—men breathed freer and deeper, they raised their heads more proudly; for centuries the all-powerful word of the czars had swept over the heads of Russians like the sword of Damocles—it now seemed to be removed, and to promise to each one a longer life, a longer unendangered existence. For where was there a subject of the czars who might not at any time be convicted of a crime—where an innocent person who might not at any moment be condemned to death? A glance, a smile, an inconsiderate word, had often sufficed to cause a head to fall! And now this eternally present danger seemed to be removed! What wonder, then, that they raised shouts of joy, that they embraced each other, that they loudly and solemnly called down the blessings of Heaven upon this noble and merciful empress!

During this time of general rejoicing among the great and noble of the realm in the brilliant imperial halls above, the palace was surrounded by dense masses of people looking up with curiosity at the bright windows, and listening with astonishment to the joyful shouts that reached their ears below. And when they learned the cause of the rejoicing above, they shrugged their shoulders and murmured low: "The empress will henceforth punish no one with death! What is that to us? That the great shall no more be put to death by the empress, is no concern of ours, the serfs of the great! The empress is powerful, but our lords and masters have yet more power over us. They will still scourge us to death, and the empress cannot hinder them!"

That a word of authority from the czarina had abolished the punishment of death, did not stir them up from their dull, expectant silence; but when a messenger from the empress came and announced that Elizabeth had ordered a flask of brandy to be given to each one of the crowd assembled below, that they might drink her health, then came life and movement to these stupid masses, then their dull faces were distorted into a friendly grin, then they screamed and howled with a brutish ecstasy, and they all rushed to the opened door to avail themselves of the promised benevolence of the empress and receive the divine liquor!

For the great, the abolition of capital punishment—for the people, a flask of brandy—these were the first rays that announced the appearance of the newly-rising sun Elizabeth in the horizon of her realm!

No,—Elizabeth did yet more!—in this hour she remembered with a grateful heart the faithful friends who had assisted her to the throne; to reward these was her next and most sacred duty!

A nod from her called to her presence those thirty grenadiers of the Preobrajensky regiment whom Grünstein had won over, and the empress with a gracious smile gave them her hand to kiss.   •

Then, rising from her throne, and glancing at the assembled magnates and princes, she said, in a clear and flattering tone: "It is service that ennobles, it is fidelity that lends fame and splendor. And service and fidelity have you rendered and shown to me, my faithful grenadiers! I will reward you as you deserve. From this hour you are free; nay, more, you are magnates of my realm; you belong, with the best of right, to their circle, for, in virtue of my imperial power, I raise you to the nobility by creating you barons, all of you, my thirty faithful grenadiers, and you, Grünstein, the leader of this faithful band! Receive them into your ranks, my counts and barons, they are worthy of you!"

Hesitating, not daring to mingle with those proud magnates, stood the new barons; but the princes and counts advanced to them with open arms, with exclamations of tenderness and assurances of friendship. The empress had spoken, the slaves must obey; and these princes and counts, these generals and field-marshals, who yesterday would hardly have thrown away a contemptuous glance upon these grenadiers, now called them friends and brothers, and were most happy to admit them into their circle.

Elizabeth gave a satisfied glance at these hearty greetings: she found it infinitely sweet and agreeable to make so many men happy in so easy a manner, and with pleasure she recollected that she had yet to reward her coachman who had guided her sledge in the great and decisive hour.

She ordered him to be called. A considerable time elapsed, and all were looking expectantly toward the door, which finally opened, and, led by four lackeys, the coachman stumbled into the hall. They had had some trouble in finding him, until at length he was discovered among the people in the court-yard, enjoying the brandy distributed by order of the empress. From this crowd they had withdrawn him in spite of his resistance, in order to bring him to his sovereign.

She received the staggering Petrovitch with a gracious smile, she praised the dauntlessness with which he had guided her sledge in that eventful night, and in gratitude for his good conduct she raised him, as she had the grenadiers, to the rank of a nobleman by naming him a baron of the Russian empire.*

Petrovitch listened to her with a stupid laugh; and when the magnates crowded around him, offering their hands and assuring him of their friendship, he tremblingly and with effort stammered some unmeaning words, and falling upon his knees, he bowed his head in the dust before these great and powerful magnates, humbly kissing the hems of their garments, not suspecting that he was their equal in rank.

And constantly more brilliant and beautiful beamed the imperial grace. None of Elizabeth's faithful friends and servants were forgotten, for she possessed a virtue rare among princes— she was grateful.

She named Lestocq her first physician, president of the medical college, and member of her privy council. She made Grünstein an imperial aide-de-camp, with the rank of brigadier-general; and Woronzow a count and her first chamberlain.

Then, at last, she repeated the name of her friend Alexis Razumovsky. Her fair brow lighted up as with a reflected

---

* Maunstein, "Mémoires, Historiques, Politiques, et Militaires sur la Russie;" Levecque, "Histoire de Russie."

sunbeam on his approaching her throne and, holding out to him both hands, she said aloud: "Alexis Razumovsky, I have you most to thank for my success in dispossessing the usurpers who had robbed me of my father's throne; for your wise counsels gave me courage and force: be then, henceforth, next to my throne, my chamberlain, Count Razumovsky!"

Bending a knee before her, Alexis gratefully kissed her beloved hand, and the counts and gentlemen surrounded him, loudly praising the great wisdom of the empress, whose divine penetration enabled her everywhere to discover and reward true service!

"Ah," sighed Elizabeth, when, on the evening of this glorious day, she was again alone with her confidential friends, "ah, my friends, I have now complied with your wishes and allowed you to make an empress of me! But forget not, Lestocq, that I have become empress only on condition that I am not to be troubled with business and state affairs. This has been a day of great exertion and fatigue, and I hope you will henceforth leave me in repose. I have done what you wished, I am empress, and have rewarded you for your aid, but now I also demand my reward, and that is undisturbed peace! Once for all, in my private apartments no one is to speak of state affairs, here I will have repose; you can carry on the government through your bureaux and *chancelleries;* I will have nothing to do with it! Here we will be gay and enjoy life. Come here, my Alexis,—come here and tell me if this imperial crown is becoming, and whether you

found me fair in my ermine-trimmed purple mantle?"

"My lofty empress is always the fairest of women," tenderly responded Alexis.

"Call me not empress," said she, drawing him closer to her. "That brings again to mind all the hardships and wearinesses I have this day encountered."

"Only yet a moment, your majesty; let me remind you that you are now empress, and, as such, have duties to perform!" pressingly exclaimed Lestocq. "You have this day exercised the pleasantest right of your imperial power—the right of rewarding and making happy. But there remains another and not less important duty; your majesty must now think of punishing. The regent, and her husband and son, are prisoners; as, also, are Münnich, Ostermann, Count Löwenwald, and Julia von Mengden. You must think of judging and punishing them."

Elizabeth had paid no attention to him. She was whispering and laughing with Alexis, who had let down her long dark hair, and was now playfully twining it around her white neck.

"Ah, you have not listened to me, your majesty," impatiently cried Lestocq. "You must, however, for a few moments remember your new dignity, and direct what is to be done with the imprisoned traitors."

"Only see, Alexis, how this new lord privy counsellor teases me," sighed the princess, and, turning to Lestocq, she continued: "I think you should understand the laws better than I, and should know how traitors are punished."

"In all countries high-treason is punished with death," said Lestocq, gloomily.

"Well, let these traitors fare according to the common usage, and kill them," responded Elizabeth, comfortably extending herself upon the divan.

"But your majesty has this day abolished the punishment of death."

"Have I so? Ah, yes, I now remember. Well, as I have said it, I must keep my word."

"And the regent, Prince Ulrich, the so-called Emperor Ivan, Counts Ostermann, Münnich, Löwenwald, as well as Julia von Mengden, and the other prisoners, are all to remain unpunished?"

"Can they be punished in no other way than by death?" impatiently asked Elizabeth. "Have we not prisons and the knout? Have we not Siberia and the rack? Punish these traitors, then, as you think best. I give you full powers, and, if it must be so, will even take the trouble to affix my signature to your sentence."

"But we cannot scourge the regent or her son?"

"No," said Elizabeth, with vehemence, "these you must permit to go free and without hinderance to Germany; your judicial powers will not extend to them. It shall not be said that Elizabeth has delivered up her aunt and cousin to torture for the purpose of securing her own advantage. Let them go hence free and unobstructed! I tell you this is my express, imperial will!"

And Elizabeth, exhausted by so great an effort, leaned her head upon the shoulder of Alexis, mechanically playing with his locks.

"And Münnich and Ostermann?" asked Lestocq.

"*Mon Dieu!* will, then, this annoyance never cease?" impatiently exclaimed the empress. "What are Münnich and Ostermann to me? I know them not; they have never injured and are wholly indifferent to me. Do with them as you and your colleagues think best, I shall not trouble myself about it. Judge, condemn, punish them, it is all one to me—only their lives must be spared, as I have promised that no one shall be punished with death."

"I may, then, announce to the council that you will confirm their sentence?"

"Yes, yes, certainly," cried Elizabeth, springing up. "Scourge, banish them, do what you please, but leave me in peace! Come, my Alexis, this good Lestocq is insufferable to-day; he will annoy us to death if we remain any longer here! Come, we will escape from him and his serious face! Oh, we have much more serious subjects of conversation. To-morrow is my grand gala dinner, and we have my toilet to examine, to be certain that every thing is in the proper order. And then the ball toilet for the evening, which is far more important. I shall open the ball with a *Polonnaise*. You promised me, Alexis, to practise with me the new tour which the Marquis de la Chetardie describes as the latest Parisian mode. Come, let us essay this tour. For a new empress, at her first court ball, there is nothing more important than that she should perform her duty as leader of the dance with propriety and grace. Quick, therefore, to the work! Give me your hand—and now, Alexis, let us commence. Sing a melody to it, and then it will go better."

Alexis began to sing a *Polonnaise*, and, taking the hand of the empress, they commenced the practice of the new *Polonnaise* tour.

"So, that is right," said he, interrupting his singing, "that is very fine. Now let go my hand and turn proudly and majestically around. Beautifully done! Now a half turn sideward. One, two, three—la, la, la, tra la!"

"Yet one more question," interposed Lestocq; "may the council of state sit in judgment upon Löwenwald and de Mengden, and will you confirm their decision?"

"One, two, three—tra, la, la!" sang Alexis, and the empress whirled and made her graceful turn, as he had taught her.

Lestocq repeated his question to the empress.

Elizabeth was precisely in the most difficult tour.

"Yes, yes," she breathlessly cried, "I deliver them all over to you; scourge them, punish them, send them to Siberia—whatever you think best! Halt, Alexis, we must try this tour over again. But, indeed, I think I shall acquit myself very well in it."

"Heavenly!" cried Alexis. "Once more, then! One, two, three—la, la, la, tra la!"

CHAPTER XVII.

PUNISHMENT.

"PUNISH them all, all!" had Elizabeth said, "but the regent, her husband, and her son—them you will permit to return to Germany!"

"We must accomplish the will of the empress, and therefore let them go!"

"We will obey her commands," said Lestocq to Alexis Razumovsky. "We must let them go free, but it would be dangerous to let them ever reach Germany. With their persons they would preserve their rights and their claims,

and Elizabeth would always stand in fear of this regent and this young growing emperor, whose claims to the imperial Russian crown are incontestable. You alone, Razumovsky, can turn away this danger from the head of the empress, by convincing her of its reality, and inducing her to change her mind. Reflect that the safety of the empress is our own; reflect that, as we have risen with her, so shall we fall with her!"

"Rely upon me," said Alexis, with a confident smile; "this regent and her young Emperor Ivan shall never pass the Russian boundary! Let them now go, but send a strong guard with them, and travel by slow marches, that our couriers may be able to overtake them at a later period. That is all you have to do in the case."

And, humming a sentimental song, Alexis repaired to the apartments of the empress.

Before the back door of the palace Elizabeth had occupied as princess, a travelling-sledge was waiting. Gayly sounded and clattered the bells on the six small horses attached to the sledge; gayly did the postilions blow their horns, and with enticing calls resounded the thundering *fanfares* through the cold winter air.

To those for whom this sledge was destined, this call sounded like a greeting from heaven. It was to them the dove with the olive-branch, announcing to them the end of their torments; it was the messenger of peace, which gave them back their freedom, their lives, and perhaps even happiness. They were to return to Germany, their long-missed home; hastening through the Russian snow-fields, they would soon reach a softer climate, where they would be surrounded by milder manners and customs. What was it to Anna that she was to be deprived of earthly elevation and power—what cared she that she henceforth would no more have the pleasure of commanding others? She was free, free from the task of ruling slaves and humanizing barbarians; free from the constraint of greatness, and, finally, free to live in conformity with her own inclinations, and perhaps,

ah, perhaps, to found a happiness, the bare dreaming of which already caused her heart to tremble with unspeakable ecstasy.

Again and again the *fanfares* resounded without. Anna, weeping, tore herself from the arms of Julia. She had in vain implored the favor of taking Julia von Mengden with her. Elizabeth had refused it, and, in this refusal, she had pronounced the sentence of the favorite—this was understood by both Julia and Anna.

They held each other in a last embrace. Anna wept hot tears, but Julia remained calm, and even smiled.

"They may send me to Siberia, if they please, my heart will remain warm under the coldness of the Siberian climate, and this great happiness of knowing that you and yours are saved they cannot rend from me; that will be for me a talisman against all misfortunes!"

"But I," sadly responded Anna—"shall I not always be tortured by the reflection that it is I who have been the cause of your misfortunes? Are you not condemned because you loved and were true to me? Ah, does love, then, deserve so hard a punishment?"

"The punishment passes, but love remains," calmly responded Julia. "That will always be my consolation."

"And mine also," sighed Anna.

"You will not need it," said Julia, with a smile. "You, at least, will be happy."

Anna sighed again, and her cheek paled. A dark and terrible image arose in her soul, and she shudderingly whispered:

"Ah, would that we were once beyond the Russian boundary, for then, first, shall we be free."

"Then let us hasten our journey," said Prince Ulrich; "once in the sledge, and every minute brings us nearer to freedom and happiness. Only hear how the horns are calling us, Anna—they call us to Germany! Come, take your son, wrap him close in your furred mantle, and let us hasten away—away from here!"

The prince laid little Ivan in the arms of his wife, and drew her away with him.

"Farewell, farewell, my Julia!" cried Anna, as she took her seat in the sledge.

"Farewell!" was echoed as a low spirit-breath from the palace.

Shuddering, Anna pressed her child to her bosom, and cast an anxiously interrogating glance at her husband, who was sitting by her.

"Be calm, tranquillize yourself—it will all be well," said the latter, with a smile.

The postilion blew his horn—the horses started; gayly resounded the tones of the silver bells; with a light whizzing, away flew the sledge over the snow. It bore thence a dethroned emperor and his overthrown family!

Rapidly did this richly-laden sledge pass through the streets, but, following it, was a troop of armed, grim-looking soldiers, like unwholesome ravens following their certain booty.

At about the same hour, another armed troop passed through the streets of St. Petersburg. With drawn swords they surrounded two closely-covered sledges, the mysterious occupants of which no one was allowed to descry! The train made a halt at the same gate through which the overthrown imperial family had just passed. The soldiers surrounded the sledges in close ranks; no one was allowed a glimpse at those who alighted from them.

But these extra precautions of the soldiery were unnecessary, as nobody wished to see the unfortunate objects. Every one timidly glanced aside, that they might not, by looking at the poor creatures, bring themselves into suspicion of favoring men suffering under the displeasure of the government. But though they looked not at them, every one knew who they were; though they dared not speak to each other, every one tremblingly said to himself: "There go Münnich and Ostermann to their trials!"

Münnich and Ostermann, the faithful servants of Peter the Great—Münnich, whom Prince Eugene called "his beloved pupil;" Ostermann, of whom the dying Czar Peter said he had never caught him in a fault; that he was the only honest statesman in Russia—Münnich and Ostermann, those two great statesmen to whom Russia was chiefly indebted for what civilization and cultivation she had acquired, were now accused of high-treason, and sent for trial before a commission commanded to find them guilty and to punish them. They were to be put out of the way because they were feared, and to be feared was held as a crime deserving death!

Firm and courageous stood they before their judges. In this hour old Ostermann had shaken off his illness and thrown away the shield of his physical sufferings! He would not intrench himself behind his age and his sickness; he would be a man, and boldly offer his unprotected breast to the murderous weapons of his enemies!

For, that he was lost he knew! A single glance at his judges made him certain of it, and from this moment his features wore a calm and contemptuous smile, an unchangeable expression of scorn. With an ironic curiosity he followed his judges through the labyrinth of artfully contrived captious questions by which they hoped to entangle him; occasionally he gave himself, as it were for his own amusement, the appearance of voluntarily being caught in their nets, until he finally by a side spring tore their whole web to pieces and laughingly derided his judges for not being able to convict him!

He was accused of having, by his cabals alone, after the death of Catharine, effected the elevation to the throne of Anna, Duchess of Courland. And yet they very well knew that precisely at that time Ostermann had for weeks pretended to be suffering from illness, for the very purpose of avoiding any intermingling with state affairs. They accused him of having suppressed the testament of Catharine, and yet that testament had been published in all the official journals of the time!

Ostermann laughed loud at all of these childish accusations.

"Ah," said he, "should I be sitting in your places, and you all, though innocent, should be standing accused before me, my word for it, I would so involve you in questions and answers that you would be compelled to confess your guilt! But you do not understand questioning, and old Ostermann is a sly fox that does not allow himself to be easily caught! The best way will be for you to declare me guilty, though I am no criminal; for as your empress has commanded that I should be found guilty, it would certainly be in me a crime worthy of death not to be guilty."

"You dare to deride our empress!" cried one of the judges.

"Aha!" said Ostermann, laughing, "I have there thrown you a bait, and you, good judicial fishes, bite directly! That is very well, you are now in a good way! Only go on, and I will help you to find me guilty, if it be only of simple high-treason. It will then be left to the mercy of your empress to declare me convicted of threefold high-treason! Go on, go on!"

But Münnich showed himself less unruffled and sarcastic in the face of his judges. These never-ending questions, this ceaseless teasing about trifles, exhausted his patience at last. He wearied of continually turning aside these laughably trivial accusations, of convincing his judges of his innocence, and making them ashamed of the nature of the proofs adduced.

"Let it suffice," said he, at length to his judges; "after hours of vain labor, you see that in this way you will never attain your end. I will propose to you a better and safer course. Write down your questions, and append to each the answer you desire me to give; I will then sign the whole protocol and declare it correct." *

"Are you in earnest?" joyfully asked the judges.

"Quite in earnest!" proudly answered Münnich.

They were shameless enough to accept his offer; they troubled him with no more questions, but wrote in the protocol such answers as would best suit the purpose of his judges.

In these answers Münnich declared himself guilty of all the crimes laid to his charge, acknowledged himself to be a traitor, and deserving death.

When they had finished their artistic labor, they handed to Münnich the pen for his signature.

He calmly took the pen, and, while affixing his signature, said with a contemptuous smile: "Was I not right? In this way it is rendered much easier for you to make of me a very respectable criminal, and I have only the trouble of writing my name! I thank you, gentlemen, for this indulgence."

Quick and decisive as were the hearings, now followed the sentences. Ostermann was condemned to be broken on the wheel, Münnich to be quartered, and the two ministers, Löwenwald and Golopkin, to the axe!

But Elizabeth had promised her people that no one should be punished with death; she must abide by that promise, and she did. She commuted the punishment of the condemned, as also of Julia von Mengden, into banishment to Siberia for life. What a grace! and even this grace was first communicated to Ostermann after his old limbs had been bound to the wheel and his executioners were on the point of crushing him!

But even in this extreme moment Count Ostermann's calm heroism did not forsake him.

"I was convinced that such would be the result!" he calmly said, quietly stretching his released limbs; "this Empress Elizabeth has not the courage to break her oath by chopping off a few heads! It is a pity. On the wheel it might have become a little warm for me, but in Siberia it will be fearfully cold."

From the windows of her palace Elizabeth had witnessed the preparations for this pretended execution; and as she knew that at last their punishment would be commuted, she was amused to see the solemn earnestness and the death-shudder of the condemned. It was a very entertaining hour that she and her friends passed at that window, and the comical face of old Ostermann, the proud gravity of Count Münnich, the folded hands and heaven-directed glances of Golopkin and Löwenwald, had often made her laugh until the tears ran down her cheeks.

"That was a magnificent comedy!" said she, retreating from the window when the condemned were released from their bands and raised into the vehicles that were immediately to start with them for Siberia. "Yes, it was, indeed, very amusing! But tell me, Lestocq, where are they about to take old Count Ostermann?"

"To the most northerly part of Siberia!" calmly replied Lestocq.

"Poor old man!" sighed Elizabeth; "it must be very sad for him thus to pass his last years in suffering and deprivation."

Lestocq seemed not to have heard her remark, and laughingly continued: "To Münnich I have thought to apply a jest of his own."

"Ah, a jest!" cried Elizabeth, suddenly brightening up. "Let us hear it. you know I love a jest, it is so amusing! Quick, therefore, let us hear it!"

"Perhaps your majesty may remember Biron, Duke of Courland," said Lestocq. "Count Münnich, as you know, overthrew him, and placed Anna Leopoldowna in the regency. Biron has ever since lived at Pelym in Siberia, and, indeed, in a house of which Münnich himself drew the plan, the rooms of which are so low that poor Biron, who is as tall as Münnich, could never stand erect in them. The good Münnich, he was very much devoted to the duke, and hence in pure friendship invented this means of reminding him, every hour in the day, of the architect of his house, his friend Münnich!"

"Ah, you promised us a jest, and you are there repeating an old and well-known story!" interposed the empress, yawning.

"Now comes the joke!" continued Lestocq. "We have transferred Biron to another colony, and Herr Münnich will occupy the poetical pleasure-house of his friend Biron at Pelym." *

"Ah, that is delightful, in fact!" cried Elizabeth, clapping her little hands. "How will Münnich curse himself for cruelty which now comes home to himself! That is very witty in you, Herr Lestocq; very laughable, is it not, Alexis? But, Alexis, you do not laugh at

* Levecque, vol. v., p. 235; Mannstein, Mémoires, vol. iii., p. 96.

all; you look sad. What is the matter with you? Who has disobliged, who has wounded you?"

Alexis sighed. "You yourself!" he said, in a low tone.

"I?" exclaimed the astonished empress. "I could not be so inhuman!"

"No, only to wound me by refusing the first request I addressed to you!"

"Name your request once more, I have forgotten it!" said Elizabeth, with vehemence.

Alexis Razumovsky fell upon his knees before her, and, imploringly raising his hands, said:

"Elizabeth, my empress, have compassion for my care and anxiety on your account; leave me not to tremble for your safety! Grant me the happiness of seeing you unthreatened and free from danger in your greatness and splendor! Oh, Elizabeth, listen to the prayer of your faithful servant—let not this Anna Leopoldowna pass the boundary of your realm—let not your most deadly enemy escape!"

"Oh, grant his prayer," cried Lestocq, kneeling beside Alexis; "there is wisdom in his words; listen to him rather than to the too great generosity of your own heart! Let not your enemies escape, but seize them while they are yet in your power!"

"Elizabeth, greatest and fairest woman on earth," implored Alexis, "have compassion for my anxiety; I shall never laugh again, never be cheerful, if you allow these your most dangerous enemies to withdraw themselves from your power!"

Elizabeth bent down to him with a smile of tenderness, and laid her left hand upon his locks, while with her right she gently raised his head to herself.

"Love you me, then, so very much, my Alexis," she asked, "that you suffer with anxiety for my safety? Ah, that makes me happy—that fills my whole heart with joy! Only look at him, Lestocq; see how beautiful he is, and then say whether one can refuse the prayer of those heavenly eyes, those pleading lips?"

"You will, then, grant my prayer?" exultingly asked Alexis.

"Well, yes," tenderly responded she, "since there is no other means of rendering you again cheerful and happy, I must, indeed, consent to the fulfilment of your wishes, and not let my enemies quit the country if it be yet possible to retain them."

"They have proceeded by slow marches, and can hardly now have arrived in Riga, where they are to rest several days," said Lestocq. "There will consequently be time for a courier yet to reach them with your counterorder."

"And he must be dispatched immediately!" said Alexis, pressing the hand of the empress to his lips. "In this hour will my kind and gracious empress sign the command for the arrest of Anna Leopoldowna, her husband, and her son!"

"Already another signature!" sighed Elizabeth. "How you annoy me with this eternal signing and countersigning! Will it, then, never have an end? I already begin to hate my name, because of being compelled so often to write it under your musty old documents. Why

did the emperor, my deceased father, give me so long a name?—a shorter one would now relieve me of half my labor!"

But in spite of her lamentings, Elizabeth nevertheless, a quarter of an hour later, subscribed the order to arrest the regent, her husband, and son, and shut them up, preliminarily, in the citadel of Riga.

"So now I hope you will again be happy and cheerful," said she, throwing away the pen, and with a tender glance at Razumovsky. "Come, look at me—I have done all you wished; let us now be gay and take our pleasure."

And while Elizabeth was jesting and laughing with Alexis, Lestocq, taking the newly-signed order, hurried away to dispatch his courier.

At length they had reached the borders of this feared, pernicious Russian empire. They now needed no longer to tremble, no longer to glance anxiously around them, or listen with fear at the slightest sound. Only a short quarter of an hour and the boundary will be passed and liberty secured!

They had made a halt at a small public house near the boundary. The horses were to be changed there, and there the soldiers of the escort were to get their last taste of Russian brandy before crossing the border.

Anna and her husband have remained in the sledge. She holds her son in her arms, she presses him to her bosom, full of exulting maternal joy: for he is now saved, this poor little emperor; Anna has now no longer to fear that her son will be torn from her—he is saved—he belongs to her; she can rejoice in his childish beauty, in the happy consciousness of safety.

She has thrown back the curtains of the sledge. She felt no cold. With joy-beaming eyes she looked forward to that blessed land beyond the boundary! There, where upon its tall staff the Russian flag floated high in the air, there freedom and happiness were to begin for her—there will she find again her youth and her maiden dreams, her cheerfulness and her pleasure—there is freedom—golden, heavenly freedom!

She is so happy at this moment that she loves all and every one. For the first time she feels a sort of tenderness for her husband, who, patiently bearing all in silence, had complained and wept only for her. Gently she reclined her head upon his shoulder, and with a cry of ecstasy the prince encircled her neck with his arms.

"Oh, my husband," she whispered, with overflowing eyes, "look there, over there! There is our future, there will we seek for happiness. Perhaps we may unitedly find it in the same path, for we have here a sweet bond to hold our hands together. Look at him, your son. Ulrich, you are the father of my child! Grant my heart only a little repose, and perhaps we may yet be happy with each other."

Prince Ulrich's eyes were suffused with tears; he experienced a moment of the purest happiness. He impressed a kiss upon the brow of his wife, and in a low tone called her by the tenderest names.

The child awoke and smilingly looked up from Anna's bosom to both of his parents. Anna lifted up the little Ivan.

"Look there, my son," said she— "there you will no longer be an emperor, but you will have the right to be a free and happy man. No crown awaits you there, but freedom, worth more than all the crowns of the world."

Little Ivan exultingly stretched forth his tiny arms, as if he would draw down to his childish heart this future and this freedom so highly lauded by his mother.

And, like the child, the parents looked smilingly out upon the broad expanse that stretched away before them.

Look only forward, constantly forward, where the skies are clear, and dream of happiness! Look forward— no, turn not backward your glance, for the horizon darkens in your rear; misfortune is closely following upon your track! You see it not, you look only forward, and still you smile.

It draws nearer and nearer, this black cloud of evil. It is the ravens, the booty-scenting ravens who are following you!

Look forward, dream yourselves happy, and smile yet. What would it help you to look back? You cannot escape the calamity!

Nearer and nearer, with a wild cry, rush on these ravens of misfortune; the air already bears detached sounds to Anna's ears.

She trembles. It is as if her boding soul scented the approaching evil. Pressing her child closer to her bosom, she gives her husband her hand.

The horses are attached to the sledge, and the soldiers leave the public house. All is ready for the train to go on over the boundary. The postilions draw the rein! Now a wild cry of "Halt! halt!"

The soldiers bear up, the postilions halt!

"Forward! forward!" shrieks Prince Ulrich, in mortal anguish.

"Halt! in the name of the empress!" cried an officer, who came rushing past upon a foaming steed, and he handed to the commander of the escort an open writing, furnished with the imperial seal.

The commander turned to the postilions.

"To the right about, toward Riga!" ordered he, and then, turning to the trembling princely pair, he said: "In the name of the empress, you are my prisoners! I am directed to conduct you to the citadel of Riga!"

With a loud groan, Anna sinks into the arms of her husband. He consoles her with the most soothing and affectionate words; he has thought, sorrow, only for her—he feels not for himself, but only for her.

For a moment Anna was overpowered by this unexpected horror; then she calmly rose erect, and pressed her son more closely to her bosom.

"We are all lost," whispered she, "prisoners forever! Poor child—poor, unhappy husband!"

"Despair not," said Prince Ulrich, "all may yet turn out well! Who knows how soon aid may reach us!"

Anna lightly shook her head, and, thinking of the last words of her friend, she murmured low: "Punishment passes, but love remains!"

CHAPTER XVIII.

THE PALACE OF THE EMPRESS.

THE new empress, Elizabeth, had rewarded and punished, and with that she thought she had finished her imperial labors and forever dismissed all her difficulties.

"I have shaken off my imperial burdens," said she to her friends; "let us now begin to enjoy the imperial pleasures. Ah! we shall lead a pleasant life in this splendid palace. My first law is this: No one shall speak to me of government business or state affairs. I will

have nothing to do with such things, do you hear? For what purpose do I have my ministers and my council? Go you with such wearisome questions to my grand chancellor, Tscherkaskoy, and my minister, Bestuscheff; they shall govern for me. I can demand that of them, as I pay them for it. If you seek an office, if you have invented any thing for promoting the welfare of the country, if you have found any official abuse, or discovered any conspiracy, then go to

Bestuscheff or to Woronzow, or also to Lestocq—spare me! But when you have a grace to demand, when you need money, when you desire a title or orders, then come to me, and I will satisfy your wishes. We have much money, many ribbons for orders, and as for titles, they are the cheapest and most convenient of all, as they cost absolutely nothing. Ah, a jest just now occurs to me. We will amuse ourselves a little to-day. We will have a title-auction. Call our courtiers, attendants, and servants. We shall have a gay time of it! We will have a game at dice. Bring the dice! I will at each throw announce the prize, and the dice shall then decide who is the winner!"

They all gathered around her; the noble gentlemen of her body-guard, consisting of the grenadiers who had been raised to nobility and created officers at the commencement of her reign. They came noisily, with singing and laughing, and saluting their empress, Elizabeth, with a thundering *viva*. .

"First of all, let us drink your health, sir captain!" said she, ordering wine to be brought, as well as brandy of the costly sort she had lately received as a present from the greatest distiller of her capital, to which she herself was very partial.

Loudly clinked their glasses, loudly was shouted a *viva* to the empress, which Elizabeth laughingly accepted by offering them her hands to kiss, and was delighted when they fell into ecstasies over the beauty and freshness of those hands.

"Now, silence, gentlemen of the body-guard!" she cried. "I, your captain, command attention!"

And, when silence was established, she continued: "We will have a game at dice, and titles and orders, gold and brandy, shall be the prizes for which you shall contend!"

"Ah, that is magnificent, that is a glorious game!" exclaimed they all.

"The first prize," said Elizabeth, "is the position of privy councillor! Now take the dice, gentlemen!"

They began to throw the dice, with laughter and shouting when they had thrown a high number—with lamentations and stamping of the feet when it was a low one.

In the meanwhile Elizabeth listlessly stretched herself upon a divan, and laughingly said to Alexis, who sat by her side: "Oh, it is very pleasant to be an empress. Only see how happy they all are, and it is I alone who make them so; for out of these common soldiers I have created respectable officers, and have converted serfs into barons and gentlemen! I thank you, Alexis, for impelling me to become an empress. It is a noble pleasure, and I should now be unwilling to return to that still and uneventful life that formerly pleased me so well! I will so manage that the Empress Elizabeth shall be as little troubled with labor and business as the princess, and the empress can doubtlessly procure for herself more pleasures than could the princess! Yes, certainly, I will now remain what I am, an empress by the grace of God!"

A thundering shout and loud laughter here interrupted Elizabeth. The dice had decided! The cook of the empress had won, and become a councillor of state.

Elizabeth laughed. "These dice are very witty," said she, "for certainly the cook must be a privy councillor! I establish you in your dignity, Feodor, your title is recognized! Now for a new trial. Two thousand rubles is the prize, which I think of more value than a title!"

There was a zealous pressing and shoving, a' pushing and puffing; every one desired to be the first to get hold of the dice and struggle for the rich prize. There were many ungentle encounters, many a thrust in the ribs, many invectives, many a gross, unseemly word; the empress saw all, heard all, laughed at all, and said to Alexis: "These gentlemen are very practical! Two thousand rubles are estimated by them at a higher rate than the proudest title. I comprehend that a title is a nonsensical thing, of which no real use can be made, but what beautiful dresses can be bought with two thousand rubles! And that reminds me that you have not yet told me how you like this dress of mine! You take so little notice of my toilet, dearest, and yet it is only for you that I change my dress seven or eight times a day; I would, every hour, please you better and better."

"Oh, no dressing is necessary for that," tenderly responded Alexis; and stooping, he whispered some words in her ear which pleased her well, and made her laugh heartily.

Meanwhile the dicing continued. Blind luck scattered her gifts in the strangest manner; under-officers of the palace attained to high titles, and high officers with laughing faces won pipes of brandy; barons of the body-guard, made of men who but a few days before had been serfs, were seen approaching the mirrors with vain coxcombry to see the effect of orders just won by a cast of the dice, or with greedy avidity pocketing the rubles which fortune had thrown to them!

It was a jovial and brilliant evening, and, in dismissing her friends, Elizabeth promised them many repetitions of it.

And she kept her word. Frenzied merry-makings, pleasures and festivals of the roughest sorts were now the principal occupation of the new empress. The amusement of her court, the providing it with new festivals and pleasures, she considered as the first and most important of her imperial duties; and these alone she endeavored to fulfil.

But who composed her court, and of what elements did it consist?"

Elizabeth found the presence of her serious official councillors very tiresome, as they knew not how to make themselves agreeable; she found the surrounding of herself with the respectable ladies of her court to be very incommodious, as there might some day be found among them one with a handsomer or more tasteful toilet than herself, or, indeed, one who might dare to be of a finer type of beauty than she! She therefore gladly avoided inviting the distinguished men of her court with their wives, or the higher class of state officials. It was far more convenient, far more agreeable, to surround herself with frivolous and handsome young men. They knew how to laugh and be cheerful, and she was thus sure that no other lady would be there to dispute with her the palm of beauty.

Elizabeth was not proud. She cared not whether noble blood flowed in the veins of those who were invited to her festivals. The youth, beauty, and agreeable qualities which the empress found in any person, alone decided the question of their admittance to the court.

Peasants, grooms, soldiers, servants, abandoned reprobates, who, by their beauty had won the favor of the empress, were seen to attain to the highest stations.*

On them were lavished the treasures of the state; they were adorned with orders and titles, and the magnates bowed to the ground before these potent favorites of the all-powerful empress, and the people shouted with transport when their beloved czarina, with her magnificent train of newly-created noblemen, made her appearance in the streets, and with gracious smiles returned the humble salutations of her kneeling slaves. That was a ruler in perfect accordance with Russian ideas; they sympathized with her inclinations and pleasures—she was blood of their blood and flesh of their flesh! The strangers were at length banished, and a real Russian sat upon the throne of the czars!

And yet Elizabeth trembled upon her imperial throne, surrounded by the band of magnates and nobles, of whom she could truly say, "I am their creator—

they are my work!" She trembled before those secret daggers, those lingering poisons, which always surround the imperial Russian throne as its truest satellites, and lay low many a high-born head; she trembled before Anna Leopoldowna, who was sighing away her days in the closed citadel of Riga, and before Anna's son, the infant Ivan, whom the Empress Anna in her testament had named as Emperor of all the Russias! She, indeed, would not work and trouble herself for her country and her people, this good empress by the grace of God, but yet she would be empress, that she might be enabled to enjoy life, and no cloud must obscure the heaven of her earthly glory!

She therefore tore herself for some short hours from the pleasures in which she was usually immersed, from the arms of her lover, the object of her deepest interest; her own safety and her own peace were concerned. That was well worth the effort to take the pen once more in hand, and affix the troublesomely long name of Elizabeth to some few official documents.

She consequently signed the command to bring back Anna Leopoldowna and her husband from the citadel of Riga to the interior of Russia, and place them in strict confinement in Raninburg.

She also signed another order, and that was to rend the young Ivan from the arms of his mother, to take him to the castle of Schlüsselburg, and there to hold him in strict imprisonment, to grow up without teachers, or any kind of instruction, and without the least occupation or amusement.

"I well know," said she, with a sigh,

---

* Schlosser's "Geschichte des Achtzehnten Yahrhunderts." Zweiter Band, s. 56, folg.; 211, folg.

as she signed the document—"I well know that it would be better for this Ivan to be executed for high-treason than to remain in this condition, but I lack the courage for it. It is so horrible to kill a poor innocent child!"

"And in this way we attain our end more safely," said Lestocq, with a smile. "Your majesty has sworn to take the life of no one; very well, you keep your word as to physical life—we do not destroy the body but the spirit of this boy Ivan! We raise him as an idiot, which is the surest means of rendering him innoxious!"

Elizabeth had signed the order, and her command was executed. They took from Anna Leopoldowna her last joy, her only consolation—they took away her son, whose smiling face had lighted her prison as with sunbeams, whose childishly stammered words had sounded to her as the voice of an angel from heaven.

They took the poor weeping child to Schlüsselburg, and his crushed and heart-broken parents first to Raninburg, and finally to the fortress Kolmogory, situated upon an island in the Dwina, near to that gulf which, on account of its never-melting ice, has obtained the name of the *White Sea*.*

No one could rescue poor Anna Leopoldowna from that fortress—no one could release her son, the poor little Emperor Ivan, from Schlüsselburg! They were rendered perfectly inoffensive; Elizabeth had not killed them, she had only buried them alive, this good Russian empress!

And, nevertheless, she still trembled

upon her throne, she still felt unsafe in her imperial magnificence! She yet trembled on account of another pretender, the Duke Karl Peter Ulrich of Holstein, who, as the son of an elder daughter of Peter the Great, had a more direct claim to the throne than Elizabeth herself.

That no party might declare for him and invite him to Russia, her ministers advised the empress herself to send for him, and declare him her successor. Elizabeth followed this advice, and the young Duke Peter Ulrich of Holstein accepted her call. Declining the crown of Sweden, he professed the Greek religion in St. Petersburg, was clothed with the title of grand prince by Elizabeth, and declared her successor to the throne of the czars.

Elizabeth could now undisturbedly enjoy her imperial splendor. The successor to the throne was assured, Anna Leopoldowna languished in the fortress of Kolmogory, and in Schlüsselburg the little Emperor Ivan was passing his childish dream-life! Who was there now to contest her rights—who would dare an attempt to shake a throne which rested upon such safe pillars of public favor, and which so many new-made counts and barons protected with their broad shoulders and nervous arms?

Elizabeth had no more need to govern, no more occasion to tremble. She let sink the hand which, with a single stroke of the pen, could give laws to millions of men, which could give them interminable sorrow and endless torments; she again took the heavy imperial crown from her head, replacing it with wreaths of myrtles and ever-fra-

---

* Levecque, vol. v., p. 233.

grant roses. She permitted Tscherkaskoy to govern, and Bestuscheff to sell to
England the dearest interests of Russia.
She permitted her ministers to govern
with unrestricted power, and was rejoiced when no one came to trouble her
about affairs of state or the interests
of her people.

CHAPTER XIX.

ELEONORE LAPUSCHKIN.

Two years had elapsed since Elizabeth's accession to the throne ; for her,
two years of pleasure and enjoyment,
only troubled here and there with occasional small clouds of ill-humor—but
those clouds overshadowed only her
domestic peace. It was not the affairs
of state, not the interests of her people,
that troubled and saddened Elizabeth ;
she asked not how many of her subjects
the war with Sweden had swept away ;
how many had fallen a sacrifice to hunger in the southern provinces of her
realm. She had quite other cares and
anxieties than those which concerned
only her ministers, not herself. What
have princes to do with the happiness
of their people ?

Elizabeth was a consummate princess ; she thought only of her own happiness, only of herself and her own sorrows. And it was a very severe, very
incurable sorrow that visited her—a sorrow that often brought tears of anger
into her eyes and curses upon her lips.
Elizabeth was jealous—jealous not of
this or that woman, but of the whole
sex. She glowingly desired to be the
fairest of all women, and constantly
trembled lest some one should come to
rob her of the prize of beauty. And
were there not, in her own court, women who might venture to enter the
lists with her ? Was there not, before
all, one woman whose aspect filled the
heart of the empress with a thirst for
vengeance, of whom she was compelled
to say that she was younger, handsomer,
and more attractive than herself—and
this one, was it not Eleonore Lapuschkin ?

For two long years had Elizabeth
borne about with her this hatred and
jealousy ; for two long years had she in
vain sought to discover some punishable
fault in her rival ; for two long years
had she in vain reminded Lestocq of his
promise to find Eleonore Lapuschkin
guilty of some crime. She had come
out pure from all these persecuting pursuits, and even the eyes of the most zealous spy could find no blot upon her es-
cutcheon. Like a royal lily she proudly
bloomed with undisputed splendor in
the midst of this court, whose petty cabals and intrigues could not soil her
fair fame. Her presence spread around
her a sort of magic. The most auda-

cious courtier, the most presumptuous cavalier, approached her with only reverence; they ventured not in her presence to use such words and jests as but too well pleased the empress; there was something in Eleonore's glance that commanded involuntary respect and awe; an elevation, a mildness, a soft feminine majesty was shed over her whole being that enchanted even those who were inimical to her. Elizabeth had perceived that, with her eyes sharpened by jealousy; her envy was yet more mighty than her vanity, and her envy told her Eleonore Lapuschkin is handsomer than the Empress Elizabeth; wherever Eleonore appears, there all hearts fly to meet her, all glances incline to her; every one feels a sort of ecstasy of adoration whom she greets with a word or a smile, for that word or that smile sanctifies him as it were, and enrolls him among the noblest and best.

And even Alexis had been unable to withstand this magic! Oh, Elizabeth narrowly watched him; she had analyzed his every word and every glance; she had seen how he always pressed near her, how he blushed with joy when she remarked his presence and returned his salutation! Yea, she, and perhaps only she, had seen Alexis covertly possess himself of the glove which Eleonore had lost the previous evening at the grand court ball, had seen him press that glove to his lips and afterward conceal it in his bosom.

As Elizabeth thought of these things her eyes filled with tears, and her whole form shook with rage. She felt unable to be angry with or to punish him, but she was resolved that Eleonore Lapuschkin should feel the whole weight of her vengeance.

"Oh," said she, while pacing her boudoir in a state of violent excitement, "I shall know how to punish this presumptuous woman! She ventures to defy me, but I will humble her! Ha, does she not give herself the appearance of not remarking that I constantly have for her a clouded brow and an unfriendly greeting? How! will she not take the pains to see that her empress looks upon her with disfavor? But she shall see and feel that I hate, that I abhor her. Oh, what a powerless creature is yet an empress! I hate this woman, and she has the impudence to think I cannot punish her unless she is guilty."

And weeping aloud, Elizabeth threw herself upon the divan. A low knock at the door recalled her attention from her angry grief. Rising, she bade the person at the door to enter.

It was Lestocq, the privy conncillor and president—Lestocq, the confidant of the empress, who came with a joyful face and cheerful smile.

Elizabeth felt annoyed by this cheerfulness of her physician. With an angry frown she turned her back upon him.

"Why were you not at the conrt ball last evening?" she then ronghly said.

"I was there," answered Lestocq.

"Ah, that is not true," cried the empress with vehemence, glad at least to have some one on whom she could discharge her anger. "It is false, I say no one saw you there! Ah, you dare, then to impose a falsehood upon your empress? You would—"

"I was at the court ball," interposed Lestocq; "I saw and noted all that occurred there. I saw that my empress beamed in all the splendor of beauty, and yet with her amiable modesty she thought Eleonore Lapuschkin handsomer than herself. I read in Elizabeth's noble brow that she was pained by this, and that she promised to punish the presumption of the insolent countess."

"And to what end have you read all that," responded Elizabeth, with vehemence. "to what end, since you are so sluggish a servant that you make no effort to fulfil any wish of your mistress? To what end, since you are so disregardful of your word as not to hold even your oath sacred?"

"I was at the ball precisely because I remembered my oath," said Lestocq, "because I was intent upon redeeming my word and delivering over to you this Countess Lapuschkin as a criminal! But you could not recognize me, as I was in the disguise of a lackey of the Countess Eleonore Lapuschkin."

Elizabeth springing up from her seat, stared with breathless curiosity into Lestocq's face.

"Well?" she anxiously asked, as Lestocq remained silent. "Speak on; then what further?"

"Illustrious empress," said Lestocq, "I am now here to redeem my word. This Countess Eleonore Lapuschkin is a criminal!"

"Ah, thank God!" cried Elizabeth, breathing more freely.

"By various intrigues and stratagems, by bribery of her servants, I have finally succeeded in spying out her secrets; and last evening, when as her lackey I conducted her from the ball and afterward waited at table at an entertainment given by her husband to some confidential friends, last evening her whole plan was made clear to me. It is a great and very important conspiracy that I have detected! This Countess Eleonore Lapuschkin is guilty of high-treason; she conspires against her legitimate empress!"

"Ah, she conspires!" exclaimed Elizabeth, with a fierce laugh. "For whom, then, does she conspire?"

"For one whose name I dare not utter without the express permission of my empress!"

"Speak, speak quickly!"

Lestocq bent down close to the ear of the empress. "She conspires for the Schüsselburg prisoner Ivan!" said he.

"I shall therefore be able to punish her," said Elizabeth, smilingly. "I shall no longer be obliged to suffer this hated woman within the walls of my capital!"

"Siberia has room for her and her fellow-conspirators!" replied Lestocq. "For this fair countess is not alone guilty, although she is the soul of the conjuration, as it is love that animates her. Eleonore Lapuschkin conspires for her lover!"

"Oh, this adored saint has, then, a lover!" exclaimed the empress. "And I believed her spotless as a lily, so pure that I felt abashed in her presence!"

"You have banished her lover to Siberia, the lover of Eleonore, Count Löwenwald. You may believe that that has caused her a mortal grief."

"Ah," joyfully exclaimed Elizabeth, "I have, therefore, unknowingly caused her tears to flow! But I will yet do it with a perfect consciousness! Relate to me in detail exactly what you know of this conspiracy!"

And Lestocq related that Eleonore Lapuschkin, in connection with her husband, the chamberlain Lilienfeld, and Madame Bestuscheff, who was the sister of the condemned Golopkin, had entered into a conspiracy for the overthrow of Elizabeth and the placing of Ivan upon the throne, and thus releasing the prisoners banished to Siberia.

"Oh, they were very gay at the yesterday's dinner of the conspirators," said Lestocq. "The husband of Countess Lapuschkin even ventured to drink the health of the Emperor Ivan, and to his speedy liberation!"*

"But that is high-treason!" exclaimed Elizabeth. "Ah, I had cause to tremble and eternally to stand in fear of my murderers! I already see them lurking around me, encircling me on all sides, to destroy me! Lestocq, save me from my murderers!"

And with a cry of anguish the empress clung convulsively to the arm of her physician.

"The incautiousness of these conspirators has already saved you, empress," said Lestocq. "They have delivered themselves into our hand, they have made us masters of the situation. What would you more? You will punish the traitors; that is all!"

"And I cannot kill them!" shrieked Elizabeth, with closed fists. "I have tied my own hands in my unwise generosity! Ah, they call me an empress, and yet I cannot destroy those I hate!"

"And who denies you that right?" asked Lestocq. "Destroy their bodies, but kill them not! Wherefore have we the knout, if it cannot flay the back of a beauty?"

"Yes, wherefore have we the knout?" exclaimed Elizabeth, with a joyous laugh. "Ah, Lestocq, you are an exquisite man, you always give good advice. Ah, this beautiful Countess Eleonore shall be made acquainted with the knout!"

"You have a double right for it!" said Lestocq, "for she has dared to speak of your majesty in unseemly language!"

"Has she done that?" cried Elizabeth. "Ah, I almost love her for it, as that gives me the right to chastise her. Lestocq, what punishment is prescribed for a subject who dares revile his empress? You must know it, you are familiar with the laws! Therefore tell me quickly, what punishment?"

"It is written," said Lestocq, after a moment's reflection, "that any one who dares so misuse his tongue as to revile the sublime majesty of his emperor or empress with irreverent language, such criminal shall have the instrument of his crime, his tongue, torn out by the roots!"

"And this time I will exercise no mercy!" triumphantly exclaimed Elizabeth.

She kept her word—she exercised no mercy! Count Lapuschkin, with his fair wife, the wife of Bestuscheff, the Chamberlain Lilienfeld, and some

---

* Levecque, vol. v., p. 241.

others, were accused of high-treason and brought before the tribunal.

It was not difficult to convict the countess of the crime charged; incautiously enough had she often expressed her attachment to the cause of the imprisoned Emperor Ivan, and her contempt for the Empress Elizabeth. And in what country is it not a crime to speak disrespectfully of the prince, though he be a criminal and one of the lowest of men?

She was therefore declared guilty; she was sentenced to be scourged with the knout, to have her tongue torn out, and to be transported to Siberia!

Elizabeth did not pardon her. She was a princess—how, then, could she pardon one who had dared to revile her? Every crime is easier to pardon than that of high-treason; for every other there may be extenuating circumstances—for that, never; it is a capital crime which a prince never pardons; how, then, could Elizabeth have done so?—Elizabeth, empress by the grace of God, as all are princes and kings by the grace of God!

The people were running to and fro in the wildest confusion in the streets of St. Petersburg; they cried and shouted *vivas* to their empress who to-day accorded to them the splendid spectacle of the knouting of some respectable ladies and gentlemen! Ah, that was a very gracious and condescending empress to provide once more a delightful spectacle for her serfs at the expense of the nobility! That was an empress after their own hearts—real Russian blood!

Shrieking and shouting they rushed to the place of execution, pressing against the barriers that separated the central point from the spectators. There stood the bearded assistants of the executioner, there lay the knouts and other instruments, and with eager glances the people devoured all: they found all these preparations admirable, they rejoiced with unrestrained delight in the prospect of seeing the handsomest woman in the realm flayed with the knout. And not the common people alone, the *noblesse* must also be present; the great magnates of the court must also come, if they would avoid exciting a suspicion that they commiserated the condemned and revolted at their punishment. They all came, these slavish magnates, perhaps with tears in their hearts, but with smiles upon their lips; perhaps murmuring secret curses, but aloud applauding the just sentence of the empress.

Now the closed carriages of the condemned were seen approaching in a long, lingering train; the train halted, the doors were opened, and in the centre of the place of execution appeared Eleonore Lapuschkin, radiant with the brilliancy of the purest beauty, her noble form enveloped in a full, draping robe, which lent to her loveliness an additional charm. She looked around with an astonished and interrogating glance, as if awaking from a confused dream. Young, amiable, the first and most celebrated lady of the court, of which she was the most brilliant ornament, she now sees herself, instead of the admirers who humbly paid their court to her, surrounded by these rough executioners, who regard her with bold and insolent glances, eagerly stretching forth their hands for their prey. One of them, approaching her, ventures to rend from her bosom the kerchief that covers it. Eleonore, shuddering, shrinks back, her cheeks are pale as marble, a stream of tears gushes from her eyes. In vain she implores, in vain her lamentations, in vain her trembling innocence, in vain her efforts to cover herself anew. Her clothes are torn off, and in a few moments she stands there naked to the girdle, with all the upper portion of her person exposed to the eager glances of the masses, who in silence stare at this specimen of the purest feminine beauty.

The proud lily is broken, shattered; she bows her head, the storm has crushed her. Incapable of resistance, she is seized by one of the executioners, who, by a sudden movement, throws her upon her back. Another then approaches and places her in the most convenient position for receiving the punishment. Soon, with rough brutality, he lays his broad hand upon her head, and places it so that it may not be hit by the knout, and then, like a butcher who is about to throttle a lamb, he caresses that snow-white back, as if taking pleasure in the contemplation of the wonderful fairness of his victim.

Now is she in the right position; he steps back, and raising the knout, brings it down upon Eleonore's back with such accuracy that it takes off a strip of skin from her neck to her girdle. Then he swings the knout anew, with the same accuracy and the same result. In a few moments her skin hangs in shreds over her girdle, her whole form is dripping with blood, and the shuddering spectators venture not a single bravo for this dexterous executioner.*

The work is finished! With a flayed back Eleonore is raised upon the shoulders of the executioner. She has not screamed, she has not moaned, she has remained dumb and without complaint, but she has prayed to God for vengeance and expiation for the shame inflicted upon her.

And again advances the executioner, with a pair of pincers in his hand. Eleonore looks at him through eyes flaming with anger.

"What would you?" she coldly asks.

"Tear out your tongue!" answers he, with a rude laugh. Two of the executioner's assistants then seizing her, grasp her head.

This time Eleonore defends herself—despair lends her strength. Freeing herself from the grasp of these barbarous executioners, she falls upon her knees, and, raising her bloody arms toward heaven, implores the mercy of God; glancing at the spectators, she implores their pity and their aid; turning her eyes toward the proud imperial palace, where Elizabeth sits enthroned, she begs there for grace and mercy.†

But as all remained silent, and as neither God nor man, nor yet the empress, had mercy upon her, a wild rage took possession of Eleonore's soul.

Raising her eyes toward heaven with flaming glances, she exclaimed:

"Woe to this merciless Elizabeth

* L'Abbé Chappe d'Auteroche, "Voyage en Sibérie," vol. ii., p. 370.
† Levecque, vol. v., p. 242.

Woe to this woman who has no compassion for another woman! What she now does to me, do Thou also to her, my God and Lord! Grant that she be flayed as she has now flayed me! Grant her a daughter, and let that daughter before her mother's eyes suffer what I now suffer, O my God! Woe to Elizabeth, and woe to you, ye cowardly slaves, who can look on and see a woman flayed and tortured! Shame and perdition to Russia and its Empress Elizabeth!"

These were Eleonore's last words.

With a wild rage her executioners seized her for the purpose of tearing out her tongue. And when that was accomplished, and her husband and son had suffered a similar martyrdom, all three were placed upon a *kibitka*, to be conveyed to Siberia.

Eleonore could no longer speak with her tongue, but her eyes spoke, and those eyes continued to repeat the prayer for vengeance she had addressed to Heaven: "Grant to this Empress Elizabeth a daughter, and let that daughter's sufferings be like mine!"

CHAPTER XX.

A WEDDING.

THE people dispersed. The great returned to their palaces, and also Alexis Razumovsky, who, that he might not excite the anger of the empress, had likewise attended the execution, returned to the imperial palace.

Elizabeth was standing before a large Venetian mirror, scrutinizing a toilet which she had to-day changed for the fourth time.

"Well," she asked of Alexis, as he entered, "was it an interesting spectacle? Was the handsome countess soundly whipped?"

And, while so asking, she was smilingly occupied in attaching a purple flower to her hair.

"She was flayed," laconically replied

Alexis. "Her blood streamed down a back that was as red as your beautiful lips, Elizabeth."

Elizabeth offered him her lips to kiss.

"Now," she jestingly asked, "who is now the handsomest woman in my realm?"

"You are and always were!" responded Alexis, embracing her.

"And now tell me," said she, with curiosity, "what did this proud countess do? How did she behave, what did she say?"

Alexis, seating himself upon a tabouret at her feet, related to her all about the fair Eleonore, and what a terrible curse she uttered.

"Ah, nonsense!" replied Elizabeth,

shrugging her shoulders, "How can one make such a stupid prayer to God! I shall never marry, and therefore never have a daughter to be scourged with the knout."

But while thus speaking, her eyes suddenly became fixed and her cheek pale. She laid her trembling hand upon her heart—tears gushed from her eyes.

Under her heart she had felt the movement of a new and mysterious life! Heaven itself seemed to contradict her words! Elizabeth felt that she was a mother, and Eleonore's words now filled her with awe and terror!

Fainting, she sank into Razumovsky's arms.

A few weeks later, a great and magnificent court festival was celebrated at the imperial palace in St. Petersburg. It was not enough that Elizabeth had chosen a successor in the person of Peter, Duke of Holstein, she must also give this successor a wife, that the throne might be fortified and assured by a numerous progeny.

She chose for him the Princess of Anhalt-Zerbst, the young and beautiful Sophia Augusta, who, embracing the Greek religion, received the name of Catharine.

It was the marriage festival of this young German princess with the heir to the Russian throne which was celebrated in the imperial palace at St. Petersburg—a festival of splendor and enthusiasm, as it was attended by two women of the most exciting beauty, Elizabeth the present and Catharine the future empress—the one gorgeous with the splendor of the present, the other irradiated with the glory of the future. People looked at the fair youthful face of Catharine, and sought to read in her majestic high forehead the hopes that Russia might cherish of her! It was, therefore, a festival of the present and future that was there and then celebrated, and the magnates humbly prostrated themselves before this new star, and threw themselves upon the earth before the ever-new sun of imperial majesty which shone upon them in the person of Elizabeth.

Catharine with a joyful spirit and a proud smile laid her hand in that of Peter, and as she stepped with him to the altar she thought: "I do this that I may one day be empress! and as I can reach that position in no other way—well, then, let them call me the wife of this underaged boy! I will suffer it until the time comes when I shall no longer suffer, but command."

With such thoughts did Catharine become the wife of the Grand-duke Peter, who, as he with a loud and solemn "yes" vowed eternal truth to his young wife, looked at the Countess Woronzow, and both exchanged a stolen smile and a glowing glance of love.

"They may henceforth call this proud Catharine my wife," thought Peter, "but I shall never love her, as my heart will ever belong to my dear Woronzow! But Elizabeth has decided that Catharine shall be my wife. I accommodate myself to her command, and obey now, that I may one day command! But then woe to the wife this day forced upon me!"

And when the ceremony was ended,

the new-married pair received with smiling faces and radiant glances the congratulations of the court, which in lond and ecstatic exclamations commended the love and happiness of this young princely pair.

On the same day a second marriage was celebrated in this same imperial palace, perhaps not so splendid, but certainly a happier one, for it was love that united the two—love had overcome Elizabeth's aversion to marriage, and decided her to raise her dear Alexis Razumovsky to the position of her husband—love, and also a little superstition! As the son born to Elizabeth some months previously had died soon after its birth, and in this dispensation Elizabeth recognized the punishment of heaven in disapproval of her connection with Alexis, she shudderingly remembered the words spoken by Eleonore Lapuschkin, and her heart was filled with fear for the children which the future might bring to her.

"I will destroy the curse which this Countess Lapuschkin has pronounced against my children," thought Elizabeth, as she now for the second time felt herself to be a mother. "If God blesses my children, the curse of no human being can affect them, and this revengeful prayer of the countess will have no more power when the priest of God has consecrated and blessed the child now quietly reposing under my heart!"

This was the reason why Elizabeth resolved to marry Alexis Razumovsky; this was the reason why she, in a solitary chapel, accompanied only by Lestocq and the priest, stood before the marriage-altar with Alexis, and became his wife.

She breathed freer when the priest had pronounced his blessing upon her; an oppressive weight was lifted from her heart; the child she was about to bear was saved and sheltered, and Eleonore's curse had no longer any power over it!

On the next day Elizabeth appointed Alexis field-marshal, and raised him in the ranks of the nobility.

"We must at any rate give our son a respectable father," said she. "I hope we shall have a son, who will be as beautiful as his father; whom I will overload with honors, and place high above all the magnates of my court. Ah, a son! No daughter, Alexis!"

"And why no daughter?" smilingly asked Razumovsky.

Elizabeth shuddered, and, clinging to her beloved, whispered:

"Has not Eleonore Lapuschkin said, 'Give her a daughter, and let her, before the eyes of her mother, experience what I now suffer!' Oh, Alexis, wish me therefore no daughter! I should always tremble for her!"

And God seemed to have listened to the anxious prayer of the empress. Again she bore a son, but again the son died shortly after his birth.

"It is very sad to lose a child, and especially a son," sighed Elizabeth, and involuntarily she thought of Anna, that poor mother whom she had robbed of her son, that he might grow up in eternal joyless imprisonment, that he might be morally murdered, and from a man be converted into an idiot!

"This is God's vengeance!" whispered something in her breast, but Elizabeth shrank from these low whisperings of her conscience, and she tremulously said: "I will not listen to it! Away, ye intrusive thoughts! I am an empress—for me there are no crimes, no laws! An empress is exalted above all law, and whatever she does is right! Away, away, therefore, ye troublesome thoughts! This boy Ivan must remain in prison; I cannot restore him to his mother. May she bear other children, and then new joys will bloom for her!"

But these thoughts would not be thus banished, they constantly haunted her; they left not her nightly conch; they constantly renewed their dismal, awful whisperings; and this all-powerful empress would loudly shriek with mortal anguish, and she was dismayed at being left alone with her thoughts.

"I will have society around me," said she, "and will never be alone; the people about me shall always laugh and jest, to cheer me and distract my thoughts. Hasten, hasten—call my court; the most jovial men shall be most welcome! And, do you hear, above all things, bring me wine, the best and strongest wine. When I drink plenty of it, I shall again become gay and happy; it drives away all cares, and renders the heart light and free!"

And they came, the merriest gentlemen of the court; it also came, the strong, fiery wine; and, after an hour, Elizabeth's brow beamed with renewed pleasure, while her heavy tongue with difficulty stammered:

"How beautiful it yet is to be an empress—for an empress there is only joy and delight, and endless pleasures!"

CHAPTER XXI.

SCENES AND PORTRAITS.

YEARS passed—famous and glorious years for Russia. Peace within her borders, and splendid victories gained over foreign enemies, particularly over the Prussians. In songs of jubilee the people praised and blessed their empress, whose wisdom had brought all to such a glorious conclusion, and had made her country great, triumphant, and happy.

The good Elizabeth! What had she to do with the victories of her soldiers, with the happiness of her realm? She knew nothing of it, and if peace prevailed, throughout the Russian empire, t was absolutely unknown in the imperial palace, where there was eternal war, a never-ending feud! There the young Catharine contended with her husband, whom she hated and abhorred; with Elizabeth, who saw in her a dangerous rival. But it was an unequal struggle in which these two women were engaged, for Elizabeth had on her side the power and dominion, while Catharine had only her youth, her beauty, and her tears!

Elizabeth hated Catharine because she dared to remain young and handsome, while she, the empress, saw that she was growing old, and her charms were withering; and Catharine hated Elizabeth because the latter denied her a right which the empress daily claimed for herself—the right to choose a lover, and to love him as long as he pleased her. She hated Elizabeth because the latter surrounded her with spies and watchers, and required of her a strict virtue, a never-violated matrimonial fidelity—fidelity to the husband who so far derided and insulted his wife as to demand that she should receive into her circle and treat with respect and kindness his own mistress, the Countess Woronzow—fidelity to this husband, who had never shown her any thing but contempt and neglect, and who had no other way of entertaining her than teaching her to march in military fashion, and stand as a sentinel at his door!

Wounded in her inmost being and her feminine honor, tired of the eternal pin-prickings with which Elizabeth tormented her, Catharine retreated into her most retired apartment, there in quiet to reflect upon her dishonorable greatness, and yearningly to dream of a splendid future. "For the future," said she, with sparkling eyes to her confidante, Princess Daschkow, "the future is mine, they cannot deprive me of it. For that I labor and think and study. Ah, when *my* future shall have become the present, then will I encircle my brows with a splendid imperial diadem, and astonish you all with my greatness and magnificence."

"But you forget your husband!" smilingly interposed Countess Daschkow. "He will a little obscure the splendor of your imperial crown, as he will always be the first in the realm. He is the all-powerful emperor, and you will be powerless, although an empress!"

Catharine proudly tossed her head, and her eyes flashed.

"I shall one day remember all the mortifications he has inflicted upon me," said she, "and an hour will come when I shall have a reckoning with him, and full retribution! Ah, talk not to me of my husband—Russian emperors have never been immortal, and why should he be so?"

"Catharine!" exclaimed the Princess Daschkow, turning pale, "you cannot think—"

"I think," interposed Catharine, with an unnatural smile, "I think the Russian emperors are not immortal, and that this good Empress Elizabeth is very fortunate in having no emperor who presumes to stand over her and have a will more potent than her own!"

"Ah, Elizabeth has no will at all!" laughingly responded the princess.

"But I shall have a will!" said Catharine, proudly.

The Princess Daschkow had spoken the truth. Elizabeth had no longer any will; she let Bestuscheff govern, and was herself ruled by Alexis Razumovsky, the field-marshal, her husband. She did whatever these two required, willingly yielding to them in all cases demanding no personal effort on her part.

On this point only had she a will of her own, which she carried through with an iron hand.

"I have not become empress that I might labor, but that I might amuse myself," said she. "I have not set the crown upon my head for the purpose of governing, but for the purpose of enjoying life. Spare me, therefore, the labor of signing your documents. I will sign nothing more, for my hand is not accustomed to holding the pen, and the ink soils my fingers, which is unworthy of an empress!"

"It is only one signature that I implore of you to-day," said Bestuscheff, handing her a letter. "Have the great kindness to make an exception of this one single case, by signing this letter to King Louis XV. of France."

"What have I to write to this King of France?" fretfully asked Elizabeth. "Why should I do it? It is a long time since he has sent me any new dresses, although he might well know that nothing is more important for an empress than a splendid and varied wardrobe! Why, then, should I write to this King of France?"

"Your majesty, it is here question of a simple act of courtesy," said Bestuscheff, pressingly; "an act the omission of which may be attended with the most disagreeable consequences, perhaps indeed involve us in a war. Think of the peace of your realm, the welfare of your people, and sign this letter!"

"But what does it contain that is so important?" asked the empress, with astonishment. "I now remember that for a year past you have been importuning me about this!"

"Yes, your majesty, I have been for the last three years daily imploring of you this signature, and you have refused it to me; and yet the letter is so necessary! It is against all propriety not to send it! For it is a letter of congratulation to the King of France, who in an autograph letter announced to you the birth of his grandson. Reflect, your majesty, that he wrote you with his own hand, and for three years you have refused to give yourself the small trouble to sign the answer I have prepared.* This prince, for whose birth you are to congratulate the king, is now old enough to express his own thanks for the sympathy you manifest for him."

Elizabeth laughed. "Well," said she, "I shall finally be obliged to comply with your wishes, that you may leave me in peace. For three years I have patiently borne your importunities for this signature. My patience is now at an end, and I will sign the letter, that I may be freed from your solicitations. Give me, therefore, that intolerable pen, but first pour out a glass of Malvoisie, and hold it ready, that I may strengthen myself with it after the labor is accomplished."

Elizabeth, sighing, took the pen and slowly and anxiously subscribed her name to this three-years-delayed letter of congratulation to the King of France.

"So," said she, throwing down her pen after the completion of her task—"so, but you must not for a long time again trouble me with any such work, and to-day I have well earned the right to a very pleasant evening. Nothing

more of business—no, no, not a word more of it! I will not have these delightful hours embittered by your absurdities! Away with you, Bestuscheff, and let my field-marshal, Count Razumovsky, be called!"

And when Alexis came, Elizabeth smilingly said to him: "Alexis, the air is to-day so fine and fresh that we will take a ride. Quick, quick! And know you where?"

Razumovsky nodded. "To the villa!" said he, with a smile.

"Yes, to the villa!" cried Elizabeth, "to see my daughter at the villa!"

She therefore now had a daughter, and this daughter had not died like her two sons. She lived, she throve in the freshness of childhood, and Elizabeth loved her with idolatrous tenderness!

But precisely on account of this tenderness did she carefully conceal the existence of this daughter, keeping her far from the world, ignorant of her high birth, unsuspicious of her mother's greatness!

The fatal words of the Countess Lapuschkin still resounded in the ears of the empress: "Give this Elizabeth a daughter, and let that daughter experience what I now suffer!"

Such had been the prayer of the bleeding countess, flayed by the executioners of the empress, and the words were continually echoing in Elizabeth's heart.

Ah, she was indeed a lofty empress; she had the power to banish thousands to Siberia, and was yet so powerless that she could not banish those words from her mind which Eleonore Lapuschkin had planted there.

* Mannstein, Mémoires, vol. iii., p. 98.

Eleonore was therefore avenged! And while the countess bore the torments of her banishment with smiling fortitude, Elizabeth trembled on her throne at the words of her banished rival—words that seemed to hang, like the sword of Damocles, over the head of her daughter!

Perhaps it was precisely for the reason that she so much feared for her daughter, that she loved her so very warmly. It was a passionate, an adoring tenderness that she felt for the child, and nevertheless she had the courage to keep her at a distance from herself, to see her but seldom, that no one might suspect the secret of her birth.

Eleonore's words had brought reflection to Elizabeth. She comprehended that her legitimate daughter would certainly be threatened with great dangers after her death; she had shudderingly thought of poor Ivan in Schlüsselburg, and she said to herself: "As I have held him imprisoned as a pretender, so may it happen to my daughter, one day, when I am no more! Ivan had but a doubtful right to my throne, but Natalie is indisputably the grand-daughter of Peter the Great—the blood of the great Russian czar flows in her veins, and therefore Peter will fear Natalie as I feared Ivan; therefore will he imprison and torment her as I have imprisoned and tormented Ivan!"

By this affectionate anxiety was Elizabeth induced to make a secret of the existence of her daughter, which was imparted to but a few confidential friends.

The little Natalie was raised in a solitary country-house not far from the city, and her few servants and people were forbidden under pain of death to admit any stranger into the constantly-closed and always-watched house. No one was to enter it without a written order of the empress, and but few such written orders were given.

Elizabeth, then, as it were to recompense herself for the trouble of signing the letter to the King of France, resolved to visit her daughter to-day with her husband.

"Rasczinsky may precede and announce us," said she. "We will take our dinner there, and he may say to our major-domo that we are going to Peterhoff. Then no one will be surprised that we make a short halt at my little villa in passing, or, rather, they will know nothing of it. Call Rasczinsky!"

Count Rasczinsky was one of the few who were acquainted with the secret, and might accompany the empress in these visits. Elizabeth had unlimited confidence in him; she knew him to be a silent nobleman, and she estimated him the more highly from the fact that he seemed much attached to the charming, beautiful, and delicate child, her daughter. She remarked that he appeared to love her as a brother, that he constantly and fondly watched over her, and that he was never better pleased than when, as a child, he could jest and play with her.

"Rasczinsky, we are about to ride out to the villa on a visit to Natalie!" she said, when the count entered.

The count's eyes beamed with pleasure. "And I may be permitted to accompany your majesty?" he hastily asked.

The empress smiled. "How impetuous you are!" said she. "Would not one think you were a dying lover, a sighing shepherd, and it was question of seeking your tender shepherdess, instead of announcing to a child of eleven years the speedy arrival of her mother?"

"Your majesty," said Count Rasczinsky, laughing, "I am not in love, but I adore this child as my good angel. I can never do or think any thing bad in Natalie's presence. She is so pure and innocent that one casts down his eyes with shame before her, and when she glances at me with her large, deep, and yet so childish eyes, I could directly fall upon my knees and confess to her all my sins!"

"You would not have many to confess," said Elizabeth, "for your sins are few. You are the pride of my court, and, as I am told, a true pattern of all knightly virtues. Remain so, and who knows, my fair young count, what the future may bring you? Love my Natalie now only as an angel of innocence; let her grow up as such, and then—"

"And then?" asked the count, as the empress stopped.

"Then we shall see!" smilingly responded Elizabeth. "But now hasten forward to announce us."

"Your majesty forgets that, to enable one to penetrate into this enchanted castle, your written command is required!"

"Ah, that is true?" said Elizabeth, stepping to her writing-table. This time she was not too indolent to write; no representations nor prayers were needed. It concerned the seeing of her daughter—how, then, could she have thought writing painful or troublesome?

With the same pen with which, a short time before, she had so unwillingly signed the congratulatory letter, she now wrote upon a sheet of paper, provided with her seal, these words:

"The Count Rasczinsky may be admitted.   ELIZABETH."

She handed the paper to the count, who pressed it to his lips.

"You can retain this paper for all time," said the empress, as she dismissed him. "I know that I can wholly confide in you. You will never sell or betray my Natalie?"

"Never!" protested the count, taking his leave.

Hastily mounting his horse, he galloped through the streets, and when, having left the city behind him, he found himself in the open country where no one could observe him, he drew the paper Elizabeth had given him from his bosom, and, waving it high in the air, shouted:

"Good fortune, good fortune! This paper is my talisman and my future! With this paper I will give Russia an empress, and make myself her emperor!"

CHAPTER XXII.

PRINCES ALSO MUST DIE.

YES, even princes must die, glorious and lofty as they are, proudly as they stand over their trembling subjects! Even to them comes the dark hour in which all the borrowed and artistically-combined tinsel of their lives falls from them; a dark hour, in which they tremble and repent, and pray to God for what they seldom granted to their fellow-men—mercy! Mercy for those false tales which they have imposed upon the people, for those false tales of the higher endowments of princes, of inherited wisdom which raises them above the rest of mankind—mercy for their arbitrariness, their pride, and their insolence—mercy for a poor beggar, who, until then, had called himself a rich and powerful prince.

And this hour came for Elizabeth. After twenty years of splendor, of absolute, unlimited power, of infallibility, of likeness to the gods, came the depressing hour in which Elizabeth ceased to be an empress, and became only a trembling earth-worm, imploring mercy, aid, amelioration of her sufferings from her Creator!

She suffered much, this poor empress, dethroned by death; she suffered, although reposing upon silken cushions, with a gold-embroidered covering for her shaking limbs.

And she was yet so young, hardly fifty, and she loved life so intensely! Oh, she would have given the half of her empire for a few more years of life and enjoyment. But what cares Death for the wishes of an empress? Here ends her earthly supremacy! Groaning and writhing, the earth-worm tremblingly submits.

Where, now, were all her favorites—those high lords of the court, those grand noblemen, created from soldiers, grooms, lackeys, and serfs—where were they now? Why stood they not around the death-bed of their empress? Why were they not there, that the remembrance of the benefits conferred upon them might drive away those terrible reminiscences of the torments she had inflicted upon others? Where were they, her counts, barons, field-marshals, and privy councillors, whom she had raised from nothing to the first positions in the realm?

None were with her! They had all hastened thence for the preservation of their ill-gotten wealth, to crawl in the dust before Peter, to be the first to pay him homage, that he might pardon their greatness and their possessions! From the death-bed they had fled to Peter, and, kneeling before him, they praised God for at length bestowing upon the happy realm the noblest and best ruler, Peter III.!

But where were Elizabeth's more particular friends, who had made her an empress?

Where was Lestocq?

Him the empress had banished to Siberia. Yielding to the prayers and calumnies of his enemies, which she was too weak to withstand, she had given him up; she had sacrificed him to procure peace and quiet for herself, and in the same hour in which she had tenderly pressed his hand, and called him her friend, had she signed his sentence of banishment! Lestocq had for nine years languished in Siberia.

Where was Grünstein? Banished, cast off, like Lestocq.

Where was Alexis Razumovsky?

Ah, well for her! He stood at her bedside, he pressed her cold hand in his; he yet, in the face of death, thanked her for all the benefits she had heaped upon him. But, alas! she was also surrounded by others—by wild, pale, terrible forms, which were unseen by all except the dying empress! She there saw the tortured face of Anna Leopoldowna, whom she had let die in prison; there grinned at her the idiotic face of Ivan, whose mind she had destroyed; there saw she the angry-flashing eye and bloody form of Eleonore Lapuschkin, and, springing up from her bed, the empress screeched with terror, and folded her trembling hands in prayer to God for grace and mercy for her daughter, for Natalie, that He would turn away the horrible curse that Eleonore had hurled at her child.

Alexis Razumovsky stood by her bedside, weeping. Overcome, as it seemed, by his sorrow, another left the death-chamber of the empress, and rushed to his horse, standing ready in the court below! This other was Count Rasczinsky, the confidant of the empress.

The bells rang in St. Petersburg, the cannon roared; there were both joy and sorrow in what the bells and cannon announced!

The Empress Elizabeth was dead; the Emperor Peter III. ascended the throne of the czars as absolute ruler of the Russian realm. The first to bow before him was his wife. With her son of five years old in her arms, she had thrown herself upon her knees, and, touching the floor with her forehead, she had implored grace and love for herself and her son; and Peter, raising her up, had presented her to the people as his empress.

In St. Petersburg the bells rang, the cannon thundered—"The empress is dead, long live the emperor!"

Before the villa stopped a foam-covered steed, from which dismounted a horseman, who knocked at the closed door. To the porter who looked out from a sliding window he showed the written order of Elizabeth for his admission. The porter opened the door, and with the loud cry, "Natalie, Natalie!" the Count Rasczinsky rushed into the hall of the house.

The bells continued to ring, the cannon to thunder. There was great rejoicing in St. Petersburg.

Issuing from the villa, Count Rasczinsky again mounted his foaming steed.

Like a storm-wind swept he over the plain—but not toward St. Petersburg, not toward the city where the people were saluting their new emperor!

Away, away, far and wide in the distance, his horse bounded and panted, bleeding with the spurs of his rider. Excited constantly to new speed, he as constantly bounds onward.

Like a nocturnal spectre flies he through the desert waste; the storm-wind drives him forward, it lifts the mantle that enwraps him like a cloud, and under that mantle is seen an angel-face, the smile of a delicate little girl, two tender childish arms clasping the form of the count, a slight elfish form tremblingly reposing upon the count's breast.

"You weep not, my angel," whispered the count, while rushing forward with restless haste.

"No, no, I neither weep nor tremble, for I am with you!" breathed a sweet, childish voice.

"Cling closer to me, my sweet blossom, recline your head against my breast. See, evening approaches!—Night will spread its protecting veil over us, and God will be our conductor and safeguard! I shall save you, my angel, my charming child!"

The steed continues his onward course.

The child smilingly reclines upon the bosom of the rider, over whom the descending sun sheds its red parting beams.

Like a phantom flies he onward, like a phantom he disappears there on the border of the forest. Was it only a delusive appearance, a *fata morgana* of the desert?

No, again and again the evening breeze raises the mantle of the rider, and the charming angelic brow is still seen resting upon the bosom of the count.

No, it is no dream, it is truth and reality!

Like a storm-wind flies the count over hill and heath, and on his bosom reposes Natalie, *the daughter of the empress!*

CHAPTER XXIII.

THE CHARMED GARDEN.

ONE must be very happy or very unhappy, to love Solitude, to lean upon her silent breast, and, fleeing mankind, to seek in its arms what is so seldom found among men, repose for happiness or consolation for sorrow! For the happy, solitude provides the most delightful festival, as it allows one in the most enjoyable resignation to repose in himself, to breathe out himself, to participate in himself! But it also provides a festival for the unhappy—a festival of the memory, of living in the past, of reflection upon those long-since vanished joys, the loss of which has caused the sorrow! For the children of the world, for the striving, for the seeker of inordinate enjoyments, for the ambitious, for the sensual, solitude is but ill-adapted—only for the happy, for the sorrow-laden, and also for the innocent, who yet know nothing of the world, of neither its pleasures nor torments, of neither its loves nor hatreds!

So thought and spoke the curious Romans when passing the high walls surrounding the beautiful garden formerly belonging to the Count Appiani. At an earlier period this garden had been well known to all of them, as it had been a sort of public promenade, and under its shady walks had many a tender couple exchanged their first vows and experienced the rapture of the first kiss of love. But for the four last years all this had been changed; a rich stranger had come and offered to the impoverished old Count Appiani a large sum for this garden with its decaying villa, and the count had, notwithstanding the murmurs of the Romans, sold his last possession to the stranger. He had said to the grumbling Romans: "You are dissatisfied that I part with my garden for money. You were pleased to linger in the shady avenues, to listen to these murmuring fountains and rustling cypresses; you have walked here, you have here laughed and enjoyed yourselves, while I, sitting in my dilapidated villa, have suffered deprivation and hunger. I will make you a proposition. Collect this sum, you Romans, which this stranger offers me; ye who love to promenade in my garden, unite yourselves in a common work. Let each one give what he can, until the necessary amount is collected, then the garden will be your common property, where you can walk as much as you please, and I shall be happy to be relieved from poverty by my own countrymen, and not compelled to sell to a stranger the garden so agreeable to the Romans!"

But the good Romans had no answer to make to Count Appiani. They, indeed, would have the enjoyment, but it must cost them nothing—in vain had they very much loved this garden, had taken great pleasure under its shady trees; but when it became necessary to pay for these pleasures, they found that they were not worth the cost, that they could very well dispense with them.

The good Romans therefore turned away from this garden, which threatened them with a tax, and sought other places of recreation; while old Count Appiani sold his garden and the ruins of his villa to the rich stranger who had offered him so considerable a sum for them. From that day forward every thing in the garden had assumed a different appearance. Masons, carpenters, and upholsterers had come and so improved the villa, within and without, that it now made a stately and beautiful appearance amid the dense foliage of the trees. It had been expensively and splendidly furnished with every thing desirable for a rich man's dwelling, and the upholsterers had enough to relate to the listening Romans of the elegant magnificence now displayed in this formerly pitiable villa. How gladly would the former promenaders now have returned to this garden; how gladly would they now have revisited this villa, which, with its deserted halls and its ragged and dirty tapestry, had formerly seemed to them not worth looking at! But their return to it was now rendered impossible; for on the same day in which the new owner took possession of the garden, he had brought with him more than fifty workmen, who had immediately commenced surrounding it with a high wall.

Higher and higher rose the wall; nobody could see over it, as no giant was sufficiently tall; no one could climb over it, as the smoothly-hammered stones of which it was built offered not the least supporting point. The garden with its villa had become a secret mystery to the Romans! They yet heard the rustling of the trees, they saw the green branches waving in the wind; but of what occurred under those branches and in those shaded walks they could know nothing. At first, some curious individuals had ventured to knock at the low, narrow door that formed the only entrance into this walled garden. They had knocked at that door and demanded entrance. Then would a small sliding window be opened, and a gruff, bearded man with angry voice would ask what was wanted, and at the same time inform the knocker that no one could be admitted; that he and his two bull-dogs would be able to keep the garden clear of all intruders. And the two great hounds, as if they understood the threats of their master, would show their teeth, and their threatening growl would rise to a loud and angry bark.

They soon ceased to knock at that door, and, as they could not gain admission, they took the next best course, of assuming the appearance of not wishing it.

Four years had since passed; they had overcome the desire to enter the premises or to look over the wall, but they told wondrous tales of the garden and of a beautiful fairy who dwelt in it, and whose soft, melodious voice was sometimes heard in the stillness of the night singing sweet, transporting songs. No one had seen her, this fairy, but she was certainly beautiful, and of course young; there were also some bold individuals who asserted that when the moon shone brightly and goldenly, the young fairy was then to be seen in the tops of the trees or upon the edge of the wall. Light as an elf, transparent as a moonbeam, she there swung to and fro, executing singular dances and singing songs that brought tears to the eyes and compassion to the hearts of those who heard them. On hearing these tales, the Romans would make the sign of the cross, and pass more quickly by the walls of this garden, which thenceforth they called " *The Charmed Garden.*" It was indeed a charmed garden! It was an island of happiness, behind these walls, concealed from the knavery of the world. Like an eternal smile of the Divinity rested the heavens over this ever-blooming, ever-fragrant garden, in whose myrtle-bushes the nightingales sang, and in whose silver-clear basins the goldfishes splashed.

Yes, it was indeed a charmed garden, and also had its fairy, who, if she did not compete with the moonbeams in rocking herself on the tops of the trees and the edges of the wall, was nevertheless as delicate as an elf, and who tripped from flower to brook and from brook to hill as lightly and gracefully as the gazelle. The whole spring, the whole youth of nature, flashed and beamed from this beautiful maiden-face,

so full of childlike innocence, purity, and peace. No storm had as yet passed over these smiling features, not the smallest leaf of this rose had been touched by an ungentle hand; freely and freshly had she blossomed in luxuriant natural beauty; she had drunk the dews of heaven, but not the dew of tears, for those deeply-dark beaming eyes had wept only such tears as were called forth by emotions of joy and happiness.

She sat under a myrtle, whose blossoming branches bent down to her as if they would entwine that pure and tender brow with a bridal wreath. With her head thrown back upon these branches, she reposed with an inimitable grace her reclining form. A white transparent robe, held by a golden clasp, fell in waves to her little feet, which were encased in gold-embroidered slippers of dark-red leather. A blushing rose was fastened by a diamond pin in the folds of her dress upon her budding bosom, finely contrasting with the delicate flush upon her cheeks. A guitar rested upon her full round arm. She had been singing, this beautiful fairy child, but her song was now silenced, and she was glancing up to the clouds, following their movements with her dreamy, thoughtful eyes. A smile hovered about her fresh, youthful lips—the smile peculiar to innocence and happiness.

She dreamed; precious, ecstatic images passed before her mental eyes; she dreamed of a distant land in which she had once been, of a distant house in which she had once dwelt. It was even more beautiful and splendid than this which she now occupied, but it had lacked this blue sky and fragrant atmosphere; it lacked these trees and flowers, these myrtle-bushes, and these songs of the nightingale, and upon a few summer days had followed long, dull winter months with their cold winding-sheet of snow, with their benumbing masses of ice, and the fantastic flowers painted on the windows by the frost. And yet, and yet, there had been a sun which shone into her heart warmer than this bright sun of Italy, and the thought of which spread a purple glow upon her cheeks. This sun had shone upon her from the tender glances of a lady whom she had loved as a tutelar genius, as a divinity, as the bright star of her existence! Whenever that lady had come to her in the solitary house in which she then dwelt, then had all appeared to her as in a transfiguration; then had even her peevish old servant learned to smile and become humble and friendly; then all was joy and happiness, and whoever saw that beautiful and brilliant lady, had thought himself blessed, and had fallen down to adore her.

Of that lady was the young maiden now thinking, of that memorable woman with the flashing eyes whose tender glance had always penetrated the heart of the child with delight, whose gentle words yet resounded like music in her ears.

Where was she now, this lady of her love, her longings? why had she been brought away from that house with its snowy winding-sheet and the ice drapery upon its windows? Where lay that house, and where had she to seek it with her thoughts? What was the language she had there spoken, and which she now secretly spoke in her heart, although nobody else addressed her in it, no one about her understood it; and wherefore had her friend and protector, he who had brought her here, who had always been with her, wherefore had he suddenly given himself the appearance of no longer understanding it?

And even as she was thinking of him, of this dear friend and protector, he came along down the alley; his tall form appeared at the end of the walk; she recognized his noble features, with the proud eagle glance and the bold arched brow.

The young maiden rose from her seat and hastened to meet him.

"How charming that you have come, Paulo," she gayly said, stretching forth her little hands toward him. "I must ask you something, and that directly, Paulo. Tell me quickly what is that language called in which we formerly conversed together, and why have we ceased to speak it since we came here to Rome?"

Paulo's brow became slightly clouded, but when he looked into her beautiful face, animated by expectant curiosity, this expression of displeasure quickly vanished from his features, and, threatening her with his finger, he said:

"Always this same question, Natalie; and yet I have so often begged of you to forget the past, and live only in the present, my dear, sweet child! The past is sunken in an immeasurable gulf behind you, which you can never pass, and if it stretches out its arms to you, it will only be for the purpose of dragging you down into the abyss with it! Forget it, therefore, my Natalie, and yield thyself to this beautiful and delightful present, to increase for you the attractions of which will ever be the dearest task of my life."

"It is true," said the young maiden, sighing, "I am wrong to be always recurring to those long-past times; you must pardon me, Paulo, but you will also acknowledge that my enigmatical past justifies me in feeling some curiosity. Only think how it began! You one day came rushing to my room, you pressed me all trembling to your heart, and silently bore me away. 'Natalie,' said you, 'danger threatens you; I will save, or perish with you!' You mounted your horse with me in your arms. Behind us screamed and moaned the servants of my house, but you regarded them not, and I trustingly clung to your heart, for I knew that if danger threatened me, you would surely save me! Oh, do you yet remember that fabulous ride? How we rested in out-of-the-way houses, or with poor peasant people, and then proceeded on farther and farther! And how the sun constantly grew warmer, melting the snow, and you constantly became more cheerful and happy, until, one day, you impetuously pressed me to your bosom, and said: 'Natalie, we are saved! Life and the future are now yours! Look around you, we are in Italy. Here you can be free and happy!'"

"And was not that a good prophecy?" asked Paulo. "Has it not been fulfilled? Are you not happy?"

"I should be so" sighed Natalie,

"could I avoid thinking so often of that past! Those words which you then spoke to me were the last I ever heard in that language, which I had always spoken until then, but of which I know not the name! From that hour you spoke to me in an unknown tongue, and I felt like a poor deserted orphan, from whom was taken her last possession, her language!"

"And yet whole peoples have been robbed of that last and dearest possession!" said Paulo, his brow suddenly darkening, "and not, as in your case, to save life and liberty, but for the purpose of enslaving and oppressing them."

Natalie, perceiving the sudden sadness of her friend, attempted to smile, and, grasping his hand, she said:

"Come, Paulo, we are naughty children, and vex ourselves with vagaries, while all nature is so cheerful and so replete with divine beauty. Only see with what glowing splendor the departing sun rests upon the tops of the cypresses! Ah, it is nowhere so beautiful as here in my dear garden. This is my world and my happiness! Sometimes, Paulo, it makes me shudder to think that the walls surrounding us might suddenly tumble down, and all the tall houses standing behind them, and all the curious people lounging in the streets, could then look in upon my paradise! That must be terrible, and yet Marianne tells me that other people live differently from us, that their houses are not surrounded by walls, and that no watchman with dogs drive away troublesome visitors from them. And yet, she says, they smilingly welcome such inconvenient people, receiving them with friendly words, while they only thank God when they finally go and leave the occupants in peace. Is it then true, Paulo, that people can be so false to each other, and that those who live in the world never dare to speak as they think?"

"It is, alas! but too true, Natalie," said Paulo, with a sad smile.

"Then never let me become acquainted with such a world," said the young maiden, clinging to Paulo's arm. "Let me always remain here in our solitude, which none but good people can share with us. For Marianne is good, as also Cecil, your servant; and Carlo—oh, Carlo would give his life for me. He is not false, like other people; I can confide in him."

"Think you so!" asked Paulo, looking deep into her eyes with a scrutinizing glance.

She bore his glance with a cheerful and unembarrassed smile, and a roguish nod of her little head.

"You must certainly wish to paint me again, that you look at me so earnestly. No, Paulo, I will not sit to you again, you paint me much too handsome; you make an angel of me, while I am yet only a poor little thing, who lives but by your mercy, and does not even know her own name!"

"Angels never have a name, they are only known as angels, and need no further designation. As there is an Angel Gabriel, so is there an Angel Natalie!"

"Mocker," said she, laughing, "there are no feminine angels! But now come, be seated. Here is my guitar, and I will sing you a song for which Carlo yesterday brought me the melody."

"And the words?" asked Paulo.

"Well, as to the words, they must come in the singing—to-day one set of words, to-morrow another. Who can know what glows in your heart at any given hour, and what you may feel in the next, and which will escape you in words unknown to yourself, and which unconsciously and involuntarily stream from your lips."

"You are my charming poetess, my Sappho!" exclaimed Paulo, kissing her hand.

"Ah, would that you spoke true!" said she, with sparkling eyes and a deeper flush upon her cheeks. "Let me be a poetess like Sappho, and I would, like her, joyfully leap from the rocks into the sea. Oh, there are yet poetesses—Carlo has told me of them. All Rome now worships the great improvisatrice, Corilla. I should like to know her, Paulo, only to adore her, only to see her in her splendor and her beauty!"

"If you wish it, you shall see her," said Paulo.

"Ah, I shall see her then!" shouted Natalie, and, as if to give expression to her inward joy, she touched the strings of her guitar, and in clear tones resounded a jubilant melody. Then she began to sing, at first in single isolated words and exclamations, which constantly swelled into more powerful, animated and blissful tones, and finally flowed into a regular dithyramb. It was a song of jubilee, a sigh of innocence and happiness; she sang of God and the stars, of happy love, and of reuniting; of blossom, fragrance, and fanning zephyrs; and in unconscious, foreboding pain, she sang of the sorrows of love, and the pangs of renunciation.

All Nature seemed listening to her charming song; no leaflet stirred, in low murmurs splashed the waves of the fountain by which she sat, and occasionally a nightingale wailed in unison with her hymn of rejoicing. The sun had descended to a point nearer the horizon, and bordered it with moving purple clouds. Natalie, suddenly interrupting her song, pointed with her rosy fingers to the heavens.

"How beautiful it is, Paulo!" said she.

He, however, saw nothing but her face, illuminated by the evening glow.

"How beautiful art thou!" he whispered low, pressing her head to his bosom.

Then both were silent, looking, lost in sweetest dreams, upon the surrounding landscape, which, as if in a silence of adoration, seemed to listen for the parting salutation of the god of day. A nightingale suddenly came and perched upon the myrtle-bush under which Natalie and her friend were reposing. Soon she began to sing, now in complaining, now in exulting tones, now tenderly soft, now in joyful trumpet-blasts; and the night-wind that now arose rustled in organ-tones among the cypress and olive trees.

Natalie clung closer to her friend's side.

"I would now gladly die," said she.

"Already die!" whispered he. "Die before you have lived, Natalie?"

Then they were again silent, the wind rustled in the trees, the fountains murmured, the birds sang, and in golden light lay the moon over this paradise of two happy beings.

But what is that which is rustling in the pines close to the wall—what is that looking out with flashing eyes and a poisonous glance? Is it the serpent already come to expel these happy beings from their paradise?

They see nothing, they hear nothing, they are both dreaming, so sure do they feel of their happiness.

But there is a continued rustling. It is unnatural! It resembles not the rustling of the evening wind! It is not the rustling of a bird, balancing itself upon a branch of the tree! What, then, is it?

An opening is made in the foliage, and it is the arm of a man that makes it. Upon the wall is to be seen the form of a man, and near him slowly rises a second form. Cautiously he glances around, and then makes a scornful grimace, while his eyes shine like those of a hyena. He has discovered the two sitting together in happy security, and enjoying the tranquil beauty of the evening in silent beatitude. He has seen them, and points toward them with his finger, while, at the same time, he lightly touches the arm of the other man, who has boldly swung himself up on the wall. The glance of the latter follows the direction in which the other points; he also now sees the reposing pair, and over his features also flits an unnatural smile. He suddenly fumbles in his bosom, and when his hand is withdrawn a small dagger glistens in it. With a bold leap,

NATALIE AND COUNT PAULO.　　　　p. 126.

the man is already on the point of springing from the wall into the garden. The other holds him back, and makes a threatening counter-movement. He, it seems, is the commander, and uses his power with an indignant negative shake of the head; his commanding glance seems to say: "Be silent, and observe!"

Staring and immovably their eyes were now fixed upon the silent pair sitting in the bright moonlight which surrounded them as with a glory. One of the men still holds the dagger in his hand, and with a powerful arm the other holds him in check. Then they whisper low together—they seem to be consulting as to what is to be done. The man with the dagger seems to yield to the arguments or persuasions of the other. He nods his consent. The first disappears behind the wall, and the armed one slowly follows him. Yet once again he glances over the wall, raising his arm and shaking his dagger toward Natalie and her friend. Then he disappeared, and all was again peaceful and still in this smiling paradise!

Was it, perhaps, only an illusive dream that bantered us, only a *fata morgana* formed by the moonbeams? Or does the serpent of evil really lurk about this paradise? Will destruction find its way into this charmed garden? Ah, no solitude and no wall can afford protection against misfortune! It creeps through the strongest lock, and over the highest wall; and while we think ourselves safe, it is already there, close to us, and nearly ready to swallow us up.

CHAPTER XXIV.

THE LETTERS.

IT was suddenly lively in the garden. Cecil, Paulo's old servant, approached from the house, with a lantern in his hand.

He comes down the alley with hasty steps, and with an anxious countenance approaches his master.

"What is it, Cecil?"

"Two letters, sir, that have just arrived. One comes from the hotel of the Russian legation, and the other from that of the Lord-Cardinal Bernis."

Paulo shuddered slightly, and his hand involuntarily grasped after the first letter, but he suddenly constrained himself, and his glance fell upon Natalie, whose eyes were fixed with curiosity upon the two letters.

"We will first see what the good Cardinal Bernis writes us!" said Count Paulo, placing the Russian letter in his pocket with apparent indifference.

"Bernis?" asked Natalie. "Is not that the French cardinal, who is at the same time a poet, and whom the pope, the great Ganganelli, so dearly loves?"

"The same," said Paulo, "and besides, the same Cardinal Bernis whom I had months ago promised to allow the pleasure of making your acquaintance! He already knows you, Natalie, although he has never yet seen your fair face; he knows you from what I have told him."

"Oh, let us quickly see what the good cardinal writes!" exclaimed Natalie, clapping her hands with the impatience of a child.

Count Paulo smilingly broke the seal and read the letter.

"You are in truth a witch," said he; "you must have some genius in your service, who listens to every wish you express, in order to fulfil it without delay! This letter contains an invitation from the cardinal. He gives a great entertainment to-morrow, and begs of me that I will bring you to it. The improvisatrice Corilla will also be there!"

"Oh, then I shall see her!" exclaimed the delighted young maiden. "At length I shall see a poetess! For we shall go to this entertainment, shall we not, Paulo?"

The count thoughtfully cast down his eyes, and his hand involuntarily sought the letter in his pocket. An expression of deep care and anxiety was visible on his features, and Cecil seemed to divine the thoughts of his master, for he also looked anxious, and a deep sigh escaped from his breast.—Natalie perceived nothing of all this! She was wholly occupied by the thought of seeing Oorilla, the great improvisatrice, of whom Carlo, Natalie's music-teacher, had told her so much, and whose fame was sounded by children and adults in all the streets of Rome.

"We go to this festival, do we not, Paulo?" repeated she, as the count still continued silent.

Recovering from his abstraction, he said: "Yes, we will go! It is time that my Natalie was introduced into this circle of influential Romans, that she may gain friends among people of importance, who may watch over and protect her when I no longer can!"

"You will, then, leave me!" cried the young maiden, turning pale and anxiously grasping the count's arm. "No, Paulo, you cannot do that! Would you leave me because I, a foolish child, desired to go to this festival, and was no longer contented with our dear and beautiful solitude? That was wrong in me, Paulo, as I now plainly see, and I desire it no longer! Oh, we will prepare other pleasures for ourselves here in our delightful paradise. You have often called me a poetess, and I will now believe I am, and no longer wish to see another. I will suffice for myself! Come, I will immediately sing you a song, a festival song, my friend!"

And taking her guitar, Natalie struck some joyous accords; but Count Paulo lightly laid his hands upon the strings so as to silence them, and drawing the tips of her fingers to his lips, with a slight shaking of his head, he said: "Not now, my charming poetess, I am not worthy of hearing you."

"And it is late," added Cecil, coming as it were to the aid of his master.

The count rose. "Yes, you are right—it is late," said he, "and I must not longer keep Natalie from her slumber. Come, my sweet child, you must retire; you must sleep, that your brow may beam with blooming freshness to-morrow!"

Natalie made no answer; with a light sigh she mechanically took the count's offered arm.

Cecil preceded them with the lantern in his hand. Thus they proceeded up the alley leading to the villa, all three silent and thoughtful. The sky had become obscured, a black cloud intercepted the light of the moon, and Natalie's charmed garden was suddenly wrapped in gloom.

A cold shudder ran through her delicate frame.

"A feeling of anxiety has come over me!" she whispered, clinging closer to the count's side.

"Poor child!" said the count. "Are you already oppressed with fear?"

"What if the wall should give way, and bad people should intrude into our garden! Ah, Marianne says that misfortune lurks everywhere in the world, lying in ambush for those who think themselves safe, destroying their happiness, and making them wholly miserable; and people only laugh and rejoice that another man's hopes have been wrecked! Ah, and I have felt so secure in my happiness! If misfortune should now actually come—if these walls should prove not high enough to keep it off! Ah, Paulo, protect me from lurking misfortune!"

They had now arrived at the door of the villa. Paulo pressed the trembling young maiden with paternal tenderness to his breast, and, lightly touching her forehead with his lips, he said : "Good-night, my love! Sleep gently, and be not anxious! So long as I live, misfortune shall never approach you! Rest assured of that!"

Thus speaking, he led her into the house, where Marianne was waiting to accompany her to her chamber.

Natalie silently followed her, but before entering her room she once more turned, and, pressing her fingers to her lips, wafted kisses in the air toward her friend.

"Good-night, Paulo!"

"Good-night, Natalie!"

The door closed behind her, and the smile instantly vanished from Paulo's lips. With impetuous haste, beckoning Cecil to follow him, he strode through the corridor leading to his own apartments.

When he had arrived there, and Cecil had closed the door behind him, the count with a deep sigh threw himself upon a chair, whilst Cecil silently busied himself in lighting the wax-candles and placing them upon the table beside his master.

"Will not your grace now read the other letter?" he timidly asked, as Count Paulo still remained buried in his silent reflections.

"Oh, this unblessed letter!" exclaimed the count, with a shudder. "I tell you, Cecil, I feel that it contains misfortune. It has lain with a heavy weight like a nightmare upon my breast and I yet felt not the strength in me to draw it forth and read it in Natalie's presence!"

"That was well!" said Cecil, "and it was for that reason that I told you in advance that the letter was from Russia, that you might be on your guard. But now, Sir Count, we are alone, and now you can read it!"

"Yes, away with this childish fear!" cried the count, with resolution. "I will be a man, Cecil, and whatever this letter may contain, I will bear it like a man!"

Drawing forth the letter, he broke the seal with a trembling hand, and threw the cover across the room. Then unfolding the letter, he read. Behind him stood Cecil, involuntarily trembling with anxious expectation.

The letter fell from the count's hands, and a deadly paleness spread over his face, which bore the expression of utter despair.

"Oh, my prophetic soul!" he sighed.

"Your presentiment is then fulfilled!" anxiously asked Cecil.

"Yes, it is fulfilled! My property is sequestrated; they refuse to send me the money I required; they command my immediate return to Russia, as my *congé* has expired and my respite is at an end!"

"And you are lost, my lord, if you do not obey this command!" said Cecil.

"And Natalie?" reproachfully asked the count. "Can I, dare I leave her?"

"She is much safer without than with you! They may not yet suspect who she is! It is very possible that it in reality only is because your leave of absence has expired, as the laws of Russia require that every absentee should return to his country once in every four years. Fulfil, therefore, this hard duty. Pretend to suppose that your recall is for no other reason than the renewal of your passport, and the giving you an opportunity to pay your homage to the empress. Appear innocent and unconcerned, and all may yet go well!"

"No," gloomily replied the count, "nothing will go well any more! The whole future stands before me in clear and distinct traits—a future full of shame and horror! Oh, would it not be better to flee from that future and seek in some remote and hidden valley a place where, perhaps, misfortune cannot reach, nor destruction overtake us!"

"How?" reproachfully asked Cecil. "Is it Count Paulo who speaks thus? Is it the pupil whom I taught to defy misfortune and rise superior to disaster with courageous self-confidence? Is it the son of my heart for whom I have left all, sacrificed all, for whom I have offered up my fatherland, my freedom, and my independence; whom I shall love until my last breath? Paulo, pluck up a good heart, my son! You have proposed to yourself a great end, which was only to be reached by thorny and dangerous paths; will you now stop at the first cross-road and return upon your steps, instead of pressing forward sword in hand? No, no, I know you better, my son; this momentary hesitation will pass away, and you will again be great and strong for the struggle and the victory!"

With a faint smile Count Paulo gave him his hand. "You know not, my friend, how great is the sacrifice you demand of me!" said he, in a subdued tone. "I must leave Natalie. I must never see her more, never more draw consolation from her glance, nor hope from her charming smile! Oh, Cecil, you have no idea of what Natalie is to me; you know not that I—"

"I know," interposed Cecil, solemnly, "I know that you have sworn upon the holy book to protect her with your life from every injury; I know that you have sworn never to give rest to yourself until you have reinstated her in her inherited rights, and that, until then, she shall be sacred to you, sacred as a sister, sacred as a daughter whose honor you will protect and defend against every outrage, against even every sinful thought. That have you sworn, and I know you will hold your word sacred and keep your oath!"

Count Paulo dropped his head upon his breast and sighed deeply.

"I must therefore leave her!" said he.

"Your own welfare demands it."

"But how is she to live during our absence? Our money will not suffice to the end. Alas! we had so surely calculated on this remittance from my estates, and now it fails us!"

"We will sell that costly ornament of brilliants which you had destined as a present for Natalie on her seventeenth birthday."

"Ah," sighed the count, "you have a means for the removal of every obstacle. I must therefore go!"

"And I go with you," said Cecil. "I would, if it must be so, be able to die for you!"

"They will destroy all three of us!" said the count. "Believe me, the knife is already sharpened for our throats! Believe also, Cecil, that I tremble not from fear of death. But I fear for Natalie! Ah, I already seem to see the approach of her murderers, to see them seize her with their bloody hands, and I shall not be there to protect her!"

While Count Paulo thus spoke, with a sad, foreboding soul, those two mysterious men, who had so threateningly watched and listened to Natalie and her friend, still remained under the wall.

The one still held the dagger in his hand, and was unquietly walking back and forth near his companion, who had calmly thrown himself upon the ground.

"You did wrong to hinder me, Beppo," he angrily said. "It would have been best to have finished them at once. The occasion could not have been more favorable—the solitary garden, the nightly stillness and obscurity. Ah, one blow would have done the business!"

"Well, and what if the gentleman who sat near her had seized you before the blow was struck? How then?" asked the other. "You are yet but a novice and a bungler, friend Giuseppo.

You yet lack discretion, the tranquil glance, the sure hand! You always suffer yourself to become excited, which is unartistic and even dangerous. We went out to-day only to obtain information; we were only to discover and observe the signora, and perhaps to watch for an opportunity. But to fall upon her in this garden would have been the extreme of stupidity, for we had all the servants and the hounds against us, and it is one of the first principles of our profession to put others in danger, but never to incur it ourselves."

"Wherefore, then, have we come here?" cried Guiseppo, with vehemence.

"To see and know her, that we may surely recognize her again when the right hour comes. And that hour will come—I will answer for it. Did not the signora tell us that this lady would probably attend the festival of Cardinal Bernis?"

"She said so."

"Well, and we have come here that we might see and know her in advance. She is very beautiful, and a truly respectable person, Giuseppo. I am pleased with the idea of this festival of the French cardinal. I think it will afford much business in our line."

CHAPTER XXV.

DIPLOMATIC QUARRELS.

In the palace of the French ambassador at Rome, Cardinal Bernis, there was an unusually busy movement to-day. From the kitchen-boys to the major-domo, all were in the most lively motion, in the most passionate activity. For this morning, while taking his chocolate, the cardinal had sent for his major-domo, and, quite contrary to the usual joviality of his manner, had very seriously and solemnly said to him: "Signor Brunelli, I to-day intrust you with a very important and responsible duty, that of making as splendid as possible the grand festival we are three days hence to give in honor of the Archduke Ferdinand. No pains must be spared, nothing must be wanting; the most luxurious richness, the most tasteful decoration, the most extravagant splendor must be exhibited. For this entertainment must excite the attention not only of Rome, but of all Europe; it must become the subject of conversation at all the courts, and, above all, it must cause the despair of all present ambassadorial housekeeping. I have very important diplomatic reasons for this. All Europe shall see how devoted France is to the empire of Austria, and what a good understanding subsists between the two courts. Therefore, Signor Brunelli, strain your inventive head, that it may on this occasion hit upon whatever is most distinguished and preëminent, for this must be an entertainment never before equalled. That is what I expect, what I demand of you; and if you satisfy my demands, it will give me pleasure to reward your zeal by a present of a hundred ducats."

Thus with solemn dignity spoke the cardinal, while sipping his chocolate; and Signor Brunelli had pledged himself by a solemn oath punctually to fulfil his master's commands, and to astonish Rome with an entertainment such as had never been recorded in the annals of diplomatic history.

With a proud step had Brunelli gone to his own private cabinet, where, having shut himself up, he had devoted several hours to serious meditation upon the deep plans presenting themselves to his mind. But Signor Brunelli had, in fact, a very experienced and inventive head, and the cardinal acted wisely in confiding in his major-domo and leaving to him the ordering of the entertainment.

He had now, with the sharp glance of a military commander, arranged his plan of battle, and felt perfectly sure of victory. He therefore rang for a servant, and commanded the attendance of the chief cook in the cabinet of the major-domo. Then with a gentleman-like listlessness he threw himself upon a divan and began to sip his coffee with the exact dignified deportment that had been displayed by his excellency the cardinal.

"Signor Gianettino," said he, to the entering cook, "I propose honoring you to-day with a very important and significant affair. I wish, on the day after to-morrow, to prepare an entertainment which in splendor and magnificence shall surpass any thing hitherto seen. You know that the major-domos of the other diplomatists have become my irreconcilable enemies through envy; they cannot forgive me for having more inventive faculties and better taste than any of them! We must bring these major-domos to despair, and with a gnashing of teeth they shall acknowledge that in all things I am their master. You, however, must aid me in this great work; in your hands, Signor Gianettino, lies a considerable part of my triumph and my laurels. For what does it help me, if the arrangements and decorations, if the whole establishment, are excellent, should there be a failure in the highest and most sublime part of the entertainment—in the food. The food, my dear sir, and a well-ordered table, is the gist of a festival, and should there be the least failure in that, the whole is profaned and desecrated, and must be covered with a mourning-veil. Take my words to heart, signor; let us have a table covered with food the mere odor of which shall set our first gourmets in ecstatic astonishment, while its judicious arrangement will give pleasure to the poetic mind! That is what I expect of you, and if you succeed in satisfying my requirements, I am ready to reward your exertions with fifty bottles of our best French wines."

Signor Gianettino returned his thanks with a pleasant, thoughtful smile, and with a majestic step repaired to his boudoir, where he was seen for a long time, walking back and forth in deep thought and with a wrinkled brow. Then, stepping to his writing-table, he sketched the plan of this inordinately great dinner, at first slowly and thoughtfully, and then with constantly more and more fire and enthusiasm, carried away by the greatness of the occasion, and animated by the importance of his mission and his calling.

Then, throwing aside the pen, and exhausted by so great an effort, he gently glided down upon the divan, at the same time ringing for a servant whom he directed to bring his breakfast and afterward to summon all the cooks and scullions to his cabinet. He then stretched himself with eminent grace upon the divan, as he had seen the major-domo do; with a serious thoughtfulness he sipped the glass of Malvoisie the servant had brought him, with sundry *pâtés* and rare *entremets*.

And they came, the cooks and scullions, they came in their white jackets, with their white aprons and snow-white caps; they came in solemn silence, fully impressed with the importance of the moment.

"Signors," said the chief cook, "it is

on a beautiful and sublime affair that I have assembled you here to-day. It concerns an increase of the fame and triumphs we have so many times gained over our diplomatic rivals, and an increase of the laurels we have won in the sacred realms of our art! I propose to prepare a banquet for to-morrow, and for that I require your support and aid, gentlemen. For what is the use of ever so good a plan of battle of a commander-in-chief, if his troops fail in courage and skill to carry out the plan of their general? Gentlemen, I doubt not your courage or skill! You will contend for the sake of the fame we have acquired and hitherto enjoyed without dispute, for the sake of the fame which the French *cuisine* has enjoyed for centuries, and which must be preserved until the end of all things! You will stand by me, gentlemen, in the praiseworthy effort to acquire new glory for France, by showing these little Austrian princes and these gentlemen diplomatists what wonderful things the French art of cookery can bring to pass. The plan is devised and sketched, and all that is now required is its execution. If this great work succeeds, then, gentlemen, you may feel assured of my eternal gratitude—a gratitude which I will prove to you by leaving all the remains of the dinner to your free use and sole benefit! Here is the plan, hasten to the work; I have assigned to each one the part he is to take in its accomplishment. Hasten, therefore! I however, by way of exception, will myself go to the market to-day and make the necessary purchases. On such an important occasion, no one, however highly placed, must decline labor and the faithful performance of duty. I go, therefore, and six of the kitchen-boys may follow me with their baskets."

Thus speaking, the chief cook, Signor Gianettino, took his hat and gold-headed cane to go to the market. Six kitchen-boys, armed with large baskets, followed him at a respectful distance.

At the great vegetable and fish market of Rome there was to-day a very unusual and extraordinary life and movement. There was a crowd and tumult, a roaring and screaming, a shouting and laughing, such as had not been heard for a long time. It was partly in consequence of the fact that the whole diplomatic corps had been for some days agitated with preparations for entertainments in honor of the Archduke Ferdinand, who had come to Rome to see the wonders of the holy city, and who could hardly find time and leisure for the festivities offered him. But for the tradesmen and dealers, for the country people in the vicinity of Rome, this presence of the Austrian prince was a happy circumstance; for these banquets and festivals scattered money among the people, and the dealers and honest country people could fearlessly raise their prices, as they were sure of a sale for their commodities. The cooks and servants of the diplomatists and cardinals were seen running hither and thither in busy haste, everywhere selecting the best, everywhere buying and cheapening.

But in one place in the market there was to-day an especial liveliness and activity among the crowd, and to that spot Signor Gianettino bent his steps.

He had seen the cook of the Spanish ambassador, the Duke of Grimaldi, among those collected there, and as this cook was one of his bitterest enemies and opponents, Signor Gianettino resolved to watch him, and, if possible, play him a trick. He therefore cautiously mingled with the crowd, and made a sign to his followers to keep at a distance from him.

It was certainly a very important affair with which the Spanish cook Don Bempo was occupied, as it concerned the purchase of a fish that a countryman had brought to the city, of such a monstrous size and weight that the like had never been seen there. It was the most remarkable specimen with which the Roman fish-market had ever been honored. But the lucky fisherman was fully aware of the extraordinary beauty of his fish, and in his arrogant pride demanded twenty ducats for it.

That was what troubled Don Bempo. Twenty ducats for one single fish, and the major-domo of the Spanish ambassador had urged upon him the most stringent economy; but he had, indeed, at the same time urged upon him to provide every thing as splendid as possible for the banquet which the Duke of Grimaldi was to give in honor of the Archduke Ferdinand; indeed, he had with an anxious sigh commanded him to outdo if possible the next day's feast of Cardinal Bernis, and to provide yet rarer and more costly viands than the French cook.

That was what Don Bempo was now considering, and what made him waver in his first determination not to buy the fish.

There was only this one gigantic fish in the market; and, if he bought it, Signor Gianettino, his enemy, of course could not possess it; the triumph of the day would then inure to the Spanish embassy, and Don Bempo would come off conqueror. That was indeed a very desirable object, but—twenty ducats was still an enormous price, and was not at all reconcilable with the recommended economy.

At any rate he dared not buy the fish without first consulting the major-domo of the duke.

"You will not, then, sell this fish for twelve ducats?" asked Don Bempo, just as Gianettino had unnoticedly approached. "Reflect, man, twelve ducats are a fortune—it is a princely payment!"

The fisherman contemptuously shook his head. "Rather than sell it for twelve ducats I would eat it myself," said he, "and invite my friends, these good Romans, as guests! Go, go, sublime Spanish Don, and buy gudgeons for your pair of miserable ducats! Such a fish as this is too dear for you; you Spanish gentlemen should buy gudgeons!"

"Bravo! bravo!" cried the laughing spectators. "Gudgeons for the Spanish gentlemen with high-nosed faces and empty pockets!"

Don Bempo blushed with anger and wounded pride. "I shall unquestionably buy this fish," said he, "for nothing is too dear for my master when the honor of our nation is to be upheld. But you must allow me time to go home and get the money from the major-domo. Keep the fish, therefore, so

...ong, and I will return with the twenty ducats for it."

And majestically Don Bempo made himself a path through the crowd, which laughingly stopped aside for him, shouting: "Gudgeons for the Spanish gentlemen! *Viva* Don Bempo, who pays twenty ducats for a fish!"

"He will certainly not come back," said the fisherman, shaking his head.

"He goes to buy gudgeons!" cried another.

"What will you bet that he returns to buy the fish?" said a third.

"He will not buy it!" interposed a fourth. "These Spaniards have no money; they are poor devils!"

"Who dares say that?" shrieked another, and now suddenly followed one of those quarrels which are so quickly excited on the least occasion among the passionate people of the south. There was much rage, abuse, and noise. How flashed the eyes, how shook the fists, what threats resounded there!

"Peace, my dear friends, be quiet I tell you!" cried the fisherman, with his stentorian voice. "See, there comes a new purchaser for my fish. Be quiet, and let us see how much France is disposed to offer us."

The disturbance subsided as suddenly as it had arisen, and all pressed nearer; all directed interrogating, curious, expectant glances at Signor Gianettino, who just at that moment approached with a proud and grave step, followed by the solemn train of six scullions with their baskets.

No one had before remarked him in the crowd, for they had been all eyes and ears for Don Bempo, and hence every one supposed he had only just then arrived.

The shrewd chief cook also assumed the appearance of having only accidentally passed that way without the intention of buying any thing.

But he suddenly stopped before the great fish as if astonished at its enormous size, and seemed to view it with admiration and delight.

"What a rare and splendid animal is this!" he finally exclaimed with animation. "Really, one must come to Rome to see such a wonder!"

"That is understood!" exultingly cried the bystanders, who had a reverence for the fishes of Rome.

"This is no niggard! *He* will not be so mean as to offer twelve ducats for such a miracle as this!"

"Twelve ducats!" cried Gianettino, folding his hands. "How can you think me so pitiful as to offer such a miserable sum for so noble a fish. No, truly, he must have a bold forehead who would offer so little money for this splendid animal!"

"Hear him! hear!" cried the people. "This is a learned man. He knows something of the value of rarities!"

"*Viva!* Long life to the French cook, *il grande ministro della cucina!*"

Gianettino bowed politely in response to the compliment, and then civilly asked the price of the fish.

The fisherman stood there with an expression of regretful sadness upon his face. "I fear it will be of little use to name the price!" said he, "the fish is as good as sold."

"Nevertheless, name the price!"

"Twenty ducats!"

"Twenty ducats!" exclaimed Gianettino, with an expression of the liveliest astonishment. "You jest, my friend! How can such a splendid animal be possibly sold for twenty ducats?"

"Hear! hear!" shouted the crowd. "He finds the price too low!"

"He is a real gentleman!"

"He will not buy gudgeons like the Spaniard!"

"In earnest, friend, tell me the price of this fish!" said Gianettino.

"I have demanded twenty ducats for it," sadly responded the fisherman, "and it is sold for that sum."

"Impossible! In that case it would not be lying here!" replied Gianettino. "Or has the man paid you the money, and now gone for a cart for the conveyance of the giant?"

"I have not yet been paid."

"The purchaser, then, has given you earnest money?"

"No, not even that. I have yet received nothing upon it."

"And you can pretend that you have sold this fish," cried Gianettino, "and that, too, for the ridiculously small sum of twenty ducats! Ah, you are a joker, my good man; you wish to excite in me a desire for this rare specimen, and therefore you say it is sold. But how can a fish that yet lies exposed for sale, and for which no one has made you a suitable offer, be already sold?"

And gravely approaching the giant of the waters, Gianettino laid his hand upon his head and solemnly said: "The fish is mine. I purchase it; you demand twenty ducats! But I shall give you what you ought to have, and what the creature is worth! I shall pay you six-and-thirty ducats for him!" *

The crowd, which had maintained an anxious and breathless silence during this negotiation, now broke out with a loud and exulting shout.

"That is a real nobleman!"

"*Evviva il ministro della cucina! Il grande Gianettino!*" *

"That is no parsimonious Spaniard! He is a French cavalier. He will buy no gudgeons, but will have the right Roman fish."

"Gentlemen," said Gianettino, modestly casting down his eyes, "I do not understand your praises, and it seems to me I only deal like a man of honor, as every one of you would do! This honest man taxes his wares too low; I give him what they are worth! That is all. If I acted otherwise I should not long remain in the service of the lofty and generous Cardinal Bernis! Justice and generosity, that is the first command of his excellency!"

"*Evviva* the French ambassador!"

"Praise and honor to Cardinal Bernis!"

And while the people were thus shouting, Gianettino, from his well-filled purse paid down the six-and-thirty ducats upon the fisherman's board. He then commanded his six attendant scullions to bear off the fish.

It was, indeed, a heavy work to place the enormous animal upon their baskets, but the active Romans cheerfully lent a hand, and when they had suc-

---

* Archenholz, "England and Italy," vol iv., p. 217.

ceeded in the difficult task, and the six youngsters bent under their heavy load, Signor Gianettino gravely put himself at the head of the train, and proudly gave the order: "Forward to the kitchen of his excellency Cardinal Bernis!"

At this moment a man was seen making his way through the crowd; thrusting right and left with his elbows, he incessantly pushed on, and, just as Signor Gianettino had fairly got his troop in motion, the man, who was no other than Don Bempo, succeeded in reaching the fisherman's table.

"Here, I bring you the twenty ducats," he proudly called out. "They will no longer say that the Spaniards buy gudgeons. The fish is mine! There are your twenty ducats!"

And, with a supercilious air, Don Bempo threw the money upon the table.

But just as proudly did the fisherman push back the money. "The fish is sold!" said he.

"Forward, march!" repeated Signor Gianettino his word of command. "Forward to the kitchen of his excellency Cardinal Bernis!"

And with solemn dignity the train began to move.

Don Bempo with a cry of rage rushed upon the fish.

"This fish is mine," he wildly cried, "I was the first to offer its price, I offered twenty ducats, and only went home to get the money!"

"And I," exclaimed Signor Gianettino, "I offered thirty-six ducats, and immediately paid the cash, as I always have money by me."

"It is Signor Gianettino, the cook of the French ambassador, and I am ruined!" groaned Don Bempo, staggering back.

"Yes, it is the cook of his excellency the cardinal!" cried the crowd.

"And the cardinal is an honorable man!"

"He is no Spanish niggard!"

"He does not haggle for a giant fish; he pays more than is demanded!"

"I hope," said Signor Gianettino to Don Bempo, who still convulsively grasped the fish, "that you will now take your hands from my property and leave me to go my way without further hinderance. It is not noble to lay hands on the goods of another, Don Bempo, and this fish is mine!"

"But this is contrary to all international law!" exclaimed the enraged Don Bempo. "You forget, signor, that you insult my master, that you insult Spain, by withholding from me by main force what I have purchased in the name of Spain."

"France will never stand second to Spain!" proudly responded Gianettino, "and where Spain *offers* twenty ducats, France *pays* six-and-thirty!— Forward, my youngsters! To the kitchen of the French ambassador!"

And urgently pushing back Don Bempo, Gianettino solemnly marched through the crowd with his retinue, the people readily making a path for him and cheering him as he went.

It was a brilliant triumph in the person of the chief cook of their ambassador, which the French celebrated to-day; it was a shameful defeat which Spain suffered to-day in the person of her ambassador's chief cook.

Proud and happy marched Signor Gianettino through the streets, accompanied by his gigantic fish, and followed by the shouts of a Roman mob.

Humiliated, with eyes cast down, with rage in his heart sneaked Don Bempo toward the Spanish ambassador's hotel, and long heard behind him the whistling, laughter, and cat-calls of the Roman people.

CHAPTER XXVI.

THE FISH FEUD.

CARDINAL BERNIS was in his boudoir. Before him lay the list of those persons whom he had invited to his entertainment of the next day, and he saw with proud satisfaction that all had accepted his invitation.

"I shall, then, have a brilliant and stately society to meet this Austrian archduke," said the well-contented cardinal to himself. "The *élite* of the nobility, all the cardinals and ambassadors, will make their appearance, and Austria will be compelled to acknowledge that France maintains the best understanding with all the European powers, and that she is not the less respected because the Marquise de Pompadour is in fact King of France."

"Ah, this good marquise," continued the cardinal, stretching himself comfortably upon his lounge and taking an open letter from the table, "this good marquise gives me in fact some cause for anxiety. She writes me here that France is in favor of the project of Portugal for the suppression of the order of the Jesuits, and I am so to inform the pope! This is a dangerous thing, marquise, and may possibly burn your tender fingers. The suppression of the Jesuits! Is not that to explode a powder-barrel in the midst of Europe, that may shatter all the states? No, no, it is foolhardiness, and I have not the courage to apply the match to this powder-barrel! I fear it may blow us all into the air."

And the cardinal began to read anew the letter of Madame de Pompadour which a French courier had brought him a few hours before.

"Ahem, that will be dangerous for the good father!" said he, shaking his head. "Austria also agrees to this magnificent plan of the Portuguese Minister Pombal, and I am inclined to think that this Austrian archduke has come to Rome only for the purpose of bringing to the pope the consent of the Empress Maria Theresa! Ha, ha! how singular! their chaste and virtuous Maria Theresa and our good Pompadour are both agreed in this matter, and in taking this course are both acting against their own will. The women love the Jesuits, these good fathers who furnish them with an excuse for every weakness, and hold a little back door open for every sin. That is very convenient for these good women! Yes, yes, the women—I think I know them."

And, smiling, the cardinal sank deeper into himself, dreaming of past, of charming times, when he had not yet counted sixty - five years. He dreamed of Venice, and of a beautiful nun he had loved there, and who for him had often left her cloister in the night-time, and, warm and glowing with passion, had come to him. He dreamed of those heavenly hours, where all pleasure and all happiness had been compressed into one blessed intoxication of bliss, where the chaste priestess of the Church had for him changed into a sparkling priestess of joy!

"Yes, that was long ago!" murmured the cardinal, as at length he awoke from his blissful dreams of the past.

"Those were beautiful times—I was then young and happy; I was then a man, and now—now am old; love has withered, and with it poesy! I am now nothing but a diplomatist."

There was a low knock at the door. The cardinal hastily but carefully returned the portrait of his beautiful nun to the secret drawer in his writing-table whence it had been taken, and bade the knocker to enter.

It was Brunelli, the major-domo of the cardinal, who came with a proud step, and face beaming with joy, to make a report of his plans and preparations for the morrow's entertainment.

"In the evening the park will be il-luminated with many thousand lamps, which will outshine the sun, so that the guests will there wander in a sea of light," said he, in closing his report.

The cardinal smiled, and with a stolen glance at the small box that contained the portrait of his beautiful nun, he said: "Spare some of the walks in the alleys from your sea of light, and leave them in a partial obscurity. A little duskiness is sometimes necessary for joy and happiness! But how is it with your *carte du diner?* What has Signor Gianettino to offer us? I hope he has has something very choice, for you know the cardinals like a good table, and my friend Duke Grimaldi has a high opinion of our cuisine."

"Ah, the Spanish ambassador, your excellency?" exclaimed Brunelli, contemptuously. "The Spanish ambassador knows nothing of the art of cookery, or he would not possibly be satisfied with his cook! He is a niggard, a poor fellow, of whom all Rome is speaking to-day, and laughing at him and his master, while they are praising you to the skies!"

And Signor Brunelli related to his listening master the whole story of the gigantic fish, and of the humiliation of the Spanish cook.

The cardinal listened with attention, and a dark cloud gradually gathered upon his thoughtful brow.

"That is a very unfortunate occurrence," said he, shaking his head, as Brunelli ended.

"But at least it was an occurrence in which France triumphed, your excellency," responded Brunelli.

"I much fear the Duke of Grimaldi

will do as you have done," said the cardinal; "he will confound my cook with France, and in his cook see all Spain insulted."

"Then your excellency is not satisfied?" asked Brunelli, with consternation. "The whole palace is full of jubilation; all the servants and lackeys and even the secretary of the legation are delighted with this divine affair!"

The cardinal paid no attention to these panegyrics of his major-domo, but thoughtfully paced the room with long strides.

"And you think Gianettino had the right of it?" at length he asked.

"He was entirely in the right, your excellency. Nothing had been paid for the fish, and Gianettino's right to purchase was perfect, and nobody could dispute it!"

"Well, when we are in the right, we must maintain our right," said the cardinal, after a pause, "and as the affair is known to all Rome, it must be fought through with *éclat!* The fish, in all its pride of greatness shall grace our table to-morrow!"

"We have no dish of sufficient size in which to serve it."

"Then let a new one be made," laughed the cardinal. "Take the measure of this Goliath, and hasten to the silversmith, that he may make a silver dish of the proper size. But see that it is completed by to-morrow morning, and that it is richly ornamented. If Rome has heard of the fish, so also must it hear of the dish. Hasten, therefore, Signor Brunelli, and see that all is done as I have ordered!"

"This is, in fact, a very diverting story," said the cardinal, laughing, when he was again alone. "We have here a monster fish which will probably swallow my friendship with the Duke of Grimaldi! Well, we shall see!"

The cardinal then rang for his bodyservant, whom he ordered to dress him.

"Court toilet?" asked the servant, astonished at being called to this service at so unusual an hour.

"No, house toilet!" said the cardinal. "I shall soon receive visitors."

The shrewd cardinal had not deceived himself! In a few minutes an equipage rolled into the court, and the footman announced his highness the Spanish ambassador, the Duke of Grimaldi.

"He is a thousand times welcome!" cried the cardinal, and as the door now opened and the Spanish duke entered, the cardinal advanced to receive him with open arms and a friendly smile.

"My dear, much-beloved friend, what a delightful surprise is this!" said the cardinal.

But the duke observed neither the open arms nor the pleasant smile, nor yet the friendly welcome of the cardinal. He strode forward with a serious, majestic *grandezza,* and placing himself directly before the cardinal, he solemnly asked: "Know you of the outrage which a servant of your house has inflicted on mine?"

"Of an outrage?" asked the cardinal, without embarrassment. "I have been told that your cook had a dispute with mine, because mine had bought a fish that was too dear for yours. That is all I know."

"Then they have not told you,"

thundered the duke, "that your servant, like an impudent street robber, has wrongfully seized my property. For that fish was mine, it belonged to the Spanish embassy, and therefore to Spain; and your servant has with outrageous insolence committed a trespass upon the property of a foreign power!"

"Did this fish, then, actually belong to the Spanish crown?" asked Bernis. "Was it already paid for, and legally yours?"

"It was not paid for, but was ordered, and my servant had gone home for the money."

"As long as it was not paid for, no one could have any claim upon it."

"You are, then, disposed to dispute the fish with me?" cried the duke.

"Should I dispute it," smilingly responded the cardinal, "that would be equivalent to a recognition of your right to it, which I have no idea of making. Besides, my friend, what does this quarrel of our cooks concern us, and what has Spain and France to do with these disputes of our servants? They may fight out their own quarrels with each other; let us give them leave to do so, and if they give each other bloody heads, very well, we will bind them up, that is all!"

"You take the affair with your usual practical indifference," said the duke with bitterness, "and I can only regret being compelled to look at it in a different light. The question here is not of a difficulty between our servants, but of an insult which Spain has received from France in the face of all Rome. Yes, all Rome has witnessed this insult, and these miserable Romans have even dared to dishonor us with irony and satire, and to mock and deride Spain, while they overload you with their praises!"

"The good Romans, as you know, are like children. This contest of our cooks has delighted them, and they shouted a *viva* to the conqueror. But I beg you not to forget that I have nothing at all to do with the victories of my cook."

"But I have something to do with the defeats of mine! Whoever insults my servant insults me; and whoever insults me, insults the kingdom I represent—insults Spain! It is therefore in the name of Spain that I come to demand satisfaction. Spain has a right to this fish! I demand my right, I demand the surrender of the fish!"

"If you take this matter in earnest," said the cardinal, "then am I sorry to be compelled also to be serious! If Spain can find offence in the fact that France has bought a fish which was too dear for the Spanish cook, I cannot see how I can here make satisfaction, as we cannot be taxed with any fault."

"You refuse me the fish, then?" exclaimed the duke, bursting with rage.

"As you say that all Rome knows of this affair and takes an interest in it, I cannot act otherwise. It must not have the appearance that France feels herself less great and powerful than Spain; that France pusillanimously yields when Spain makes an unjust demand!"

"That is to say, you wish to break off all friendly relations with us?"

"And can those relations be seriously endangered by this affair?" asked the cardinal, with vivacity. "Is it possible that this trifling misunderstanding between two servants can exercise an influence upon a long-cherished friendship and harmony of two powers whose relations, whether friendly or otherwise, may uphold or destroy the peace of Europe?"

"Honor is the first law of the Spaniard," proudly responded the duke, "and whoever wounds that can no longer be my friend! France has attacked the honor of Spain, and all Rome has chimed in with the insulting acclamations of France—all Rome knows the story of this fish!"

"Then let us show to these silly Romans that we both look upon the whole affair merely as a jest. When you tomorrow laughingly eat of this fish, the good Romans will feel ashamed of themselves and their childish conduct."

"You propose then, to-morrow, when the nobility of Rome, when all the diplomatists are assembled, to parade before them this fish which to-day sets all tongues in motion?" asked the duke, turning pale.

"The fish was bought for this dinner, and must be eaten!" said the cardinal, laughing.

"Then I regret that I cannot be present at this festival!" cried the duke, rising. "You cannot desire that I should be a witness to my own shame and your triumph. You are no Roman emperor, and I am no conquered hero compelled to appear in your triumphal train! I recall my consent, and shall not appear at your to-morrow's festival!"

"Reflect and consider this well!"

said the cardinal, almost sadly. "If you fail to appear to-morrow, when the whole diplomacy are assembled at my house for an official dinner, that will signify not only that the duke breaks with his old friend the cardinal, but also that Spain wishes to dissolve her friendly relations with France."

"Let it be so considered!" said the duke. "Better an open war than a clandestine defeat! Adieu, Sir Cardinal!"

And the duke made for the door. But the cardinal held him back.

"Have you reflected upon the consequences?" he asked. "You know what important negotiations at this moment occupy the Catholic courts. Of the abolition of the greatest and most powerful of orders, of the extirpation of the Jesuits, is the question. The pope is favorable to this idea of the Portuguese minister, Pombal, but he desires the coöperation of the other Catholic courts. Austria gives her consent, as do Sardinia and all the other Italian states; only the court of Spain has declared itself the friend and defender of the Jesuits, and for your sake has France hitherto remained passive on this most important question, and has affected not to hear the demands of her subjects; for your sake has France stifled her own convictions and joined in your support. Therefore, think well of what you are about to do! To break off your friendly relations with France, is to compel France to take sides against Spain; and if the powerful voice of France is heard against the Jesuits, the single voice of Spain will be powerless to uphold them."

"Well, then, let them go!" cried the duke. "What care I for the Jesuits when the defence of our honor is concerned? Sir Cardinal, farewell; however France may decide, Spain will never submit to her arrogance!"

The duke abruptly left the room, slamming the door after him.

Cardinal Bernis saw his departure with an expression of sadness.

"And such are the friendships of man," he murmured to himself; "the slightest offence is sufficient to destroy a friendship of many years. "Well, we must reconcile ourselves to it," he continued after a pause, "and, at all events, it has its very diverting side. For many months I have taken pains to support Grimaldi with the pope in his defence of the Jesuits, and now that celebrated order will be abolished because a French cook has bought a fish that was too dear for the Spanish cook! By what small influences are the destinies of mankind decided!

"But now I have not a moment to lose," continued the cardinal, rousing himself from his troubled thoughts. "Grimaldi has rendered it impossible for me longer to oppose the views of the Marquise de Pompadour; I must now give effect to the commands of my feminine sovereign, and announce to the pope the assent of France to his policy. To the pope, then, the letter of the marquise may make known the will of Louis!"

The cardinal hastily donned his official costume, and ordered his carriage for a visit to the Vatican.

10

CHAPTER XXVII.

POPE GANGANELLI (CLEMENT XIV).

Two men were walking up and down in the garden of the Quirinal, engaged in a lively discourse. One of them was an old man of more than sixty years. Long white locks waved about his forehead, falling like a halo on both sides of his cheeks. An infinite mildness and clearness looked out from his dreamy eyes, and a smile of infinite kindness played about his mouth, but so full of sorrow and resignation that it filled one's heart with sadness and his eyes with tears. His tall, herculean form was bent and shrunken; age had broken it, but could not take away that noble and dignified expression which distinguished that old man and involuntarily impelled every one to reverence and a sort of adoration. To his friends and admirers this old man seemed a super-terrestrial being, and often in their enthusiasm they called him their Saviour, the again-visible Son of God! The old man would smile at this, and say: "You are right in one respect, I am indeed a son of God, as you all are, but when you compare me with our Saviour, it can only be to the crucified. I am, indeed, a crucified person like Him, and have suffered many torments. But I have also overcome many."

And, when so speaking, there lay in his face an almost celestial clearness and joyfulness, which would impel one involuntarily to bow down before him, had he not been, as he was, the vicegerent of God upon earth, the Pope Ganganelli.

The man who was now walking with him formed a singular contrast with the mild, reverence-commanding appearance of the pope. He was a man of forty, with a wild, glowing-red face, whose eyes flashed with malice and rage, whose mouth gave evidence of sensuality and barbarity, and whose form was more appropriate for a Vulcan than a prince of the Church. And yet he was such, as was manifested by his dress, by the great cardinal's hat over his shoulder, and by the flashing cross of brilliants upon his breast. This cardinal was very well known, and whenever his name was mentioned it was with secret curses, with a sign of the cross, and a prayer to God for aid in avoiding him, the terror of Rome, the Cardinal Albani.

Sighing and reluctantly had the pope finally resolved to have the cardinal near his person, that he might attempt by mild and gentle persuasion to soften his stubborn disposition; but the cardinal had replied to all his gentle words only with a contemptuous shrug of the shoulders, with low murmured words, with a darkly-clouded brow.

"It is in no one's power to change and make a new being of himself," he finally said, in a harsh tone, as the pope continued his exhortations and representations. "You, my blessed father, cannot convert yourself into a monster such as you describe me; and I, Cardinal Albani, cannot attain to the sublime godliness which we all admire in your holiness. Every one must walk in his own path, taking especial care not to disturb others in theirs."

"But that is exactly what you do," gently replied Ganganelli. "All the streets of Rome bear witness to it. Did you not yesterday, in one of these streets, with force and arms rescue a bandit from the hands of justice, and with your murderous dagger take the life of the servant of the law?"

"They wanted to lead one of my servants to death, who had done nothing more than obey my commands," vehemently responded the cardinal. "I liberated him from their hands as was natural; and if some of the *sbirri* were killed in the encounter, that was their fault. Why did they not voluntarily give up their prisoner and then run away?"

"And was it really your command that this bandit fulfilled?" asked the pope, shuddering. "You know he killed a young nobleman, the pride and hope of his family, and was caught in the act, which he did not attempt to deny?"

"That young nobleman had mocked and made a laughing-stock of me in a public company," calmly replied the cardinal; "hence it was natural that he must die. Revenge is the first duty of man, and whoever neglects to take it is dishonored!"

"And such men dare to call themselves Christians!" exclaimed Ganganelli, with uplifted arms—"and such men call themselves priests of the religion of love!"

"I am a priest of love!" said Albani.

"But of what love?" responded the pope, with an appearance of agitation—"the priest of a wild, beastly passion, of a rough animal inclination. You know nothing of the soft and silent love that ennobles the heart and strengthens it for holy resolutions; which inculcates virtue and decency, and lifts up the eyes to heaven—of that love which is full of consolation and blessed hope, and desires nothing for itself."

"God save me from such a love!" said the cardinal, crossing himself. "When I love, I desire much, and of virtue and perfection there is, thank God, no question."

"Repent, amend, Francesco," said the pope. "I promised your uncle, the very worthy Cardinal Alessandro Albani, once more to attempt the course of mildness, and exhort you to return to the path of virtue. Ah, could you have seen the poor old man, with tears streaming from his blind eyes—tears of sorrow for you, whom he called his lost son!

"My uncle did very wrong so to weep," said the cardinal. "Blind as he was he yet kept a mistress.* How, then, can he wonder that I, who can see, kept several? Two eyes see more than none; that is natural!"

* Joseph Gorani's "Secret Memoirs of the Italian Courts," vol. ii., p. 131.

"But do you, then, so wholly forget your solemn oath of chastity and virtue?" excitedly exclaimed the pope. "Look upon the cross that covers your breast, and fall upon your knees to implore the pardon of God."

"This cross was laid upon my breast when I was yet a boy," gloomily responded the cardinal; "the fetters were attached to me before I had the strength to rend them; my will was not asked when this stone was laid upon my breast! Now I ask not about your will when I seek, under this weight, to breathe freely as a man! And, thank God, this weight has not crushed my heart—my heart, that yet glows with youthful freshness, and in which love has found a lurking-hole which your cross cannot fill up. And in this lurking-hole now dwells a charming, a wonderful woman, whom Rome calls the queen of song, and whom I call the queen of beauty and love! All the world adjudges her the crown of poesy, and only you refuse it to her."

"Again this old complaint!" said the pope, with a slight contraction of his brow. "You again speak of her—"

"Of Corilla," interposed the cardinal—"yes, of Corilla I speak, of that heavenly woman whom all the world admires; to whose beautiful verses philosophers and poets listen with breathless delight, and who well deserves that you should reward her as a queen by bestowing upon her the poetic crown!"

"I crown a Corilla!" mockingly exclaimed the pope. "Shall a Corilla desecrate the spot hallowed by the feet of Tasso and Petrarch? No, I say, no; when art becomes the plaything of a courtesan, then may the sacred Muses veil their heads and mourn in silence, but they must not degrade themselves by throwing away the crown which the best and noblest would give their heart's blood to obtain. This Corilla may bribe you poor earthly fools with her smiles and amorous verses, but she will not be able to deceive the Muses!"

"You refuse me, then, the crowning of the renowned improvisatrice Corilla?" asked the cardinal, with painfully suppressed rage.

"I refuse it!"

"And why, then, did you send for me?" exclaimed the cardinal with vehemence. "Was it merely to mock me?"

"It was for the purpose of warning you, my son!" mildly responded the pope. "For even the greatest forbearance must at length come to an end; and when I am compelled to forget that you are Alessandro Albani's nephew, I shall then only have to remember that you are the criminal Francesco Albani, whom all the world condemns, and whom I must judge! Repent and reform, my son, while there is yet time; and, above all things, renounce this love, which heaps new disgrace upon your family and overwhelms your relatives with sorrow and anxiety!"

"Renounce Corilla!" cried the cardinal. "I tell you I love her, I adore her, this heavenly, beautiful woman! How can you ask me to renounce her?"

"Nevertheless I do demand it," said the pope with solemnity, "demand it in the name of your father, in the name of God, against whose holy laws you have sinned—you, His consecrated priest."

"But that is an impossibility!" passionately exclaimed Francesco. "One must bear a heart of stone in his bosom to require it; and that you can do so, only proves that you have never known what it is to love!"

"And that I can do so, should prove to you that I have indeed known it, my son!" sadly responded the pope.

"Whoever has known love, knows that there can be no renunciation!"

"And whoever has known love, can renounce!" exclaimed the pope, with animation. "Listen to me, my son, and may the sad story of a short happiness and long expiation serve you as a warning example! You think I cannot have known love? Ah, I tell you I have experienced all its joys and all its sorrows—that in the intoxication of rapture I once forgot my vows, my duties, my holy resolutions, and, doubly criminal, I also taught her whom I loved to forget her own sacred duties and consent to sin! Ah, you call me a saint, and yet I have been the most abject of sinners! Under this Franciscan vesture beat a tempestuous, fiery heart, that derided God and His laws, a heart that would have given my soul to the evil one, had he promised to give me in exchange the possession of my beloved! She was beautiful, and of a heavenly disposition; and hence, when she passed through the aisles of the church, with her slight fairy form, her angelic face veiled by her long dark locks, her eyes beaming with love and pleasure, a heavenly smile playing about her lips—ah, when she thus passed through the church, her feet scarcely touching the floor, then I, who awaited her in the confessional, felt myself nearly frantic with ecstasy, my brain turned, my eyes darkened, there was a buzzing in my ears, and I attempted to implore the aid and support of God."

"You should have appealed to Cupid!" said the cardinal, laughing. "In such a case aid could come only from the god of ancient Rome, not of the modern!"

The old man noticed not his words. Wholly absorbed in his reminiscences, he listened only to the voice of his own breast, saw only the form of the beautiful woman he had once so dearly loved!

"God listened not to my fervent prayers," he continued, with a sigh, "or perhaps my stormily-beating heart heard not the voice of God, because I listened only to her; because with intoxicated senses I was listening to the modest, childishly-pure confession which she, kneeling in the confessional, was whispering in my ears; because I felt her breath upon my cheeks and in every trembling nerve of my being. And one day, overcome by his glowing passion, the monk so far forgot his sworn duty as to confess his immodest and insane love for the wife of another man!"

"Ah, she was, then, married?" remarked the cardinal.

"Yes, she was married, sold by her own parents, sacrificed at the shrine of mammon, married to a man whom she did not and could not love, and who pursued her with an insane jealousy. Ah, she suffered and suffered with the uncomplaining calmness of an angel. And I, did I not also suffer? We wept together, we complained together, until our hearts at length forgot complaining, and an unspeakable, a terrible happiness, made us forget our troubles. I had forgotten all—my God, my clerical vows; she also had forgotten all—her husband, her vow of fidelity; and if a thought of these things sometimes intruded upon our moments of happiness, it only caused us to plunge into new delights, and to lull ourselves anew into a blessed forgetfulness!"

"And the good, jealous husband remarked nothing?" asked the cardinal.

"He remarked nothing! He loved me, he confided in me, he called me his friend; and when he was compelled to take a long journey, he confided to me his house and his wife, establishing me as the guard of her virtue!"

The cardinal broke out into loud laughter. "These good husbands," said he—"they are all alike to a hair. Every one has a friend in whom he confides, and it is that very friend who betrays him. They must all fulfil their destinies, these good husbands! Relate further, holy father! Your story is very entertaining. I am curious to hear the end!"

"The end was terrible, replete with horror and shame," said the pope. "We lived blessed days, heavenly nights; oh, we were so happy that we hardly had a thought for our criminality, but only for our love. One night there was a knocking at the closed door of the house, and we shudderingly recognized the voice of the husband demanding admission."

"And you were not at all in a situation to grant it to him," laughingly interposed the cardinal. "He might perhaps have been not a little astonished, this good husband, that you watched by night as well as by day the temple of his wedded happiness."

"With tears of anguish and terror she conjured me to fly, to save her from the derision of the world and the anger of her husband; she led me to a secret stairway, and I, like a madman pursued by the furies, was hastening to descend, when my foot slipped and I fell down the stairs with a loud clattering noise. I felt the blood oozing from my breast and pouring from my mouth in a warm stream—my limbs pained me frightfully—but I picked myself up and with extremest suffering fled to my cloister, when, having reached my cell, I fell senseless. A long illness now confined me to my bed and tortured my body with frightful pains; but far more frightful were the tortures of my soul, more frightful the voices that day and night whispered to me of my crime and guiltiness! My conscience was fully awakened, it spoke to me in a voice of thunder, and like a worm I turned upon my bed of pain, imploring of God a little mercy for the torments that burned my brain! This time God permitted Himself to be found by me; I heard his voice, saying: 'Go and repent, and thy sins shall be forgiven thee! Shake off the sinfulness that weighs upon thy head, and peace will return to thy bosom.' I heard this voice of God, and wept with repentant sorrow. I vowed to obey and reconcile myself to God by renouncing my love and never again seeing its object! It was a great sacrifice, but God demanded it, and I obeyed!"

"That is, this sickness had restored you from intoxication to sobriety; you were tired of your mistress!"

"I had, perhaps, never loved her more warmly, more intensely, than in those dreadful hours when I was struggling with my poor tortured heart and imploring God for strength to renounce her and separate myself from her forever. But God was merciful and aided my weakness with His own strength. Letters came from her, and I had the cruel courage to read them; I had condemned myself to do it as an expiation, and while I read her soft complainings, her love-sorrows, I felt in my heart the same sorrows, the same disconsolate wretchedness; tears streamed from my eyes, and I flayed my breast with my nails in utter despair! Ah, at such moments how often did I forget God and my repentance; how often did I press those letters to my lips and call my beloved by the tenderest names; my whole soul, my whole being flew to her, and, forgetting all, all, I wanted to rush to her presence, fall down at her feet, and be blessed only through her, even if my eternal salvation were thereby lost! But what was it, what then restrained my feet, what suddenly arrested those words of insane passion upon my lips and irresistibly drew me down upon my knees to pray? It was God, who then announced Himself to me—God, who called me to himself —God, who finally gave me strength to withstand my love and always leave her letters unanswered until they finally ceased to come—until her complaints, which, however, had consoled me, were no longer heard! The sacrifice was made, God accepted it, my sin was expiated, and I was glad, for my heart was forever broken, and never, since then, has a smile of happiness played upon my lips. But in my soul has it become tranquil and serene, God dwells there, and within me is a peace known only to those who have struggled and overcome, who have expiated their sins with a free will and flayed breast."

"And your beloved, what became of her?" asked the cardinal. "Did she pardon your treason, and console herself in the arms of another?"

"In the arms of death!" said Ganganelli, with a low voice. "My silence and my apparent forgetfulness of her broke her heart; she died of grief, but she died like a saint, and her last words were: 'May God forgive him, as I do! I curse him not, but bless him, rather; for through him am I released from the burden of this life, and all sorrow is overcome!' She therefore died in the belief of my unfaithfulness; she did, indeed, pardon me, but yet she believed me a faithless betrayer! And the consciousness of this was to me a new torment and a penance which I shall suffer forever and ever! This is the story of my love," continued Ganganelli, after a short silence. "I have truly related it to you as it is.* May you, my son, learn from it that, when we wish to do right, we can always succeed, in spite of our own hearts and sinful natures, and that with God's help we can overcome all and suffer all. You see that I have loved, and nevertheless had strength to renounce. But

* Joseph Gorani, "Secret Memoirs," vol. ii., p. 26.

it was God who gave me this strength, God alone! Turn you, also, to God; pray to Him to destroy in you your sinful love; and, if you implore Him with the right words, and with the right fervor, then will God be near you with His strength, and in the pains of renunciation will He purify your soul, preparing it for virtue and all that is good!"

"And do you call that virtue?" asked the cardinal. "May Heaven preserve me from so cruel a virtue! Do you call it serving God when this virtue makes you the murderer of your beloved, and, more savage than a wild beast, deaf to the amorous complaints of a woman whom you led into love and sin, whose virtue you sacrificed to your lust, and whom you afterward deserted because, as you say, God called to yourself, but really only, because satiated, you no longer desired her. Your faithlessness cunningly clothes itself in the mantle of godliness, nothing further. No, no, holy father of Christendom, I envy you not this virtue which has made you the murderer of God's noblest work. That is a sacrilege committed in the holy temple of nature. Go your way, and think yourself great in your bloodthirsty, murderous virtue! You will not convert me to it. Let me still remain a sinner—it at least will not lead me to murder the woman I love, and provide for her torment and suffering, instead of the promised pleasure. Believe me, Corilla has never yet cursed me, nor have her fine eyes ever shed a tear of sorrow on my account. You have made your beloved an unwilling saint and martyr—possibly that may have been very sublime, and the angels may have wept or rejoiced over it. I have lavished upon my beloved ones nothing but earthly happiness. I have not made them saints, but only happy children of this world; and even when they have ceased to love me, they ·have always continued to call me their friend, and blessed me for making them rich and happy. You have set a crown of thorns upon the head of your beloved, I would bind a laurel-crown upon the beautiful brow of my Corilla, which will not wound her head, and will not cause her to die of grief. You are not willing to aid me in this, my work? You refuse me this laurel-wreath because you have only martyr-crowns to dispose of? Very well, holy father of Christendom, I will nevertheless compel you to comply with my wishes, and you shall have no peace in your holy city from my mad tricks until you promise me to crown the great improvisatrice in the capitol. Until then, *addio*, holy father of Christendom. You will not see me again in the Vatican or Quirinal, but all Rome shall ring with news of me!"

With a slight salutation, and without waiting for an answer from the pope, the cardinal departed with hasty steps, and soon his herculean form disappeared in the shadow of the pine and olive trees. But his loud and scornful laugh long resounded in the distance.

CHAPTER XXVIII.

THE POPE'S RECREATION HOUR.

THE pope followed his retreating form with a glance of sadness and a shake of the head.

"He is past help," murmured he; "he runs to his ruin, and the voice of warning is unheeded. But how, if he should happen to be right? How, if he with his worldly wisdom and his theory of earthly happiness, should be more conformable to the will of God than we with our virtue and our doctrine of renunciation? Ah, yes, the world is so beautiful, it seems made entirely for pleasure and enjoyment, and yet men wander through it with tearful eyes, disregarding its beauty, and refusing to share its pleasures. All, except man, is free on earth. He alone lies in constraining bands, and his heart bleeds while all creation rejoices. No, no, that cannot be; every individual does what he can to render mankind free and happy, and I also will do my part. God has laid great power in my hand, and I will use it so long as it is mine."

Thus speaking, the pope left the garden, and hastened up to his study.

"Signor Galiandro," said he, to his private secretary, "did you not speak to me to-day of several petitions received, in which people begged for dispensations from monk and cloister vows?"

Signor Galiandro smilingly rummaged among a mass of papers that covered the pope's writing-table.

"In the last four weeks some fifty such petitions have been received. Since your holiness has released several monks and nuns from their vows, all these pious brides of Christ and these consecrated priests seem to have tired of their cloister-life, and long to be out in the world again."

"Whoever does not freely and willingly remain in the house of the Lord, we will not retain them," said Ganganelli. "Compelled service of the Lord is no service, and the prayer of the lips without the concurrence of the heart is null! Give me all these petitions, that I may grant them! The love of the world is awakened in these monks and nuns, and we will give back to the world what belongs to the world. With their resisting and struggling hearts they will make but bad priests and nuns; perhaps it will be better for them to become founders of families. And they who honestly do their duty, equally serve God, whether they are in a cloister or in the bosoms of their families." *

The pope seated himself at his writ-

* Ganganelli's own words.—See Gorani, vol. ii., p. 41.

ing-table, and after having carefully examined all the petitions for dispensations, signed his consent, and smilingly handed them back to his secretary.

"I hope we have here made some people happy," said he, rising, "and therefore it may, perhaps, be allowed us also to be happy in our own way for a quarter of an hour."

He lightly touched the silver bell suspended over his writing-table, and at the immediately opened door appeared the pleasant and well-nourished face of brother Lorenzo, the Franciscan monk, who performed the whole service of the pope.

"Lorenzo," said Ganganelli, with a smile, "let us go down into the poultry-yard. You must show me the young chickens of which you told me yesterday. And hear, would it be asking too much to beg of you to bring my dinner into the garden?"

"I would that you could ask too much," said brother Lorenzo, waddling after his master, who was descending the stairs leading to the court-yard. "I really wish, your holiness, that it were asking too much, for then your dinner would at least be a little more desirable and heavier to transport! Was such a thing ever heard of? the father of Christianity keeps a table like that of the poorest begging monk, and is satisfied with milk, fruit, bread, and vegetables, while the fattest of capons and ducks are crammed in vain for him, and his cellar is replete with the most generous wines."

"Well, well, scold not," said Ganganelli, smiling; "have we not for years felt ourselves well in the Franciscan cloister, it never once occurring to us to wish ourselves better off? Why should I now quit the habits of years, and accustom myself to other usages? When I was yet a Franciscan monk, I always had, thanks to our simple manner of living, a very healthy stomach, and would you have me spoil it now, merely because I have become pope? It has always remained the same human body, Lorenzo, and all the rest is only falsehood and fraud! How few years is it since you and I were in the cloister, and you served the poor Franciscan monk as a lay brother! You then called me brother Clement, and they all did the same, and now you no longer call me brother, but holy father! How can your brother of yesterday be your father of to-day? We are here alone, Lorenzo; nobody sees or hears us. We would for once cease to be holy father, and for a quarter of an hour become again brother Clement."

"Ahem! it was not so bad there," simpered Lorenzo. "It was yet very pleasant in our dear cloister, and I often think, brother, that you were far happier then than now, when every one falls upon his knees to kiss your slipper. It must be very dull to be always holy, always so great and sublime, and always revered and adored!"

"Therefore let us go to our ducks and hens," said the pope. "The people have made a bugbear of me, before which they fall upon the earth. But the good animals, who understand nothing of these things, they cackle and grunt, and gabble at me, as if I were nothing but a common gooseherd and by no means the sainted father of Christendom! Come, come to my dear brutes, who are so frank and sincere that they cackle and gabble directly in my face as soon as their beaks and snouts are grown. They are not so humble and devoted, so adoring and cringing, as these men who prostrate themselves before me with humble and hypocritical devotion, but who secretly curse me and wish my death, that there may be a change in the papacy! Come, come, to our honest geese!"

Brother Lorenzo handed to the pope the willow basket filled with corn and green leaves, and both, with hasty steps and laughing faces, betook themselves to the poultry-yard; the ducks and geese fluttered to them with a noisy gabbling as soon as they caught sight of the provender-basket, and Ganganelli laughingly said: "It seems as if I were here in the conclave, and listening to the contention of the cardinals as they quarrel about the choice of a new pope. Lorenzo, I should well like to know who will succeed me in the sacred chair and hold the keys of St. Peter! That will be a stormy conclave!—Be quiet, my dear ducks and geese! Indeed, you are in the right, I forgot my duty! Well, well, I will give you your food now—here it is!"

And the pope with full hands strewed the corn among the impatiently gabbling geese, and heartily laughed at the eagerness with which they threw themselves upon it.

"And is it not with men as with these dear animals?" said he, laughing; "When one satisfies them with food, they become silent, mild, and gentle. Princes should always remember that,

and before all things satiate their subjects with food, if they would have a tranquil and unopposed government! Ah, that reminds me of our own poor, Lorenzo! Many petitions have been received, much misery has been described, and many heart-rending complaints have been made to me!"

"That is because they know you are always giving and would rather suffer want yourself than refuse gifts to others," growled Lorenzo. "Hardly half the month is past, and we are already near the end of our means!"

"Already?" exclaimed the pope, with alarm. "And I believe I yet need much money. There is a father of fourteen children who has fallen from a scaffolding and broken both legs. We must care for him, Lorenzo; the children must not want for bread!"

"That is understood, that is Christian duty," said Lorenzo, eagerly. "Give me the address, I will go to him yet to-day! And how much money shall I take with me?"

"Well, I thought," timidly responded Ganganelli, that five scudi would not be too much!"

Lorenzo compassionately shrugged his shoulders. "You can never learn the value of money," said he; "I am now to take *five* scudi to these *fourteen* children."

"Is it not enough?" joyfully asked Ganganelli. "Well, I thank God that you are so disposed! I only feared you would refuse me so much, because my treasury, as you say, is already empty. But if we yet have something left, give more, much more! At least a hundred scudi, Lorenzo!"

"That is always the way with you; from extreme to extreme!" grumbled Lorenzo. "First too little, then too much! I shall take to them twenty scudi, and that will be sufficient!"

"Give them thirty," begged Ganganelli, "do you hear, thirty, brother Lorenzo. Thirty scudi is yet a very small sum!"

"Ah, what do you know about money?" answered Lorenzo, laughing; "these geese here understand the matter better than you, brother Clement."

"Well, it is for that reason I have made you my cashier," laughed Ganganelli. "A prince will always be well advised when he chooses a sensible and well-instructed servant for that which he does not understand himself. To acknowledge his ignorance on the proper occasion does honor to a prince, and procures him more respect than if he sought to give himself the appearance of knowing and understanding every thing. Come, Lorenzo, let us go into the garden; you see that these fowls care nothing for us now; as they are satiated, they despise our provender. Come, let us go farther!"

"Yes, into the garden!" exclaimed Lorenzo, with a mysterious smile. "Come, brother Clement, I have prepared a little surprise for you there! Come and see it!"

And the two old men turned their steps toward the garden.

"Follow me," said Lorenzo, preceding the pope, and leading him to a more solitary and better screened part of the garden. "Now stoop a little and creep through here, and then we are at the place."

The pope carefully followed the directions of his leader, and worked his way through the obstruction of the myrtle-bushes until he arrived at a small circular place, in the centre of which, shaded by tall olive-trees, was a turf-seat surrounded by tendrils of ivy, and before which was a small table of wood yet retaining its natural covering of bark.

"See, this is my surprise!" said Lorenzo.

Ganganelli stood silent and motionless, with folded hands. A deep emotion was visible in his gentle mien, and tears rolled slowly down over his cheeks.

"Well, is it not well copied, and true to nature?" asked Lorenzo, whose eyes beamed with satisfaction.

"My favorite spot in the garden of the Franciscan convent!" said Ganganelli in a tone trembling with emotion. "Yes, yes, Lorenzo, you have represented it exactly, you know well enough what gives me pleasure! Accept my thanks, my dear good brother."

And, while giving his hand to the monk, his eye wandered with gentle delight over the place, with its beautiful trees and green reposing bank, and thoughtfully rested upon each individual object.

"So was it," he murmured low, "precisely so; yes, yes, in this place have I passed my fairest and most precious hours; what have I not thought and dreamed as a youth and as a man, how many wishes, how many hopes have there thrilled my bosom, and how few of them have been realized!"

"But one thing has been realized,"

said Lorenzo, "greater than all you could have dreamed or hoped! Who would ever have thought it possible that the poor, unknown Franciscan monk would become the greatest and most sublime prince in the whole world, the father of all Christendom? That is, indeed, a happiness that brother Clement, upon his grass-bank in the Franciscan convent, could never have expected!"

"You, then, consider it a happiness," said Ganganelli, slowly letting himself down upon the grass-bank. "Yes, yes, such are you good human beings! wherever there is a little bit of show, a little bit of outward splendor, you immediately conclude that there is great happiness. This proves that you see only the outward form, paying no regard to what is concealed under that form, and which is often very bitter. Believe me, Lorenzo, in these times there is no very great happiness in being pope and the so-called father of Christendom. The princes have become very troublesome and disobedient children; they are no longer willing to recognize our paternal authority, and if the holy father does not manifest a complaisant friendliness toward these refractory princely children, and wink at their independence, they will renounce the whole connection and quit the paternal mansion. We should then, indeed, be the holy father of Christendom, but no longer have any children under the paternal authority! For having so expressed myself, I shall never be pardoned by the cardinals and princes of the Church; it has made them my deadly enemies, and yet it is

with these principles alone that I have succeeded in bringing the refractory Portuguese court again under my paternal control!

"But here in this pleasant place let us dismiss such unpleasant thoughts," the pope more cheerfully continued, after a pause. "Here I will forget that I am pope; here I will never be any thing more than brother Clement, of the Franciscan convent, nor shall the cares and troubles of the pope, nor his holiness or infallibility, accompany him to this dear quiet place. Here I will be only a man, and forgetting my cramping highness and my forced splendor, will here right humanly enjoy the sun and this soft green grass, and in deep draughts inhale this sweet balsamic air. Ah, how happy one may yet be if he can for a moment escape from the envelope of dignity by which he is kept a chrysalis, and freely exercise the butterfly wings of manhood! And hear me for once, brother Lorenzo, so very human has your pope here become, that he feels a right fresh human appetite. If all here is as it used to be at the convent, then must you have something to appease my hunger."

Brother Lorenzo nodded with a sly smile. Stepping to the side of the grassy bank, and slipping aside a small door concealed by the grass, he disclosed a walled excavation, filled with fruits and pastry.

"I see you have forgotten nothing!" joyfully exclaimed Ganganelli, taking some of the fragrant fruit which Lorenzo tendered him. "Ah, you make me very happy, Lorenzo."

Saying this, he threw his arm around

Lorenzo's neck, and silently pressed him to his bosom.

Brother Lorenzo was equally silent, but he no longer laughed; his usually cheerful face assumed a wonderfully clear and pleased expression, and two large tears rolled down over his cheek —but they were tears of joy.

CHAPTER XXIX.

A DEATH-SENTENCE.

An approaching bustling, a vehement calling and screaming, disturbed the two old men. It was Lorenzo who was called, and he quickly glided through the bushes to look after the cause of this disturbance. But soon he returned with a melancholy face and depressed mien.

"Brother Clement," said he, "it is already all over with our enjoyment, which has been so great for me that I forgot to remind you that the pope cannot neglect the hour in which he gives audience. That hour has now come, and your anteroom is already filled with princes and prelates."

"And yet you speak of the great happiness of being pope," said Ganganelli, rising with a sigh from the grassy bank. "I am not allowed an hour for recreation, and yet people think—but no," said Ganganelli, interrupting himself and laughing, "we should not be ungrateful, and it would be ungrateful for me now to complain. If I have not had an hour for recreation, well, I have had half an hour and even that is much!"

And, beckoning to brother Lorenzo to follow him, the pope crept through the bushes that separated the place from the more frequented part of the garden.

As he then walked up the grand alley, his face and his whole form assumed a very different appearance. The mild friendliness had vanished from his features, pride and dignity were now expressed by them, and his tall, erect form had in it something noble and imposing; it was no longer the stooping form of age, but only that of a somewhat elderly hero. The brother Clement had been transformed into the prince of the Church, who was about to receive his vassals.

They now saw a tall, manly form hastening down the alley directly toward the pope.

"Who is it?" asked Ganganelli, half turning toward Lorenzo, who was following him.

"It is Juan Angelo Braschi, the former treasurer, to whom you yesterday sent the cardinal's hat."

"Ah, the beautiful Braschi," sadly

murmured Ganganelli. "The beloved of the favorite of my nephew, of the Cardinal Rezzonico. Ah, how bad the world is!"

In fact, he whom Ganganelli called the "beautiful" Braschi, well deserved that epithet. No nobler or more plastic beauty was to be seen; no face that more reminded one of the divine beauty of ancient sculpture, no form that could be called a better counterfeit of the Belvedere Apollo. And it was this beauty which liberal Nature had imparted to him as its noblest gift, which helped Juan Angelo Braschi, the son of a poor nobleman of Cesara, to his good fortune, his highest offices and dignities. Not for his merits, but solely for his beauty, did the women bestow upon him their love; and as among these women there were some who exercised an important influence upon powerful cardinals, Braschi had quickly mounted from step to step, crowding aside those who had nothing but their merits and services to speak for them.

With a free and noble demeanor, Braschi now approached the pope, who remained standing at some distance awaiting him, with a calm and proud self-possession. Braschi dropped upon one knee, and, pressing the hem of the pope's garment to his lips, said:

"Pardon me, most holy father, that I have ventured to seek you here. But my lively gratitude would not be longer restrained. It impelled me toward you with the wings of the wind. I must be the first to fall at your feet to stammer out to you my inexpressible thanks."

Proudly nodding his head, the pope motioned him to rise.

"It is well," said he, "and you have lent your gratitude an abundance of words. It is true you were only treasurer, and I have permitted you to take a great step in making you a cardinal. But remember, my lord cardinal, that I have promoted you only because I wished to take from you the office of treasurer, as I need a man for that post whose honesty no one could call in question!" *

Thus speaking, he passed on with a ceremonious salutation, leaving the new cardinal rooted to the earth with terror, his beautiful brow distorted with rage.

"He shall expiate that," muttered Braschi, gnashing his teeth, as the pope slowly pursued his way. "By the Eternal, the proud Franciscan shall expiate that! Ah, the day will come when he will fully remember these words!"

Meantime, Ganganelli wandered calmly on, followed by his faithful Lorenzo, with a smile of joy at this dismissal and humiliation of the proud and handsome Cardinal Braschi.

The pope suddenly stopped, and, turning to Lorenzo, said:

"What a strange thought has passed through my head! I have made this miserable coxcomb Braschi a cardinal because he was not honest enough for a treasurer, but in doing so I have paved the way for him to the papal throne! Would it not be strange, Lorenzo, if I have thus myself provided my successor? His dishonesty and intriguing disposition has made him a cardinal. Why can

* The pope's own words.—See Gorani, vol. ii., p. 27.

it not also make him a pope? The world is indeed so strange!" *

"What dreams those are," murmured Lorenzo, shrugging his shoulders; "the idea that a Braschi could be the successor of the noble Ganganelli!"

Many cardinals and princes of the Church, many noblemen and foreign ambassadors, were assembled in the pope's audience-room, and as Ganganelli entered, they all received him with joyful acclamations, and humbly fell upon their knees before the head of the Church, the vicegerent of God, who, with solemn majesty, bestowed upon them his blessing, and then condescendingly conversed with them. That was a ceremony to which the pope was obliged to subject himself once a week, and which he reckoned as not one of the least of the troubles attendant upon his exalted position. Hence he was well pleased when this hour was over, and he at length was relieved of the presence of all these eulogistic and flattering gentlemen.

Only Cardinal Bernis had remained behind, and to him Ganganelli, giving him his hand, and drawing a deep breath, said:

"What a mass of false and hypocritical phrases we have again been obliged to swallow! These cardinals have the impudence to speak to me of their love

and veneration; they do not hesitate so to lie with the same lips which to-day have already pronounced blessings and pious words of edification! But let us forget these hypocrites. Business is over, and it is kind of you to come and chat with me for one little hour. You know I love you very much, my good friend Bernis, although you do pay homage to the heathen divinities, and, as a real renegade, have constituted yourself a priest of the muses."

"Ah, you speak of my youthful sins," said the cardinal, smiling. "They are long since past, and sleep with my youthful happiness."

"That must be a wide bed which enables them all to find place side by side," responded Ganganelli, laughing, and holding up his forefinger threateningly to the cardinal.

"But what is that you are drawing from your breast-pocket with such an important air?"

"A letter from the Marquise de Pompadour, holy father," seriously replied the cardinal—"a letter in which I am commanded to communicate to you, the father of Christendom, the acquiescence of France in your proposed abolition of the order of the Jesuits. Here is a private letter addressed to me by the marquise, and here the official letter signed by King Louis, which is destined for your holiness."

The pope took the papers, and while he was reading them his face turned deadly pale, and a dark cloud gathered upon his brow.

"France also acquiesces," said he, when he had finished the reading. "How is it, then—were you not your

* Juan Angelo Braschi, whom Pope Clement XIV. made a cardinal, was in fact Ganganelli's successor, and took possession of the papal chair as Pius VI. He was chosen after a very stormy conclave, and indeed the different parties voted for him on the ground that he belonged to no party, and because they thought he was so very much occupied with his own beauty that he would think of nothing else, and, while occupied with the care of his face, would leave the cares of state to others.

self against the abolition of the order, and were you not in accordance with the Spanish ambassador, your friend of many years?"

"This friendship of many years is to-day destroyed by a fish, and drives us a helpless wreck upon the wildly-rolling waves," said the cardinal, shrugging his shoulders.

Ganganelli paid no attention to him. Serious and thoughtful, he walked up and down the room, while his heaven-ward-directed eye seemed to address a great and all-important question to the Being there above, which received no answer.

"I clearly see how it will be," finally murmured the pope, as if talking to himself. "I shall complete the work I have begun—it is God Himself who has opened the way for it, but this way will at the same time lead me to my grave."

"What dark thoughts are these?" said Bernis, approaching him. "This bold and high-hearted resolution will not bring you death, but fame and im-mortality."

"It will at least lead me to immortal-ity," said the pope, with a faint smile. "The dead are all immortal. But think not so little of me as to suppose I would now timidly shrink from doing that which I have once recognized as right and necessary. Only there are necessi-ties of a very painful and dreadful kind. Such a necessity is war. And is it not a war that I commence, and does it not involve the destruction of all those thousands who call themselves the fol-lowers of Loyola, and belong to the So-ciety of Jesus? Ah, believe me, this Society of Jesus is a hydra, and we shall never succeed in entirely extirpating it. I may now cleave the head with my sword, and with the same blow I may separate my own head from my body; but a day will come when the head of this hydra will have grown again, and when it will rise from the dead with renewed vitality, while I shall be mouldering in my grave. Say not, therefore, that I know not how to destroy them, and if you do say it, at least add that I lacked not the will, but that I gave for it my own life."

Thus speaking, the pope slightly nod-ded an adieu to the cardinal, and with-drew into his study, the door of which he carefully closed after him.

There was he long heard to walk the room with measured steps. Then all was still. No one ventured to disturb him. Hours passed. Lorenzo, with a fearful presentiment, knelt before the door. He laid his ear to the keyhole and tried to listen. All was still with-in, nothing stirred. At length he ven-tured to call the pope's name—at first low and tremulously, then louder and more anxiously, and as no answer was received, he at last ventured to open the door.

At his writing-table sat the pope; his face deadly pale, with staring eyes and great drops of perspiration on his fore-head. Immovable sat he there, his right hand, which held a pen, resting on a parchment lying upon the table before him.

Like an image of wax, so stiff, so mo-tionless was he, that Lorenzo, shudder-ing, made the sign of the cross upon his brow. Then, noiselessly advancing, he timidly and anxiously touched the pope's shoulder. Ganganelli shuddered, and a slight trembling pervaded his members; he then drew a long breath, and, casting a dull glance at his faithful friend, said:

"Lorenzo, let my coffin be ordered, and pray for my soul. I have just now signed my own death-sentence. See, there it lies. I have signed the decree abolishing the order of the Jesuits! I must therefore die, Lorenzo. It is all over and past with our shady place and our recreations. My murderers are already prowling around me, for I tell you I have myself signed my death-sentence!" *

---

* The pope's own words.—See Gorani, vol. ii., p. 41.

CHAPTER XXX.

THE FESTIVAL OF CARDINAL BERNIS.

AND this day of the festival had finally come. With what joyful impatience, with what anxious desire, had Natalie looked forward to it—how had she importuned her friend, Count Paulo, with questions about Cardinal Bernis, about the people she would meet there, about the manners and usages with which she would have to conform!

"I am anxious and fearful," said she, with amiable modesty; "they will find occasion to laugh at me, and you will be compelled to blush for me, Paulo. But you must tell these wise men and great ladies that it is my very first appearance in society, and that they must have consideration for the awkwardness and ineptitude of a poor child who knows nothing of the world, its forms, or its laws."

"For you no excuse will be necessary," responded Paulo, pressing the delicate tips of her fingers to his lips.

"Only be quite yourself, perfectly true and open, inoffensive and cheerful! Forget that you are in an assemblage; imagine yourself to be in our garden, under the trees and among the flowers, and speak to people as you speak to your trees and flowers."

"But will the people give me as true and cordial answers as my trees and flowers?" asked Natalie, thoughtfully.

"They will say to you more beautiful and more flattering things," said Paulo, smiling. "But now, Natalie, it is time to be thinking of your toilet. See, the sun is already sinking behind the pines, and the sky begins to redden! The time to go will soon arrive, and your first triumph awaits you!"

"Oh, it will not have long to wait," said Natalie, laughing, and, light and graceful as a gazelle, she tripped to the house.

Count Paulo gazed after her with a melancholy rapture. "And I am to leave this angel," thought he, "to lose the brightest and noblest jewel of my life, and drive myself out of paradise. And wherefore all this? Perhaps to chase a phantom that will never become a reality, to follow a chimera which may be only a meteor that dances before me and dissolves into mist when I think to reach it? No, no, the world is not worth so much that one should sell himself and his soul's happiness for its splendor and its greatness. Natalie herself shall decide. Loves she me, and is she satisfied with the quiet circumscribed existence that I can henceforth only offer her, then away, ye vain dreams and ye proud desires for greatness; then shall I be, if not the greatest, certainly the happiest of human beings!"

It was a wonderfully brilliant festival that Cardinal Bernis had to-day prepared for his guests—a festival hitherto unequalled in Rome. The walls were decorated with garlands and festoons of flowers, the flaming candelabras among which found their reflection in the tall Venetian mirrors that rose in their golden frames from the floor to the ceilings; and in the corners of the rooms were niches, here furnished with orange-trees, and there with heavy silk curtains, behind which were grottoes adorned with shells, in the midst of which were fountains where splashed waters rendered fragrant by oil of roses and other essences. And ever-new surprises, new grottoes and groves in those rich halls offered themselves to the eyes of the beholders. Now one suddenly found himself in a quiet boudoir lighted only by a solitary lamp, where the most artistic engravings and the rarest drawings were spread out upon a table; then again one entered a hall sparkling with a thousand lights and resounding with music, where the gayly-dressed crowd undulated in mazy waves; then again grottoes opened here and there, or one stepped out through the open doors into the garden where one could enjoy the balsamic coolness of the evening in walks brilliantly lighted with colored lamps, or listen to the music of performers concealed in the shrubbery, or, again, fleeing from the throng and the lights, seek a resting-place upon some grassy bank or under some myrtle-bush, whether for solitary musing or for encircling in sweet and silent familiarity, the waist of some chosen fair one who, understanding the stolen glance, had strayed here unnoticed.

But the central point of the festival was the monstrous gigantic hall which the cardinal had caused to be erected in the centre of the garden expressly for this occasion. The walls of muslin and flowers were held together by more than a hundred gilded pillars, the girandoles attached to each of which diffused a sea of light. Silken carpets covered the floor, and the *plafond* of this gigantic hall was formed by the thousand-starred arch of heaven. Here, also, niches and grottoes were everywhere to be found; in them one could, in the midst of the constantly moving and noisy crowd, enjoy quiet and repose.

Only one of these niches was inaccessible, as it appears, to the company, and yet it was precisely this which excited the curiosity of all, and which all, whispering, approached, anxious to get a peep behind the closed thick silken curtains, before which two richly gallooned servants of the cardinal walked back and forth with solemn earnestness, but respectfully requesting every one to comply with the cardinal's wishes and not approach the mysterious drapery, but await his own time for the solution of the enigma! A few steps led up to this closed and covered niche; these steps were strewed with roses, that was plainly seen; but, to what did these steps lead, and what was thus carefully concealed?

A precious surprise, certainly, for it was the forte of the cardinal to prepare surprises for the agreeable entertainment of his guests. The ladies and gentlemen, the cardinals and princes of the Church, crowded around him begging for an explanation of the mystery, a disclosure of the secret.

"I am myself uninitiated," said Cardinal Bernis, laughing; "some divinity may have taken a seat there, or perhaps it is a sphinx which will from thence give us the solution of her enigma. But let us see what belated guests are now coming to us."

And the cardinal with zealous precipitation approached the principal entrance to the hall, the *portières* of which had just been drawn aside, and behind was seen Natalie at the hand of Paulo.

As if blinded by the sudden flood of light, she stood for a moment still, a purple glow flushing her delicate cheeks, and clinging to Paulo's arm, she whispered: "Protect me, Paulo, I am so frightened by this crowd!"

Just at that moment the doorkeeper cried with a loud voice: "Princess Natalie Tartaroff and Count Paulo!"

At the sound of these strange names all glanced toward the door, and all flaming, curious, prying eyes were fixed with astonishment and admiration upon the young maiden.

But Natalie did not remark it. She glanced at Paulo with a glad smile, and a proud happiness beamed from her features. She had, then, a name; she was no longer an abandoned, nameless orphan. At length the enigma of her birth was solved, and what she had so often prayed for, Count Paulo had vouchsafed her as a surprise to-day.

He had at the same time announced her name to herself and the world, and she not only had a name, but she was a princess; she took a rank in the company, and Count Paulo and Carlo had no reason to be ashamed of her. But where was Carlo? At the thought of him this feeling of effervescing pride vanished from the young maiden's heart; she even forgot that she was a princess, to remember only that Carlo, her music-teacher, had promised her to be present at this festival, and to wonder that she could not discover him in this gay and confused assemblage.

She did not remark that, since her appearance, a deep stillness had supervened in the hall, that all eyes were upon her, that people secretly whispered to each other, and gave utterance to murmured expressions of astonishment and delight; she saw not how the beauties here and there turned pale and indignantly bit their proud lips; she saw not how the eyes of the men glowed and flashed, and what eagerly-lusting glances the cardinals and princes of the Church cast upon her.

She was so unconstrained, this charming child, she knew not how handsome she was! But she was to-day of a wonderfully touching beauty. Like a white and delicate lily stood she there in the heavy white satin robe that enveloped her graceful form, and the brilliants that adorned her hair, neck, and arms, shone and sparkled like sunlighted dew-drops in the calyx of the flower. So beautiful was she that even Cardinal Bernis stood speechless and as if blinded before her, finding no expression for his joyful surprise and astonishment.

"Oh," at length he smilingly said, with a low bow, "I shall have to quarrel with Count Paulo! He promised us the presence of a mortal woman, and now he leads into our circle a divinity who must look down upon us poor human beings with a smile of contempt."

Natalie smiled. "I know," said she, with her clear, sweet, childish voice—"I know that Cardinal Bernis is a poet, and therefore it will not be very difficult for him to change a young maiden into a divinity. Nor is this the first time he has done so! I remember a lovely poem of his, the complaint of a shepherd, who considers the object of his love a divinity because she is so beautiful, and at last she proves to be no divinity, but, on the contrary, a regular little quarrelsome wrangler who has nothing beautiful about her but her hands and face! Take care, cardinal, that it does not prove with you and me

as with the shepherd in your charming poem!"

She said that with such childish ingenuousness, and in so cheerful and jesting a tone, that the cardinal listened to her as if intoxicated, and with unconcealed admiration he looked into that delicate, childlishly pure face, over which no trace of sorrow nor any sigh of care had ever yet passed.

Without answering, he took her arm, and, beckoning Count Paulo to his side, led the princess to the circle of ladies.

Behind those closed curtains that still concealed the mysterious niche, it had meanwhile become stirring. Busy servants hastened hither and thither, lighting the lamps and arranging the festoons and draperies. It seems they had here erected a little stage, and the large wall-picture that formed the background of this stage bore the appearance of a decoration. A side-curtain, serving as a partition, formed a second room, which seemed destined for a sort of greenroom, in the centre of which was a large and well-lighted mirror, and before it stood a young woman regarding herself with the greatest attention, here plucking at her dress and there arranging her train or an ornament. She was evidently the one who was to appear upon the stage; her costume betrayed it! It was not the fashionable costume of the day, such as was worn by the distinguished ladies of Roman society; it was an ideal Greek dress that seemed to have been made for the purpose of displaying and rendering yet more voluptuous and enticing the great beauty of the wearer.

She was very beautiful, this woman,

with her sparkling black eyes, and dark shining hair which had been gathered into a Grecian knot behind—beautiful, with the laurel-wreath resting upon her high forehead—beautiful, in the transparent Grecian robe which only so far concealed the luxuriant forms of her full figure as to allow them to be divined—beautiful, with those full, round, and entirely uncovered arms with their jewelled bracelets—beautiful, with her graceful neck, her fully-exposed, naked shoulders, and her voluptuously swelling bosom.

She was, in her appearance, a Greek, only her face was not Grecian. It was wanting in the noble forms, the still cheerfulness and repose of Grecian beauty, modest even in its voluptuousness. It was only the face of a sensual and passionate Roman woman, and no Lais would have ventured such a smile as played upon the dark-red lips of this Roman woman, or such glowing glances as she shot like arrows from her dark eyes.

Standing before the glass she viewed herself, her lips murmuring low words, occasionally turning her eyes from the mirror to the little table standing near it, upon which lay several open books.

What murmured she, and what read she in those books? Singular! she was uttering single, isolated, unconnected words, which had nothing in common with each other but the sound of melody ;—they were rhymes, but without connection or sense, without inward mental correlation.

"So," she now said to herself, with a satisfied smile, "I am now perfectly armed and prepared. All these rhymes of Tasso and Petrarch are now implanted in my mind and ready for use, and I have not to fear embarrassment in repeating any of them. Ah, they shall admire me, these good Romans ; I will animate and inflame them, and excite all my enamored cardinals to such an ecstasy that they must finally prevail upon the silly, obstinate old pope against his own will, to fulfil my only desire. I will attain my end, even if I am compelled to pawn my honor and my salvation for it! Bah! honor, what can honor be to a woman? Beauty is our honor, further nothing! And fair, it seems to me, I yet am! And if I am fair," she more glowingly continued, after a pause, "how comes it that Carlo has ceased to love me? Ah, the false one, to betray and desert me when I love him most!"

A dark flush of anger now overspread her cheeks, and, threateningly raising her hands, with compressed lips she continued : "And to desert me for another woman—me, the pride and delight of all Rome—me whom all the princes and cardinals worship! Ah, while thousands lie at my feet, imploring for a glance or a smile, this little, unknown singer dares to scorn me and deride my love!"

"And why should he not dare it?" asked a voice behind her, and the face of a young man became visible.

"Carlo!" she cried, hastening to meet him with outspread arms.

He almost ungently checked her. "You forget," said he, "that this little, insignificant, and unknown singer loves you no longer, Corilla! Grant, then, henceforth, to the thousands who languish at your feet, a few of your enticing smiles and glowing glances—I have nothing against it, and am not at all jealous!"

"But you should be!" cried she, stamping her feet with rage. "I tell you I will not suffer you to leave me; I will be loved by you, and no one shall you dare to look at, and no one shall you dare to love, but me alone."

Carlo broke out into a scornful laugh, and then seriously and proudly said: "I am a Neapolitan, and with us men do not allow themselves to be constrained to love, and no woman there dares utter the command, 'Thou shalt love me!'—I will not, Signora Corilla!"

"You will not!" screamed she, gnashing her teeth. "Then woe to you and to her!"

"I fear no serpents!" said Carlo, laughing, "and if an adder attempts to sting me, I tread it under foot!"

"But fear at least for her you love!" she threateningly said. "Oh, you think I shall not be able to discover this secret love of yours, and not spy out this new divinity to whom you have consecrated your heart? Tremble therefore now, for I know her! I know the garden in which she lives, and there is a place in the wall just opposite her favorite seat; whoever knows that place and possesses a steady hand and a sharp dagger will know how to hurl it so as to pierce her bosom."

Carlo felt a deadly terror, he felt his heart stand still, but he collected himself and said, with a contemptuous smile: "Cardinal Francesco Albani indeed possesses among his *bravi* many such skilful hands, and surely it will not require many of your highly-prized glances to induce him to favor you with the loan of one of them."

The signora slightly bit her lips. "You mock me," she almost sadly said, "and yet you should remember that it is only love that makes me so savage and fills my heart with a thirst for vengeance! Carlo, I so warmly love you!"

And the beautiful, glowing woman humbly and imploringly bent before her beloved.

The latter laughingly said: "How well you know how to say that—with what variations and modulations! I yesterday heard you say the same to Cardinal Albani; to be sure, it sounded a little different, but not less warm and glowing!"

"You know why I do that!" said she. "He is an enamored fool, whom I would win with tender words that I may make him my instrument. You know the object for which I strive, and which I must attain at any price! Ah, Carlo, when once they have crowned me in the capitol, then, I am sure, you will be compelled to love me again!"

"Never again!" he harshly and roughly said.

"Is that your last word?" shrieked she, with flashing eyes and the wild rage of a tigress.

"It is my last word!"

She flew to him like a mad person, seized his hands and fixedly stared him in the face.

"Ungrateful!" said she, gnashing her teeth. "Is it thus you reward my love, is this your return for all I have done for you? Can you forget that it was I who withdrew you from poverty and baseness? What were you but a poor, unnoticed singer in the streets, on whom people bestowed scanty alms? Was it not I who rescued you from that shame, and clothed you and gave you a home? Was it not I who gave you a name and procured you consideration and respect by making you my singer and companion, and allowing you to play upon the harp at my improvisations? How, has not all Rome admired you when you sang the canzones I wrote for you, thereby procuring you honor and respectability, and making you a popular man from a low beggar? Go, you cannot leave me, for you are my creature, my property!"

He wildly thrust her aside, and his eyes flashed with indignation. "Signora," said he, his lips tremulous with rage, "you have rent the last band that bound me to you, and in twitting me of your benefits you have annihilated them! We now have nothing in common with each other, except perhaps mutual hatred, and that, I hope, will have a longer duration than our love!"

And Carlo turned toward the door. Corilla rushed after him with an exclamation of terror.

"You will leave me now!" cried she, with anguish, "now, in this hour when you are so indispensable to me? now, when I am to celebrate a new triumph before this notable assembly? when all eyes are expectantly turned to the curtain behind which I am to appear? No, no, Carlo, from compassion remain with me only one hour, only this evening!"

Carlo smiled contemptuously. "I will remain," said he, "for I have promised *her* that she shall hear you!"

"She has therefore come?" cried Corilla, with an outburst of joy.

"She is now here," he laconically said.

Corilla no longer listened to him, she walked back and forth with a triumphant mien, a cruel, malicious smile playing upon her lips.

At this moment there was a slight knock at the door, which was opened, and a man who appeared upon the threshold glanced into the room with a grinning laugh.

Corilla gave him a sign, and, at the same time pointed at Carlo, who, having turned his back toward her, seemed to have no suspicion of what was occurring behind him. But he saw it, nevertheless, in the tall mirror that stood in the middle of the room; he saw Corilla make signs of intelligence with that man who was in the livery of Cardinal Francesco Albani; he saw the man make answer with his fingers, and then draw forth a dagger, which he threateningly swung over his head.

Oh, Carlo had very well understood what that man said, as he also did that language of the fingers, the much-used language of the Romans and Neapolitans.

The man had said: "She is here, that beautiful lady! She can no longer escape us!"

"You will strike her?" had Corilla asked.

The man had swung the dagger over his head and held up two fingers of his right hand. That signified: "In two hours she will be dead."

" Good! you shall be satisfied with me," had been Corilla's answer.

The door was again closed. Corilla turned smiling to Carlo, her former rancor seemed to have vanished; she was in high spirits.

" Carlo," said she, " how good you are not to leave me! Let us now begin. I feel myself glowing with inspiration. Ah, I shall enrapture these good Romans, I think! "

" How long will this improvisation last? " Carlo gruffly asked

" Well, one or two hours, according to the delight we give our public."

" If this farce continues longer than an hour and a half, I shall throw down my harp and go away," said Carlo, in a tone of severity. " I swear it to you by the spirit of my mother! Remember it; I shall show you the time every quarter of an hour."

" You are a tyrant," said she, laughing. " But I suppose I must submit. Give, therefore, the signal that we are ready."

CHAPTER XXXI.

THE IMPROVISATRICE.

ALL the guests of the cardinal were assembled in the gigantic hall, and all eyes were anxiously bent upon the mysterious curtain, which still remained closed.

Now resounded a little bell, and Cardinal Bernis smilingly turned to Natalie, who sat by his side.

" I think this mystery is about to be unveiled," said he.

" And I am quite anxious about it," said the young maiden, gracefully laying her hand upon her heart. " My heart beats as violently as if a mystery were about to be unveiled in my own breast. Do you believe in presentiments, Sir Cardinal? "

Bernis had not time to answer her. Just at that moment the curtain drew up, a general " Ah! " of admiration was heard, and, suddenly carried away by their feelings, the whole audience broke into extravagant and long-enduring applause, crying and shouting, " *Evviva Corilla! l'improvisatrice Corilla!* "

And in fact it was an admirable picture which was there presented to the audience. Those flower-strewed steps led up to an altar, upon the centre of which, between wreaths of flowers, shot up two dark-red flames. Against that altar leaned, exalted and august as a Grecian priestess, the improvisatrice Corilla. Her eyes raised to the heavens, her features lighted up with a rosy glow by the red flames, her half-raised right arm resting upon an urn, while her left arm was stretched upward toward heaven, she thus resembled an inspired priestess, just receiving a message from on high, listening with ecstasy, with suppressed breath and parted lips, to the voice of the Deity, and forgetting the world in a blissful intoxication, she seemed about to take her flight to the empyrean!

And while Corilla, as if absorbed in spiritual contemplation, continued to stand immovable there, began the low notes of a harp, which, gradually becoming fuller and stronger, at length resounded in powerfully-rushing and exultant tones. From Corilla all eyes were now turned upon Carlo, who, in the light dress of a Greek youth, his harp upon his arm, was leaning against a pomegranate tree placed in the background of the stage, and with his pale, serious face, with his noble, manly features, formed a beautiful contrast to the inspired and love-beaming priestess Corilla.

Natalie, feeling something like a slight puncture in her heart, involuntarily carried her hand to her bosom. It was a strange, a wonderful feeling, which stirred within her, partly partaking of joy at seeing and hearing her friend Carlo, as people were murmuring praises of his beauty, and of his great skill upon the harp, and partly a feeling of painful emotion. She knew not why, but as her glance met his, it quickly turned toward Corilla, and quite sadly she said to herself: "She is much handsomer than I!"

Carlo now opened his lips, and to a beautifully simple melody he sweetly sang an introductory song, as it were to prepare the audience for the coming solemnity. Having finished this, two lovely *amourettes* came forward, with silver vases in their hands, and hastened down the steps to the audience, politely requesting them to furnish themes for the great improvisatrice Corilla.

Then, returning to the altar, they threw into the urn the small scraps of paper on which the guests had proposed themes. The harp again resounded, and with a solemn earnestness, her face and glance still directed upward, Corilla drew one of the little strips of paper from the urn. Accident, or perhaps her own dexterity, had favored her.

"Sappho's lament before throwing herself from the rocks"—that was the theme proposed.

Corilla's face immediately took an expression of sadness; her eyes flashed with an unnatural fire; her previously raised arm fell powerless by her side; her head, like a broken rose, sank upon her breast; her other hand convulsively grasped the urn, and in this position she in fact resembled an abandoned mourner, weeping over the ashes of her lost happiness. She was now the repudiated and forsaken one who, ready to resign her life, was brooding upon thoughts of death. And while her face took this expression, and she, staring upon the earth before her, seemed to be meditating upon irremediable fate, thought Corilla: "This is a charming theme which the good Cardinal Albani has thrown into the urn for me. I found it directly by the small pin which, according to his promise, he inserted in the paper. This cardinal is an agreeable imp, and I must give him a kiss for his complaisance. Besides, the Tasso rhyme will here be the most appropriate!"

Again she directed her gaze, with a gloomy expression, toward the heavens, and with a violently heaving bosom, with feverishly flitting breath, she began the lament of Sappho. Now like rattling thunder, now like the gentle breathings of the flute, rolled this sweet and picturesque language of Italy from her lips—like music sounded those full, artistic rhymes, of which but few of the hearers had the least suspicion that they came from Tasso. To improvise in the Italian language is an easy and a grateful task! What wonder, then, that Corilla acquitted herself so charmingly? The audience paid no attention to the thoughts expressed; they asked not after the quintessence; they were satisfied with the agreeable sound, without inquiring into the sense of her words; it was their melody which was admired. They listened not for the thought, but only for the rhyme, and with ecstatic smiles and admiring glances they nodded to each other when, thanks to the studies which Corilla had made in Tasso, Marino, and Ariosto, she seemed of herself to find rhymes for the most difficult words.

An immense storm of applause resounded when she ended; and as if awakening from an intoxicating ecstasy, Corilla glanced around with an expression of astonishment on her features; she looked around as if she knew not whence she came, and in what strange surroundings she now found herself.

After a short pause, which Carlo filled out with his harp, she again put her hand into the urn and drew out a new theme; again the inspiration seemed to pass over her, and the holy Whitsuntide of her muse to be renewed. Constantly more and more stormily resounded the plaudits of her hearers; it was like a continued thunder of enthusiasm, a real salvo of joy. It animated Corilla to new improvisations; she again and again recurred to the urn, drawing forth new themes, and seemed to be absolutely inexhaustible.

"It is now enough," whispered Carlo, just as she had drawn forth a new theme. "You have but a quarter of an hour left!"

"Only this theme yet," she begged in a low tone. "It is a very happy one, it will win for me the hearts of all these cardinals and gentlemen!"

"Yet a quarter of an hour, and then your time is up," said he. "Remember my oath, I shall keep my word!"

An inexplicable anxiety, a tormenting uneasiness, came over him; he had hardly strength and recollection sufficient to enable him to accompany Corilla, who was discussing in verse the question, "Which Rome was the happiest, ancient or modern?"

Carlo's eyes, fixed and motionless, rested upon Natalie; it fearfully alarmed him not to be near her, not to be able to watch every one of her steps, every one of her motions; it seemed to him as if he saw that savage man with his naked dagger lurking near her! And she, was she not pale as a lily; seemed she not, in that white robe, to be already the bride of death?

"I must hasten to her, I must protect her or die!" thought he, and, with a threatening glance at Corilla, he showed her the hour. Corilla read in the expression of his face that he was in earnest with his threat, and as if her inspiration lent wings to her words, she spoke on as in a storm of inward agitation, and with words of fire she decided that modern Rome was the happiest, as she had the holy father of Christendom, her pope, and his cardinals!

The applause, the general delight, was now unbounded; cardinals were to be seen weeping with enthusiasm and joy; others with heartfelt emotion were showering words of blessing upon the improvisatrice, and all pressed toward the tribune in order to accompany her down the steps and in among the company.

A sudden thought of rescue had like a flash of lightning arisen in Carlo's soul.

"Natalie must first be completely separated from this society, and then I will seek this man and render him incapable of mischief!" thought he.

By main strength he made himself a path through the crowd surrounding Corilla, and now stood near Cardinal Bernis, at whose side still remained Natalie and Count Paulo.

"You have struck the lyre like an Apollo," exclaimed the cardinal to the singer.

Carlo bowed with a smile, and hastily said: "And are you ignorant, your eminence, that a much greater poetess and improvisatrice than our Corilla is in your society?"

The cardinal smilingly threatened him with his finger. "Poor Carlo, has it already come to this?" said he. "You are jealous of our delight in Corilla, and would lessen her fame, that you may make her more your own!"

"I speak the truth," said Carlo; "a poetess is among us whom the muses themselves have consecrated, an improvisatrice, not of human composition, but by the grace of God, to whom the angels whisper the rhymes, and the muses the ideas!"

"And who, then, is this divinely-gifted artist, this consecrated daughter of the muses?" wonderingly asked the cardinal.

Carlo indicated Natalie, and bowed to the ground before her.

"Princess Tartaroff?" asked the cardinal, with astonishment.

"That she is a princess, I know not," said Carlo, "but I am quite certain she is a poetess!"

What was it that at this moment stirred the soul of the young maiden? She now felt a pride, a blessed joy, and yet had she previously felt so sad at Corilla's triumph! It seemed as if enthusiasm raised its wings in her, as if the word, the right word, pressed to her lips, as if she must utter in song her rejoicings and lamentings for her simultaneously felt pleasures and pains! A pure and genuine child of Nature, she felt in herself the natural impulse to pour out in words, tones, and even in tears, what agitated her soul, and to which she was unable to give a name.

Cardinal Bernis had first turned imploringly to Count Paulo, praying for his permission to invite the young princess to surprise and delight the company with some of her improvisations. Others, overhearing this, mingled in the conversation, and added their requests to those of the cardinal; and, the feeling becoming general, the requests for an improvisation became universal and pressing; people, momentarily forgetting the great and celebrated improvisatrice Corilla, with a feverish curiosity turned to the new and unknown star. Corilla stood almost alone —only Cardinal Albani remaining by her side; but his tender words were not competent to appease the violent storm of jealousy that raged in her soul.

The solicitations of the curious Romans became constantly more urgent, and Count Paulo, unable longer to resist them, finally consented to leave the decision to his ward, the young princess herself.

And Natalie? She was so real and ingenuous a child of Nature, that she felt no timidity in the presence of this crowd; she was so full of faith and confidence, so full of trust and human love. She thought, "Why should I not give a little pleasure to these good people who approach me with such warm sympathies? And why should I tremble before them? Did not Paulo tell me that I should feel as if I were in my garden, and it was only my trees and flowers that were looking at me with human faces? Well, then, I will so think and feel, and speak only to my dear trees and flowers!"

Beckoning Carlo with a charming smile, guided by his hand, she hastily ascended the steps. And as they saw her there upon the stage, this delicate, lovely maiden—as they looked upon her spiritual maiden beauty, with the childlike expression of her noble features, with eyes that beamed with pleasure and inspiration—there arose such a storm of applause that Natalie slightly trembled, and with a sweet smile she said to Carlo: "The people here are much more boisterous than the zephyrs in our garden, but they are not so melodious, and it almost saddens the heart!"

Cardinal Bernis now approached with the silver vase. On this occasion he had taken it upon himself to collect the themes, and with a respectful bow he handed them to the princess. With a gracious smile she took one of the papers and unfolded it. The subject given was, "Longing for home."

That was a theme well calculated to inspire Natalie, and to reawaken in her all her longings, sorrows, loves, and remembrances. She suddenly felt something like a cold shudder in her heart, and, glancing around with a feeling of solitude and desertion, she saw nothing but curious faces and strange, staring eyes! She, also, was repudiated and homeless, and an excessive longing for the distant unknown home of her childhood now took possession of her.

Perhaps Carlo had read her thoughts upon her brow; low and plaintive melodies poured from his harp, as it were the rustling murmurs of far-off remembrances, the sighing and sobbing of a yearning heart. And Natalie, carried away by these tones, forgetful of all around her, mindful only of the happiness of her childhood and of the lady she had so dearly loved, began to sing.

Of what she said and what she sang she was unconscious. She stood there as if elevated by inward inspiration; her eye flashed as she stared into the far distance, and the images she saw there caused her to smile and weep at the same time; all the glow, all the child-like purity of her soul, came in words from her lips in a stream of inspiration, of painful ecstasy!

She saw nothing, heard nothing! She saw not the ladies weeping with emotion, not the rapturous glances of the men; she had entirely forgotten all those strange, unknown people; and when the constantly increasing storm of applause finally reminded her of them, it was all over with her inspiration—the words died upon her lips, and with a sad smile she hastened the conclusion.

And now arose a shout and an outbreak of rapture which caused Natalie to tremble with anxious timidity. She cast a searching glance around her; it seemed to her that Paulo must come to her relief, that he must rescue and redeem her from the enthusiastic and flattering men who surrounded her. She saw him not! Where was Paulo, where was Carlo? These inquisitive lord cardinals had formed a circle around her, she seemed to herself a prisoner; it alarmed her to thus find herself the central point of all these attractions.

Not far from her stood Corilla, with glowing cheeks and anger-flashing eyes. "I will avenge this affront or die!" thought she, as, grasping Albani's hand with convulsive violence, she whispered to him: "Free me from this woman, and I will realize all your wishes."

Francesco Albani smiled. "Then you are mine, Corilla, and no power on earth shall take you from me. That child is dead. See, see how she makes herself a path through the crowd—ah, it is too sultry for her here in the hall, she approaches the garden door, she slips out. Ah, give me your hand, Corilla. Yet a few moments and the fairest woman on earth is mine!"

Light as a gazelle, timid and trembling, Natalie had fled the crowd, and now, stepping out into the garden, she breathed easier, it seeming to her that she had escaped a danger.

"This night air will cool and refresh me, and I shall soon succeed in finding Paulo," thought she, constantly wandering farther and farther into the garden. But the brightness of the illuminated alleys annoyed her. A more obscure and secluded path opening, Natalie entered it. Ah, she needed solitude and stillness, and what knew she, this simple, harmless child of Nature—what knew she whether it was proper and seemly for a young woman thus alone to venture into these dark walks? She knew not that she incurred any risk, or that one needed protection among people!

Ever farther resounded the noise of the festival—the clang of the music sounded fainter and fainter. Natalie wandered farther and farther, happy, because alone!

Alone? What, then, was it that noiselessly and cautiously haunted her steps, following every movement she made, constantly nearing her the farther she found herself, as she supposed, from all other living beings? What was it inaudibly creeping through the bushes, even its dark shadow imperceptible, that followed her like a ghost?

It became stiller and stiller, and nearer crept the gloomy form that lurked in her steps. Now with a sudden spring he rushes upon the maiden. What gleams in his hand? It is a dagger. He swings it high, that he may sink it deep. Then some one rushes from the bushes, seizes the murderer's arm, wrests the dagger from his hand, hurls him to the earth, and a dear, well-known voice cries: "Fly, Natalie, fly quickly to Count Paulo! This serpent will no longer follow you! I have him fast, the assassin!"

And Carlo broke out into a happy and triumphant laugh.

Natalie made no answer, she was paralyzed with terror; there was a roaring in her ears, it darkened before her eyes, and she fell senseless to the earth!

But her disarmed murderer sought to free himself from Carlo's grasp. Struggling with his captor, he finally succeeded in half rising. Carlo thought not of his own danger, but only of Natalie's, and it was only on her account that he now loudly called for help, at the same time exerting a superhuman strength to hold on upon his prisoner.

Voices were heard, lights approached, and Paulo's cry of anguish resounded.

"Here, here!" anxiously cried Carlo, his strength already beginning to fail him. And his call being recognized, people soon came with lights. Count Paulo was already distinguishable, already Cardinal Bernis, with a light in his hand, was hastening on in advance of the rest.

With a last powerful effort the prisoner succedded in freeing himself.

"She is saved for this time, but my dagger will yet make her acquaintance!" said he, with a scornful laugh, and like a serpent he glided away among the bushes.

"She is saved!" cried Carlo, sinking back toward Count Paulo, and pointing with a happy smile to Natalie, who, awaking from her momentary stupefaction, stretched forth her arms toward the count.

"Paulo," she whispered low, "let us hasten from here! I dread these people! I fear them! Let us go! But take him with us, that they may not kill him, my saviour, my friend Carlo!"

CHAPTER XXXII.

THE DEPARTURE.

THE morning dawned. Count Paulo rose from the arm-chair in which he had passed the night. He had occupied the whole fearfully anxious night in writing; he now laid the pen aside and stood up.

His face had an expression of firmness and decision; he had formed a firm resolution, had come to an irrevocable determination.

With a firm step advancing to the door opening into the adjoining chamber, he called to his friend Cecil.

The latter immediately made his appearance, and, entering the count's chamber, laconically said: "All is ready."

Count Paulo smiled sadly. "You are then sure there are no other means of saving her and ourselves?" he asked.

"None whatever," said Cecil. "Every moment's delay increases her and your danger. The occurrence of last night is a proof of it. They sought the death of Natalie—without Carlo's help she would have been murdered, and all our plans would have come to an end."

"Her life is threatened, and yet you can urge me to go and leave her here alone and unprotected?"

"Was it you who saved her from the danger of last night?" asked Cecil.

"Believe me, it is your presence that threatens her with the most danger. Precisely because you are at her side, they suspect her and watch her every step; the circumstance that she is with you creates distrust, and in Natalie they will think they see her whose mysterious flight has long been known in Russia. And Catharine will have her tracked in all countries and upon all routes. Therefore, save Natalie, by seeming to give her up. Return home and relate to them a fable of a false princess by whom you had been deceived, and whom you abandoned as soon as you discovered the deception. They will everywhere lend you a believing ear, as people gladly believe what they wish, and by this means only can you assure the future of Natalie and yourself."

"That is all just and true. I myself have so seen and recognized it," said the count; "and yet, my friend, I nevertheless still waver, and it seems to me that an internal voice warns me against that which I am about to do!"

Cecil smilingly shook his head. "Trust not such voices," said he; "it is the whispering of demons who envelop themselves in our own wishes, who entice us to what we would, by seeming to warn us against what we fear. Nothing but your departure can give you safety. Leave Natalie here in quiet solitude, and without you she will be well concealed in the solitude of this garden, and you, in the mean time, will pursue your affairs in Russia, and deceive the enemy, while you yourself seem to be the deceived party. They threaten you with the confiscation of your property, and they will fulfil those threats if you do not obey the call of the government. Go, therefore, go! We will secretly sell your property; and when this is accomplished, then, laden with treasure, let us return to Natalie, no longer fearing their threats."

"And when all this is done," exclaimed Count Paulo, glowing, "it shall be our task to conduct Natalie back in triumph to the country to which she belongs, there to place the diadem upon her fair brows, and to raise her above all other mortal beings!"

"God grant us the attainment of our ends!" sighed Cecil.

"We must and shall attain them!" responded Paulo, with enthusiasm. "I must fulfil this great task of my life, or die! Away, now, with all wavering or hesitation! What must be, shall be! They shall not say of the man who took compassion upon the deserted and threatened orphan and raised her for his objects, that he gave up his plans on account of his own egotistical wishes, and pusillanimously failed to finish the work he began! No, no, history shall not so speak of me: It shall at least represent me as a brave man capable of sacrificing his heart and his life for the attainment of his higher ends!

Seal these letters, Cecil. They contain my last will, and my bequest to Natalie, which I wish to place in her own hands. Ah, Cecil, I have been an enthusiastic fool until this hour! I thought—alas, what did I not think and dream!—I thought that all these plans and objects were not worth so much as one sole smile of her lips, and that if she would say to me 'I love thee,' this sweet word would not be too dearly purchased with an imperial crown. Perhaps, ah, perhaps, I think so yet, but I will never more suffer myself to be swayed by such thoughts. We must go—Natalie's happiness demands it. And besides, she will not lack friends and protectors. It was not without an object that I last evening presented her to the most notable people of Rome; not without an object that I consented to her showing herself as a poetess. They now know her name, which is repeated with highest praise in every quarter of the city; all Rome is to-day enthusiastic in her praise, and all Rome will protect and defend her. Add to which, I shall yet recommend her to the special protection of Cardinal Bernis!"

"And it was exactly in his house where she was almost murdered!" said Cecil. "Without that singer, Carlo, she would have been forever lost! If, then, you would choose a protector for her, let it be Carlo."

Count Paulo's brow darkened. "This singer loves her!" said he.

"Precisely for that reason," smilingly responded Cecil. "One who loves will best know how to protect her."

Count Paulo made no answer; he

12

continued thoughtfully walking back and forth. Then he said with decision: "Seal these letters, Cecil. I will take them to Natalie myself."

"You will, then, see her again?" asked Cecil, while folding the letters. "You will render the parting more painful!"

"I will it!" said Paulo, with decision, and, taking the letters, he left the room with a firm and resolute step.

He found Natalie in her room. She did not hear him coming, and thus did not turn to receive him. She was sitting motionless at the window and dejectedly looking out into the garden, her head supported by her hand.

The events of the previous evening had made a great change in her. She now felt older, more experienced, more earnest. A dark shadow had passed over her sunbright happiness, a dark power had threateningly approached her; the seriousness of life had been suddenly unfolded to her and had brushed off the ether-dust of harmless and joyful peace from her childish soul. The happy child had become a conscious maiden, and new thoughts, new feelings had sprung up within her. The first tears of sorrow had, with a mighty creative power, called all these slumbering blossoms of her heart into existence and activity, and her unconscious-feelings had become conscious thoughts.

But what had not happened, what had she not experienced and felt since last evening? First, had not a new happiness broken in upon her, had she not now a name, was she not a princess? Then, had she not achieved a triumph—a triumph in the presence of Corilla? But then, also, how many *desillusions* had she not experienced in a few hours? How had her heart been cooled by the rich flow of words in Corilla's poesy! Her whole soul had languished for the acquaintance of a poetess, and she had heard only a rhymed work of art. And then the last terrible event! Why had they wished to murder her? Who were her unknown enemies, and why had she enemies?

"I should have been dead had he not rescued me!" murmured she, and her lovely face was illuminated by a sunny smile. "Yes, without Carlo I should have been lost—I have to thank him for my life! Oh," said she then aloud, "to him therefore belongs my existence, and for every joy I am yet capable of feeling I am indebted to him, my friend Carlo! Ah, how shall I ever be able to reward him for all this happiness?"

And while she was thus speaking, Count Paulo, pale and silent, stood behind her; she saw him not, and after a pause she continued: "How strange it is! To-day, when I think of him, my heart beats as never before, and I feel in it something like heavenly bliss, and yet at the same time like profound sorrow. Ah, what can it be, and why do I, to-day, think only of him? I could weep because he does not yet come! How strange it all is, and at the same time how sad! Seems it not to me that I love Carlo more than any one else, more even than Paulo, who formerly was the dearest to me? How is it now, and am I, then, really so ungrateful to Paulo?"

Count Paulo still stood behind her, pale and silent. A painfully ironic smile flitted over his face, and he thought: "I came to ask a question, and Natalie has already given me the answer before I had time to ask it. Perhaps it is better thus. I have now nothing to ask!"

The young maiden became more and more deeply absorbed in her thoughts. Count Paulo laid his hand lightly upon her shoulder. She was startled, and involuntarily cried, "Carlo!"

"No, Paulo!" said he, with a melancholy smile, "but at all events a friend, Natalie, though a friend who is about to leave you!"

"You leave me?" she anxiously exclaimed.

"That means only outwardly, only with my body, never with my soul," said he, deeply moved. "That, Natalie, will remain with you eternally, that will never leave you—do you hear, never! Always remember this, my charming child, my sweet blossom! Never entertain a doubt of me, and if my voice does not reach you, if you receive no news of me, then think not, 'Paulo has abandoned me!' no, then think only, 'Paulo is dead, but my name was the last to linger upon his lips, and his last sigh was for me!'"

"You desert me?" said she, wringing her hands. "What am I, what shall I do, without you? You have been my protector and my reliance, my teacher and my friend! Alas, you were all to me, and I have ever looked up to you as my lord and father."

Count Paulo sadly smiled. "Love me always as your father," said he;

"while I live you shall never be an orphan, that I swear to you!"

"And must you go," cried she, clinging to him; "well, then let me go with you! You will be my father—well, I demand my right as your daughter; to accompany her father is a daughter's right."

"No," he firmly said, "you must remain while I go; but I go for you, to assure your future power and splendor. Remember this, Princess Natalie, forget it not, and when one day they brand me as a traitor, then say: 'No, he was no traitor, for he loved me!' And now hear what I have yet to say," continued the count, after a pause, while the still weeping Natalie looked up to him through her tears. "But look at me, Natalie—no, not that sad glance, I cannot bear it! Leave me my self-possession and my courage, for I need them! Weep not!"

And Natalie, drying her eyes with her long locks, sought to smile.

"I no longer weep," said she, "I listen to you."

Paulo placed two sealed letters in her hand.

"Swear to me," said he, "to hold these letters sacred as your most precious possession."

"I swear it!" said she.

"Swear to me to discover them to no human eye, to betray their possession to no human ear! Swear it to me by the memory of your mother, who now looks down from heaven upon you and receives your oath!"

"Then she is dead?" said the young maiden, sadly drooping her head upon her breast.

"You have not yet sworn!" said he.

The young maiden raised her head, and, turning her eyes toward heaven as if in the hope of encountering the tender maternal glance, she solemnly said: "By the sacred memory of my mother I swear to discover these papers to no human eye, to betray their existence to no human ear, but to hold them sacred as my most precious and mysterious treasure!"

"Swear, further," said Count Paulo, "that, whenever a danger may threaten you, you will sooner forget all other things than these papers, that they shall be the first which you will endeavor to save. Yes, swear to me that you will ever bear them upon your heart and never permit them to be separated from you!"

"I swear it!" said Natalie. "I will defend the possession of these papers, if necessary, with my life!"

"And thereby will you defend your honor," said Paulo, "for your honor rests in these papers. Yet ask me not what they contain. You must not yet know, there is danger in knowing their contents! But when a whole year has passed without my return or your hearing from me, and if in this whole year no messenger comes to you from me, then, Natalie, then open these letters; you will then possess my testament, and you will consider it a sacred duty to execute it!"

Natalie, sobbing, said: "Ah, why did not that dagger pierce my heart yesterday? I should then have died while I was yet happy!"

"You will yet do so!" said Count Paulo, with a slight tincture of bitterness; "Carlo and your future yet remain to you!"

She looked at him with a clear, bright glance, but without answering. She had again become an enigma to herself. Now, when her friend, when Paulo, was about to leave her, it seemed to her she had done wrong to love another, even for a moment, better than him, her benefactor and protector; indeed, as if she in fact loved no one so well as him, as if she could resign and leave all others to insure Paulo's permanent presence!

But she was suddenly startled, and a glowing flush overspread her cheeks. She had, quite accidentally, glanced through the window into the garden, and had there discovered Carlo, as with slow and hesitating steps he descended the alley leading to the villa.

Count Paulo had followed her glance, and, as he now observed the singer, he said: "He shall henceforth be your protector! Promise me to love him as a brother. Will you?"

He looked at her with a fixed and searching gaze, and she cast not down her eyes before that penetrating and interrogating glance, but met it directly with clear and innocent eyes.

"Yes, I will love him as a brother!" she said.

"One thing more, and then let us part!" said Paulo. "Marianne is honest and true—let her never leave you. I have amply provided her with funds for the necessary expenses for the next six months, and I hope long before the expiration of that time to send a further supply. If I do not, then conclude I am dead, for only with my life can I be robbed of the sweet duty of caring for you! And now let me go to Carlo!"

Slightly nodding to her, he hastily left the room.

At that moment Carlo mounted the steps leading to the door of the villa. Paulo met him with a hearty greeting.

"Let us go down into the garden," said he, "I have many things to say to you."

The two men remained a long time in the garden. Natalie, standing at the window, occasionally saw them, arm in arm, at some turning of the walks, and then they would again disappear as they pursued their way in earnest conversation. Strange thoughts flitted through the soul of the young maiden, and when she saw the two thus wandering, arm in arm, she thoughtfully asked herself: "Which is it, then, that I most love? Is it Carlo, is it Paulo?"

"I now understand you perfectly," said Count Paulo, as they again approached the house after a long and earnest conversation. "Yes, it seems to me I know you as myself, and know I can confide in you. You have perfectly tranquillized me, and I thank you for your confidence. It was then Corilla, that vain improvisatrice, who would have destroyed her? That is consoling, and I can now depart with a lighter heart. Against such attacks you will be able to protect her."

"I will protect her against every attack," responded Carlo. "You have my oath that the secret you have confided to me shall be held sacred, and you have thereby secured her from every outbreak of my passion. She stands so high above me that I can only adore her as my saint, can love her only as one loves the unattainable stars!"

CHAPTER XXXIII.

AN HONEST BETRAYER.

At about the same time Cecil was hastening through the streets of Rome, often looking back to see if any one was following him, and viewing with suspicious eyes every one whom he met. He finally stopped before the backdoor of a palace, and, after having satisfied himself that he had not been followed, he lightly knocked three times at the door. Upon its being opened, a grim, bearded Russian face presented itself.

Cecil drew a ring from his bosom and showed it to the porter.

"Quick! conduct me to his excellency," said he.

The Russian nodded his recognition of the token, and beckoned Cecil to follow him. After a short reflection, Cecil entered and the door was closed.

Guided by his conductor through a labyrinth of rooms and corridors, Cecil finally succeeded in reaching a little boudoir, whose heavily-curtained windows hardly admitted a ray of dim twilight.

The conductor, bidding Cecil to wait here, left him alone.

In a few moments a concealed door was opened, and a man of a tall, proud form entered.

"At length!" he said, on perceiving Cecil. "I had begun to doubt your coming."

"I waited until I could bring you decisive intelligence, your excellency," said Cecil.

"And you bring it to-day?" quickly asked the unknown.

"In an hour we leave Rome for St. Petersburg!"

Uttering a loud cry of joy, the stranger walked the room in visible commotion. Cecil followed him with timid, anxious glances, and, as he still kept silence, Cecil said:

"Your excellency, I have truly performed what you required of me. I have persuaded the count to make the journey, notwithstanding his opposition to it, and, as you commanded, his ward remains behind in Rome, alone and unprotected."

"Ah, you praise your acts because you desire your reward," said his excellency, contemptuously opening his writing-desk, and drawing forth a well-filled purse. "You there have your pay, good man!"

Cecil indignantly rejected the money. "I am no Judas, who betrays his master for money," said he. "Please remember, your excellency, for what I promised to fulfil your excellency's commands, and what reward you promised me!"

"Ah, I now remember! You required my promise that no harm should befall the count!"

"Only on that condition did I promise my assistance," said Cecil. "When your emissary sought me and called me to you, I only followed him, as you well know, most noble count, because you gave me to understand that my master's life and safety were concerned. I came to you. Allow me, your excellency, to repeat your own words. You said: 'Cecil, you have been represented to me as a true friend of your master. Fidelity is so rare a virtue, that it deserves reward. I will reward you by saving your life. Quickly leave this traitorous count, and break off all connection with him, else you are lost. I am secretly sent here in order to capture the count and his criminal ward, and take them to St. Petersburg. What there awaits the count may easily be imagined.' Thus speaking, your excellency then showed me the command for the count's arrest, signed by the empress. Upon which I asked: 'Is there no means of saving the count?' 'There is one,' said you. 'Persuade the count to return immediately to St. Petersburg, leaving his ward behind him here, and I swear to you, in the name of the empress, that no harm shall come to him.'"

"Well," impatiently cried the count, "what is the use of repeating all that, as I know it already?"

"Only because your excellency seems to forget that what I did was not done for your miserable gold, but for a totally different reward—the safety of a man whom I love as my own son."

"You have my word—no harm shall come to him."

"I doubt not your excellency's word," firmly and decidedly responded Cecil; "your word is all-powerful, and when you let your commanding voice be heard, all Russia trembles and bows before you. But here your voice resounds only between these walls, and nobody hears it but I alone. Give me an evidence of your word—a safety-pass, signed by your own hand, for my master, and then destroy the order for his arrest which you now hold!"

"Ah, it seems you would prescribe conditions?" said the count, proudly.

"Certainly I will," said Cecil. "I have complied with your conditions, and now it is your turn, Sir Count, to comply with mine, for you knew them before!"

A dark glow of anger showed itself in the count's face, and, passionately starting up, he approached Cecil, raising his arm threateningly against him.

"Sir Count," said Cecil, stepping back, "you mistake! I am no Russian serf, I am a free man, and no one has a right so to threaten me!"

The count had already let his arm fall, seeming suddenly to have changed his mind, and in a more friendly manner he said:

"You are right, Cecil, and what you desire shall be done."

Taking a large sealed paper from a drawer in his writing-desk, he handed it to Cecil.

"That is the order for the arrest; destroy it yourself!" said he.

Taking the paper, Cecil read it with attention. "It is, as you say, the order for the arrest. It is destroyed!"

With a satisfied smile, he tore the

paper into a thousand pieces, and placed these in his bosom.

The count had stepped to the table and hastily written a few lines upon another piece of paper. This he handed to Cecil. "I hope you are now satisfied," said he.

Cecil took the paper and read it.

"This is a safety-pass in due form," said he — "a valid instruction to all boundary guards and officials to let us pass without molestation. Your Excellency, we are quits. I complied with your wish, as you now have with mine, and my dear master is saved!"

"It being understood that you start immediately," said the count.

"The post-horses are already ordered, and we shall set out as soon as I return home. Farewell, therefore, Sir Count; I thank you for enabling me to save the man whom I most loved. I thank you!"

Cecil was approaching the door, when he suddenly stopped, and his face took a sad expression. "I have deceived my dear master, in order to save him," said he, "and in order to redeem the promise I made his father on his death-bed, swearing that I would watch over and protect the son at the risk of my heart's blood. But if the son knew what I have done, he would call me a betrayer and curse me, for he holds his word dearer than his own life! He leaves the princess in the belief that it is necessary for her safety, and repairs to Russia, to return with increased wealth. Sir Count, what is to become of Natalie?"

"That," low and mysteriously replied the count, "that can be decided only by the will of her who has sent me.

Until that decision no hair of her head can be touched, and the princess will follow me to Russia only with her own free will! But you must know that the empress hates no one more than her own son. How, then, if she should be disposed to pass him over, and select another as her successor?"

"Oh, would to God that I rightly understand you!" exclaimed Cecil.

"We shall, one day, perfectly understand each other," said the count, with a significant smile. "Now, hasten to redeem your word, and leave Rome with your master!"

As soon as Cecil left the room, the count's face assumed a knavishly malicious expression. With a loud laugh he threw himself upon the silken divan.

"Thus are all these so-called good men real blockheads, stupid fools, who believe every word spoken to them with a friendly mien! This honest man really believes that his highly-prized master is now saved, because he bears in his bosom the fragments of the order for his arrest. Worthy dunce; as if there were no duplicate, and as if every promise were countersigned by the Divinity himself! Go home with your count — my word shall be fulfilled. No hair of his head shall be touched, but his proud back shall be curled, and in the mines of Siberia he may learn to bow before a higher power!"

Thus speaking, the count pulled a bell whose silken cord hung over the divan, and, as no one instantly appeared, he pulled it again, this time more violently. But yet some minutes passed, and still the bell was unanswered. The count gnashed his teeth with rage, and muttered vehement curses.

At length the door opened, and with an imploring face a servant appeared upon the threshold.

"Miserable hound, where were you?" cried the count to him.

The servant fell upon his knees and crept like a dog to his master's feet.

"Excellency, we had, as your grace commanded, so long as the gentleman was with you, withdrawn from the anteroom and waited in the corridor, where the bell could not be heard," stammered the servant.

"I will teach you wretches to keep me waiting," exclaimed the count, and seizing the knout that lay upon the table before him, he laid it with merciless rage upon the poor servant, until his own arm sank powerless, and he felt himself exhausted with fatigue.

"Now go, you hound!" said he, replacing the knout upon the table; and the flagellated serf, rising respectfully, with his hand wiped away the blood which ran in streams from his wounds.

"Now go and send my officers to me!" cried the count. The servant staggered out to obey the command, and soon the persons thus ordered made their appearance and remained standing in silence at the door.

The count lay stretched out upon the divan, playing with the knout, whose leathern thongs were still dripping with his servant's blood.

"Let a courier take horse immediately, and give him the order countersigned by her imperial majesty for the arrest of Count Paulo Rasczinsky. The courier will follow him with it to the Rus-

sian frontier, and then by virtue of this order arrest him at the next station and send him to St. Petersburg in chains! This is the command for the courier; he will answer with his head for its execution!"

One of the officers bowed, and went to dispatch the courier.

"Is our reconnoitrer returned?" asked the count of the two who remained.

"He is."

"What news brings he? Does he know the cause of the murderous attack at the festival of the French cardinal? Yet why do I ask you? Make yourselves scarce, and let him come to speak for himself!"

The officers were no sooner gone, than a wild-looking, bearded churl made his appearance upon the threshold of the door and greeted the count with a grinning laugh.

"What know you of the murderous attack?" asked the count, in Italian.

"A friend of mine was charged with the affair," said the bravo. "He is in the pay of the most holy Cardinal Albani. We served long together under the same chief, and I know him intimately. He carries the most skilful dagger in all Rome, and it is the greatest wonder that he missed on this occasion."

"Was it done by order of the cardinal?"

"No! The lord cardinal had lent this bravo to the celebrated improvisatrice Corilla—the order came from her."

"It is well!" said the count. "Do you know all the *bravi* in Rome?"

"All, your excellency. They are all my good friends."

"Well, now listen to what I have to say to you. You must hold the life of the Princess Tartaroff as sacred as your own! Know that she is no moment unwatched; that wherever she appears she is surrounded by secret protectors. Whoever touches her is lost—my arm will reach him! Say that to your friends, and tell them that the Russian count keeps his word. Four thousand sequins are yours in four weeks, if until then the princess meets with no accident. Away with you, and forget not my words!"

"Ah, these words, your excellency, are worth four thousand sequins, and these one does not so easily forget!" said the bandit, leaving the room.

Again the count rang, and ordered his private secretary, Stephano, to be called.

"Stephano," said the count to him, "the first step is taken toward the accomplishment of our object. The work must succeed; I have pledged my word for it to the empress, and who can say that Alexis Orloff ever failed to redeem his word? This princess is mine! Count Paulo Rasczinsky is just now leaving Rome, and she has no one to protect her!"

"But it is not yet to be said that she is already yours!" said Stephano, shrugging his shoulders. "As you will not employ force, your excellency, you must have recourse to stratagem. I have hit upon a plan, of which I think you will approve. They describe this so-called little princess as exceedingly innocent and confiding. Let us take advantage of her confiding innocence—that will be best! Now hear my plan."

Stephano inclined himself closer to the ear of the count, and whispered long and earnestly; it seemed as if he feared that even the walls might listen to him and betray his plans; he whispered so low that even the count had some trouble in understanding him.

"You are right," said the count, when Stephano had ended; "your plan must and will succeed. First of all, we must find some one who will incline her in our favor, and render her confiding."

"Oh, for that we have our good Russian gold," said Stephano, laughing.

"And besides," continued the count, "our incognito is at an end. All Rome may now learn that I am here! Ah, Stephano, what a happy time awaits me! This Natalie is beautiful as an angel!"

"God grant that you may not fall in love with her!" sighed Stephano. "You are always very generous when you are in love."

CHAPTER XXXIV.

ALEXIS ORLOFF.

Two things principally occupied the Romans during the next weeks and months, offering them rich material for conversation. In talking of these they had forgotten all other events; they spoke no more of the giant fish which had destroyed the friendship of France and Spain; they no longer entertained each other with anecdotes in connection with the festival of Cardinal Bernis, at which the *entrée* of that fish upon his long silver platter was hailed with shouts and *vivats*—yea, even that Russian princess, who had momentarily shown herself on the horizon of society, all these were quickly forgotten, and people now interested themselves only about the extirpation of the order of the Jesuits, which Pope Clement had now really effected, and of the arrival of the Russian ambassador-extraordinary, the famous Alexis Orloff, whose visit to Rome seemed the more important and significant as they well knew in what near and confidential relations his brother, Count Gregory Orloff, stood with the Empress Catharine, and what participation Alexis Orloff had in the sudden death of the Emperor Peter III.

The order of the Jesuits, then, no longer existed; the pious fathers of the order of Jesus, were stricken out of the book of history; a word of power had annihilated them! With loud complaints and lamentations they filled the streets of the holy city, and if the prayer of humility and resignation resounded from their lips, yet there were very different prayers in their hearts, prayers of anger and rage, of hatred and revenge! They were seen wringing their hands and loudly lamenting, as they hastened to their friends and protectors, and besieged the doors of the foreign embassies. With them wept the poor and suffering people to whom the pious fathers had proved themselves benefactors. For, since they knew that their existence was threatened, they had assiduously devoted themselves to works of charity and mercy, and to strengthening, especially in Rome, their reputation for piety, benevolence, and generosity. Prodigious sums were by them distributed among the poor; more than five hundred respectable impoverished Romans, who had been accused of political offences, were secretly supported by them. In this way the Jesuits, against whom the cry of denunciation had been raised for years in all Europe, had nevertheless succeeded, at least in the holy city, in gaining for themselves a very considerable party, and thus securing protection and support in the time of misfortune and persecution. But while the people wept with them, and many cardinals and princes of the Church secretly pitied them, the ambassadors of the great European powers alone remained insensible to their lamentations. No one of them opened the doors of their palaces to them, no one afforded them protection or consolation; and although it was known that Cardinal Bernis, in spite of the horror which had for years been felt of this order in France, was personally favorable to them, and had long delayed the consent of the court of France to their abolition, yet even Bernis now avoided any manifestation of kindness for them, lest his former friend, the Spanish ambassador, might think he so far humiliated himself as to favor the Jesuits for the sake of recovering the friendship and good opinion of the Duke of Grimaldi. But Grimaldi himself now no longer dared to protect the Jesuits, however friendly he might be to them, and however much they were favored by Elizabeth Farnese, the Spanish queen-mother. King Charles, her son, had finally ventured to defy her authority, and in an autograph letter had commanded the Duke of Grimaldi to receive no more Jesuits in his palace. And while, as we have said, the whole diplomacy had declared against the order of the holy fathers of Jesus, it must have been the more striking that this Russian Count Orloff had compassion upon them, that he opened the doors of his palace to them, and lent a willing ear to the complaints of the unfortunate members of the order.

This Russian count gave the good Romans much material for reflection and head-shaking; the women were occupied with his herculean beauty, and the men with his wild, daring, and reckless conduct. They called him a barbarian, a Russian bear, but could not help being interested in him, and eagerly repeating the little anecdotes freely circulated respecting him.

They smilingly told that he had been the first who had had the courage to defy the powerful republic of Venice, which, for recruiting sailors for his fleet in their territories for the war against the Turks, wished to banish him from proud and beautiful Venice. But Alexis Orloff had laughed at the senate of the republic when they sent him the order to leave. He had ordered the two hundred soldiers, who formed his retinue, to arm themselves, and, if necessary, to repel force with force; but to the senate he had answered that he would leave the city as soon as he pleased, not before! But, as it seemed that he was not pleased to leave the city, he remained there, and now the angry and indignant senate sent him the peremptory command to leave Venice with his soldiers in twenty-four hours. A deputation of the senate came in solemn procession to communicate to the Russian count this command of the Council of Three. Alexis Orloff received them, lying upon his divan, and to their solemn address he laughingly answered: "I receive commands from no one but my empress! It remains as before, that I shall go when I please, and not earlier!"

The senators departed with bitter murmurs and severe threats. Count Alexis Orloff remained, and the cowardly senate, trembling with fear of this young Russian empire, had silently pocketed the humiliation of seeing this overbearing Russian within their walls for several weeks longer.* This evidence of the haughty insolence of Count Orloff was related among the Romans with undisguised pleasure, and they thanked him for having thus humiliated and insulted the proud and imperious republic. But they suspiciously shook their heads when they learned that he seemed disposed to display his pride and arrogance in Rome! They told of a *soirée* of the Marchesa di Paduli which Alexis Orloff had attended. As they there begged of him to give some proof of the very superior strength which had acquired for him the name of "the Russian Hercules," he had taken one of the hardest apples from a silver plateau that stood upon the table and playfully crushed it with two fingers of his left hand. But a fragment of this hard apple had hit the eye of the Duke of Gloucester, who was standing near, and seriously injured it. The sympathies of the whole company were excited for the English prince, and he was immediately surrounded by a pitying and lamenting crowd. Count Orloff alone had nothing to say to him, and not the slightest excuse to make. He smilingly rocked himself upon his chair, and hummed a Russian popular song in praise of his empress." †

And was it not also an insult for Alexis Orloff now to show himself a friend to the Jesuits, whom the decree of God's vicegerent had outlawed and proscribed? Was it not an insult that he loudly and publicly promised to these persecuted Jesuits a kind reception and efficient protection in Russia, and invited them to found new communities and new cloisters there?

But Alexis Orloff cared little for the dissatisfaction of the Romans. He said to his confidant Stephano: "There is no greater pleasure than to set at defiance all the world, and to oppose all these things which the stupid people would impose upon us as laws. The friend and favorite of the Empress Catharine has no occasion for complying with such miserable laws; wherever I set my foot, there the earth belongs to me, and I will forcibly maintain my pretensions whenever they are disputed! In Russia I am the serf of the empress, in revenge for which I will, at least abroad, treat all the world as my serfs. This gives me pleasure, and wherefore is the world here but to be enjoyed?"

"A little also for labor," said Stephano, with a sly smile.

"For that I have my slaves, for that I have also you!" responded Orloff, laughing. "There is only one labor for me here in Rome, and that is to create as much disturbance as possible in the city; to set the people at odds with the government, so that they may have their hands full, and find no time for observing our nice game with our little princess, or to interfere with it. We must have freedom of action, that is the most important. Hence we must protect these pious Jesuits, and offer support to the enemies of this too-enterprising pope, by which means we shall

<hr />

* Archenholz, "Italien," vol. iv., p. 53.
† Gorani, vol. ii., p. 28.

ultimately attain our own ends, and that is enough for us!"

"We have not yet advanced a step with our Princess Natalie," said Stephano, shrugging his shoulders; "that, it seems, is an impregnable fortress!"

"It must, however, yield to us," laughingly responded Alexis Orloff, "and she shall yet acknowledge us as conquerors. We are undermining, Stephano, and when the building crushes her in its crashing fall, will she first discover that she has long been in danger. And what said you—that we have not yet advanced a step? And yet Rasczinsky is gone, and we have known how to keep Cardinal Bernis, who would have interested himself for the little one, so very much occupied with the affair of the Jesuits, that he has yet had no time to think of the princess. Ah, these Jesuits are very useful people. We strew them like snuff in the faces of these diplomatists, and, while they are yet rubbing their weak eyes and crying out with pain, we shall quietly draw our little fish into our net, and take her home without opposition!"

"And if the fish will not go into the net?"

"It must go in!" impatiently cried Orloff. "Bah! have I at the right time succeeded in towing our emperor, God bless him! into eternity, and shall I doubt in the fulness of time of enclosing this beautiful child in my arms? Look at me, Stephano—what is wanting for it in me? Are not all these beautifu. women of Rome enraptured with the Russian Hercules? How, then, can it be that a woman of my own country can withstand me? The preliminaries are the main thing, and if we only had some one to prepare her for my appearance, all would then go well. And such a one we will find, thanks to our rubles! But enough of politics for the present, Stephano. Call my valet. It is time for my toilet, and that is a very important affair."

CHAPTER XXXV.

CORILLA.

CORILLA was alone. Uneasy, full of stormy thoughts, she impetuously walked back and forth, occasionally uttering single passionate exclamations, then again thoughtfully staring at vacancy before her. She was a full-blooded, warm Italian woman, that will neither love nor hate with the whole soul, and nourishes both feelings in her bosom with equal strength and with equal warmth. But, in her, hatred exhaled as quickly as love; it was to her only the champagne-foam of life, which she sipped for the purpose of a slight intoxication—as in her intoxication only did she feel herself a poetess, and in a condition for improvisation.

"I must at any rate be in love," said she, "else I should lose my poetic fame. With cool blood and a tranquil mind there is no improvising and poetizing. With me all must be stirring and flaming, every nerve of my being must glow and tremble, the blood must flash like fire through my veins, and the most glowing wishes and ardent longings, be it love or be it hate, must be stirring within me in order to poetize successfully. And this cannot be comprehended by delicate and discreet people; this low Roman populace even venture to call me a coquette, only because

I constantly need a new glow, and because I constantly seek new emotions and new inspirations for my muse."

Love, then, for the improvisatrice Corilla, was nothing more than a strong wine with which she refreshed and strengthened her fatigued poetic powers for renewed exertions; it was in a manner the tow which she threw upon the expiring fire of her fantasy, to make it flash up in clear and bright flames.

It was only in this way that she loved Carlo, and wept for him, except that in this case her love had been of a longer duration, because it was *he* who gave up and left *her!* That was what made her hatred so glowing, that was what made her seek the life of the woman for whom Carlo had deserted her.

"This is a new situation," said she, "which I am called to live through and to feel. But a poetess must have experienced all feelings, or she could not describe them. For my part, I do not believe in the revelations of genius—I believe only in experiences. One can describe only what one has felt and experienced. Whoever may attempt to describe the flavor of an orange, must first have tasted it!"

That this attempt to murder Natalie had failed, was to her a matter of little moment. She had experienced the emotion of it, and just the same would it have been a matter of indifference to her had the dagger pierced Natalie's breast—she was sufficiently a child of the South to consider a murder as only a venial sin, for which the priest could grant absolution.

There was only one thing which exclusively occupied Corilla, following and tormenting her day and night, and that was her poetic fame. She desired that her name should stand high in the world, glorified by all Europe, and for this purpose she desired above all things to be crowned as a poetess in the capitol of the holy city; for this fame she would willingly have given many years of her life.

That was the aim of all her efforts, and how much would she not have borne, ventured, and suffered for its attainment! How many intrigues were planned, how much cunning and dissimulation, flattery, and hypocrisy, had been employed for that purpose, and all, all as yet in vain!

Therefore it was that Corilla now wept, and with occasional outbreaks of passionate exclamations violently paced her room. Her cheeks glowed, her eyes flashed—she was very beautiful in this state of excitement. That she must have acknowledged to herself as her glance accidentally encountered her own face in the glass.

With a smile of satisfaction she remained standing before the mirror, and almost angrily she said:

"Ah, why I am now alone, why does no one see me in my beautiful glow? My face might now produce some effect, and gain me friends! Why, then, am I now alone?"

But it seems that Corilla had only to express a wish in order to see it suddenly fulfilled; for the door was at that moment opened, and a servant announced Count Alexis Orloff.

Corilla smiled with delight, and let that smile remain upon her lips, as she very well knew it was becoming to her, and that she had conquered many hearts with it; but secretly her heart throbbed with fear, and timidly she asked herself, "What can that Russian count want of me?"

But with a cheerful face she advanced to receive him; she seemed not to remark that a dark cloud lay upon his brow, and that his features bore an almost threatening expression.

"He is a barbarian," thought she, "and barbarians must be treated differently from other men. I must flatter this lion, in order to fetter him!"

"It is a serious matter that brings me to you, signora," said Alexis, gloomily.

"A serious matter?" she cheerfully asked. "Ah, then I pity you, count. It is difficult to speak with me of serious matters!"

"You rather do them!" said Alexis, carelessly throwing himself upon a divan. "You would not play with such serious things as, for instance, a dagger, and therefore you hurl it from you, altogether indifferent whether you thereby quite accidentally pierce the heart of another."

"I do not understand you, count," said Corilla, without embarrassment, but at the same time she looked at him with such a charming and enticing expression, that Alexis involuntarily smiled.

"I will make myself intelligible to you," said he, in a milder tone. "You must understand, that I know you, Corilla. That assassin who followed the Princess Tartaroff at the festival of Cardinal Bernis, was employed by you, Signora Maddalena Morelli Fernandez, called Corilla!"

"And what if it were true, Signor Alexis Orloff, called the handsome Northern Hercules?" asked she, roguishly imitating his grave seriousness. "If it were really true, what further?"

Alexis looked in her face with an expression of astonishment. "You are wonderfully bold!" said he.

"None but slaves are without courage!" responded she. "Freedom is the mother of boldness!"

"You do not, then, deny the hiring of that bravo?"

"I only deny your right to inquire," said she.

"I have a right to it," he responded with vehemence. "This Princess Tartaroff is a subject of the Empress of Russia, my mistress, who watches over and protects all her subjects with maternal tenderness."

"That good, tender empress!" exclaimed Corilla, with an ambiguous smile. "But in order properly to watch and preserve all her children and subjects, she should keep them in her own country. Take this Princess Tartaroff with you to Russia, and then she will be safe from our Italian daggers. Take her with you; that will be the best way!"

"You, then, very heartily hate this poor little princess?" asked Alexis, laughing.

"Yes," said she, after a short reflection, "I hate her. And would you know why, signor? Not for her beauty, not for her youth, but for her talents! And she has great talents! Ah, there was a time when I hated her, although I knew her not. But now, now it is different. I now not only hate, but fear her! For she can rival me, not only in love, but in fame! Ah, you should have seen her on that evening! She was like a swan to look at, and her song was like the dying strains of the swan. And all shouted applause, and all the women wept; indeed, I myself wept, not from emotion, but with rage, with bitterness, for they had forgotten me—forgotten, for this new poetess; they overwhelmed her with flatteries, leaving me alone and unnoticed! And yet you ask me if I hate her!"

Quite involuntarily had she suffered herself to be carried away by her own vehemence, her inward glowing rage. With secret pleasure Count Orloff read in her features that this was no comedy which she thus improvised, but was truth and reality.

"If you so think and feel," said he, "then we may soon understand each other, signora. A real hatred is of as much value as a real love; indeed, often of much greater. One can more safely confide in hatred, as it is more enduring. I will therefore confide in you, signora, if you will swear to me to betray no word of what I shall tell you."

"I swear it!" was Corilla's response.

"Listen, then! This Princess Tar-

13

taroff is an impostor; no princely blood flows in her veins, and if she gives herself out to be a princess, it is because she therewith connects plans of hightreason. More I need not say to you, except that my illustrious empress has charged me to bring this fraudulent princess to her at St. Petersburg, that she may there receive her punishment! This I have sworn to do, and must redeem my promise to transport her from here, without exciting attention, and without subjecting her to any personal injury. Do you now comprehend why I come?"

"I comprehend," said Corilla. "An empress would avenge herself, and therefore a poor poetess must forego her own little private revenge! But how, if I should not believe a word of this long story; if I should consider it a fable invented by you to assure the safety of your princess?"

"That you may be compelled to believe it, listen further to me."

And Alexis Orloff spoke long and zealously to her, affording her a glance into his most secret intrigues, into his finely-matured plans, while Corilla followed him with intense expectation and warmly-glowing cheeks.

"I comprehend it all, all!" said she, when Alexis had finally ended; "it is a deep and at the same time an infernal plan—a plan which must excite the envy and respect of Satan himself!"

"And yourself?" laughingly asked Alexis.

"Oh, I," said she—"I belong, perhaps, to the family of devils, and therefore take pleasure in aiding you! You need a negotiator who has a wide con-

science and an eloquent tongue! I can furnish you with such a one. Ah, that will make a droll story. Said you not that the singer Carlo watched this golden treasure like a dragon? Well, it shall be his brother who shall contend with this dragon. His own brother—will not that be pleasant, count?"

"And are you sure of him?" asked Count Orloff. "How if his brother should win him from us?"

"Have no anxiety; this Carlo Ribas is so virtuous that he hates no one so much as his brother Joseph, merely because he passed some years in the galleys for forgery. He is now free, and has secretly come here. As he was aware that I knew his brother, he came to me to beg for my countenance and support. I will send him to you."

"And you will also not forget my request, that you will in all societies speak of the great love which the Empress Catharine cherishes for her near relation, the Princess Tartaroff?"

"I will not forget it. In your hands, count, I lay my revenge—you will free me from this rival?"

"That will I," said he, with an inhuman laugh. "And when the work is completed, and you have faithfully stood by me, then, signora, you may be sure of the gratitude of the empress. · Catharine is the exalted protectress of the muses, and in the fulness of her grace she will not forget the poetess Corilla. You may expect an imperial reward."

"And I shall gratefully receive it," said Corilla, with a smile. "A poetess is always poor and in want of assistance. The muses lavish upon their votaries all joys but those of wealth."

"Ah!" exclaimed Corilla, when the count had left her, "I shall in the end obtain all I desire. I shall not only be crowned with fame, but blessed with wealth, which is a blessing almost equal to that of fame! Money has already founded many a reputation, but not always has fame attracted money to itself! I shall be rich as well as famous!"

"That you already are!" exclaimed the Cardinal Francesco Albani, who, unremarked, had just entered the room.

"I am not," said she, with vehemence, "for they refuse me the prize of fame! Have you been with the pope, your eminence, and what did he say?"

"I come directly from him."

"Well, and what says he?"

"What he always says to me—no!"

Corilla stamped her feet violently, and her eyes flashed lightnings.

"How beautiful you are now!" tenderly remarked the cardinal, throwing an arm around her.

She rudely thrust him back. "Touch me not," said she, "you do not deserve my love. You are a weakling, as all men are. You can only coo like a pigeon, but when it comes to action, then sinks your arm and you are powerless. Ah, the woman whom you profess to love begs of you a trifling service, the performance of which is of the highest importance to her, the greatest favor, and you will not fulfil her request while yet swearing you love her! Go! you are a cold-hearted man, and wholly undeserving of Corilla's love!"

"But," despairingly exclaimed the cardinal, "you require of me a service that it is not in my power to perform. Ask something else, Corilla—ask a human life, and you shall have it! But I cannot give what is not mine. You demand a laurel-crown, which only the pope has the power to bestow, and he has sworn that you shall not have it so long as he lives!"

"Will he, then, live eternally?" cried Corilla, beside herself with rage.

The cardinal gave her an astonished and interrogating glance. But his features suddenly assumed a wild and malicious expression, and violently grasping Corilla's hand, he murmured:

"You are right! 'Will he, then, live forever?' Bah! even popes are mortal men. And if we should choose for his successor a man better disposed toward you than— Corilla," said the cardinal, interrupting himself, and, in spite of her resistance, pressing her to his bosom—"Corilla, swear once more to me that you will be mine, and only mine, as soon as I procure your coronation in the capitol! Swear it once more!"

She gave him such a sweet, enticing, and voluptuous smile, that the cardinal trembled with desire and joy.

"When you in the capitol adorn Corilla with the laurel-crown, then will she willingly lay her myrtle-crown at your feet," said she, with a charming expression of maiden modesty.

The cardinal again pressed her passionately to his bosom.

"You shall have the laurel-crown, and your myrtle-crown is mine!" he excitedly exclaimed. "You will soon see whether Francesco is a cold-hearted man! Farewell, Corilla!"

And with a hasty salute he left the

room. The astonished Corilla dismissed him with a smile.

"If it is to succeed at all, it can be only through him," said she. "Poor Francesco, he will bring me a full laurel-crown! And what can I give him in return? An exfoliated myrtle-crown, that is all! No heart with it!"

CHAPTER XXXVI.

THE HOLY CHAFFERERS.

CARDINAL FRANCESCO ALBANI, meantime, hastened through the streets with the sprightliness of youth. He noticed neither the respectful salutations and knee-bendings of those he passed, nor their visible shuddering and alarm when under the cardinal's hat they recognized the fierce and inhuman Francesco Albani.

He stopped before the palace of Cardinal Juan Angelo Braschi. The equipage of the new cardinal was drawn up before his door.

"Ah," gleefully remarked Albani, "he is therefore yet at home, and I shall meet with him!"

Hastily entering the palace, and pushing past the servant who would have preceded him, he entered the cardinal's cabinet unannounced.

"Be not troubled, your eminence," said Albani, with a smile, "I will not detain you long. I know your habits, and know that Signora Malveda usually expects you at this hour, because Cardinal Razzonico is not then with her! But I have something important to say to you. You know I am a man who, without forms and circumlocutions, al-ways come directly to the point. I do so now. You desire to be the successor of Ganganelli?"

Braschi turned pale, and timidly cast down his eyes.

"Why are you shocked?" cried Albani. "Every cardinal hopes and wishes to become the father of Christendom—that is natural; I should also wish it for myself, but I know that that cannot be. I have permitted these lord cardinals, who, in the conclave, invoke the Holy Spirit, to look too much into my cards. I was not so prudent as you, Braschi, and therefore you are much the more likely to become God's vicegerent! Would you not like to be pope, if Ganganelli should happen to die? And how high would you hold my voice—how much would it be worth to you?"

"More than all I possess, infinitely more!" said the shrewd Braschi. "Were I sure of your voice, I might then have a definite hope of becoming a pope; for your voice carries many others with it. How, then, can you expect me to estimate what is inestimable?"

"Would you give me twenty thousand?" asked Albani.*

"Threefold that sum if I possessed it, but I have nothing! I am a very poor cardinal, as you well know. My whole property consists of six thousand scudi, and that trifling sum I dare not offer you."

"Borrow, then, of Signora Malveda!" said Albani. "Cardinal Rezzonico is rich and liberal. Let us speak directly to the point. You would be pope, and I am willing to forward your views. How much will you pay?"

"If Signora Malveda will lend me four thousand scudi, I should then have ten thousand to offer you!"

"Well, so be it! Ten thousand scudi will do, if you will add to it a trifling favor."

"Name it," said Braschi.

"You know that Ganganelli opposes the crowning of our famous improvisatrice, Corilla, in the capitol. This is an injustice which Ganganelli's successor will have to repair. Will you do it?"

"Braschi gave the cardinal a sly glance. "Ah," said he, "Signora Corilla seems to be less liberal than Signora Malveda? She will allow you no discount of her future laurel-crown, is it not so? I know nothing worse than an ambitious woman. Listen, Albani; it seems that we must be mutually useful to each other; I need your voice to

become pope, and you need mine to become a favored lover. Very well, give me your voice, and in return I promise you a laurel-crown for Signora Corilla, and eight thousand scudi for yourself!"

"Ah, you would haggle!" contemptuously exclaimed Albani. "You would be a very niggardly vicegerent of God! But as Corilla is well worth two thousand scudi, I am content. Give me eight thousand scudi and the promise to crown Corilla!"

"As soon as I am pope, I will do both. My sacred word for it! Shall I strengthen my promise by swearing upon the Bible?"

Cardinal Albani gave the questioner a glance of astonishment, and then broke out with a loud and scornful laugh.

"You forget that you are speaking to one of your kind! Of what use would such a holy farce be to us who have no faith in its binding power? No, no, we priests know each other. Such buffoonery amounts to nothing. One written word is worth a thousand sworn oaths! Let us have a contract prepared—that is better. We will both sign it!"

"Just as you please!" said Braschi, with a smile, stepping to his writing-desk and rapidly throwing some lines upon paper, which he signed after it had been carefully read by Albani.

"At length the business is finished," said Albani. "Now, Cardinal Braschi, go to your signora, and surprise her with the news that she holds in her arms a pope *in spe*. Pope Clement will soon need a successor; he must be very ill, the poor pope!"

<hr />

* Gorani (vol. ii., p. 131) says of this cardinal: "He is excessively vindictive, and keeps in his pay many so-called *bravi*, to whom he deputes his vengeances. Miscreants find protection with him, and he admits them to his table, that they may always be in readiness to execute his bloody commands. With this cruelty he is also avaricious, and sells his protection; whence his palace serves as a refuge for bankrupts and murderers."

So speaking, he took leave of the future pope with a friendly nod, and departed with as much haste as he had come.

"And now to these pious Jesuit fathers!" said he, stepping out upon the grass. "It was very prudent in me that I went on foot to Corilla to-day. Our cursed equipages betray every thing; they are the greatest of chatterboxes! How astonished these good Romans would be to see a cardinal's carriage before these houses of the condemned! No, no, strengthen yourselves for another effort, my reverend legs! Only yet this walk, and then you will have rest."

And the cardinal trudged stoutly on until he reached the Jesuit college. There he stopped and looked cautiously around him.

"This unfortunate saintly dress is also a hinderance," murmured he. "Like the sign over a shop-door it proclaims to all the world: 'I am a cardinal. Here indulgences, dispensations, and God's blessings are to be sold! Who will buy, who will buy?' I dare not now enter this scouted and repudiated sacred house. I might be remarked, suspected, and betrayed. Corilla, dear, beautiful woman, it costs me much pains and many efforts to conquer you; will your possession repay me?"

The cardinal patiently waited in the shadow of a taxus-bush until the street became for a moment empty and solitary. Then he hastened to a side-door of the building, and, sure of being unobserved, entered.

A deep and quiet silence pervaded these long and deserted cloister-passages. It seemed as if a death-veil lay upon the whole building,—as if it were depopulated, desolated. Nowhere the least trace of that busy, stirring life, usually prevailing in these corridors—no longer those bands of scholars that formerly peopled these passages—the doors of the great school-room open, the benches unoccupied, the lecturer's chair, from which the pious fathers formerly with such subtle wisdom explained and defended their dangerous doctrines, these also are desolate. The reign of the Jesuits was over; Ganganelli had thrust them from the throne, and they cursed him as their murderer! He had suppressed their sacred order, he had commanded them to lay aside their peculiar costume and adopt that of other monkish orders, or the usual dress of abbés. But from their property he had not been able to expel them in this college Il Jesu—within their cloisters his power had not been able to penetrate. There they remained, what they had been, the holy fathers of Jesus, the pious defenders of craft and Christian deception, the cunning advocates of regicide, the proud servants of the only salvation-dispensing Church!—there, with rage in their hearts, they meditated plans of vengeance against this criminal pope who had condemned them to a living death; who, like a wicked magician, had changed their sacred college into an open grave! He had killed them, and he, should he nevertheless live?

With these fatal questions did the holy fathers occupy themselves, reflecting upon them in their gloomy leisure, and in low whisperings consulting with their prior. And in such secret consultation did Cardinal Francesco Albani find the prior with his confidant in the retectorium.

"Do not let me disturb you," he said, laughing; "I see by your faces you are engaged in conversation upon the subject in which I yesterday took a part. That is very well—we can resume it where we yesterday broke off, and again knot the threads which I yesterday so violently rent. With which knot shall we begin?"

The eyes of the pious Jesuit father flashed with joy. Francesco Albani was inclined to favor their plans and wishes; they saw that in his cunning smile, in his return to them.

"We were speaking of the sacred and important duty you will have to perform to-morrow, your eminence," said the prior, with a winning smile.

"Ah, yes, I remember," said the cardinal, with apparent indifference. "We spoke of the to-morrow's communion of his holiness the pope."

"And of the fact that you, your eminence, would to-morrow have to discharge the important duty of pouring the sacred wine into the golden chalice of the vicegerent of God," said the prior.

"Yes, yes, I now remember it all," said Albani, with a smile. "You spoke to me of a wonderful flask of wine, which, by means of the golden tube, you would gladly help to the honor of being drunk by his holiness from the communion chalice."

"It is so precious a wine that only the vicegerent of God is worthy of wetting his lips with it. It must touch the lips of no other mortal!"

"I know such a wine," said Albani; "it thrives best in the region of Naples,* and whoever drinks of it becomes a partaker of eternal blessedness."

"Yes, you are right, it is a wonderfully strengthening wine!" said the prior, folding his hands and directing his eyes toward the heavens. "We thank God that He has left us in possession of so precious an essence! The pope, they say, is suffering, and needs strengthening. See how closely we follow the teaching of Him whose name we bear, and who has commanded, 'Love your enemies, bless those who curse you!' Instead of avenging ourselves, we would be his benefactors, and refresh him with the most precious of what we possess!"

"And you would be so unselfish as to keep from him all knowledge of your benevolence, you would bless him quite secretly! But how if I should betray you, and communicate your precious secret to his holiness the pope? Yes, yes, I shall open my mouth and speak, unless I am prevented by a golden lock put upon my lips."

"We shall willingly apply such a lock!" said the pleased prior.

"But, that it may entirely close my mouth, the lock will need to be very heavy!" responded Albani, with a laugh.

"It is so—it weighs six thousand scudi!" said the prior.

"That is much too light!" exclaimed Albani, laughing; "it will hardly cover my mouth. It still remains that I am to undertake a very hazardous affair.

---

* The celebrated poison, *Acqua Tofana*, is prepared only in Naples.

Reflect, if any one should discover my possession of this strange wine; if Ganganelli should perceive that it is not wine from his own cellar that I have poured into the cup for him! It is dangerous work that you would assign to me, a work for which I might lose my head, and you venture to offer me a poor six thousand scudi for it! Adieu, then, pious fathers, keep you your golden lock, and I my unclosed lips. I shall know when and where to speak!"

And the cardinal moved toward the door. Hastening after him, the prior handed him a small flask, the contents of which were clear and pure as crystal water, timidly and anxiously whispering, "Ten drops of this in Ganganelli's communion wine, and ten thousand scudi are yours!"

"Give the ten thousand scudi at once!" said Albani, with decision.

"And the drops?"

"The pope's wine is too strong; I will reduce it a little with this pure water.*

---•••---

CHAPTER XXXVII.

"SIC TRANSIT GLORIA MUNDI!"

On the following day there was a solemn high office in St. Peter's. All Rome flocked there, to see this great and touching spectacle. A dense crowd thronged the streets, and all shouted and cried when the pope, surrounded by his Swiss guard, appeared in their midst in his gilded arm-chair, and received the greetings of the people with a bland smile.

Toward St. Peter's waved the human throng, and to St. Peter's the pope was borne. The features of Ganganelli had an expression of sadness, and as he now glanced down upon the thousands of his subjects who, shouting, followed him, he asked in his heart, "Who among you will be my murderers? And how long will you yet allow me to live?

Ah, were I yet the poor Franciscan monk I was, then no one would take the pains to assassinate me. Why, then, does the world, precisely now, seem so fair to me, now, when I know that I must leave it so soon?" And the pope shed a secret tear while, surrounded by royal splendor, he imparted his blessing to the thousands who reverently knelt at his feet.

The bells rung, the organ resounded, the wide halls of St. Peter's were penetrated by the marvellous singing of the

---

* The poison, *Acqua Tofana*, is pure and clear as water, without taste or smell. It is prepared from opium and Spanish flies, combined with some other ingredients, which, however, are only known to the makers of it. That the *Acqua Tofana* is made from the foam sometimes found upon the lips of the dying, is an idle tale. Aliessandro Borgia was the first to bring it into use.

Sistine chapel. Thousands and thousands of wax tapers lighted the noble space of the church, thousands and thousands of people pressed into the sacred halls. Under his canopy, opposite the high altar, sat the vicegerent of God upon his golden throne, surrounded by the consecrated cardinals and bishops, protected by the Swiss guard! Who could have ventured to attack the holy father—who would have been so foolhardy as to attempt to penetrate that thick wall of Swiss guards and princes of the Church—who could have been successful in such an attempt? No human being! But where the people could not penetrate, where there was no room for the swinging of a dagger, there the malignant poison lurked unseen!

Ganganelli sat upon his golden throne, intoxicated by the clang of the organ and charmed by the singing of the high choir, and the pope, looking down upon the human crowd, again asked himself: "Who among you are my murderers?"

The singing ceased, the organ was silent, and only the solemn tones of all the bells of St. Peter's resounded through the church. A death-like stillness else; the people lay upon their knees and crossed themselves; before the altar kneeling priests murmured prayers.

It was a solemn, a sublime moment, for the pope must now receive the communion—the vicegerent of God must drink the blood of the Lamb. But still the pope remains sacred; he cannot, like other mortals, make use of his earthly feet; he must not like them approach the altar. Sitting upon his throne, he has partaken of the holy wafer, and, as it was unbecoming his dignity to descend to the altar in order to come to Christ, the latter must decide to come to him!

The golden chalice at the high altar contains the blood of the Lamb; the Cardinal Francesco Albani performs the holy office. He has blessed the host, and under his consecrated hand will now be effected the miracle of turning the wine into the blood of Christ!

And Cardinal Albani lays the golden tube in the cup, and another cardinal passes the other end of the tube to the pope.

Through this sacred tube will he sip the consecrated wine, the blood of the Redeemer!

Rushing and thundering recommences the high office, the trumpets renew their blasts, the drums roll, the bells ring, the organ rattles its song of jubilee, the trombones crash in unison. It is the greatest, most sublime moment of the whole ceremony. The pope having put the golden tube to his lips, sips the wine changed into blood.

While the pope drinks, the two cardinals who to-day are on service approach the sacred throne. They hold a torch in the right hand, and a small bundle of tow in the left, and, according to the custom, set the tow on fire.

It flashes up in a bright flame, is soon extinguished, and a small, almost imperceptible quantity of ashes floats from it to the feet of the pope.

"*Sic transit gloria mundi!*" (So passes the glory of the world!) exclaimed Francesco Albani, with proud presumptuousness and with maliciously-scornful glances, while with an expression of savage triumph he stares in the paling face of the pope. "*Sic transit gloria mundi!*" repeated Albani, in a yet louder and more thundering voice.

The bells ring, the hymn resounds, the trombone and organ clang; the audience are on their knees in prayer. A bustle arises, a suppressed murmur—the holy father of Christendom has fainted upon his throne like any common mortal man.

He has had a vision, the poor pope! It seemed to him that he had seen the face of his murderer, and, as his sentence of death, resounded the scoffing words of Albani: "*Sic transit gloria mundi!*"

CHAPTER XXXVIII.

THE VAPO.

SINCE Paulo had left her, and she found herself alone, Natalie felt sad, solitary, in the paradise that surrounded her. No longer did she sing in emulation of the birds, no longer did she hop with youthful delight and the impetuosity of a young roe through the charming alleys. Sadly, and with downcast eyes, sat she under the myrtle-bush by the murmuring fountains, and frequent heavy sighs heaved her laboring breast.

"All is changed, all!" she often thoughtfully said to herself. "A great and terrible secret has been unveiled within me—the secret of my utter abandonment! I have no one on earth to whom I belong! Once I never thought of that. Paulo was all to me, my friend, my father, my brother; but Paulo has abandoned me, I belong not to him, and hence I could not go with him. And who is left to me? Carlo!" she answered herself in a low tone, and with a melancholy smile. "But Carlo has not filled the void that Paulo's absence has left in my heart. At first I thought he could, but that was only a short deception. Carlo is good and kind, always devoted, always ready to serve me. He always conforms himself to my will, is all subjection, all obedience. But that is terrible, unbearable!" exclaimed the almost weeping young maiden. "Who, then, shall I obey, before whom shall I tremble, when all obey me and tremble before me? And yet Carlo is a man. No," said she, quite low, "were he so, I should then obey him, and not be me; then would he give me commands, and not I him! No, Carlo is no man—Paulo was so! Where art thou, my friend, my father?"

And the young maiden yearningly spread her arms in the air, calling upon her distant friend with tender, low-whispered words and heart-felt longings.

But the days slowly passed, and still no news came from him. Natalie dreamily and sadly sank deeper into herself; her cheeks paled, her step became less light and elastic. In vain did her true friends, Marianne and Carlo, exhaust themselves in projects and propositions for her distraction and amusement.

"You should go into the world and amuse yourself in society, princess," said Carlo.

"I hate the world and society," said Natalie. "People are all bad, and I abominate them. What had I done to these people, how had I offended them even in thought, and yet they would have murdered me the very first time I appeared among them? No, no, leave me here in my solitude, where I at least have not to tremble for my life, where I have Carlo to guard and protect me."

The singer pressed the proffered hand to his lips.

"Then let us at least make some excursions in the environs of Rome," said he.

"No," said she, "I should everywhere long to be back in my garden. Nowhere is it so beautiful as here. Leave me my paradise—why would you drive me from it?"

"Alas!" despairingly exclaimed Carlo, "you call yourself happy and satisfied; why, then, are you so sad?"

"Am I sad?" she asked, with surprise. "No, Carlo, I am not sad! I sometimes dream, nothing more? Let me yet dream!"

"You will die," thought Carlo, and with an effort he forced back the cry of despair that pressed to his lips; but his cheeks paled, and his whole form trembled.

Seeing it, Natalie shook off her apathy, and with a lively sympathy and tender friendship she inquired the cause of his disquiet. She was so near him that her breath fanned his cheek, and her locks touched his brow.

"Ah, you would kill me, you would craze me!" murmured he, sorrowfully, sinking down, powerless, at her feet.

She looked wonderingly at him. "Why are you angry with me?" she innocently said, "and what have I done, that you so wrongfully accuse me?"

"What have you done?" cried he, beside himself,—the moment had overcome him, this moment had burst the bands with which he had bound his heart, and in unfettered freedom, in glowing passion, his long-concealed secret forced its way to his lips. He must at length for once speak of his sorrows, even if death should follow; he must give expression to his torment and his love, even should Natalie banish him forever from her presence!

"What have you done?" repeated he. "Ah, she does not even know that she is slowly murdering me, she does not even know that I love her!"

"Am I not to know?" she reproachfully asked. "Would you, indeed, have saved my life had you not loved me? Carlo, I am indebted to you for my life, and you say I murder you!"

"Yes," he frowardly exclaimed, "you murder me! Slowly, day by day, hour by hour, am I consumed by this frightful internal fire that is destroying me. Ah, you know not that you are killing me. And have you not destroyed my youthful strength, and from a man converted me into an old, trembling, and complaining woman? Is it not for your sake that I have fled the world, leaving behind me all it offered of fame and wealth and honor? Is it not your fault that I have ceased to be a free man, to have a will of my own, and have become a slave crawling at your feet? Ah, woe is me, that I ever came to know you! You are an enchantress, you have made me your hound, and, whining, I lie in the dust before you, satisfied when you touch me with your foot."

At first, Natalie had listened to him with terror and astonishment; then an expression of noble pride was to be read upon her features, a glowing flush flitted over her delicate cheeks, and with flashing eyes and a heaving bosom she sprang up from her seat. Proud as a queen she rose erect, the blood of her ancestors awoke in her; she at this moment felt herself free as an empress, as proud, as secure—and, stretching her arm toward the outlet of the garden, she said in a determined tone: "Go, Signor Carlo! Leave me, I tell you! We have no longer any thing in common with each other!"

Carlo seemed as if awakened from a delirium. Breathless, with widely-opened eyes, trembling and anxious, he stared at the angry maiden. He knew nothing of what he had said; he comprehended not her anger, only his infinite suffering; he was conscious only of his long-suppressed, long-concealed secret love. And, grasping Natalie's hands with an imploring expression, he

constrained the young maiden, almost against her will, to remain and reseat herself upon the grassy bank before which he knelt.

As he looked up to her with those glowing, passionate glances, a maiden fear and trembling for the first time came over her, an anxiety and timidity inexplicable to herself! Her delicate, transparent cheeks paled, tears filled her eyes, and, folding her hands with a childishly supplicating expression, she said in a low, tremulous tone: "My God, my God! Have mercy upon me! I am a wholly abandoned, solitary orphan! Rescue me yet from this trouble and distress, from this terrible loneliness!"

"Fear nothing, my charming angel," whispered Carlo, "I will be gentle as a lamb, and patient, very patient in my sorrow; I have sworn it and will keep my oath! But you must bear me' You must, only this one time, allow me to express in words my love and my sorrow, my misery and my ecstasy. Will you allow me this, my lily, my beautiful swan?"

He would have again grasped her hand, but she withdrew it with a proud, angry glance.

"Speak on," said she, wearily leaning her head against the myrtle-bush. "Speak on, I will listen to you!"

And he spoke to her of his love; he informed her of his former life, his poverty, his want, his connection with Corilla, whom he had quitted in order to devote himself wholly to her, to obey, serve, and worship her all his life, and, if necessary, to die for her! "But you," he despairingly said, " you know not love! Your heart is cold for earthly love; like the angels in heaven, you love only the good and the sublime, you love mankind collectively, but not the individual. Ah, Natalie, you have the heart of an angel, but not the heart of a woman!"

The young maiden had half dreamingly listened to him, her head leaned back and her glance directed toward the heavens. She now smiled, and, with an inimitable grace, laying her hand upon her bosom, said in a very low tone: "And yet I feel that a woman's heart is beating there. But it sleeps! Who will one day come to awaken it?"

Carlo did not understand these low, whispered words; he understood only his own passion, his own consuming glow. And anew he commenced his love-plainings, described to her the torments and fierce joys of an unreturned love, which is yet too strong and overpowering to be suppressed. And Natalie listened to him with a dreamy thoughtfulness. His words sounded in her ears like a wonderful song from a strange, distant world which she knew not, but the description of which filled her heart with a sweet longing, and she could have wept, without knowing whether it was for sorrow or joy.

"Thus, Natalie," at length said Carlo, entirely exhausted and pale with emotion—"thus love I you. You must sometime have learned it, and have known that even angels cannot mingle with mortals unloved and unpunished. I should finally have been compelled to tell you that you might torture no longer in cruel ignorance; that you, learning to understand your own heart, might tell

me whether I have to hope, or only to fear!"

"Poor Carlo!" murmured Natalie. "You love me, but I do not love you! This has even now become clear to me; and while you have so glowingly described the passion, I have for the first time comprehended that I yet know nothing of that love, and that I can never learn it of you! This is a misfortune, Carlo, but as we cannot change, we must submit to it."

Carlo drooped his head and sighed. He had no answer to make, and only murmuringly repeated her words: "Yes, we must submit to it!"

"And why can we not?" she almost cheerfully asked, with that childlike innocence which never once comprehended the sorrow she was preparing for Carlo—"why can we not joyfully submit? We both love, only in a different manner. Let each preserve and persevere in his own manner, and then all may yet be well!"

"And it shall be well!" exclaimed Carlo, with animation. "You cannot love me as I love you, but I can devote my whole life to you, and that will I do! At home, in my charming Naples, a beautiful custom is prevalent. When one loves, he is adopted as a *vapo*, a protector, who follows the steps of the one he loves, who watches before her door when she sleeps, who secretly lurks at a distance behind her when she leaves her house, who observes every passer-by in order to preserve her from every murderous or other inimical attack, or in case of need to hasten to her assistance. Such a *vapo* protects her against the jealousy of her husband or the vengeance of a dismissed lover.* Natalie, as I cannot be your lover, I will be your *vapo*. Will you accept my services?"

Giving him her hand, she smilingly said, "I will."

Carlo pressed that hand to his lips, and bedewed it with a warm tear.

"Well, then, I swear myself your *vapo*," said he, with deep emotion. "Wherever you may be, I shall be near you, I shall always follow to warn and to protect you; should you be in danger, call me and you will find me at your side, whether by night or by day; I shall always watch over you, and sleep at the threshold of your door, and should a dream alarm you, I shall be there to tranquillize you. So long as I live, Natalie, so long as your

*Archenholz. "England and Italy," vol v., p. 187.

vapo has a dagger and a sure hand, so long shall misfortune fail to penetrate into your dwelling. You cannot be mine, or return my love, but I can care for you and watch over you. In accepting me for your *vapo*, you have given me the right to die for you if necessary, and that of itself is a happiness!"

Thus speaking, Carlo rose, and, no longer able to conceal his deep emotion and suppress his tears, he left Natalie, and hastened into the obscurest alleys of the garden.

The young maiden watched his retreat with a sad smile.

"Poor Carlo!" murmured she, "and ah! yet much poorer Natalie! He loves at least. But I, am I not much more to be pitied? I have no one whom I love. I am entirely isolated, and of what use is a solitary paradise?"

CHAPTER XXXIX

THE INVASION.

CORILLA had kept her word. She had sent to Alexis Orloff, Carlo's brother, Joseph Ribas, the galley-slave, and with a malicious smile she had said to the latter, "You will avenge me on your treacherous brother?"

Count Orloff warmly welcomed Corilla's *protégé*.

"If you give me satisfaction," said he, "you may expect a royal recompense, and the favor of the exalted Empress of Russia. First of all, tell me what you can do?"

"Not much," said Joseph Ribas, laughing, "and the little I can will yet be condemned as too much. I can very dexterously wield the dagger, and reach the heart through the back! Because I did that to a successful rival at Palermo, I was compelled by the police to flee to Naples. There a good friend taught me how to make counterfeit money, an art which I brought to some perfection, and which I successfully practised for some years. But the police, thinking my skill too great, finally relieved me from my employment, and gave me free board and lodging for ten years in the galleys. Ah! that was a happy time, your excellency. I learned much in the galleys, and something which I can now turn to account in your service. I learned to speak the Russian language like a native of Moscow. Such a one was for seven years my inseparable friend and chain-companion, and as he was too stupid or too lazy to learn my language, I was forced to learn his, that I might be able to converse with him a little. That, your excellency, is about all I know: to wield the dagger, make counterfeit money, speak the Russian language, and some other trifling tricks, which, however, may be of no service to your excellency."

"Who knows?" said Orloff, laughing. "Do you understand, for example, how to break into a house and steal gold and diamonds, without being caught in the act?"

"That," said Joseph, thoughtfully, "I should hope to be able to accomplish. I have, indeed, as yet had no experience in that line, but in the galleys I have listened to the soundest instructions, and heard the experiences of the greatest master of that art, with the curiosity of an emulous student!"

Orloff laughed. "You are a sly fellow," said he, "and please me much. If you act as well as you talk, we shall soon be good friends! Well, to-morrow night you make your first essay. The business is an invasion."

"And that shall be my master-piece!" responded Joseph Ribas.

"If you succeed, I will, in the name of my illustrious empress, immediately take you into her service, and you become an officer of the Russian marine."

Joseph Ribas stared at him with astonishment. "That is certainly an immense honor and a great good fortune," said he, "only I should like to know if the Russian marine engages in sea-fights, and if the officers are then obliged to stand under fire?"

"Yes, indeed," cried Orloff, laughing, "but in such cases you can conceal yourself behind the cannon until the fight is over!"

"I shall remember your wise suggestion in time of need!" seriously responded Joseph Ribas, bowing to the count.* "And where, your excellency, is to be the scene of my present activity? Where am I to gain my epaulets?"

"I will myself conduct you to the spot and show you the house where a rich set of diamonds and some thousands of scudi are lying in company with your epaulets!"

"And as I have rather long fingers, I shall be able to grasp both the epaulets and the treasure," laughingly responded Ribas.

---

* And, in fact, Ribas did remember it! At a later period, having become a Russian admiral, he was intrusted with the command of the flotilla which was to descend the Danube to aid in the capture of Killa and Ismail. But during the investment of Ismail (December 21, 1790), Ribas concealed himself among the reeds on the bank of the Danube, and did not reappear until the danger was over and he could in safety share in the booty taken by his sailors. But this cowardice and avarice of their admiral very nearly caused a mutiny among the sailors. It was not suppressed without the greatest efforts. (See "Mémoires Secrètes sur la Russie, par Masson," vol. iii., p. 381.)

It was in the evening after this conversation of Orloff with Joseph Ribas, a wonderfully brilliant evening, such as is known only under Italian skies.

Natalie inhaled the soft air with delight, and drank in the intoxicating odor of the flowers which poured out their sweetest fragrance in the cool of the evening. She was on this evening unusually cheerful; with a smiling brow and childish gayety, as in happier days, she skipped down the alleys, or, with her guitar upon her arm, reposed upon her favorite seat under the myrtle-bush near the murmuring fountains.

"I am to-day so happy, ah, so happy," said she, "in consequence of having dreamed of Paulo—in my dream he was near me, spoke to me, and that is a sure sign of his speedy return! Oh, certainly, certainly! In my dream he announced it to me, and I distinctly heard him say: 'We shall meet again, Natalie. I shall soon be with you!'"

"Ah, may this dream but prove true!" sighed Marianne, Natalie's faithful companion. She was standing, not far from her mistress, with Carlo, and both were tenderly observing the young maiden, who now smilingly grasped her guitar and commenced a song of joy for Paulo's expected return!

"I have no faith in our count's return!" whispered Marianne while Natalie was singing. "It is a bad sign that no news, not a line, nor even the shortest message, has yet come from him. Something unusual, some great and uncontrollable misfortune, must have prevented his writing!"

"You do not think they have imprisoned him?" asked Carlo.

"I fear it," sighed Marianne. "And if so, what fate then awaits our poor princess? Helpless, alone, without means! For if the count is imprisoned, he will no longer be in a condition to send money, as he promised. And we now possess only a thousand scudi, with double that amount in diamonds!"

"Then we are still rich enough to keep off deprivations for a time!" said Carlo.

"But when at length these last resources are exhausted?" asked Marianne—"when we no longer have either money or diamonds—how then?"

"Oh, then," exclaimed Carlo, with a beaming face, "then will we labor for her! That also will be a pleasure, Marianne!"

While the two were thus conversing, Natalie, with a happy smile and cheerful face, was still singing her hymn of joy for Paulo's approaching return, to the accompaniment of the rustling trees, the murmuring fountains, and the chirping birds in the myrtle-bush. It was a beautiful night, and as the bright full moon now advanced between the pines, illuminating Natalie's face and form, the partially intoxicated and perfectly happy Carlo whispered: "Only look, Marianne!—does she not resemble a blessed angel ready to spread her wings and with the moonlight to mount up to the stars?—Only look, seems it not as if the moonbeams tenderly embraced her for the purpose of leading an angel back to its home?"

"May she, at least, one day, with such a happy smile, take her departure for the skies!" sighed Marianne, piously folding her hands.

At this moment a shrill, cutting wail interrupted Natalie's song. A string of her guitar had suddenly snapped asunder; frightened, almost angry, Natalie let the instrument fall to the earth, and again the strings resounded like lamentations and sighs.

"That is a bad omen," sighed Natalie. "How, if that should be true, and not my dream?"

And, trembling with anxiety, the young maiden stretched forth her hands toward her friends.

"Carlo,—Marianne," she anxiously said, "come here to me, protect me with your love from this mortal fear and anguish which has suddenly come over me. See, the moon is hiding behind the clouds. Ah, the whole world grows dark and casts a mourning-veil over its bright face!"

And the timid child, clinging to Marianne's arm, concealed her face in the bosom of her motherly friend.

"And you call that an omen!" said Carlo, with forced cheerfulness. "This time, princess, I am the *fatum* which has alarmed you! It is my own fault that this string broke. It was already injured and half broken this evening when I tuned the guitar, but I hoped it would suffice for the low, sad melodies you now always play. Yes, could I have known that you would have so exulted and shouted, I should have replaced it with another string, and this great misfortune would not have occurred."

While speaking, he had again attached the string and drawn it tight.

"The defective string is quickly repaired, and you can recommence your hymn of joy," he said, handing back the guitar to Natalie.

She sadly shook her head. "It is passed," said she, "I can exult and sing no more to-day, and have an aversion to this garden. See how black and threatening these pines rise up, and do not these myrtle-bushes resemble large dark graves? No, no, it frightens me here—I can no longer remain among these graves and these watchers of the dead! Come, let us go to our rooms! It is night—we will sleep and dream! Come, let us immediately go into the house."

And, like a frightened roe, she fled toward the house, the others following her.

In an hour all was silent in the villa. The lights were successively extinguished in Natalie's and Marianne's chambers; only in Carlo's little chamber yet burned a dull, solitary lamp, and occasionally the shadow of the uneasy singer passed the window as he restlessly walked his room. At length, however, this lamp, also, was extinguished, and all was dark and still.

About this time a dark shadow was seen creeping slowly and cautiously through the garden. Soon it stood still, and then one might have supposed it to be a deception, and that only the wind shaking the pines had caused that moving shadow. But suddenly it again appeared in a moonlighted place, where no bush or tree threw its shade, and, as if alarmed by the brightness, it then again moved aside into the bushes.

This shadow came constantly nearer and nearer to the house, and, as the walks were here broader and lighter, one might distinctly discern that it was a human being, the form of a tall, stately man, that so cautiously and stealthily approached the house. And what is that, sparkling and flashing in his girdle —is it not a dagger, together with a pistol and a long knife? Ah, a threatening, armed man is approaching this silent, solitary house, and no one sees, no one hears him! Even the two large hounds which with remarkable watchfulness patrol the garden during the night, even they are silent! Ah, where, then, are they? Carlo had himself unchained them that they might wander freely—where, then, can they be?

They lie in the bushes far from the house, cold, stiff, and, lifeless. Before them lies a piece of seductively smelling meat. That was what had enticed them to forget their duty, and, instead of growling and barking, they had with snuffling noses been licking this tempting flesh. Their instinct had not told them it was poisoned, and therefore they now lay stiff and cold near the food that had destroyed them.

No, from those hounds he had nothing more to fear, this bold, audacious man; the hounds will no more betray him, nor warningly announce that Joseph Ribas, the venturesome thief and galley-slave, is lurking about the house to steal or murder, as the case may be.

He has now reached the house. He listens for a moment, and as all remains still, no suspicious noise making itself heard, with pitch-covered paper, brought with him for the purpose, he presses in one of the window panes. Then, passing his hand through the vacancy caused by the absent pane of glass, he opens one wing of the French window, and by a bold leap springing upon the parapet, he lets himself glide slowly down into the room.

Again all is still, and silent lies the solitary, peaceful villa. Suddenly appears a small but bright light behind one of these dark windows.

That is the thief's lantern, which Joseph Ribas has lighted to illuminate his dark, criminal way.

He cautiously ascends the stairs leading to the second story, and not a step jars under his feet, not one, nor does the slightest noise betray him.

He is now above, in the long corridor. Approaching the first door, he listens long. He hears a loud breathing—some one sleeps within. With one sole quick movement he turns the key remaining in the lock. The door is now locked, and the sleeper within remains undisturbed. Joseph creeps along to the next door, and again he listens to ascertain if there be anything stirring within. But no, he hears nothing! All is still behind this door.

He draws a pistol from his girdle, cocks it, and, thus prepared to resist every attack, he suddenly opens the door. No one is in the room, no one but Joseph Ribas the thief, who, with flashing eyes, suspiciously and carefully examines every hole and corner.

But no, no one is there. Calm and sure, Joseph Ribas steps into the room, drawing and bolting the door behind him. No one can now surprise him, no one can fall upon him from behind. But yes, there is also a door on each side, right and left. He listens at the first, he thinks he hears a light breathing; here also he quickly shoves a bolt and passes over to the other door, which stands ajar. Cautiously he pushes it open and looks in. A small, dull lamp is burning there, lighting the lovely face of the sleeping Princess Natalie.

"That is she!" low murmured Ribas, as with eager glances he observes the young and charming maiden. He is drawn forward as if with invisible bands—he penetrates into this sacred asylum of the slumbering maiden. But he forcibly checks his advance. "I have sworn not to touch her, and I will keep my word, that I may secure my epaulets!" he muttered to himself, and, retreating into the first chamber, he bolts the door, to make all sure, that leads into Natalie's chamber.

"Now to the work!" said he, with decision. "Here stands the bureau, the treasure must be here."

And, placing the dark lantern upon a table, he draws forth his picklock and chisels, and commences breaking open the bureau. Right—his thievish instinct has not deceived him, he has found all, all. Here is the little box of sparkling diamonds, and here the full purses of money.

With a knavish smile, Joseph Ribas conceals the brilliants in his bosom, and deposits the money in his capacious pockets.

"It is a pity that this is not mine," he muttered, with a grin, "but toward this count I must act as an honorable thief, and I have promised to bring it all truly to him."

The work is completed, the malicious

criminal act is performed. He can now go, can again creep away from the house his feet have soiled.

Why goes he not? Why does he linger in these rooms? Why directs he such wild and eager glances to the door behind which Natalie sleeps?

He cannot withstand the temptation, and even at the risk of awaking Natalie, he must see her once more! And, moreover, what had he to fear from an isolated young girl? He will only have one more look at her. Nothing more!

He noiselessly pushes back the bolt; noiselessly, upon tiptoe, with closed lantern, he creeps into the room and to Natalie's bedside.

She is wonderfully beautiful, and she smiles in her slumber. How charming is that placid face, that half-uncovered shoulder, that arm thrown up over her head, where it is half concealed under her luxuriant locks! Wonderfully beautiful is she. Dares he to touch that arm and breathe a kiss, a very light kiss, upon those fragrant lips? Why not? No one sees him, nor will Count Alexis Orloff ever know that his commands have been disobeyed.

But as he bent down, as his breath comes only in light contact with her cheek, she stirs! Maiden modesty never slumbers; it watches over the sleeping girl, it protects her. It is her good genius who never deserts her.

Drawing herself up, Natalie opens her eyes and starts up from her couch. Then she sees a large, threatening masculine form close before her, close before her that wildly-laughing face.

A shriek of anguish and terror bursts from her lips, and in a tone of alarm she calls: "Carlo, Carlo! Help! help. Carlo! Save—"

More she did not say. With a wild rage, angry, and ashamed of his own folly, Joseph Ribas rushes upon her.

"One more cry!" he threateningly said—"one more call for help, and I will murder you!"

But at this moment a small curtained door which Ribas had not remarked and hence not fastened, was suddenly opened, and Carlo rushed in.

"I am here, Natalie!—I am here!"

Rushing upon the stranger, and grasping him with gigantic strength, he thrust him down from the bed.

Joseph Ribas turned toward his new and unexpected enemy. The lamp lighted his face, and falling back Carlo shrieked, "My brother!"

Joseph Ribas broke out into a loud, savage laugh. "At length we meet, my brother," said he. "But this time you shall not hinder me in my work. This time I am the conqueror!"

"No, no, that you are not!" cried Carlo, beside himself with pain and rage. "Confess what you want in this house—confess, or you are a dead man!"

And with a drawn dagger he rushed upon his opponent!

A frightful struggle ensued. Natalie, in her night-dress, pale as a lily, knelt upon her bed and prayed. She had folded her hands over her breast, directly over the place where the papers confided to her by Paulo, in a little silken bag, always hung suspended by a golden chain.

"Grant, O my God," prayed she— "grant that I may keep my promise to

THE INVASION. p. 212.

Paulo, and that I may defend these papers with my life!"

And the two brothers were still struggling and contending; like two serpents they had coiled around each other, and held each other in their toils.

"Flee, flee, Natalie!" groaned Carlo, with a weakened voice—"flee away from here! I yet hold him, you are yet safe! Flee!"

But in this moment the maiden thought not of her own danger. She thought only of Carlo. Springing from her bed, with flashing eyes she boldly threw herself between the contending men.

"No, no," said she, courageously, "I will not flee—I shall at least know how to die!"

A shriek resounded from Carlo's lips, his arms relaxed and fell from his enemy, leaving his brother free.

"Ah, finally, finally!" gasped the panting Joseph. "That was an amusing carnival farce, my virtuous brother! Farewell! I am this time triumphant!"

With a wild leap he sprang to the door; brandishing his bloody dagger in his right hand, he ran through the corridor, down the stairs, and out into the garden.

"Saved!" said he, breathing more freely. "I think this Russian will be satisfied with me! I bring the money and the diamonds, and at the same time have effectually opened a vein for this troublesome protector! Ah, it seems to me I have very successfully put in practice my studies in the high-school of the galleys!"

And, humming a jovial song, Joseph Ribas swung himself into a tree close to the wall, and let himself down on the other side.

Above, in Natalie's chamber, Carlo long lay stretched on the floor, pale, with the death-rattle in his throat. In a bright stream flowed the blood from the wound made by his brother's dagger. Natalie knelt by him. No tear was in her eye, no lamentation escaped her lips. She seemed perfectly calm and collected in her excess of sorrow; she only sought with her robe and her hair to cover Carlo's wound and stop the flow of blood.

A happy smile played upon Carlo's blue lips.

"I die," he murmured, "but I die for thee! Thy *vapo* has kept his word, he has defended thee until his last breath! How good is God! He lets me die in thy service!"

"No, no, you must not die!" cried Natalie, her calmness giving place to the wildest sorrow. "No, Carlo, you must live! Oh, say not that you die! Ah, you love me, and yet you would leave me alone! Only live, and I also will love you, Carlo, as warmly and as glowingly as you love me! Do but remain with me and my heart, my life shall be yours!"

"Too late! too late!" murmured Carlo, with dying lips. "Remember me, Natalie—I have dearly loved you. I die happy, for I die in your arms!"

"No, no, you shall live in my arms!" sobbed she. "I will be yours—your bride!"

"Kiss me, my bride," he falteringly stammered.

She bent over him, and with hers she

touched his lips, already stiffening in death. She laid her warm, glowing cheek to his cold and marble-pale face; that full, fresh life pressed that which was cold and expiring to her bosom in an ardent struggle with death! In vain!

Death is inexorable. What he has once touched with his hand, that is past recovery, it is his.

The blood no longer flowed from Carlo's wound, the breath no longer rattled in his throat—it was silent; but a blessed smile still lay upon his lips. With this smile had he died, happy, blessed in the embrace of her he had so truly loved.

When Marianne, after long and vain efforts to open the door, had finally managed, by tying her bed-clothes to-gether, to let herself down into the garden, and had thence hastened into the house, and up into Natalie's chamber, she found there all silent and still. Nothing stirred. Natalie lay in a death-like swoon.

He, Carlo, already stiffened in death, and she, the senseless Natalie, with her head reclining against the marble face of her friend!

Poor Natalie! Why must Marianne succeed in awaking thee from thy swoon? Why did you not let her continue in her insensibility, Marianne? In sleep, she at least would not have realized that she was now left entirely alone, entirely abandoned, with no one to defend her against her cruel and artful enemies, of whose existence she never once dreamed!

CHAPTER XL.

INTRIGUES.

COUNT ORLOFF lay in a comfortable, careless position upon his divan, leisurely smoking his long Turkish pipe. Before him stood Joseph Ribas, laughingly relating in his own comic manner the occurrences of the preceding night.

"You are a wonderful man," said Orloff, when Joseph had finished. "You have honestly earned your epaulets, and to-day you will for the first time appear at my dinner-table as a Russian officer. Ah, I prophesy a great future for you. You have the requisite skill and address to make your fortune. You are shrewd, daring, and you recoil from no means, finding them all good and useful when they forward your aims. With such principles one may go far in this world, and Russia in fact offers you the best opportunity for bringing all these fine talents into use."

"And, moreover, I commenced my Russian career with a good omen," said Joseph. "I have placed a murder at the head of my Russian deeds! That is a promising commencement, is it not, Sir Count? You must know that better than any one."

"Indeed yes, I must best know that," said the count, laughing, and continually stroking his long black beard. "By a fair and well-timed murder one can always make his fortune in Russia. A well-timed and well-executed murder is with us often rewarded with a barony and the title of count. Indeed, sometimes with the highest and tenderest imperial favor and grace. Ah, a murder at the right moment is an excellent thing, only one must be quite sure of himself, and not fail of hitting the right man. An unsuccessful murder is a very bad, and, indeed, a very dangerous thing. I would have nothing to do with one, and never have had any thing to do with one. Whatever I have undertaken I have always boldly and successfully accomplished. The good Emperor Peter III. knew that, and consequently trembled when I, with Passeb and Bariatinsky, entered his chamber. The good emperor! He did not tremble long, it was soon finished. Yes, yes, that was a deed done at the right time, and therefore has the great Catharine been so grateful to us, and honored us above all the illustrious grandees of her empire." *

"My little opening murder has, indeed, less significance," sighed Joseph Ribas. "What was it but to help a

---

* Of the tragic and horrible events connected with Catharine's accession to the throne, and of the strangulation of Peter, in which he took so active a part, Orloff spoke in Rome with the greatest freedom and evident pleasure.—Gorani, vol. ii., p. 23.

humble musician to the blessedness and harmony of the spheres!"

"But that musician was your brother!"

Ribas shrugged his shoulders. "That is, he was so considered; but in reality I believe he was only a half-brother. My mother, of blessed memory, had many little adventures, and I think Carlo's birth was somewhat connected with them. Nor am I sure that it was not a necessary work to kill him, as it was surely my duty to avenge my father's injured honor, which is all I have done! Upon these grounds has a good, honest priest this day given me absolution, and I now stand before you pure and sinless as a maiden! We can therefore begin anew, your excellency. Have you still any commands for me?"

"You now have a very noble and sublime part to play," said Orloff, laughing. "You must now appear as the benefactor of our Russian princess, and as the mediating forerunner of my own person!"

"That will be indeed a charming rôle," said Ribas, rubbing his hands with delight. "I shall admirably acquit myself as benefactor and mediator. But give me some details, Sir Count!"

"You shall have them," said Orloff, "from the mouth of Stephano.—Stephano!"

The person called immediately appeared at the door of a side-room.

"Stephano," said Orloff, "now to the work, friend. The courier who arrived to-day has brought us good news and full powers. Count Paul Raczinsky is sent to Siberia for high-treason—his property is confiscated and falls to the state. I have an unlimited power, signed by the empress herself, to seize and sell his possessions here in the name of the empress. Take with you some attorney and officers and go to this villa. But, first of all, help our little Joseph Ribas to his uniform and epaulets, that he may be properly costumed for a rescuer and benefactor. And now, away with you! Instruct him well, Stephano. Ah, I should like to be present at this delightful comedy!"

And Count Orloff broke out into a hearty laugh.

"This whole affair is very entertaining and romantic," he said to himself, as soon as he was alone. "I am truly very thankful to Catharine for intrusting it to me. I love the adventurous and romantic. Indeed, whom else could she have chosen for this business? I should like to know who would dare to enter the lists with me, the Russian Hercules, and who would be so bold as to contend with me for this prize?"

Thus speaking, he rose from the divan and stepped to the great Venetian mirror, before which he long remained attentively viewing himself.

"Ahem! this tender Empress Catharine knows how to judge of manly beauty," murmured he, with a self-satisfied smile, "and I cannot blame her for so often giving me the preference over my brother Gregory. Besides, I shall first appear before this little Princess Natalie in my antique dress. Catharine has often told me I was enchanting in my antique costume. Well, we will also let this enchantment work a little here. But first we must think of what is near est to us. This Corilla has rendered us a service, and we must be grateful. They say she loves diamonds. I shall therefore send her these diamonds which her *élève* Joseph Ribas last night made the property of the Russian crown. And with them I will send a little billet, written with my own hand. Who knows but that this will give her more pleasure than the sparkling brilliants!"

In that, however, the handsome Count Orloff was mistaken. The poetess Corilla therein resembled to a hair the prima-donnas and heroines of the stage of the present day. She attached a great value to diamonds, and knowing that Russia was very rich in gold and diamonds, she always had an especially bewitching smile for Russian grandees. Had Count Orloff come in person to bring the diamonds, she would undoubtedly have more admired him, apparently been more pleased with his presence than with his costly gift; but, as he was not there, there was no necessity for dissimulation.

She read Count Orloff's billet with a satisfied smile; but soon laid it aside for the delight of examining the jewels.

"How that shines, and how that sparkles," said the exhilarated poetess; "not even a lover's eyes flash so brightly, nor is his smile so proud, so full of rich certainty, as the sparkling of these gems! They are enchanters, and a word from me can change these *solitaires* and rosettes into a beautiful villa, or into a fragrant park with silent arbors, intoxicating odors, and sweetly-singing birds. All that is promised me by these stones—a lover's promises do not express half so much. And only to think that it is Carlo, my former lover, to whom I am indebted for these diamonds! From love to him I wished to destroy Natalie, and that wish procured me the favor of the Russian count, and consequently these brilliants. Poor Carlo! these diamonds outlast you. How bright and beautiful were your glances that are now extinguished by death—but this cruel, inexorable death has no power over diamonds! It cannot strangle these as thou wert strangled, poor Carlo! I shall remember thee this evening, Carlo, and hope the thought of thee may inspire me for a right beautiful improvisation on death! I shall take pains still to bring to mind thy beautiful form overflowed with blood. Yes, it will inspire in me a very effective improvisation, and I will at the same time make a selection from my dear poets of some striking rhymes upon death and the grave. And when I have the rhymes, the thoughts and words will come of themselves. Rhymes, rhymes, these are the main thing with poets!"

And while the improvisatrice was thus speaking to herself, she had mechanically adorned her person with the brilliants, attaching the beautiful collar to her neck, the long pendants to her ears, and placing the splendid diadem upon her brow.

She looked exceedingly beautiful in these ornaments, and consequently rejoiced that her friend Cardinal Francesco Albani came at this precise moment.

"He will be ravished!" said she, with a smile, advancing to meet him with the proud and imposing dignity of a queen.

"You are beautiful as a goddess!" exclaimed the cardinal, "and whoever sees you thus has seen the protecting divinity of ancient Rome, the sublime Juno, queen of heaven!"

"Were I Juno, would you consent to be my Vulcan?" roguishly asked Corilla.

"No," said Albani, laughing; "the noble Juno was not exactly true to her Vulcan, and I require a faithful love! Would you be that, Corilla?"

"We shall see," said she, changing the arrangement of the diadem before the glass—"we shall see, my worthy friend. But forget not the conditions—first the laurel-crown!"

"You shall have it!" triumphantly responded the cardinal.

"Are you certain of that?" asked Corilla, with flashing eyes and glowing cheeks.

Cardinal Francesco Albani smiled mysteriously.

"Pope Ganganelli is ill," said he, "and it is thought he will die!"

CHAPTER XLI.

THE DOOMING LETTER.

GROANING, supported by his faithful Lorenzo's arm, Pope Ganganelli slowly moved through the walks of his garden. Some months had passed since the suppression of the order of the Jesuits—how had these few months changed poor Clement! Where was the peace and cheerfulness of his face, where was the sublime expression of his features, the firm and noble carriage of his body—where was it all?

Trembling, shattered, with distorted features, and with dull, half-closed eyes, crawled he about with groans, his brow wrinkled, his lips compressed by pain and inward sorrow.

No one dared to remain with him; he spoke to no one. But Lorenzo was yet sometimes able to drive away the clouds from his brow, and to recall a faint smile to his thin pale lips.

He had also to-day succeeded in this, and for the first time in several weeks had Ganganelli, yielding to his prayers, consented to a walk in the garden of the Quirinal.

"This air refreshes me," said the pope, breathing more freely ; "it seems as if it communicated to my lungs a renewed vital power and caused the blood to flow more rapidly in my veins. Lorenzo, this is a singularly fortunate day for me, and I will make the most of it.

Come, we will repair to our Franciscan Place!"

"That is an admirable idea," said Lorenzo, delighted. "If your holiness can reach it, you will recover your health, and all will again be well."

Ganganelli sighed, and glanced toward heaven with a sad smile.

"Health!" said he. "Ah, Lorenzo, that word reminds me of a lost paradise. The avenging angel has driven me from it, and I shall never see it again."

"Say not so!" begged Lorenzo, secretly wiping a tear from his cheek. "No, say not so, you will certainly recover!"

"Yes, recover!" replied the pope. "For death is a recovery, and in the end perhaps the most real."

They silently walked on, and, making a path through the bushes, they at length arrived at the place, with the construction of which Lorenzo had some months before surprised the pope, and which Ganganelli had since named the "Franciscan Place."

"So," joyfully exclaimed Lorenzo, while the exhausted pope glided down upon the grass-bank—"so, brother Clement, now let us be cheerful! You know that here we have nothing more to do with the pope. You have yourself declared that here you would be brother Clement, and nothing more; now brother Clement was always a healthy man, full of juvenile spirits and strength."

"Ah, my friend," responded Ganganelli, "I fear the pope has secretly followed brother Clement even to this place, and even here no longer leaves him free! No, no, it is no longer brother Clement who sits groaning here, it is the vicegerent of God, the father of Christendom, the holy and blessed pope! And if you knew, Lorenzo, what this vicegerent of God has to suffer and bear, how his blood like streams of fire runs through his veins, carbonizing his entrails and parching the roof of his mouth, so that the tongue fast cleaves to it, and he has no longer the power to complain of his misery! And such a crushed earthworm this miserable, infatuated people call the vicegerent of God, before whom they bow in the dust! Ah, foolish children, are you not yourselves disgusted with your masquerade, and do you not blush for this jest?"

"See you not," said Lorenzo, with forced cheerfulness, "that since you are here you have, against your will, again become brother Clement, and inveigh against God's vicegerent who holds his splendid court in the Vatican and Quirinal! Yes, yes, that was what brother Clement used to do in the Franciscan convent; he was always scolding about the pope."

"And yet he let men befool him and make a pope of him," said Ganganelli. "Ah, Lorenzo, they were indeed good purposes that decided me, and good and holy resolutions were in me when I bore this crown of St. Peter for the first time. Ah, I was then so young, not in years, but in hopes and illusions. I was so enthusiastic for the good and noble, and I wished to serve it, to honor and glorify it in the name of God!"

"And in the end you have done so!" solemnly responded Lorenzo.

"I have wished to do so!" sighed Ganganelli, "but there it has ended. I have been hemmed in everywhere; wherever I wished to press through, I have always found a wall before me—a wall of prejudices, of ancient customs, once received as indifferent, and at this wall my cardinals and officials held watch, taking care that my will should be broken against it, and not be able to break through, in order to let in a little freedom, a little fresh air, into our walled realm! They have curbed and weakened my will, until nothing more of it subsists, and of my holiest resolutions they have made a scarecrow before which foreign kings and princes cry murder, and prophesy the downfall of their kingdoms if I adhere to my innovations. Ah, the princes, the princes! I tell you, Lorenzo, it is the princes who have undermined the happiness of the world with their ideas of absolute power; they are the robbers of all mankind; for freedom, which is the common property of all men, that have they, like regular lawless highwaymen, appropriated for themselves alone. They plundered the luck-pennies of all mankind, and coined them into money adorned with their likenesses, and now all mankind run after this money, thinking: 'If I gain that, then shall I have recovered my part of human happiness which once belonged to all in common!' It has come to this, Lorenzo, through the rapacity of princes, and yet they still tremble upon their thrones, and fear that the people may one day awake from their stupid slumber, all rising as one man, and cry in the paling faces of their robbers: 'Give back what you have taken from us—we will have what is ours; we require freedom and human right; we will no longer remain slaves to tremble before a bugbear; we will be free children of God, and have no one to fear but the God above us and the consciences within our own breasts!' Come down, therefore, from your usurped thrones, become once more human—labor, enjoy, complain, and rejoice, as other men do; live not upon the sweat of your subjects, but nourish yourselves by your own efforts, that justice may prevail in the world, and humanity regain its rights!"

And Ganganelli's eyes flashed, his sunken cheeks were feverishly flushed, while he was thus speaking. Lorenzo observed it with anxious eyes; and when the pope made a momentary pause, he said: "You are again altogether the good and brave brother Clement, but even he should think about sparing himself!"

"And to what end should he spare himself?" excitedly exclaimed Ganganelli; "Death sits within me and laughs to scorn all my efforts, burying himself deeper and deeper in my inward life. You must know, Lorenzo, that my cause of sorrow is precisely this, that I now live in vain, and that I cannot finish what I began! I wished to make my people happy and free; that was what alarmed all these princes, that was an unheard-of innovation, and they have all put their heads together and whispered to each other, 'He will betray to mankind that they have rights of which we have robbed them. He wishes to give back to mankind his inherited portion of the booty! But what will then become of us? Will not our slaves rise up against us, demanding their human rights? We cannot suffer such innovations, for they involve our destruction!' Thus have they cried, and in their anxiety they have decided upon my death! Then they threw me in a crumb exactly suited to my dreams of improving the happiness of the people; they all consented that I should relieve mankind from that dangerous tapeworm, Jesuitism, and with secret laughter thought, 'It will be the death of him!' And they were right, these sly princes, it will be the death of me! I have abolished the order of Jesuits—in consequence of which I shall die—but the Jesuits will live, and live forever!"

The echo of approaching footsteps was now heard, and, sinking with fatigue, he directed Lorenzo to go and meet the intruder, and by no means to let any one penetrate to him.

Returning alone, Lorenzo handed the pope a letter.

"The courier whom you sent out some days since, has returned," said he. "This is his dispatch."

Taking the letter, with a sad smile, the pope weighed it in his hand. "How light is this little sheet," said he, "and yet how heavy are its contents! Do you know what this letter contains, Lorenzo?"

"How can I? A poor cloister brother is not all-knowing!"

"This letter," said the pope, with solemnity, "brings me life or death. It is the answer of the learned physician, Professor Brunelli, of Bologna!"

"You have written to him?" asked Lorenzo, turning pale.

"I wrote him, particularly describing my condition and my sufferings; in God's name I conjured him to tell me the truth, and Brunelli is a man of honor; he will do it! Am I right, therefore, in saying that the contents of this letter are very heavy?"

Lorenzo trembled, and, grasping the pope's hand, he hastily and anxiously said: "No, read it not. Of what use will it be to learn its contents? It is tempting God to endeavor to learn the future in advance! Let me destroy this fatal letter!"

"Of what use is it to know its contents?" asked the pope. "That I may either prepare for death, or resume a cheerful, hopeful life. Leave me, Lorenzo; I must read this letter!"

And, while his faithful servant respectfully stood back, Ganganelli broke the seal.

A pause ensued—a long, excruciating pause! Lorenzo, kneeling, prayed— Pope Ganganelli read the letter of the physician of Bologna. His face had assumed a mortal pallor; while reading, his lips trembled, and tear-drops rolled slowly down over his sunken cheeks.

Falling from his hand, the letter rustled to the earth; with hanging head and folded hands sat the pope. Lorenzo was still upon his knees, praying. Ganganelli suddenly raised his head, his eyes were turned heavenward, a cheerful, God-given peace beamed from his eyes, and with a clear, exulting voice, he said: "Lord, Thy will be done! I resign myself to Thy holy keeping."

"The letter, then, brings good news?" asked Lorenzo, misled by the joyfulness of the pope. "There is, then, no ground for the presentiments of death, and the learned doctor says you will live?"

"The life eternal, Lorenzo!" said Ganganelli. "This letter confirms my suppositions! Brunelli is a man of honor, and he has told me the truth. Lorenzo, would you know what signifies this consuming fire, this weariness and relaxation of my limbs? It is the effect of *Acqua Tofana!*"

Oh, my God!" shrieked Lorenzo, "you are poisoned!"

"Irretrievably," calmly responded the pope; "Brunelli says it, and I feel in my burning entrails that he speaks the truth."

"And are there no remedies?" lamented Lorenzo, wringing his hands. "No means at least of prolonging your life?"

"There is such a means; and Brunelli recommends it. The application of the greatest possible heat, the production of a continual perspiration, which may a little retard the progress of the evil, and perhaps prolong my life for a few weeks!" *

"Lorenzo, it is my duty to struggle every day with death. I have yet

* Archenholz, vol. v., 127.

much to complete before I die, yet much labor before I go to my eternal rest, and, as far as I can, I must bring to an end what I have commenced for the welfare of my people! Come, Lorenzo, let us return to the Vatican; set pans of coals in my room, procure me furs and a glowing hot sun! I would yet live some weeks!"

With feverish impetuosity Ganganelli grasped Lorenzo's arm and drew him away. Then, suddenly stopping, he turned toward his favorite place.

"Lorenzo," he said, in a low tone, and with deep sadness, "it was yet very pleasant in the Franciscan cloister. Why did we not remain there? Only see, my friend, how beautifully the sun glitters there among the pines, and how delightfully this air fans us! Ah, Lorenzo, this world is so beautiful, so very beautiful! Why must I leave it so soon?"

Lorenzo made no answer; he could not speak for tears!

Ganganelli cast a long and silent glance around him, greeting with his eyes the trees and flowers, the green earth and the blue sky.

"Farewell, farewell, thou beautiful Nature!" he whispered low. "We take our last leave of each other. I shall never again see these trees or this grassy seat. But you, Lorenzo, will I establish as the guardian of this place, and when you sometimes sit here in the still evening hour, then will you think of me! Now come, we must away. Feel you not this cool and gentle air? Oh, how refreshingly it fans and cools, but I dare not enjoy it—not I! This cooling cuts off a day from my life!"

And with the haste of a youth, Ganganelli ran down the alley. Bathed with perspiration, breathless with heat, he arrived at the palace.

"Now give me furs, bring pans of coals, Lorenzo, shut all the doors and windows. Procure me a heat that will shut out death—!"

But death nevertheless came; the furs and coverings, the steaming coal-pans with which the pope surrounded himself, the glowing atmosphere he day and night inhaled, and which quite prostrated his friends and servants, all that could only keep off death for some few weeks, not drive it away. More dreadful yet than this blasting heat with which Ganganelli surrounded himself, yet more horrible, was the fire that consumed his entrails and burned in his blood.

Finally, withered and consumed by these external and internal fires, the pope greeted Death as a deliverer, and sank into his arms with a smile.

But no sooner had he respired his last breath, no sooner had the death-rattle ceased in his throat, and no sooner had death extinguished the light of his eyes, than the cold corpse exhibited a most horrible change.

The thin white hair fell off as if blown away by a breath of air, the loosened teeth fell from their sockets, the formerly quietly smiling visage became horribly distorted, the nose sank in and the eyes fell out, the muscles of all his limbs became relaxed as if by a magic stroke, and the rapidly putrefying members fell from each other.

The pope's two physicians, standing

near the bed, looked with terror upon the frightful spectacle.

"He was, then, right," murmured the physician Barbi, folding his hands, "he was poisoned. These are the effects of the *Acqua Tofana!*"

Salicetti, the second physician, shrugged his shoulders with a contemptuous smile. "Think as you will," said he, "for my part I shall prove to the world that Pope Clement XIV. died a natural death."

Thus saying, Salicetti left the chamber of death with a proud step, betaking himself to his own room, to commence his history of Ganganelli's last illness, in which, despite the arsenic found in the stomach of the corpse and despite the fact that all Rome was convinced of the poisoning of the pope, and named his murderer with loud curses, he endeavored to prove that Ganganelli died of a long-concealed scrofula! *

And while Ganganelli breathed out his last sigh, resounded the bells of St. Peter's, thundered the cannon of Castle Angelo, and the curious people thronged around the Vatican, where the conclave was in solemn session for the choice of a new pope. Thousands stared up to the palace, thousands prayed upon their knees, until at length the doors of the balcony, behind which the conclave was in session, were opened, and the papal master of ceremonies made his appearance upon it.

At a given signal the bells became silent, the cannon ceased to thunder, and breathlessly listened the crowd.

The master of ceremonies advanced to the front of the balcony. A pause—a silent, dreadful pause! His voice then resounded over the great square, and the listeners heard these words: "*Habemus pontificem maximum Pium VI!*" (We have Pope Pius VI.)

And the bells rang anew, the cannon thundered, drums beat, and trumpets sounded; upon the balcony appeared the new pope, Juan Angelo Braschi, Pius VI., bestowing his blessing upon the kneeling people.

As they now had a new pope, nothing remained to be done for the deceased pope but to bury him; and they buried him.

In solemn procession, followed by all the cardinals and high-church officials, surrounded by the Swiss guards, the tolling of the bells, and the dull rolling of the muffled drums, the solemn hymns of the priests, moved the funeral *cortége* from the Vatican to St. Peter's church. In the usual open coffin lay the corpse of the deceased pope, that the people might see him for the last time. As they passed the bridge of St. Angelo, when the coffin had reached the middle of the bridge, arose a shriek of terror from thousands of throats! A leg had become severed from the body and hung out of the coffin, swinging in a fold of the winding-sheet. Cardinal Albani, who walked near the coffin, was touched on the shoulder by the loosely-swinging limb, and turned pale, but he yet had the courage to push it back into the coffin. The people loudly murmured, and shudderingly whispered to each other: "The dead man has touched his mur-

---

* Archenholz, vol. v., p. 125; Gorani, vol. ii., p. 43.

derer. They have poisoned him, our good pope! His members fall apart. That is the effect of *Acqua Tofana*." *

The infernal work had therefore proved successful, the vengeance was complete—Ganganelli was no more, and upon the papal throne sat Braschi, the friend of the Jesuits and of Cardinal Albani, to whom he had promised the crowning of the improvisatrice Corilla.

And as this cost nothing to the miserly Pope Pius, he this time found no inconvenience in keeping his sacred promise, though not so promptly as Corilla and the passionate cardinal desired.

Not until 1776, almost two years after Braschi had mounted the papal throne, took place the crowning of the improvisatrice in the capitol at Rome.

She had therefore attained the object of her wishes. She had finally reached it by bribery and intrigue, by hypocritical tenderness, by the resignation of her maiden modesty and womanly honor, and by all the arts of coquetry.

But this triumph of hers was not to be untroubled. The *nobili* shouted for her, and the cardinals and princes of the Church, but the people accompanied her to the capitol with hissing and howling. Poems came fluttering down on

all sides; the first that fell upon Corilla's head, Cardinal Albani eagerly seized and unfolded for the purpose of reading it aloud. But after the first few lines his voice was silenced—it was an abusive poem, full of mockery and scorn.

But nevertheless she was crowned. She still stood upon the capitol, with the laurel-crown upon her brow, cheered by her respectable protectors and friends. But the people joined not in those cheers, and, as the exulting shouts ceased, there swelled up to the laurel-crowned poetess, from thousands of voices, a thundering laugh of scorn, and this scornful laugh, this hissing and howling of the people, accompanied her upon her return from the capitol, following her through the streets to her own door. The people had judged her!

Corilla was no poetess by the grace of God, and only by the grace of man had she been crowned as queen of poesy!

Mortified, crushed, and enraged, she fled from Rome to Florence. She knew how to flatter the great and win princes. She was a princess-poetess, and the people rejected her!

But the laurel was hers. She was sought and esteemed, the princes admired her, and Catharine of Russia fulfilled the promise Orloff had made the improvisatrice in the name of the empress. Corilla received a pension from Russia. Russia has always promptly and liberally paid those who have sold themselves and rendered services to her. Russia is very rich, and can always send so many thousands of her best and noblest to work in the mines of Siberia, that she can never lack means for paying her spies and agents.

---

* Archenholz relates yet another case, where the Acqua Tofana had a similar violent and sudden effect. "A respectable Roman lady, who was young and beautiful, and had many admirers, made in the year 1718 a similar experiment, to rid herself of an old husband. As the dose was rather strong, death was followed by the rapid and violent separation of the members. They employed all possible means to retain the body in a human form until the funeral was over. The face was covered with a waxen mask, and by this means was the condition of the corpse concealed. This separation of the members seems to be the usual effect of this poison, and is said to occur as soon as the body is cold."—Archenholz, vol. v., p. 126.

CHAPTER XLII.

THE RUSSIAN OFFICER.

WITH Carlo's death, Natalie had lost her last friend; with the stolen money and diamonds, Marianne was robbed of her last pecuniary means. But Natalie paid no attention to Marianne's lamentations. What cared she for poverty and destitution—what knew she of these outward treasures, of this wealth consisting in gold and jewels? Natalie knew only that she had been robbed of a noble, spiritual possession—that they had murdered the friend who had consecrated himself to her with such true and devoted love, and, weeping over his body, she dedicated to him the tribute of a tear of the purest gratitude, of saddest lamentation.

But so imperfect is the world that it often leaves no time for mourning—that in the midst of our sorrow it causes us to hear the prosaic voices of reality and necessity, compelling us to dry our eyes and turning our thoughts from painfully-sweet remembrances of a lost happiness to the realities of practical life.

Natalie's delicately-sensitive soul was to experience this rough contact of reality, and, with an internal shudder, must she bend under the rough hand of the present.

Pale, breathless, trembling, rushed Marianne into the room where Natalie, in solitary mourning, was weeping for her lost friend.

"We are ruined, hopelessly ruined!" screamed Marianne. "They will drive us from our last possession, they will turn us out of our house! All the misfortunes of the whole world break over and crush us!"

The young maiden looked at her with a calm, clear glance.

"Then let them crush us," she quietly said. "It is better to be crushed at once than to be slowly and lingeringly wasted!"

"But you hear me not, princess," shrieked Marianne, wringing her hands. "They will drive us from here, I tell you; they will expel you from your house!"

"And who will do that?" asked the young maiden, proudly rising with flashing eyes. "Who dares threaten me in my own house?"

"Without are soldiers and bailiffs and the officers of the Russian embassy. They have made a forcible entrance, and with force they will expel you from the house. They are already sealing the doors and seizing every thing in the house."

A dark purple glow for a moment overspread Natalie's cheeks, and her glance was flame. "I will see," said she, "who has the robber-like boldness to dispute my possession of my own property?"

With proud steps and elevated head she strode through the room to the door opening upon the corridor.

The bailiffs and soldiers, who had been placed there, respectfully stood aside. Natalie paid no attention to them, but immediately advanced to the officer who, with a loud voice, was just then commanding them to seal all the doors and see that nothing was taken from the rooms.

"I wish to know," said Natalie, with her clear, silver-toned voice—"I wish to know by what right people here force their way into my house, and what excuse you have for this shameless conduct?"

The officer, who was no other than Stephano, bowed to her with a slightly ironical smile.

"Justice needs no excuse," said he. "On the part and by command of her illustrious majesty, the great Empress Catharine, I lay an attachment upon this house and all it contains. It is from this hour the sacred possession of her Russian majesty."

"It is the exclusive property of the Count Paulo!" proudly responded Natalie.

"It was the property of Count Paul Rasczinsky," said Stephano. "But convicted traitors have no property. This criminal count has been convicted of high-treason. The mercy of the empress has indeed changed the sentence of death into one of eternal banishment to Siberia, but she has been pleased to approve the confiscation of all he possessed. In virtue of this approval, and by permission of the holy Roman government, I attach this house and its contents!"

Natalie no longer heard him. Almost unconscious lay she in Marianne's arms. Paulo was lost, sentenced to death, imprisoned, and banished for life—that was all she had heard and comprehended—this terrible news had confused and benumbed her senses.

"Sir!" implored Marianne, pressing Natalie to her bosom, "you will at least have some mercy upon this young maiden; you will not thrust us out upon the streets; you will grant us a quiet residence in this house until we can collect our effects and secure what is indisputably ours!"

"Every thing in this house is the indisputable property of the empress!" roughly responded Stephano.

"But not ourselves, I hope!" excitedly exclaimed Marianne. "This imperial power does not extend over our persons?"

Stephano roughly replied: "The door stands open, go! But go directly, or I shall be compelled to arrest you for opposing the execution of the laws, and stirring up sedition!"

"Yes, let us go," cried Natalie, who had recovered her consciousness—"let us go, Marianne. Let us not remain a moment longer in a house belonging to that barbarous Russian empress who has condemned the noble Count Paulo as a criminal, and, robber-like, taken forcible possession of his property!"

And, following the first impulse of her noble pride, the young maiden took

Marianne by the hand and drew her away.

"They, at least, shall not forcibly eject us," said she; "no, no, we will go of our own free will, self-banished!"

"But where shall we go?" cried Marianne, wringing her hands.

"Where God wills!" solemnly responded the young maiden.

"And upon what shall we live?" wailed Marianne. "We are now totally destitute and helpless. How shall we live?"

"We will work!" said Natalie, firmly. A peculiar calm had come over her. Misfortune had awakened a new quality in her nature, sorrow had struck a new string in her being; she was no longer the delicate, gentle, suffering, unresisting child; she felt in herself a firm resolution, a bold courage, an almost joyful daring, and an invincible calmness.

"Work! *You* will work, princess?" whispered Marianne.

"I will learn it!" said she, and with a constantly quickened step they approached the outlet of the garden.

The gate which led out into the street was wide open; soldiers in the Russian uniform had been stationed before it, keeping back with their carbines the curious Romans who crowded around in great numbers, glad of an opportunity to get a peep into the so-long-closed charmed garden.

"See, there she comes, the garden fairy!" cried they all, as Natalie neared the gate.

"How beautiful she is, how beautiful!" they loudly exclaimed.

"That is a real fairy, a divinity!"

Natalie heard none of these expressions of admiration—she had but one object, one thought. She wished to leave the garden; she wished to go forth; she had no regrets, no complaints, for this lost paradise; she only wished to get out of it, even if it was to go to her death.

But the soldiers stationed at the gate opposed her progress.

Natalie regarded them with terror and amazement.

"They cannot, at least, oppose my voluntary resignation of my property," said she. "Away with these muskets and sabres! I would pass out!"

And the young maiden boldly advanced a step. But those weapons stretched before her like a wall, and Natalie was now overcome by anguish and despair; the inconsolable feeling of her total abandonment, of her miserable isolation. Tears burst from her eyes, her pride was broken, she was again the trembling young girl, no longer the heroic woman; she wept, and in tremulous tones, with folded hands, she implored of these rough soldiers a little mercy, a little compassion.

They understood not her language, they had no sympathy; but the crowd were touched by the tears of the beautiful girl, and by the sad lamentations of her companion. They screamed, they howled, they insulted the soldiers, they swore to liberate the two women by force, if the soldiers any longer refused them a passage. Dumb, unshaken, immovable, like a wall stood the soldiers with their weapons stretched forth.

Through the hissing and tumult a

loud and commanding voice was suddenly heard to ask, "What is going on here? What means this disturbance?" An officer made his way through the crowd, and approached the garden gate. The soldiers respectfully gave way, and he stepped into the garden.

"Oh, sir," said Natalie, turning to him her tearful face, "if you are an honorable man, have compassion for an abandoned and unprotected maiden, and command these soldiers, who seem to obey you, to let me and my companion go forth unhindered."

The Russian officer, Joseph Ribas, bowed low and respectfully to her. "If it is the Princess Tartaroff whom I have the honor of addressing," said he, "I must in the name of my illustrious lord, beg your pardon for what has improperly occurred here; at his command I come to set it all right!"

Thus speaking, he returned to the soldiers, and in a low tone exchanged some words with their leader. The latter bowed respectfully, and at his signal the soldiers shut the gate and retired into the street.

"Am I to be detained here as a prisoner?" exclaimed Natalie. "Am I not allowed to leave this garden?"

"Your grace, preliminarily, can still consider this garden as your own property," he respectfully responded. "I am commanded to watch that no one dare to disturb you here, and for this purpose my lord respectfully requests that you will have the goodness to permit me to remain in your house as the guardian of your safety."

"And who is this generous man?" asked Natalie.

"He is a man who has made a solemn vow to protect innocence everywhere, when he finds it threatened!" solemnly responded Joseph Ribas. "He is a man who is ready to shed his blood for the Princess Tartaroff, who is surrounded by enemies and dangers; a man," he continued, in a lower tone, "who knows and loves your friend and guardian, Count Paulo, and will soon bring you secret and sure news from him!"

"He knows Count Paulo!" joyfully exclaimed Natalie. "Oh, then all is well. I may safely confide in whoever knows and loves Count Paulo, for he must bear in his bosom a noble heart!"

And, turning to Joseph Ribas with a charming smile, she said, "Sir, lead me now where you will. We will both gladly follow you!"

"Let us, first of all, go into the villa, and send away those troublesome people!" said the Russian officer, preceding the two women to the house.

The bailiffs and soldiers were still there, occupied with sealing the doors and closets. Joseph Ribas approached them with angry glances, and, turning to Stephano, said, "Sir, I shall call you to account for this over-hasty and illegal proceeding!"

"I am in my right!" morosely answered Stephano. "Here is the command to attach this villa. It has fallen to the Russian crown as the property of the traitor Rasczinsky."

"There is only the one error to be corrected," said Joseph Ribas, "that this villa was not the property of Count Rasczinsky, as he some months ago sold it to his friend, my master. And as, so far as I know, the illustrious count, my master, never was a traitor, you will please to respect his property!"

"You will first have to authenticate your assertions!" responded Stephano, with a rude laugh.

"Here is the documental authentication!" said Joseph Ribas, handing a paper to Stephano. The latter, after attentively reading the documents, bowed reverentially, and said: "Sir, it appears that I was certainly mistaken. This deed of gift is *en règle*, and is undersigned by his grace the Russian ambassador. You will pardon me, as I only acted according to my orders."

Joseph Ribas answered Stephano's reverential bow with a haughty nod. "Go," said he, "take off the seals in the quickest possible time, and then away with you!"

But as Stephano was about retiring with his people, Joseph Ribas beckoned him back again.

"You have, therefore, recognized this deed of gift?" asked he, and as Stephano assented, he continued: "You therefore cannot deny that my master is the undisputed possessor of this villa, and can do with it according to his pleasure?"

"I do not deny it at all!" growled Stephano.

Joseph Ribas then drew forth another paper, which he also handed Stephano. "You will also recognize this deed of gift to be regular and legal! It is likewise undersigned and authenticated by our ambassador."

Stephano, having attentively read it, almost indignantly said:

"It is all right. But the count is crazy, to give away so fine a property!"

And still grumbling, he departed with his people.

Clinging to Marianne's side, Natalie had observed the whole proceeding with silent wonder; and, with the astonishment of innocence and inexperience, she comprehended nothing of the whole scene, nor was a suspicion awakened in her childishly pure soul.

"He is, then, really going?" she asked, as Stephano was slowly moving off.

"Yes, he is going," said Joseph Ribas, "and will never venture to disturb you again. Henceforth you will be in undisputed possession of your property. My lord has made this villa and garden forever yours by a regular legal deed of gift."

"And who is your lord?" asked Natalie. "Tell me his name—tell me where I may find him, that I may return him my thanks?"

"Yes, conduct us to him," said the weeping Marianne. "Let me clasp his feet and implore his further protection for my poor helpless princess."

"My lord desires no thanks," proudly responded Ribas. "He does good for its own sake, and protects innocence because that is the duty of every knight and nobleman."

"At least tell me his name, that I may pray for him," sobbed Marianne.

"Yes, his name," said Natalie, with a charming smile. "Ah, how I shall love that name!"

"His name is his own secret," said Ribas. "The world, indeed, knows and blesses him, calling him the bravest of the brave. But it is his command that you shall never be informed of it. He desires nothing, no thanks, no acknowledgments—he wishes only to secure your peace and happiness, and thus redeem the solemn vow he made to his friend, Count Paulo Rasczinsky, to guard and preserve you as a father, and to watch over you as your tutelar genius!"

"Thanks, thanks my God!" cried Marianne, with her arms raised toward heaven. "Thou sendest us help in our need, Thou hast mercy on suffering innocence, and sendest her a saviour in her greatest distress!"

The young maiden said nothing. Her radiant glance was directed heavenward, and, folding her hands over her bosom, with a happy, grateful smile she murmured:

"I am therefore no longer alone, I have a friend who watches over and protects me. Whoever he may be, he is sent by Count Paulo. Whatever may be his name, I shall be forever grateful to him!"

CHAPTER XLIII.

ANTICIPATION.

FROM that day had a new and marvellous life commenced for Natalie. She
felt herself surrounded by a dreamy,
magic, fantastic, supernatural life; it
seemed as if some invisible genius
hovered over her, listening to all her
thoughts, realizing all her wishes! And
Joseph Ribas was the merry, always-
cheerful, always-serviceable Kobold of
this invisible deity!

"My lord is not satisfied with the
modest furnishing of your villa," said
he to Natalie, on the first day. "He
begs to be allowed to adorn your chamber with a splendor suited to your rank
and your future greatness!"

"And in what is my future greatness
to consist?" asked the young maiden,
with curiosity.

"That will be made known to you at
the proper time," mysteriously replied
Joseph Ribas.

"Who will tell me?"

"He, the count."

"I shall therefore see him!" she joyfully exclaimed.

"Perhaps! Will you, however, first
allow me to have your room properly
furnished?"

"This villa belongs to your lord,"
said Natalie. "It is for him, as lord and
master, to do as he pleases in it."

And, satisfied, Ribas hastened away,
to return in a few hours with more than
fifty workmen and artists, in order to
commence the improvements.

Until now the villa had been finished
and furnished with simple elegance.
One missed nothing necessary for com-
fort or convenience, for pleasantness or
taste. But it was still only the elegant
and fashionable residence of a private
person. Now, as by the stroke of a
magic wand, this villa in a few days was
converted into the splendid palace of
some sultan or caliph. There were
heavy Turkish carpets on the floors,
velvet curtains with gold embroidery at
the windows and on the walls, the richest and most comfortable divans and
arm-chairs, covered with gold-embroidered stuffs; vases ornamented with the
most costly precious stones, noble bronze
statues, beautiful paintings, and between
them the rarest ornaments, glistening
with jewels, which modern times have
designated by the name of ribs; there
were delicate little trifles of inestimable
value, and with refined taste and judgment every thing was sought out which
luxury and convenience could demand.
With childish astonishment and ecstasy,
Natalie wandered through these rooms,
which she hardly recognized in their

splendid ornamentation, and stood before these treasures of trifles which she hardly dared to touch.

"This lord must be either a magician or a nabob," thoughtfully remarked Marianne; "it must have required millions to effect all this."

Natalie asked neither whether he was a magician, a millionnaire, or a nabob; she only thought she was to see him, and be allowed to thank him—nothing further.

"Will he come now?" she constantly asked of the humble and slavishly devoted Joseph Ribas; "will he come now that his house is prepared for his reception?"

"It is adorned only for you, princess," humbly replied Ribas. "The count, my master, wishes for nothing but to see you in a habitation worthy of you!"

But what was this luxury, what cared she for these treasures, the value of which she was incapable of estimating, and which were indifferent to her? She who had no conception of wealth or of money!—she, who knew not that there was poverty in the world, and who, raised in an Eden separated from the world, had no idea that hunger had ever made its appearance within it—she knew only the sorrows of the happy, the deprivations of the rich; she had never had either to struggle against real misfortune or to experience real want and deprivation.

Now, indeed, a deeper sorrow had entered into her life; she had lost her beloved paternal friend, Count Paulo; and Carlo, also, had been torn from her! That was certainly a more profound sorrow, and she had wept much for both of them,—but yet that was no real misfortune. She had never yet lost the whole substance of her life; for those two, however much she might always have loved them, had, nevertheless, not entirely filled out her life; they had been a part of her happiness, but not that happiness itself.

And she awaited happiness! She awaited it with ecstasy and devotion, with feverish hope and glowing desire! She knew not and asked not in what this happiness was to consist, and yet her heart yearned for it; she called for this unknown and nameless happiness with a throbbing bosom and tremulously whispering lips!

She was so much alone, she had so much time for dreaming, and intoxicating herself with fantastic imaginations! She was surrounded by a fabulous world, and she was the fairy of that world! But out of that fabulous world she sometimes longed to be, out of the ideal into the real; she yearned for truth and actuality. Then she would call Joseph Ribas to her side and bid him relate to her of that unknown lord, his master.

He told her of his battles and his heroic deeds, of his wonderful acts of bravery, and the young maiden tremblingly and shudderingly listened to him. She feared this man, who had shed streams of blood, and whose enemies with their dying lips had lauded as the greatest of heroes! And Joseph Ribas smiled when he saw her turn pale and tremble, and he would speak to her of his generosity and humanity, of his knighthood and virtue; he related to her how, on one occasion, at the risk of his life he had protected and saved a persecuted young maiden; how on another he had taken pity on a helpless old man, and singly had defended him against a host of bloodthirsty enemies. He also spoke to her of the sorrow of his master on account of the ingratitude and deceptions he had experienced, and Natalie's eyes filled with tears as, with reproachful glances, she asked of Heaven how it could have permitted the virtue of this noble unknown hero to be so severely tried, and the baseness of mankind to trouble him.

"That is it, then," Ribas would often say; "he diffuses happiness everywhere around him, while he himself has it not! He makes glad and cheerful faces wherever he appears, and his own is the only serious and sad brow. Mankind have made him hopeless, and for himself he no longer believes in happiness!"

Ah, how then did the heart of this innocent child tremble, and how she longed to find some means for restoring his belief in happiness.

"But why does he not come to those who love him?" asked she. "Why does he decline the thanks of those whose hearts are truly devoted to him? Ah, in our humid eyes and joy-beaming faces he would recognize the truthfulness of our feelings! Why, then, comes he not?"

"I will tell you," said Ribas, with a smile; "he hates women, because the only one he ever loved was false to him, and now his love is changed to ardent hatred of all women!"

"I shall therefore never see him!" sighed the girl, hanging her head with the sadness of disappointment.

This expectation, this constantly increasing impatience, rendered her inaccessible to any other feeling, any other thought. He of whom she did not know even the name, was sent by Paulo, and therefore had she believed and confided in him from the first. Now had she already forgotten that she had confided in him on Paulo's account; she believed in him on his own account, and Paulo had retreated into the background. Occasionally also the bloody image of poor Carlo presented itself to her mind, and she secretly reproached herself for having mourned him for so short a time, for having so soon forgotten that faithful self-sacrificing friend.

But even these reproaches were soon silenced when with a throbbing bosom she thought of this new friend, who like a divinity hovered over her at an infinite and unattainable distance, and whose mysteriously active nearness replaced both of those friends she had lost, and for whom she could no longer mourn!

CHAPTER XLIV.

HE!

"IT is now high time!" said Joseph Ribas one day, as, coming from Natalie, he entered the boudoir of Count Alexis Orloff. "Now, your excellency, the right moment has come! You must now show yourself, or this curious child will consume herself with a longing that has changed her blood to fire! She thinks of nothing but you; with open eyes she dreams of you, and without the least suspicion that any one is listening to her, she speaks to you, ah, with what modest tenderness and with what humble devotion! I tell you, your excellency, you are highly blessed. There is no child more innocent, no woman more glowing with love. And she knows it not; no, she has not the least suspicion that she already loves you with enthusiasm, and thirsts for your kisses as the rose for the morning dew! She knows nothing of her love!"

"She shall learn something of it!" said Orloff, laughing. "It will be a pleasant task to enlighten this little unknowing one as to her own feelings. And I flatter myself I understand how to do that."

"Endeavor, above all things, your excellency, to realize the ideal she bears in her heart. She expects to see nothing less than an Apollo, whose radiant beauty will annihilate her as Jupiter did Semele!"

"Well, in that, I hope she has not deceived herself," responded Orloff, with a self-satisfied glance into the mirror. "If I am not Jupiter, yet they call me Hercules, and he, you know, was the son of Jupiter, and, indeed, his handsomest son!"

"And be you not only a Hercules, but a Zephyr and Apollo, at the same time. Make her tremble before your heroic character, and at the same time win her confidence in your humble, modest love—then is she yours. You must cautiously and noiselessly spread your nets, you must not wound her delicate sensitiveness by a word or look, or she will flee from you like a frightened gazelle!"

"Oh, should she wish to flee, my arms are strong enough to hold her!"

"Yet it is better to hold her so fast by her own enthusiasm, that she shall not wish to flee," said Ribas. "You must entirely intoxicate her with your humble and respectful love—then is she yours!"

"Does she know I am coming?" thoughtfully asked Orloff.

"No, she knows nothing of it. She sits in the garden and sighs, occasionally grasping the golden guitar that lies on her arm, and asks of the flowers: 'What is the name of my unknown friend? In what star does he dwell, and how shall I invoke him?'"

"I will, then, surprise her!" said Orloff. "Let her anticipate my coming, but do not promise it. It begins to grow dark. Where is she, evenings?"

"Always in the garden. There she sighs and dreams of you!"

"Persuade her to go into the house, and let it be well lighted up! I would appear to her in the full splendor of the lights! Ha, you ragamuffins, you hounds, bring me my oriental costume, the richest, handsomest; hasten, or I will throttle you!"

And Count Orloff hurried into his toilet-chamber, to the trembling slaves who there awaited him.

With a sly smile Joseph Ribas returned to the villa. As he had previously said, he found Natalie dreaming in the garden, the guitar upon her arm.

"You ought to go into the house this evening," said he, "the air is damp and cold, and may injure you."

"Of what consequence would that be?" she sadly responded. "Who would ask whether I was ill or not? Who would weep for my death?"

"He!"

"Oh, he!" sighed she. "He hates all women!"

"Excepting you!" whispered Ribas. "Princess, go into the house! Take care of your precious life. It is not I who beg it of you!"

"Who is it, then?" she hastily interposed.

"It is he! He begs it of you!"

Natalie, springing up, hurried into the house.

"I will never again go into the garden in the evening!" said she. "It is his command! Thank God, there is yet something in which I can obey, and he commands it of me! But why these lights?" asked she, almost blinded by the brilliancy of the girandoles and chandeliers, the mirrors, and jewels.

"The count has so commanded!" said Ribas. "He loves a bright light! But, princess, cannot you remain in this boudoir for one evening? Only see how beautiful it is, how enticingly cool, with these fountains that refresh the air and diffuse fragrance! How delightfully still and snug it is! Reposing upon these velvet cushions, you can look through the whole suite of rooms, which in fact, to-night, flash and sparkle like the heavens, and yet in this boudoir there is a sweet twilight, refreshing to eye and heart!"

"No, no," said she, with a charming smile. "I also like brightness and light! It is too dusky here!"

"Nevertheless, remain here!"

"And why?"

"He wishes it!" said Ribas, mysteriously.

"He wishes it?" cried Natalie, turning pale, and trembling. Then, suddenly, a purple flush spread over her brow, and, reeling, she was obliged to hold by a chair to prevent falling. "Ah," she stammered, "can it be possible? Can this happiness be intended? Is it true, what I read in your eyes? Is it? Comes he here?"

"Hope always!" said Ribas, suddenly disappearing through a side-door.

Natalie, benumbed by surprise, sank down upon the divan. A feeling of boundless anxiety, of immeasurable ecstasy suddenly overcame her. She could have fled, but she felt as if spell-bound; she could have concealed herself from him, and yet was joyfully ready to purchase with her life the happiness of seeing him. It was a strange mixture of delight and terror, of happiness and despair. She spread her arms toward heaven, she sought to pray, but she had no words, no thoughts, not even tears!

A slight rustle made her rise. Almost with terror flew her glance through the suite of rooms. There below she saw the approach of something strange, singular, magical. It was a never-before-seen form, but surrounded by a wonderfully bright halo, enveloped in rich, glittering garments, such as she had never before seen. It was a strange, unknown face, but of a sublime heroic beauty, proud and noble, bold and mild.

"That is he!" she breathlessly and sadly murmured—"yes, that is he! That is a man and a hero! Ah, I shall die under his glance!"

He still continued to approach, and with every forward step he made she felt her heart contract with anxiety, admiration, and a feverish sadness.

Now he stood on the threshold of the boudoir—his glance fell upon her. And she? She lay, or rather half knelt upon the divan, motionless, pale as a marble statue, with that divine smile which we admire in ancient sculpture.

Touching was she to behold, white and delicate as a lily, so humble and devoted, so shelter-needing and love-imploring!

But Count Orloff felt neither sympathy nor compassion. He saw only that she was beautiful as an angel, an admirable woman, whom he desired to possess!

Proud as a king, and at the same time very reverential and submissive, he approached and sank upon his knee before the divan upon which she reclined in trembling yet blissful sadness.

"Princess Natalie," he murmured low, "will you be angry with your slave for daring to intrude upon you without knowing whether he would be welcome?"

She breathed freer. It was a relief to her to hear his voice—it made her feel easier. He was no magician, no demon, he was a man, and spoke to her with human words! That gave her courage and strength, it gave her back the consciousness of her own dignity. She was ashamed of her anxiety, her trembling, her childish helplessness. Yet she could say nothing, answer nothing. She only gave him her hand, with a charming smile, an inimitable grace, and welcomed him with a silent inclination of the head.

Taking her hand he pressed it to his lips. His touch seemed to kindle in her an electric glow, and with something like alarm she withdrew her hand.

"Are you, then, angry with me?" he asked, in a tone of sadness.

"No," said she, "I am not angry, but I fear you. You are so great a hero, and your sword has done so many brave deeds. I looked at your sword, and it alarmed me."

Count Orloff gave her a surprised and interrogating glance. Why said she that? Had she some suspicion, some mistrust, or was it only a presentiment, an inexplicable instinct, that made her tremble at his sword?

"No, she suspects nothing," thought he, as he gazed upon that pure, innocent, childish brow, which was turned toward him in pious confidence, and yet with timid hesitation.

He loosened his sword from his girdle, sparkling with diamonds, and humbly laid both at Natalie's feet.

"Princess," said he, "the empress herself girded me with this sword, and I swore it should never leave my side but with my life. You are dearer to me than my life or my honor, and I therefore break my sacred oath. Take my sword, I am now without arms, and you will no longer have occasion to tremble before me."

She smilingly shook her head. "You still remain a hero, though without arms—it lies in your eyes!"

"I would close my eyes," said he, "but then I should not see you, princess, and I have already so long languished for a sight of you!"

"Why, then, came you not sooner?" she asked, now feeling herself entirely cheerful and unembarrassed. "Oh, did you but know how impatiently I have awaited you!"

And with childish innocence she began to relate how much she had thought of him, how often she had dreamed of him, how she had sometimes spoken aloud to him, and almost thought she heard his answers!

Count Orloff listened to her with surprise and delight. Thus had he not expected to find her, so childishly cheerful, so charmingly innocent, and yet at the same time with so much maidenly reserve, so much natural dignity. Now she laughed like a child, now was her face serious and proud, now again tender and timid. She was at once a timid child and a glowing woman; she was innocent as an angel, and yet so full of sweet, unconscious maiden coquetry. She enchanted, while inspiring devotion, she excited passions and desires, while, with a natural maiden dignity, she kept one within the bounds of respect. She was entirely different from what Orloff had expected; perhaps less beautiful, less dazzling, but infinitely more lovely. She enchanted him with her smile, and her innocent childish face touched him.

"Speak on, speak on!" said he, when she became silent. "It is delightful to listen to you, princess."

"Why do you call me so?" asked she, with a slight contraction of her brow. "It is such a strange, cold word! It does not at all belong to me, and it is only within the last few months that I have been thus addressed. With wise and tender forbearance, Paulo long delayed informing me that I was a princess, and that was beautiful in him. To be a princess and yet an orphan, a poor, deserted, helpless child, living upon the charity of a friend, and tremulously clinging to his protecting hand! See, that is what I am, a poor orphan; why, then, do you call me princess?"

"Because you are so in reality," responded Orloff, pressing the hem of her garment to his lips—"because I am come to lead you to your splendid and powerful future!—because I will glorify you above all women on earth, and make you mistress of this great empire."

She regarded him with a dreamy smile. "You speak as Paulo often spoke to me," said she. "He also swore to me that he would one day place an imperial crown upon my head, and elevate me to great power! I understood him as little as I understand you!"

A slight scornful smile momentarily passed over Orloff's features. "Catharine has therefore rightly divined," thought he, "and her wise mind rightly understood this Rasczinsky. There was, indeed, question of an imperial crown, and this was to have been the new little empress!"

Aloud he said: "You will soon understand me, princess, and it is time you knew of what crown Paulo spoke."

"I know it not," said she, "nor do I desire to know it! Perhaps it was a jest, with which he sought to console me when I complained of being a homeless orphan, a poor child, who knew not even the name of her mother!"

"Do you not know that?" exclaimed Orloff, with astonishment.

She sadly shook her head. "They would never tell it me," said she. "But I have her image in my heart, and that, at least, I shall never lose or forget!"

"I knew your mother," said Orloff; "she was beautiful as you are, and mild and merciful."

"You knew her!" exclaimed the young maiden, grasping his hand and looking at him with a confiding friendliness. "Oh, you knew her! You will now be doubly dear to me, for those bright eyes have seen my mother, and perhaps this hand which now rests in mine has also touched hers!"

"That," said Count Orloff, with a smile, "I should not have dared to do; it would have been high-treason!"

"Was she, then, so great and sublime a princess?" asked Natalie.

"She was an empress!"

"An empress!" And the young maiden sprang up with beaming eyes and glowing cheeks. "My mother was an empress!" said she, breathing hard.

"Empress Elizabeth of Russia."

Overcome by the feelings suddenly excited by this news, Natalie sank again upon her seat and covered her face with her hands. Tears gushed out between her delicate, slender fingers; her whole being was in violent feverish commotion. Then, raising her arms toward heaven, with a celestial smile, while the tears overflowed her face, she said: "I am, then, no longer a homeless orphan; I have a fatherland, and my mother was an empress!"

Count Orloff respectfully kissed the hem of her garment.

"You are the daughter of an empress," said he, "and will yourself be an empress! That was what Paulo wished, and therefore have they condemned him as a criminal. What he was unable to accomplish must be done by me, and for that purpose have I come. Princess Natalie, your fatherland calls you, your throne awaits you! Follow me to your crowning in the city of your fathers—follow me, that I may place the crown of your grandfather, Peter the Great, upon your noble and beautiful head!"

CHAPTER XLV.

THE WARNING.

FROM this time forward, Alexis Orloff was the inseparable companion of Natalie. With the most reverential submission, and at the same time with the tenderest affection, seemed he to be devoted to her, and equally to adore her as his empress and his beloved.

He took pains to represent to her that she was necessarily and inevitably destined to become an empress.

And she had comprehended him but too well. Ambition was awakened in this young maiden of eighteen years; it was an imperial crown that called her—why should she not listen to this call coming from the lips of one in whom she had unlimited confidence, and toward whom she felt infinitely grateful?

He had unfolded and explained all to her. He had told her of her mother, the good Empress Elizabeth, who had made Russia so great and happy; he had explained to her how Count Paulo Rasezinsky had flown with her on the day of her mother's death, in order to preserve her from the pursuits of her mother's successor, the cunning and cruel Peter III., and to insure her the realm at a later period. He had then spoken to her of Catharine, who had forcibly possessed herself of the throne of her unworthy husband, and taken the reins of government into her own hands. He had spoken to her of Catharine's cruelty and despotic tyranny; he had told her that all Russia groaned under the oppression of this foreigner, and that a universal cry was heard through the whole realm, of lamentation and longing, a cry for her, the Russian princess, the grand-daughter of Peter the Great, the daughter of the beloved Elizabeth.

"You are called for by all these millions of your oppressed subjects now trodden in the dust," said he; "toward you they stretch forth their trembling hands, from you they expect relief and consolation, from you they expect happiness!"

"And I will bring them happiness," exclaimed Natalie, with emotion. "I will dry the tears of misery and console the suffering. Oh, my people shall love me as my mother once did!"

"The noblest of the land have pledged their property and their lives to give you back to your people," said Orloff; "we have solemnly sworn it upon the altar of God, and for the attainment of this end no one of us will shun want or death, treason or revolt. Look at me, Natalie! I stand before you as a traitor to this empress, to whom I have sworn faith and obedience; she has heaped favors upon me, and at one time I was even passionately devoted to her! But Count Paulo awoke me from that intoxication; he roused me from the condition of a favorite of the empress; he taught me to see the cruel, bloodthirsty empress in her true form; he spoke to me of your sacred rights, and when I recognized and comprehended them, I collected myself, vowed myself your knight, devoting myself to the defence of your rights, and swore to leave no artifice, no dissimulation, nor even treason itself, unessayed for the promotion of this great, this sublime object! Princess Natalie, for your sake I have become a traitor! The admiral of the Russian fleet, he whom the world calls the favorite of the empress, Count Alexis Orloff, lies at your feet and swears to you eternal faith, devotion, and adoration!"

"Alexis Orloff!" she joyfully exclaimed, "at length, then, I have a name by which I can call you! Alexis, was not that the name of my father? Oh, that is a good omen! You bear the name of my father, whom my mother so dearly loved!"

"And whom the empress, impelled by love, raised to the position of her husband," whispered Orloff, bending nearer to her and pressing her hand to his bosom. "Could you, indeed, love as warmly and devotedly as your mother loved her Alexis?"

The young maiden blushed and trembled, but a sweet smile played upon her lips, and although she cast down her eyes and did not look at him, yet Count Orloff saw that he had given no offence, and might venture still further.

He gently encircled her delicate form with his arm, and, inclining his mouth so close to her ear that she felt his hot breath upon her cheek, whispered: "Will Natalie love her Alexis as Elizabeth loved Alexis Razumovsky? Ah, you know not how boundlessly, how immeasurably I love you! Yes, immeasurably, Natalie. You are my happiness, my life, my future. Command me, rule me, make of me a traitor, a murderer! I will do whatever you command; at your desire I could even murder my own father! Only tell me, Natalie, that you do not hate me; tell me that my love will not be rejected by you; that this passion, under which I almost succumb, has found an echo in your heart, and that you will one day say to me, as Elizabeth said to your father, 'Alexis, I love you, and will therefore make you my husband!' You are silent, Natalie; have you no word of sympathy, of compassion for me? Ah, I offer up all to you, and you—"

He could proceed no further; he saw her turn toward him; he suddenly felt a glowing kiss upon his lips, and then, springing up from her seat, she fled through the rooms like a frightened roe, and took refuge in her boudoir, which she locked behind her.

Orloff glanced after her with a triumphant smile. "She is mine," thought he; "I am here living through a charming romance, and Catharine will be satisfied with me!"

Yes, she was his; she now knew that she loved him, and with joyful ecstasy she took this new and delightful feeling to her heart; she welcomed it as the joy-promising dawn of a new day, a

16

precious new life. She permitted this feeling to stream through her whole being, her whole soul; she made it a worship for her whole existence.

"You see," said she to Marianne, "so had I dreamed the man whom I should one day love. So brave, so proud, so beautiful. Ah, it is so charming to be obliged to tremble before the man one loves; it is so sweet to cling to him and think: 'I am nothing of myself, but all through thee! I am the ivy and thou the oak; thou wilt hold and sustain me, and if a storm-wind comes, thou wilt not waver, but stand firm and great in thy heroic strength, and protect me, and impart courage and confidence even to me!'"

She loved him, and clung to him with boundless confidence, but she was yet so full of tender maiden timidity that she could confess to him nothing of this love; and since that kiss she shyly avoided him, and constantly left his often-renewed love-questions unanswered.

At this Alexis secretly laughed. "She will come round," said he; "she will finally be compelled to it by her own feelings. I will give her time and leisure to come to a knowledge of herself!"

And for some days he kept away from the villa, pretending pressing business, and left the poor isolated princess to her languishing love-dreams.

It was precisely in these days that, on one forenoon, a carriage of indifferent appearance, adorned with no heraldic arms, stopped before the villa; a man closely enveloped in a mantle, his hat pressed deeply down over his forehead, issued from the carriage and rang the bell.

Of the servant who answered the bell he hastily inquired if the princess was at home and alone; these questions being answered in the affirmative, and the servant having asked his name in order to announce him, the stranger said, almost in a commanding tone: "The princess knows my name, and will gladly welcome me; therefore lead me directly to her!"

"The princess receives no one," said the servant, placing himself in a position to prevent the stranger's entrance.

"She will receive me," said the unknown, dropping some gold-pieces into the servant's hand.

"I will conduct you to her," said the suddenly mollified servant, "but I do it on your own responsibility!"

Princess Natalie was in her boudoir. She was alone and thinking, in a languishing reverie, of her friend who had now been two days absent. On hearing a light knock at the door, she sprang up from her seat.

"It is he!" she murmured, and with glowing cheeks she hastened to the door.

But on finding there a strange and closely-enveloped form, Natalie timidly drew back.

The stranger entered, closing the door behind him, threw back his mantle and took off the hat that shaded his face.

"Cardinal Bernis!" cried Natalie, with surprise.

"Ah, then you yet recognize me, princess!" said Bernis. "That is beautiful in you, and therefore you will not be angry with me for falling upon you unannounced. I knew that I should find you alone, and this was a too fortunate circumstance for me to let it pass unimproved. I must speak to you, princess, even at the hazard of proving tiresome."

Natalie said, with a soft smile: "You were the friend of Count Paulo, and therefore can never prove tiresome to me! I bid you welcome, cardinal!"

"It is precisely because I was Count Paulo's friend, that I have come!" said Bernis, seriously. "The count loved you, princess, and what I did not know at the time is known to me now. Because he loved and was devoted to you, he hazarded his life, and more than his life, his liberty."

"And they have robbed him of that precious liberty," sighed Natalie. "For his fidelity to me they have condemned him to a shameful imprisonment!"

"You know that!" exclaimed Bernis, with astonishment, "you know that, and nevertheless—" then, interrupting himself, he broke off, and after a pause continued: "Pardon me one question, and if you deem it indiscreet, please remember that it is put to you by an old man and a priest, and that his only object is, if possible, to be useful to you. Do you love Count Paulo Rasczinsky?"

"I love him," said she, "as one loves a father. I shall always be grateful to him, and shall never esteem myself happy until I have liberated him and restored him to his country!"

"You liberate him!" sadly exclaimed Bernis. "Ah, then you know not, you do not once dream, that you are yourself surrounded by dangers, that your own liberty, indeed your life itself, is threatened."

"I know it," calmly responded the young maiden, "but I also know that strong and powerful friends stand by my side, who will protect and defend me with their lives."

"But how if these friends are deceiving you—if precisely they are your bitterest enemies and destroyers?"

"Sir Cardinal!" exclaimed Natalie, reddening with indignation.

"Oh, I may not anger you," he continued, "but it is my duty to warn you, princess! They have undoubtedly deceived you with false pretensions, and in some deceitful way obtained your confidence. Tell me, princess, do you know the name of this count whom you daily receive here?"

"It is Count Alexis Orloff," said the young maiden, blushing.

"You know him, know his name, and yet you confide in him!" exclaimed the cardinal. "But it cannot be that you know his history: have you any idea to whom he is indebted for his prosperity and greatness?"

"The Empress Catharine, his mistress," said Natalie, without embarrassment.

The cardinal looked, with increasing astonishment, into her calm, smiling face. "I now comprehend it all," he then said; "they have laid a very shrewd and cunning plan. They have deceived you while telling you a part of the truth!"

"No one has deceived me," indignantly responded Natalie. "I tell you,

Sir Cardinal, that I am neither deceived nor overreached, easy as you seem to think it to deceive me!"

"Oh, it is always easy to deceive innocence and nobleness," sadly remarked the cardinal. "Listen to me, princess, and think, I conjure you, that this time a true and sincere friend is speaking to you."

"And how shall I recognize that?" asked the young maiden, with a slight touch of irony. "How shall I recognize a friend, when, as you say, it is precisely my pretended friends who are my enemies?"

"Recognize me by this!" said the cardinal, drawing a folded paper from his bosom and handing it to the princess.

"That is Count Paulo's handwriting!" she joyfully exclaimed.

"Ah, you recognize the handwriting," said the cardinal, "and you see that this letter is addressed to me. Count Paulo therefore considers me his friend!"

"May I read this letter?"

"I beg you to do so."

Natalie unfolded the letter and read: "Warn the Princess Tartaroff; danger threatens her!"

"That is all?" she asked with a smile.

"That is all!" said the cardinal; "but when Paulo considered these few words of sufficient importance to send them to me, you may well suppose they are of the utmost significance."

"Count Paulo is in Siberia," said Natalie, shaking her head; "how could he have written you from thence?"

"How he succeeded in doing so, I know not, but the firm, determined will of man often conquers supposed impossibilities! Enough—in a mysterious, enigmatical manner was this letter put into the hands of our ambassador at St. Petersburg, with the most urgent prayer that he would immediately send it to me by a special courier, with all the necessary particulars."

"And was that done?" asked Natalie.

"It was done! I know why your life is threatened! Princess Tartaroff, you are the daughter of the Empress Elizabeth; and therefore it is that this Empress Catharine, upon her usurped throne, trembles with fear of you—therefore was it that she said to her favorite: 'Go, and deliver me from this troublesome pretender. But do it in a sly, cautious, and noiseless manner. Avoid attracting attention, murder her not, threaten her not; I wish not to give people new reasons for calling me a bloodthirsty woman. Entice her with flatteries into our net, induce her to follow you voluntarily, that the people of no country in which she may be, may have an occasion to accuse us of using force.' Thus did Catharine speak to her favorite; he understood her and swore to execute her commands, as he did when Catharine ordered him to throttle her husband, the Emperor Peter; as he also did when she ordered him to shoot poor Ivan, the son of Anna Leopoldowna, for the criminal reason that he had a greater right to the imperial crown of Russia than this little German princess of Zerbst!"

"And he shot that poor innocent Ivan?" shudderingly asked Natalie. "Ah, this Catharine is bloodthirsty as a hyena, and her friends and favorites are hangmen's servants—ah, history will brand this murderer of Ivan!"

"It will," solemnly responded Cardinal Bernis, "and people will shudder when they hear the name of the man who strangled the Emperor Peter, who shot Ivan, and who, at the command of Catharine, has come to Italy to ensnare the noble and innocent Princess Tartaroff with cunning and flatteries and convey her to St. Petersburg. Shall I tell you this man's name? He is called Alexis Orloff!"

The young maiden sprang up from her seat, her eyes flashed, and her cheeks glowed.

"That is false," said she—"a shameful, malicious falsehood!"

"Would to God it were so!" cried the cardinal. "But it is too true, princess! Oh, listen to me, and close not your ears to the truth. Remember that I am an old man, who has long observed men, and long studied life. I know this Russian diplomacy, and this Russian craft; they have in them something devilish; and these Russian diplomatists, they poison and confound the shrewdest with their deceitful smiles and infernal cunning. Guard yourself, princess, against this Russian diplomacy, and, above all things, be on your guard against this ambassador of the Russian empress, Alexis Orloff!"

"Ah, you dare to defame him!" cried the young maiden, trembling with anger. "You have, therefore, never seen him; you have never read in his noble face that Count Alexis Orloff can never betray. He is a hero, and a hero never descends to a murder! Ah, if the whole world should rise up against him, if it should point the finger at him and say: 'That is a murderer!' I would cry in the face of the whole world: 'Thou liest! Alexis Orloff can never be a murderer! I know him better, and know that he is pure and clear of every crime. You may continue to call him a betrayer! I know why he suffers himself to be so called! I know the secret of his conduct, and a day will come when you will all learn it; when you will all feel compelled to fall down at his feet and confess, "Alexis Orloff is no false betrayer!" For the sake of her to whom he has vowed fidelity has he borne this shame. For her whom he loved has he staked his blood and his life! Alexis Orloff is a hero!'"

She was strangely beautiful while speaking with such spirit and animation. The cardinal observed her noble and excited features with an admiration mingled with the most painful emotions.

"Poor child!" he murmured, dropping his head—"poor child, she loves him, and is therefore lost!"

"You, then, do not believe me?" he asked aloud.

"No," said she, with a glad smile—"no, all the happiness I ever expect, all the good that may hereafter come to me, shall receive only from the hands of Alexis Orloff!"

"Poor child!" sighed the cardinal. "In many a case even death may prove a blessing!"

"Then will I also joyfully receive even that from his hands!" cried the young maiden, with enthusiasm.

"It is in vain, she is not to be helped!" murmured the cardinal, with a melancholy shake of the head, and, grasping the hand of the young maiden, with a compassionate glance at her fair face, he continued: "I would gladly aid you, and thereby expiate the evil you once suffered at my festival! But you will not consent to be aided. You rush to your destruction, and it is your noblest qualities, your innocence, and your generous confidence, which are preparing your ruin! May God bless you and preserve you! How glad I should be to find myself a liar and false prophet!"

"And you will so find yourself!" exclaimed Natalie.

"You believe it, because you are in love, and when a woman loves she believes in the object of her love, and smilingly offers up her life for him! Like all women, you will do so! You will sacrifice your life to your love; and when this barbarian thrusts the dagger in your heart, you will say with a smile: 'I did it! I, myself—'"

And, bowing to her with a sad smile, slowly and sighing, the cardinal left the room.

Some hours later came Alexis Orloff. Natalie received him with an expression of the purest pleasure, and, extending both hands to him, smilingly said:

"Know you yet what my mother said to her lover?"

Looking at her, he read his happiness in her face. With an exclamation of ecstasy he fell at her feet.

"I know it well, but you, Natalie, do you also know it?" he passionately asked.

Natalie smiled. "Alexis," said she,

"I love you, and therefore will I raise you to my side as my husband!" and with a charming modest blush she drew the count up to her arms.

"You do not deceive me, and this is no dream?" he cried, while glowingly embracing her.

"No," said she, "it is the truth, and I owe you this satisfaction. You have been slandered to me to-day. Ah, they shall see how little I believe them. Alexis, call a priest to bless our union, and make me your wife. Whatever then may come, we will share it with each other. If I am one day empress, you will be the emperor, and I will always honor and obey you as my lord and master."

On the evening of this day a very serious and solemn ceremony took place in the boudoir of Princess Natalie. An altar wreathed with flowers stood in the centre of the room, and before the altar stood Natalie in a white satin robe, the myrtle-crown upon her head, the long bridal veil waving around her delicate form. She was very beautiful in her joyful, modest emotion, and Count Alexis Orloff, who, in a rich Russian costume stood by her side, viewed her with ecstatic and warm desiring glances. The inhuman executioner led the lamb to the slaughter without pity or compunction!

At the other side of the altar stood the priest, a reverend old man, with long flowing silver hair and beard. Near him the sacristan, not less reverend in appearance. No one else was present except Marianne, who, in tears, knelt behind her mistress, and with folded hands prayed for her beloved princess, who was now marrying Count Alexis Orloff.

The solemn ceremony was at an end, and the young wife sank weeping into the arms of her husband, who, with tenderest whisperings, led her into the next room.

Marianne, overcome by her tears and emotions, hastened to her own room, and the reverend priest remained alone with his sacristan.

They silently looked at each other, and their faces were distorted by a knavish, grinning laugh.

"It was a wonderful scene," said the priest, who was no other than Joseph Ribas. "In earnest, I was quite affected by it myself, and I came near weeping at my own sublime homily. Confess, Stephano, that a consecrated priest could not have better gone through the ceremony."

"We have both performed our parts," simpered Stephano, the sacristan, "and I think the count must be satisfied with us."

At that moment the count returned to the room. Natalie had begged to be left alone—she needed solitude and prayer.

The priest, Joseph Ribas, and the sacristan, Stephano, gave him sly, interrogating glances.

"I am satisfied with you," said Orloff, with a smile. "You are both excellent actors. This new little countess was pleased and touched by your discourse, Joseph, my very worthy priest. Where did you learn this new villany?"

"In the high school of the galleys, your excellency," said Ribas. "Only

there is one taught such precious things. We had a priest there, a real consecrated priest, who was sentenced for life. From *ennui* he gave lessons to the smartest among us in his art, and taught us how to fold the hands, roll the eyes, and render the voice tremulous. But now, your excellency, one thing! You desired to know who it was that warned your princess to-day. I can now give you information on that point. It was the French Cardinal Bernis!"

"They are, therefore, beginning to observe our movements," thoughtfully remarked Orloff, "and these gentlemen diplomatists wish to take a hand in the game. Ah, we understand the French policy. It is the same now that it was when they helped to make the Princess Elizabeth empress. At that time they interposed, that Russia might be so occupied with her own affairs as to have no time for looking into those of France. Precisely so is it to-day. They would compassionate the daughter as they did the mother. With the help of Natalie they would again bless Russia with a revolution, that we might not have time to observe the events now fermenting in France. But this time we shall be more cautious, my shrewd French cardinal. Stephano, let every preparation be made for our immediate departure. We are no longer safe and unobserved here. Therefore we will go to Leghorn."

"We alone, or with the princess?" asked Stephano.

"My wife will naturally accompany me," said Orloff, with a derisive smile.

"Will she consent to leave Rome?" asked Joseph Ribas.

"I shall request her to do so," proudly replied Orloff, "and I think my request will be a command to her."

And the proud count was not mistaken. His request was a command for her. He told her she must leave Rome because she was no longer in safety there, and Princess Natalie believed him.

"We will go to Leghorn, and there await the arrival of the Russian fleet," said he. "When that fleet shall have safely arrived, then our ends will be attained, then we shall have conquered, for then it will be evident that the empress has conceived no suspicion; and I am the commander of that fleet, which is wholly manned with conspirators who all await you as their empress. Will you follow me to Leghorn, Natalie?"

She clung with tender submissiveness to his bosom.

"I will follow you everywhere," murmured she, "and any place to which you conduct me will be a paradise for me!"

CHAPTER XLVI.

THE RUSSIAN FLEET.

UNSUSPECTINGLY had she followed Orloff to Leghorn; full of devoted tenderness, full of glowing love, she was only anxious to fulfil all his wishes and to constantly afford him new proofs of her affection.

And how? Did he not deserve that love? Was he not constantly paying her the most delicate attentions? Was he not always as humbly submissive as he was tender? Did it not seem as if the lion was subdued, that the Hercules was tamed, by his tender Omphale, whom he adored, at whose feet he lay for the purpose of looking into her eyes, to read in them her most secret thoughts and wishes?

She was not only his wife, she was also his empress. Such he called her, as such he respected her and surrounded her with more than imperial splendor.

The house of the English Consul Dyke was changed into an imperial palace for Natalie, and the young and beautiful wife of the consul was her first lady of honor. She established a court for the young imperial princess, she surrounded her with numerous servants and a splendid train of attendants whose duty it was to follow the illustrious young empress everywhere, and never to leave her!

And Natalie suspected not that this English consul received from the Empress of Russia a million of silver rubles, and that his wife was rewarded with a costly set of brilliants for the hospitality shown to this Russian princess, which was so well calculated to deceive not only Natalie herself, but also the European courts whose attention had been aroused. Natalie suspected not that her splendid train, her numerous servants—that all these who apparently viewed her as their sublime mistress, were really nothing more than spies and jailers, who watched her every step, her every word, her every glance. Poor child, she suspected nothing! They honored and treated her as an empress, and she believed them, smiling with delight when the people of Leghorn—whenever she with her splendid retinue appeared at her husband's side—shouted with every demonstration of respect for her as an empress.

And finally, one day, the long-expected Russian fleet arrived!

Radiant with joy, Alexis Orloff rushed into Natalie's apartment.

"We have now attained our end," said he, dropping upon one knee before his wife; "I can now in truth greet you as my empress and mistress! Natalie, the Russian fleet is here, and only waits to convey you in triumph to your empire, to the throne that is ready for you, to your people who are languishing for your presence! Ah, you are now really an empress, and marvellous will you be when the imperial crown encircles your noble head!"

"I shall be an empress," said Natalie, "but you, Alexis, will always be my lord and emperor!"

"Natalie," continued the count, "your people call for you!—your soldiers languish for you, the sailors of all these ships direct their eyes to the shore where their empress lingers. The admiral's ship will be splendidly adorned for your reception, and Admiral Gluck will be the first to pay homage to you. Therefore adorn yourself, my charming, beautiful empress—adorn yourself, and show yourself to your faithful subjects in all the magnificence of your imperial position. Ah, it will be a wonderful and intoxicating festival when you celebrate the first day of your greatness!"

And Count Orloff called her attendants. Smiling, perfectly happy at seeing the pleasure and satisfaction of her husband, Natalie suffered herself to be adorned, to be enveloped in that costly gold-embroidered robe, those pearls and diamonds, that sparkling diadem, those chains and bracelets.

She was dressed, she was ready! With a charming smile she gave her hand to her husband, who viewed her with joyous glances, and loudly praised the beauty of her celestial countenance.

"They will be enchanted with the sight of you," said he.

Natalie smilingly said: "Let them be so! I am only happy when I please you!"

In an open carriage, attended by her retinue, she proceeded to the haven, and all the people who thronged the streets shouted in honor of the beautiful princess, astonished at the splendor by which she was surrounded, and estimating Count Orloff a very happy man to be the husband of such an empress!

And when she appeared upon the shore, when the carriages stopped and Princess Natalie rose from her seat, there arose from all the ships the thousand-voiced cheers of their crews. Russian flags waved from every spar, cannon thundered, and drums rolled, and all shouted: "Hail to the imperial princess! Hail, Natalie, the daughter of Elizabeth!"

It was a proud, an intoxicating moment, and Natalie's eyes were filled with tears. Trembling with proud ecstasy, she was compelled to lean upon Orloff's arm to preserve herself from falling.

"No weakness now!" said he, and for the first time his voice sounded harsh and rough. Surprised, she glanced at him—there was something in his face that she did not understand; there was something wild and disagreeable in the expression of his features, and he avoided meeting her glance.

He looked over to the ships. "See," said he, "they are letting down the great boat; Admiral Gluck himself is coming for you. And see that host of gondolas that follow the admiral's boat! All his officers are coming to do homage to you, and when you, in their company, reach the admiral's ship, they will let down the golden arm-chair to take you on board. That is an honor they pay only to persons of imperial rank!"

Her glance passed by all these unimportant things; she saw only his face; she thoughtfully and sadly asked herself what change had come over Alexis, and what was the meaning of his half-shy, half-angry appearance?

The boats came to the shore, and now came the admiral with his officers; prostrating themselves before her, they paid homage to this beautiful princess, whom they hailed as their mistress.

Natalie thanked them with a fascinating smile; and, graciously giving her hand to the admiral, suffered herself to be assisted by him into the great boat.

As soon as her foot touched it, the cannon thundered, flags were waved on all the ships, and their crews shouted, "Viva Natalie of Russia!"

Her eyes sought Orloff, who, with a scowling brow and gloomy features, was still standing on the shore.

"Count Alexis Orloff!" cried she, with her silvery voice, "we await you!"

But Alexis came not at her call! He hastily sprang into an officer's boat, without giving her even a look.

"Alexis!" she anxiously cried.

"He follows us, your highness," whispered the wife of Consul Dyke, while taking her place near the princess. "It would be contrary to etiquette for him to appear at the side of the empress at this moment. See, he is close behind us, in the second gondola!"

"Shove off!" cried Admiral Gluck, he himself taking the rudder in honor of the empress.

The boats moved from the land. First, the admiral's boat, with the princess, the admiral, and the Englishwoman; and then, in brilliant array, the innumerable crowd of adorned gondolas containing the officers of the fleet.

It was a magnificent sight. The people who crowded the shore could not sufficiently admire the splendid spectacle.

When they reached the admiral's ship, the richly-gilded arm-chair was let down for Natalie's reception. She tremblingly rose from her seat—a strange, inexplicable fear came over her, and she anxiously glanced around for Orloff. He sat in the second boat, not far from her, but he looked not toward her, not even for a moment, and upon his lips there was a wild, triumphant smile.

"Princess, they wait for you, seat yourself in the arm-chair!" said Madame Dyke, in a tone which to Natalie seemed to have nothing of the former humility and devotion—all seemed to her to be suddenly changed, all! Shudderingly she took her seat in the swinging chair—but, nevertheless, she took it.

The chair was drawn up, the cannon thundered anew, the flags were waved, and again shouted the masses of people on the shore.

Suddenly it seemed as if, amid the shouts of joy and the thundering of the cannon, a shriek of terror was heard, loud, penetrating, and heart-rending. What was that? What means that tumult upon the deck of the admiral's ship? Seems it not as if they had roughly seized this princess whose feet had just now touched the ship? as if they had grasped her, as if she resisted, stretching her arms toward heaven? and hark, now this frightful cry, this heart-rending scream!

Shuddering and silent stand the people upon the shore, staring at the ships. And the cannon are silenced, the flags are no longer waved, all is suddenly still!

Once more it seems as if that voice was heard, loudly shrieking the one name—"Alexis!"

Trembling and quivering, Alexis Orloff orders his boat to return to the shore!

In the admiral's ship all is now still. The princess is no longer on the deck. She has disappeared! The people on shore maintained that they had seen her loaded with chains and then taken away! Where?

All was still. The boats returned to the shore. Count Orloff gave his hand to the handsome Madame Dyke, to assist her in landing.

"To-morrow, madame," he whispered, "I will wait upon you with the thanks of my empress. You have rendered us an essential service!"

The people at the landing received them with howls, hisses, and curses!—but Count Orloff, with a contemptuous smile, strewed gold among them, and their clamors ceased.

Tranquil and still lay the Russian fleet in the haven. But the ports of the admiral's ship were opened, and the yawning cannon peeped threateningly forth. No boats were allowed to approach the ship; but some, impelled by curiosity, nevertheless ventured it, and at the cabin window they thought they saw the pale princess wringing her hands, her arms loaded with chains. Others also asserted that in the stillness of the night they had heard loud lamentations coming from the admiral's ship.

On the next day the Russian fleet weighed anchor for St. Petersburg! Proudly sailed the admiral's ship in advance of the others, and soon became invisible in the horizon.

On the shore stood Count Alexis Orloff, and, as he saw the ships sailing past, with a savage smile he muttered: "It is accomplished! my beautiful empress will be satisfied with me!"

CHAPTER XLVII.

CONCLUSION.

She was satisfied, the great, the sublime empress—satisfied with the work Alexis Orloff had accomplished, and with the manner in which it was done.

In the presence of her confidential friends she permitted Orloff's messenger, Joseph Ribas, to relate to her all the particulars of the affair from the commencement to the end, and to the narrator she nodded her approval with a fell smile.

"Yes," said she to Gregory Orloff, "we understand women's hearts, and therefore sent Alexis to entrap her. A handsome man is the best jailer for a woman, from whom she never runs away." And, bending nearer to Gregory's ear, she whispered: "I, myself, your empress, am almost your prisoner, you wicked, handsome man!"

And ravished by the beauty of Gregory Orloff, the third in the ranks of her recognized favorites, the empress leaned upon his arm, whispering words of tenderness in his ear.

"And what does your sublime majesty decide upon respecting your prisoner?" humbly asked Joseph Ribas.

"Oh, I had almost forgotten her," said the empress, with indifference. "She is, then, yet living, this so-called daughter of Elizabeth?"

"She is yet alive."

The empress for some time thoughtfully walked back and forth, occasionally turning her bold eagle eye upon her two favorite pictures, hanging upon the wall. They were battle-pieces from Casanova's master-hand—battle-pieces full of terrible truth; they displayed the running blood, the trembling flesh, the rage of the opponents, and the death-groans of the defeated. Such were the pictures loved by Catharine, and the sight of which always inspired her with bold thoughts.

As she now glanced at these sanguinary pictures, a pleasant smile drew over the face of this Northern Semiramis. She had just come to a decision, and being content with it, expressed her satisfaction by a smile.

"That bleeding feminine torso," said she, pointing to one of the pictures, "look at it, Gregory, that wonderful feminine back reminds me of the vengeance Elizabeth took for the beauty of Eleonore Lapuschkin. Well, Elizabeth's pretended daughter shall find me teachable; I will learn from her mother how to punish. Let this criminal be conducted to the same place where the fair Lapuschkin suffered, and as she was served so serve Elizabeth's daughter! Only the knout may be swung a little more powerfully. We have no desire to tear out the tongue of this child. Whip her, that is all, but whip her well and effectually. You understand me ? "

And while she said this, that animated smile deserted not Catharine's lips for a moment, and her features constantly displayed the utmost cheerfulness.

"I think," said she, turning to Gregory, "that is bringing an expiatory offering to the fair Eleonore Lapuschkin, and we here exercise justice in the name of God! — As to you," she then said to Joseph Ribas, "we have reason to be satisfied with you, and you shall not go without your reward. Moreover, our beloved Alexis Orloff has especially recommended you to us, and spoken very highly of your information and talents. You shall be satisfied." *

 *   *   *   *

It was a dark and dreadfully cold night. St. Petersburg slept; the streets were deserted and silent. But there, upon the place where Elizabeth once caused the beautiful Lapuschkin to be tortured, there torches glanced, there dark forms were moving to and fro, there a mysterious life was stirring. What was being done there ?

No spectators are to-night assembled around these barriers. Catharine has commanded all St. Petersburg to sleep at this hour, and accordingly it slept. Nobody is upon the place—nobody but

the cold, unfeeling executioners and their assistants—nobody but that pale, feeble, and shrunken woman, who, in her slight white dress, kneels at the feet of her executioners. She yet lives, it is true, but her soul has long since fled, her heart has long been broken. The chains and tortures of her imprisonment have done that for her. It was Alexis Orloff who murdered Natalie's heart and soul. For him had she wept until her tears had been exhausted—for him had she lamented until her voice had become extinct. She now no longer weeps, no longer complains ; glancing at her executioners, she smiles, and, raising her hands to God, she thanks Him that at last she is about to die.

She is yet praying when her executioners approach and roughly raise her up, when they tear off her light robe, and devour with their brutal eyes her noble naked form. Her soul is with God, to whom she yet prays. But when they would rend from her bosom the chain to which Paulo's papers are attached, she shudders, her eyes flash, and she holds the papers in her convulsively clinched hands.

"I have sworn to defend them with my life ! " she exclaims aloud. "Paulo, Paulo, I will keep my word ! "

And with the boldness of a lioness she defends herself against her executioners.

"Leave her those papers ! " commanded Joseph Ribas, who was present by order of the empress. "She may keep them now—they will directly be ours ! "

"Oh, Paulo, I have kept the promise I made thee ! " murmured Natalie. She then implores to be allowed to read

---

* Joseph Ribas was rewarded by the empress with the place of an officer and teacher in the corps of cadets. Afterward, upon the recommendation of Betzkoi, he was made the tutor of Bobrinsky, one of the sons of the empress by Gregory Orloff. "He accompanied Bobrinsky in all his travels," says Massen, "and inoculated the prince with all the terrible vices he himself possessed." At a later period, as we have already said, he became an admiral and a favorite of Potemkin, the fourth of Catharine's lovers.

them, and Joseph Ribas grants her the desired permission.

With trembling hands she breaks the seal and reads by the light of a torch held up for her. A melancholy smile flits over her features, and her arms fall powerless.

"Ah, they are the proofs of my imperial descent, nothing further. How little is that, Panlo!"

And now, lifting her up, they raise her high upon the backs of the executioners.

The knout whistles as it whirls through the air, the noble blood flows in streams. She makes no complaint, she prays. Only once, overcome by pain, only once she loudly screams: "*Mercy, mercy for the daughter of an empress!*"

THE END.

www.ingramcontent.com/pod-product-compliance
Lightning Source LLC
Chambersburg PA
CBHW031419020726
47499CB00005B/1497